F

ICT

MING TEA
MURDER

MING TEA MURDER

Tea Shop Mystery #16

LAURA CHILDS

BERKLEY PRIME CRIME, NEW YORK

THE BERKLEY PUBLISHING GROUP
Published by the Penguin Group
Penguin Group (USA) LLC
375 Hudson Street, New York, New York 10014

USA • Canada • UK • Ireland • Australia • New Zealand • India • South Africa • China

penguin.com

A Penguin Random House Company

This book is an original publication of The Berkley Publishing Group.

Berkley Prime Crime Books are published by The Berkley Publishing Group.
BERKLEY® PRIME CRIME and the PRIME CRIME logo are
trademarks of Penguin Group (USA) LLC.

Library of Congress Cataloging-in-Publication Data

Childs, Laura.
Ming tea murder / by Laura Childs.—First edition.
pages ; cm
ISBN 978-0-425-28164-2
1. Browning, Theodosia (Fictitious character)—Fiction. I. Title.
PS3603.H56M56 2015
813'.6—dc23
2014045914

FIRST EDITION: May 2015

PRINTED IN THE UNITED STATES OF AMERICA

10 9 8 7 6 5 4 3 2 1

Cover illustration by Stephanie Henderson.
Cover design by Lesley Worrell.

ACKNOWLEDGMENTS

Heartfelt thanks to the usual suspects—Sam, Tom, Amanda, Troy, Bob, Jennie, Dan, and all the fine folks at the Berkley Publishing Group who handle design, publicity, copywriting, bookstore sales, and gift sales. An extra special thank-you to all the tea lovers, tea shop owners, bookstore folks, librarians, reviewers, magazine writers, websites, radio stations, and bloggers who have enjoyed the adventures of the Indigo Tea Shop gang and who help me keep it all going.

And to you, dear readers, I promise many, many more mysteries featuring Theodosia, Drayton, Haley, Earl Grey, and the rest of the crazy Charleston cast—as well as a few surprises!

MING TEA
MURDER

1

With drums banging and the sweet notes of a Chinese violin trembling in the air, the enormous red-and-gold dragon shook its great head and danced its way across the rotunda of the Gibbes Museum in Charleston, South Carolina. It was the opening-night celebration for the reconstruction of a genuine eighteenth century Chinese tea house, and the crème de la crème of society had turned out in full force for this most auspicious occasion.

And even though black-tie events weren't exactly topmost in Theodosia Browning's comfort zone, there had been no easy way to refuse this particular invitation, especially when your handsome, hunky boyfriend was the museum's public relations director. So here she was, applauding the music, mesmerized by the spectacle of the enormous dragon's gaping jaws as it snapped and slapped above the heads of the excited crowd.

Yes, the event was most impressive, Theodosia decided. Glowing red Chinese lanterns, stands of bamboo, elegant orchids, and miniature *penjing* trees had transformed the cold, marble rotunda into an exotic Asian garden. And then there was the food. Serving tables were laden with tempting bites of shrimp dumplings, honey-glazed pork buns, chicken satay, and miniature crispy duck rolls. Delicious!

Of course, the real treasure was the Chinese tea house itself, purchased and deconstructed in Shanghai, then rebuilt board-by-board inside the museum. The blue-tiled, exotically peaked roof, gleaming cypress walls, and intricately carved sandalwood screens seemed tailor-made for an emperor and his courtesans.

"I'm anxious to take a look inside," Theodosia told Max, who was gazing about proudly if not a little distractedly.

"We pulled it off," said Max. "I can't believe we actually pulled it off." He sounded surprised that his PR efforts had yielded such a turnout.

"Of course you did," Theodosia told him. "Because nobody would pass up an opportunity to enjoy a fancy celebration like this." *Except . . . maybe me?*

Theodosia had a smile that could light up a tea room—and often did, since she was the proprietor of the Indigo Tea Shop on nearby Church Street. But tonight she'd been smiling so exuberantly that her face felt like it was about ready to crack. She'd flitted about on Max's arm, chatting and rubbing shoulders with Charleston's old guard, most of them big-buck donors who were thrilled that their money had made it possible to import this masterpiece of a tea house.

But Theodosia was also counting the seconds to midnight.

Because when the clock struck the proverbial witching hour, she planned to cut and run like Cinderella. She'd kick off her pinchy black satin heels, climb into her pumpkin coach—which, in this case, was her venerable six-year-old Jeep—and head home to her cozy little cottage where her dog, Earl Grey, awaited her.

Shaking her head and forcing another smile because Max was saying something to her again, she leaned toward him, and said, "Excuse me?"

"I need to schmooze a couple more board members," said Max. "You'll be okay?"

"I'll be perfect," said Theodosia.

"Go check out the photo booth," Max urged, "while I huddle with Edgar Webster, one of our illustrious donors." He grinned. "Maybe take a selfie." As a fun perk for the guests, Max had convinced the museum director to let him bring in a photo booth. And just as he'd predicted, there'd been a constant parade of guests in and out of the booth all night long. Everyone was seemingly thrilled with the notion of immortalizing themselves in photos, even if they were the small black-and-white variety.

"I'll do that," Theodosia told him. "It'll be fun." As she turned to push her way through the crowd, she caught sight of herself in a fragment of mirror. And as always, the image gave her pause.

Is that really me with that mass of auburn hair framing my face and blue eyes looking so expectant? Hmm, I don't look half-bad for being in my midthirties.

She'd swiped a hint of blusher on the apples of her cheeks, smudged on the bare minimum of mascara. But with her confident bearing, winning smile, and fair southern belle skin, she looked almost like a noblewoman who might have been portrayed in some delectable English painting. Perhaps something John Constable might have done.

"You're looking very lovely tonight," said a voice behind her.

Theodosia whirled about to find Drayton, her dear friend and tea master, smiling at her.

"If not a bit mischievous," continued Drayton.

Theodosia smiled and gave an offhand wave. "Ah, I think I might be a tad underdressed." She'd worn a simple black cocktail dress, an armful of colorful bead bracelets, and heels, while most of the other women were glitzed and glammed in the latest runway creations from Dior and Oscar de la Renta.

"Nonsense," said Drayton. "An LBD is always perfectly appropriate." Drayton was sixtyish, tall, and debonair. Tonight his gray hair was slicked back straight, and he wore a slim-cut tuxedo with his trademark bow tie. He was the buttoned-up old guard to Theodosia's more playful boho cool.

"Did you get a gander at all the jewels these women are wearing?" Theodosia asked him. "I mean, a cat burglar would have a field day here."

Drayton's bushy brows rose in twin arcs. "Please don't interject a criminal element into the occasion. Even if it is only imaginary."

"Okay, then I'll just compliment you on all your lovely *penjing*, because they certainly add to the Asian atmosphere." *Penjing* were basically Chinese bonsai, miniature trees that had been cut, trimmed, and wired so they could exist in small, moss-encrusted ceramic pots. Drayton, a master at creating windblown-style trees and miniature forests, had lent the museum a dozen of his trees. Most had spectacularly twisted trunks and leaves that were smaller than a lady's pinky nail.

"They do look nice, don't they? Particularly my Chinese elm." Drayton prided himself on his composure and modesty, but he also appreciated a compliment now and then.

"You've been inside the tea house?" said Theodosia. They both had to take a step back, since the crowd was pressing so hard around them.

"It's a marvel," exclaimed Drayton. "I took the liberty of exploring while all that Chinese-dragon business was going on." He paused and smiled. "You should run over and take a quick peek, too. You'll love it."

"I'm going to," said Theodosia. "But first I promised Max

I'd check out his photo booth." She looked around, saw that Max was backed up against a wall talking to a rather red-faced man, a board member by the name of Edgar Webster. Neither of them looked happy.

"*Photo* booth?" spat out Drayton. Clearly he wasn't a fan. "What is this fixation everyone has today with memorializing themselves? And then posting every single silly photograph on . . ." Drayton made a face. "On the *Internet?*"

"Come on," Theodosia cajoled. "It's not as bad as all that."

"I'm just not sure a photo booth is apropos for an event such as this."

"Still, it's fun. And everyone seems to love it."

"You see," said Drayton, "that's why I'm not everyone." Drayton was a self-proclaimed Luddite who mistrusted smartphones, DVDs, and CDs. In fact, he was an old-fashioned vinyl record kind of guy.

"But you're perfect just the way you are," Theodosia assured him. She glanced around again, but Max and Webster had apparently moved on.

"Oh my," said Drayton. As he gazed into the crowd, his placid expression suddenly changed to one of horror.

"What?" Then Theodosia caught sight of the small, blond woman who was speed walking toward them on clacking kitten heels.

"I'm going to let *you* handle this encounter," said Drayton as he quickly slipped away.

"You look like you're having a *marvelous* time," cooed Charlotte Webster. She slalomed to a stop in front of Theodosia and grinned like the Cheshire cat, practically upending her glass of champagne in the process. Charlotte was the bubbly socialite who presided over the Broad Street Garden Club, was a sometime customer at Theodosia's Indigo Tea Shop, and was married to Edgar Webster.

"It's a thrilling night," Theodosia, mustering yet another

smile, told Charlotte. Since Charlotte's husband, a prominent businessman and philanthropist, had put up the largest chunk of money to import the tea house, Theodosia pretty much had to make nice with his wife.

"I was just chatting with Percy Capers," said Charlotte. She fluttered a pudgy hand and adjusted her necklace, a string of sparkling diamonds with a large yellow diamond as the center stone. "You know, the museum's curator of Asian art?"

Theodosia nodded. She'd met Capers a couple of times.

"Anyway, Mr. Capers was regaling me with horror stories about importing this lovely tea house. Shipping it across the Pacific, shepherding it through customs, misplacing some of the actual parts. Why, do you know there are no *nails* whatsoever in the construction? That the entire thing is held together with dozens of wooden pegs?"

"I've heard that."

"Is that the craziest thing ever?" said Charlotte. "Wooden pegs?"

"I guess that's how they built them two hundred years ago," said Theodosia.

"Two hundred years? That's how old that thing is?" said Charlotte. She took a quick glug of champagne. "Well, I certainly hope we got our money's worth, then." She giggled loudly, patted Theodosia on the arm, and toddled off.

Charlotte was a real character, Theodosia thought to herself. And then, because she really didn't want to be unkind, decided that the Websters, as civic-minded underwriters of the tea house, really had done a wonderful thing.

As Theodosia slipped past one of the food tables, she accepted a miniature egg roll from a black-uniformed waiter. Then, when another waiter held out a tray filled with champagne glasses, she took a glass. As she sipped and surveyed the crowd, she was struck again by how fancy and formal everyone looked. Of course, many of the guests, board members as well as donors, were friends and neighbors who lived in the nearby Historic District. One of the Ravenels was conspiring with a Clayton and a Tisdale. And Mr. Pinckney was talking to a large man with a rather pronounced Texas bray.

The pounding of drums suddenly started up again, loud and hard, and Theodosia turned to see what was going on now. Oops, it was dragon time again. The Chinese dragon was humping its way through the crowd once more, tossing its head from side to side, its dragon beard fluttering with every move.

Theodosia had witnessed a dragon parade in San Francisco's Chinatown once, when she'd been roaming up and down Grant Street popping into tea shops, looking for unusual varieties and blends. But seeing this guy up close and personal was a lot more fun. And, from the enthusiasm generated by the crowd, they obviously thought so, too.

Edging her way through a clutch of suitably enthralled guests, Theodosia headed for the photo booth. Maybe she could slip in and take a quick photo right now. She wasn't all that hot to pose, but it would make Max happy. Give him a small souvenir of tonight's museum triumph.

Dodging around an enormous celadon pot filled with leafy bamboo plants, Theodosia darted past a red Chinese lantern supported by a heavy wooden post. Over here, in an alcove off the rotunda where the photo booth was located, it was a little darker, a little quieter.

Perfect.

Theodosia rounded a stone lion-dog statue, heading for the photo booth. The drums were pounding furiously now, the erhu—the Chinese violin—pouring out high, pleading notes. Finishing the last sip of champagne, she set her glass down on a small rosewood table and turned toward the photo booth.

Was it still occupied, she wondered, or could she dart in for a quick photo?

"Hello?" Theodosia called out, giving a couple of sharp knocks on the shiny, bright yellow exterior. She didn't want to go crashing in and photobomb someone. That would be just plain rude.

"Is someone in there?" she called again.

When there was no reply, Theodosia took a step forward. And just before her hand parted the flimsy black curtain, the toe of her strappy black stiletto slid into a patch of something sticky.

"Oh no," she groaned. All she needed was to ruin her best pair of shoes because some exuberant guest had spilled a glop of sweet-and-sour sauce.

Theodosia glanced down, expecting to see sauce, fragments of an exploded pork bun, or a puddle of champagne. After all, this art opening had turned into a fairly raucous party.

Only what she saw instead was a small, dark puddle.

A spilled drink?

No, Theodosia decided. Champagne or tea would have been much more translucent.

As she pulled her foot back and stared at the floor again, taking a longer, harder look, her heart began to flutter. Then it began to dance a little jitterbug. Because whatever was on the floor was decidedly dark and sticky.

No, it couldn't be. Could it?

Slowly, tentatively, her heart in her throat, Theodosia reached forward and slowly parted the curtains. And saw . . . nothing.

It was pitch-black inside the photo booth. Lights out.

Somehow that didn't feel right to her. What was going on?

She pushed the curtains a little farther apart.

And that's when she saw him. A large man, sprawled on a narrow wooden bench, bent all the way forward so his forehead pressed tightly against the front panel of the booth. His eyes were closed, and he looked like he was passed out cold.

"Excuse me," said Theodosia. "Sir?" Her mouth felt dry,

her breathing was fast and thready. "Are you okay, sir?" She paused. "Do you need help?"

No answer.

Theodosia glanced backward, looking for a museum guard, one of the museum staff, anyone who might be able to lend a hand.

But everyone had their backs to her. They were still cheering and clapping like mad as the musicians played wildly and the Chinese dragon continued his energetic prance.

Tentatively now, Theodosia touched a finger to the side of the man's throat. To where she figured a pulse point might be.

She felt . . . nothing. In fact, he felt cool. Practically lifeless.

A loud pounding sounded inside Theodosia's head, and she could feel the tiny hairs on the back of her neck prickle and rise.

No . . . please no.

And, as her eyes gradually adjusted to the darkness inside the photo booth, as her mind slowly wrapped itself around what might have just happened, that's when she saw the first telltale evidence of foul play. Just above where her fingertip had come into contact with the man's throat, a trail of dark, sticky liquid dribbled from his ear!

Blood? Has to be.

Theodosia snatched her hand away and backed out of the photo booth as fast as humanly possible. Then she screamed as loud as she could, her voice rising in volume as it mingled with the urgent, shrill notes of the erhu.

2

It was amazing. Or maybe it wasn't. That a gaggle of wealthy, sophisticated people could scatter in mere minutes, like rats fleeing a sinking ship.

Who wanted to get involved in what appeared to be a brutal, spur-of-the-moment murder?

No one, apparently. Death was too nasty, far too unseemly for this well-heeled, fashionable crowd.

So when a gang of uniformed police officers and EMTs descended upon the museum, when the dancing dragon was shooed away and the stunned musicians were silenced, Theodosia was left with a handful of museum folks. Everyone fumbled for explanations and tried to relate the story as best they could.

"How could this happen?" exclaimed Max. He touched a hand to his forehead as if he couldn't quite process the event. The tall, dark-haired, and olive-skinned Max now looked pale as a ghost.

A uniformed officer with brush-cut gray hair, a solemn expression, and a nametag that said D. HICKS hastened to take charge. "It happened," he said. "So let's move on from there. Because what I really need to know right now is: *Who is this fellow?*" He peered into the darkness of the photo booth at the dead man.

"I don't know," said Theodosia. "I'm not sure. I never saw his face. When I found him, he was just, uh, kind of slumped forward like that. Like he is now."

"You didn't touch him?" Hicks asked.

Theodosia grimaced. "Well, I kind of did."

"Explain, please," said Hicks.

Theodosia hunched her shoulders. "I'm sorry, but I reached in and touched an index finger to his throat."

"To see if the man was still breathing?"

"That's right. It seemed like the smart thing to do. The *responsible* thing to do."

"And was he breathing?"

"No. At least I don't think he was." Theodosia was nervous and felt like she was fumbling the interview when she should be trying to be a little more helpful. "And he certainly isn't breathing anymore."

"That's fairly obvious," said Max.

"So my question still stands," said Hicks. "Who is he?" Even the two EMTs who'd come rushing in with a clattering gurney stood on the sidelines now, watching and listening. The situation looked pretty darn strange, and their curiosity was ramped up.

Drayton, who'd been standing behind Theodosia and observing what was slowly turning into a freak show, held up a hand, and said, "I think I might be of some help."

"Oh yeah?" said Hicks. He looked like he was normally a fairly easygoing guy, but tonight his jaw was set firmly and his eyes were pinpricks of intensity. "You believe you can identify this man?"

Drayton nodded. "I think this unfortunate gentleman might be . . ."

"Edgar!" A shrill scream echoed from halfway across the room. It rose in volume, like steel wheels grinding against metal rails, then tapered to a high-pitched whine. "Is that my Edgar?"

Charlotte Webster suddenly stumbled toward them. She was half staggering, half running, looking like a crazed zombie woman. Her blond hair stuck straight up, her bright red lipstick was hopelessly smeared, and she wore a look of utter anguish on her doughy face.

The small crowd parted silently for her as she lurched up to the photo booth. She stopped, peered inside, and let out a sound that sounded like *"Whump?"* Then she slumped so visibly that Drayton had to reach out and steady her.

"Is it him?" Hicks asked. "Is that your husband?"

But Charlotte wasn't about to be hurried.

She fanned herself madly with one hand. "When I couldn't find Edgar in the crowd," she said, "I started to panic." Now tears streamed like rivers down her cheeks. "And now . . ." She put a hand to her chest as if she was suddenly experiencing stabbing heart pain. Then she swallowed hard and pointed at the dead man. "And now I *recognize* him," she said in a high, quavering voice. "We . . ." She shook her head, almost unable to continue.

"Take your time," said Hicks.

"I mean . . ." said Charlotte. "I can't quite believe this, but earlier tonight we actually *argued* over Edgar's choice of tuxedos. He wanted to wear the Armani. I told him I much preferred the Brioni." Her lower lip trembled and her finger shook as she pointed at the dead man, who was still slumped like a slab of meat inside the photo booth. "That's Edgar's Brioni. I'd know it anywhere."

"Oh dear," said Theodosia.

"That's Edgar Webster?" said Max. "I was just talking to him!"

"I think I . . ." Charlotte mumbled. Then her eyes rolled

back in her head until only the whites showed. Her knees trembled and buckled. In front of a dozen horrified onlookers, Charlotte dropped to the marble floor like a sack of potatoes. Potatoes encased in a fashionable red silk dress, anyway.

Drayton and Percy Capers, the Asian curator, immediately leapt to Charlotte's aid. Together they hauled her back onto her feet and led her, stumbling and blubbering, to a nearby bench.

"Well, you certainly don't see that every day," said a gruff voice.

Theodosia whirled around, ready to chastise whoever had made what she considered a fairly rude and insensitive comment. And was met with the steady, dark gaze of Detective Burt Tidwell.

"You," she said. Burt Tidwell headed the Robbery and Homicide Division of the Charleston Police Department. He was a bear-sized man with a strange, bullet-shaped head and huge hands. Brilliant, shrewd, and driven, he was not a man to be trifled with.

"You," Tidwell fired back at Theodosia. They'd met on any number of occasions. Socially, at the Indigo Tea Shop, and, more recently, when Theodosia had been pulled into a bizarre murder case.

Tidwell extended a hand and gave an impatient flick of his wrist. "Please move," he said as a kind of blanket warning to everyone in his immediate vicinity. "Everyone step back. You are all compromising my crime scene with your sticky little strands of DNA."

"*Your* crime scene?" said Hicks. He put his hands on his hips. "I don't think so." Suddenly, a turf war seemed to be brewing.

Tidwell directed a withering gaze at him. "I prefer to take over from here. Good work, though, Officer Hicks. I'm thrilled that you were able to keep so many guests from stampeding."

"Look here," said Theodosia, stepping in again. "It wasn't his fault. When I saw that poor man . . ." She pointed inside the photo booth.

"Edgar Webster," said Max.

"When I saw him slumped inside," said Theodosia, "I started screaming. Which meant the band quit playing, and then . . . well . . ." She stopped abruptly, aware that at least a dozen pairs of eyes were staring at her with increasing curiosity. "They all . . . all the guests, that is . . . got scared and ran off."

"A fine narrative," said Tidwell. "Very helpful indeed."

"You don't have to be so dismissive," said Theodosia, pulling it together and speaking more clearly now. "I was startled, and I'm afraid my screams launched everyone into panic mode."

Tidwell glanced around. "Who is in charge here, please? Besides me?"

"That would be me." Elliot Kern, the director of the museum, stepped forward and extended his hand. He was well turned out in an Ermenegildo Zegna power suit. His sparse gray hair was a fringed cap, a hawk nose dominated his face, and he exuded a faint patrician air. In an earlier century he could have been one of the wheeling, dealing members of the Medici family.

"I'm assuming you have a list of everyone who was in attendance here tonight?" said Tidwell.

"Of course," said Kern. "Absolutely." He seemed more than eager to lend assistance.

"Then I will be needing that list," said Tidwell. Like many large men, he'd taken to wearing vests under his sport coats. And tonight, the small pearly buttons on Tidwell's vest seemed to yawn and strain, defying every dreary law of physics.

"Is there anything I can do?" asked Max. But both Tidwell and Elliot Kern ignored him.

"Again, people," said Tidwell, raising his voice to a

frightening rumble, "you must clear away from here." A few more people shuffled backward as the EMTs looked anxious and edged their gurney closer.

"No, no," said Tidwell, holding up a big paw. "We cannot load him up yet. We must wait for the crime-scene team to arrive. Since we haven't determined the primary cause of death, their small ministrations are going to be quite necessary in helping gather as much information as possible."

Theodosia noted that Tidwell seemed to veer between blustering and decorous. Typical. She edged a little closer, ignoring his warning to back off.

"What was the cause of death?" Theodosia asked. She figured she already knew what it was, but she wanted to get it straight from the horse's mouth.

"If you want an official statement," Tidwell said brusquely, "you're welcome to make an appointment and meet with the medical examiner of Charleston County."

"Okay, then," said Theodosia. "How about unofficially? You're an experienced investigator. What do *you* think might have been the cause of death?" She glanced at Charlotte Webster, who was still sitting on a bench, bent over with her face in her hands.

Tidwell offered a mirthless smile, a smile that seemed to imply his superiority as an investigator. Then he extended a hand toward the dead man. "You see there . . . how the blood has oozed out? Very dark, almost black, dribbling down the side of our victim's face?"

"Yes." Theodosia wished he hadn't phrased it quite so graphically.

"Off the record, I'd say that a thin, sharp object had been inserted into our victim's right ear."

Not our *victim*, Theodosia thought. Your *victim*.

"Dear lord," said Drayton. All the blood seemed to drain from his face.

Theodosia was appalled but fascinated at the same time.

"And this particular sharp object entered his brain, too?" she asked.

"Well, yes," said Tidwell. "A sharp object, inserted rather deftly, would most definitely impact that particular area."

"Deftly," said Theodosia, frowning. "That's a strange way to describe such a brutal, up-close murder. Your choice of words almost implies a certain elegance."

Tidwell's mouth twitched slightly upward at the corners, and he rocked back on his heels. "No, Miss Browning, the elegance lies in how adroitly this particular murder will be solved."

Theodosia gazed at Tidwell, the feisty, obstinate, ex-FBI agent, who could be both courtly and brusque at the same time. "But . . ." she said. She hesitated, thought for a moment, and decided to voice her opinion anyway. "But the killer . . . the murderer . . . he had to have been a guest here tonight. It couldn't have been someone who just wandered in off the street."

"Very good, Miss Browning," said Tidwell. "My thoughts exactly."

"Now the mu shu pork has really hit the fan," murmured Max.

Theodosia lifted her gaze from the dead man to the elegant Chinese tea house. Red lights, set on a timer, had suddenly blinked on and shone down upon the enormous central gallery. Now the tea house shimmered in brilliant red light, while everything around it was bathed in a darker bloodred.

Theodosia shivered, as if a chill wind had suddenly swept across her grave. A killer had walked quietly among them with murder in his heart.

Who could it be?

3

A *Brown Betty* teapot rested on the small wooden table where Theodosia and Drayton sat. Bone china teacups were filled with freshly brewed Assam. Haley, the Indigo Tea Shop's young chef and baker extraordinaire, hovered nearby. It was a half hour before the Indigo Tea Shop was slated to open, and the three of them were still mulling over the ill-fated events of last night.

Theodosia took a fortifying sip of tea, and said, "I think Max feels partially responsible for everything that happened."

"Nonsense," said Drayton. Dressed in his customary tweed jacket with a starched white shirt and red bow tie, he looked just this side of imposing. "Max had nothing remotely to do with that murder."

"It was his idea to bring in the photo booth," offered Haley. She was in her early twenties, with stick-straight blond hair and a waifish figure. Even though she favored T-shirts and flowing, mid-length skirts, the ethereal looking

Haley was, in reality, a stiff-backed martinet. She ran the kitchen as if it were a military operation. Even now, cream scones, apple muffins, and cranberry nut bread baked in the oven, each pan of goodies timed out precisely. Luncheon ingredients had already been prepped, and woe to the deliveryman who showed up late for his allotted time.

"Still," said Theodosia, "Max feels just awful."

"As do we all," said Drayton. "It's a crying shame to import that lovely tea house all the way from China only to have the opening reception ruined."

"It wasn't just the reception that was ruined," said Haley. "It was people's lives."

Drayton pursed his lips. "Well, I certainly didn't mean to make *light* of that."

"We know you didn't," said Theodosia. She was the peacemaker in the group, always ready to smooth things over or offer a quick suggestion. Unless, of course, her own feathers got ruffled. Then, as Drayton was wont to say, *Hell hath no fury . . .*

But this morning Theodosia was in a thoughtful mood. Edgar Webster's murder simply made no sense to her. Webster was a businessman who'd served on the board of directors at the museum and was well regarded in the community. He'd also done a wonderful service for the art-loving public in helping to spearhead the importation of that treasure of a tea house.

And, what really bothered Theodosia was that Webster and his wife, Charlotte, had been in the seemingly safe company of friends. Though most of the crowd had been made up of Charleston's old-money families or newly crowned titans of industry, they were, for the most part, well-mannered titans.

Except for one.

But which one?

Theodosia knew that beneath the old-world gentility of

Charleston there ran a few undercurrents of greed, anger, and hatred. But from what she'd observed at the museum, everyone had been in a congenial, almost hale-hearty mood. They'd been drinking Chinese tea and French champagne. They'd snacked on wonderful little dim sum treats. And they'd genially patted one another on the back, congratulating themselves on how civic-minded they'd been in donating funds to help purchase the tea house.

But one of them had murder in his heart.

Theodosia shook her head. It was almost incomprehensible. If you weren't safe in a museum, with people you knew and trusted, where were you safe?

Drayton pushed back from the table and stood up abruptly. "We need to ready the tea shop." Consulting the antique Patek-Philippe watch that was wrapped around his wrist, he nodded as if to underscore his words. "Yes, it's definitely time to get moving."

"I'm all set," said Haley. She prided herself on always having it together.

"We know that," Drayton said, smiling slightly. He was secretly pleased that Haley was such a stickler for punctuality and planning. He greatly admired those traits in a person.

"You're right," said Theodosia, pulling herself up from the table. "This is Friday, so it's likely to be busy."

"Fridays are always busy," said Drayton. He was starting to bustle about, unfurling white linen tablecloths and draping them across tables. "It's the end of the work week, so people tend to slack off."

"You mean relax," said Theodosia. "There's a difference."

She was following in his footsteps now, setting out small plates along with cups and saucers. They were lovely mismatched pieces of Shelley Chintz, Aynsley, and Spode that she'd picked up at various Charleston antique shops and tag sales.

"That's what the Indigo Tea Shop is all about, don't you

think?" said Theodosia. "Relaxing?" She loved the notion that the tea shop served as a little oasis of calm for their work-weary customers.

With its brick fireplace, battered hickory tables, and leaded-glass windows, the Indigo Tea Shop exuded a cozy ambiance. Since it was autumn again, the pegged wooden floors had just gotten their annual red-tea wash, and the highboys were crammed with candles, tea towels, tea cozies, and antique silverware. A new crop of dried grapevine wreaths hung on the walls alongside antique prints that were also for sale.

And once the tables were set, the candles lit, and the faint strains of Vivaldi playing over the stereo system, the Indigo Tea Shop pretty much oozed its own blend of British and Victorian charm.

"I'm going to make a pot of that Grand Pouchong from Taiwan," Drayton announced. He was bustling about at the front counter, where floor-to-ceiling cupboards were stacked with tins that held the world's most exotic teas. Everything from delicately fruited Nilgiris to malty Assams to rich, dark oolongs.

"Sounds like a fabulous idea," said Theodosia. After Webster's demise she was craving a little fabulosity in her life.

Drayton carefully measured in the leaves and added a tiny bit extra. "And a pinch for the pot," he told her.

"That always makes it better," Theodosia agreed. Between Haley's baked goods and Drayton's tea offerings, the Indigo Tea Shop was redolent with the most amazing aromas.

"Uh-oh," said Drayton. He was gazing past the filmy curtains that framed the front window. "Here come our first customers of the morning."

The tea shop was half-filled and bustling when Delaine Dish burst through the front door around ten o'clock. Dressed in a bright fuchsia-colored skirt suit and matching jaunty hat and wearing great flashes of gleaming gold jewelry, she looked like (and was) a miniature volcano.

"Hello!" Delaine cried out to anyone who was even remotely in her vicinity. "Good morning!"

Theodosia hurried over to greet Delaine, who was the proprietor of Cotton Duck, one of Charleston's premier clothing boutiques. Loud, gossipy, and self-centered, Delaine was not only a handful, she was certified mad as a hatter.

And this morning Delaine wasn't alone.

"Theo," Delaine said in a slightly grudging tone of voice, "I'd like you to meet my great aunt Astra." She nodded in an offhand way at the tiny lady who accompanied her. "She's here for a short visit. Well, hopefully it's short." She focused an intense gaze on Aunt Astra, who was dressed in a sedate gray dress and wearing what Theodosia always thought of as "old lady shoes." That is, they were black leather lace-ups with clunky, low heels. Although now that Theodosia thought about it, maybe they were the latest in hipster fashion.

As Drayton ambled over to greet Delaine, she felt obliged to mumble another hasty introduction. Which prompted Drayton, always the proper gentleman, to give a formal half bow and lead Aunt Astra to a table.

Delaine rolled her eyes as she watched him being so solicitous.

"That woman on his arm is barely even a blood relative," Delaine confided to Theodosia. "She's, like, my great aunt once removed. And she's about a hundred years old." Delaine's head whipped around. "But, Theo, she's no doddering old fool. She's still got all her buttons, and her tongue is sharp as a razor blade. That old bat will cut you to the quick if you don't watch out."

"Then I'll be sure to watch out," Theodosia said with some amusement. Surely Delaine had to be embroidering her words?

"And she's constantly harping at me," said Delaine. "Criticizing me." She snuck a quick peak Aunt Astra's way to make sure she couldn't be overheard. "I've nicknamed her Aunt Acid because of all her bile and bitterness."

"How long is she staying with you?"

"Too long," said Delaine. She frowned, and then pressed an index finger against the frown lines forming between her brows, as if willing them to disappear. "I'm going to try to ship her off to my cousin in Goose Creek as soon as I can make suitable arrangements."

"Come on," said Theodosia, leading Delaine to her table. "You need to sit down and relax. Have yourself a nice cup of tea." She settled Delaine alongside Aunt Astra and gave them a quick summary of the day's specials.

When Theodosia returned with a plate of cream scones and a pot of English breakfast tea, Delaine shot a nervous glance at Aunt Astra, and said, "I'm sorry I missed all the excitement last night."

"Don't be," said Theodosia. "It was pretty brutal."

"You're talking about the actual murder?" said Delaine.

"I'm talking about everything," said Theodosia. Fresh in her mind was the furor that had ensued.

"Hmm," said Delaine, savoring that little bit of excitement. "There was a delicious article about the murder in this morning's *Post and Courier.* But they didn't elaborate on what poor Edgar Webster was stabbed with. The reporter just kind of danced around it." She paused. "Didn't mention where or how he was stabbed, either."

Theodosia dropped her voice. "He was stabbed with some sort of long, thin blade." She hesitated. "Inserted in his ear."

"Oh my," said Delaine, fully relishing the details. "You mean like an ice pick?"

"I suppose it was something like that," said Theodosia. "But the police haven't revealed any specific details. I suppose they want to conduct a thorough autopsy first."

"It would be fairly easy to conceal a weapon like that," said Delaine.

"That's exactly the problem," Theodosia agreed. "A small weapon the size of an ice pick could have easily disappeared into someone's pocket or handbag." And disappear it had, she thought, since so many people had been stampeding their way out the door as the police and EMTs were rushing in. The weapon could have gone out the door in that first mad scramble of people. It could have just disappeared—poof!—into the dark of the night.

Aunt Astra's eyes got progressively larger as she listened and methodically chewed her scone.

Delaine gave a faint smile. "I can just picture all of Charleston's blue bloods positively *fighting* to get out of the way of a murder investigation. Nobody wants their family name dragged through the mud or attached to something as sordid as *murder*." She took a demure sip of tea and the feather atop her hat bobbed. "You know, Edgar Webster may have moved in the upper echelons of Charleston society, but he wasn't very well liked."

Theodosia leaned forward. "Why would you say something like that?"

Delaine waved a hand. "No reason, really."

"No, there has to be *some*thing," said Theodosia. "You started to let the cat out of the bag, so now I'd like to hear exactly what you have to say."

"So would I," said Aunt Astra, touching a napkin to her lips as she finally spoke up.

Delaine made an unhappy face. "Well, you know about the trouble between him and his little wifey, Charlotte, right?"

"No, I certainly don't," said Theodosia. "What about him and Charlotte?"

Now Aunt Astra looked seriously interested. "There were problems in their marriage?" she asked.

Delaine pursed her lips. "I would have to say they had what might be termed an *open* marriage."

"Ah," said Aunt Astra, relishing this juicy tidbit.

"Okay," said Theodosia. She was surprised but not startled. Both Charlotte and Edgar had larger-than-life personalities and were involved in charities and major social functions all over town. So they were independent people. And, of course, temptation lurked everywhere.

"Their marriage was open on one side, anyway," Delaine said, selecting her words carefully.

"I'm assuming you meant on Edgar Webster's side," said Theodosia. She pondered this for a moment. "Charlotte must have been awfully upset about him stepping out on her."

"Believe it," said Delaine. "Why . . . up until a couple of weeks ago, Edgar was carrying on like a madman with Cecily Conrad."

"What do you mean by 'up until a couple of weeks ago?'" Theodosia asked.

"Webster and Cecily recently broke up," said Delaine. "Of course, they chose to conduct their big brouhaha in front of about a million people at the Valhalla Country Club. And from what I understand, the fur flew like crazy."

"Why did they break up?" Theodosia asked. *And was it even a legitimate breakup if Edgar was still married to Charlotte?*

Delaine scooped up a blob of Devonshire cream and deposited it on her scone. "Webster just got fed up with Cecily, I guess. She's a very pretty girl, nice eye candy and all that, but she was a complete money-grubber. She talked Webster into buying her a new BMW as well as bankrolling her new furniture shop. So she probably sank her talons into him to the tune of at least a half-million dollars."

"That's a major chunk of change," said Theodosia.

"But Webster was demanding his money back," said Delaine.

"You mean calling in his loan?" said Theodosia.

Delaine nodded. "You might say that. Only, from the chatter I heard, Cecily never considered it a loan. She thought it was her due. That's what their big fight was all about."

"Money!" spat out Aunt Astra. "That's always a huge motive to kill someone!"

"Of course it is, dear," said Delaine. "Even though we all know Charlotte Webster is rich as Croesus."

"So his wife controlled all the money?" said Theodosia.

"Pretty much," said Delaine. "Don't you know Charlotte's been living fat and sassy on a ginormous inheritance? Edgar Webster did okay with his business, but he was a piker compared to his wife. I'd say he was mainly along for the ride."

"But now poor Charlotte is stuck in a terrible middle ground," said Theodosia. "Her husband not only cheated on her, he got himself murdered."

"With a nasty ex-girlfriend talking smack about him," said Delaine.

Theodosia shook her head. "Charlotte must be brokenhearted as well as angry."

"Mostly angry," said Delaine. "She's an extremely volatile woman, you know."

"She is?" said Theodosia. "How so?"

"Didn't you ever hear about the Corvette incident?" asked Delaine. "About how Charlotte drove her husband's classic 1976 Corvette right into an antique lamppost on Tradd Street just because he came sneaking into the house at four AM?"

"Sounds right to me," said Aunt Astra.

But Delaine wasn't finished. "And how about the time Charlotte had a bloody blue hissy fit right in the middle of a Broad Street Garden Club meeting?"

"What happened there?"

"Somebody proposed planting lowly zinnias in the garden

between the Library Society and the Governor Aiken Gates, when what Charlotte really wanted were Juliet roses."

"That does sound a bit unreasonable," said Theodosia.

"Oh, Charlotte's unreasonable," said Delaine, touching an index finger to her lips and then helping herself to another scone. "In fact, the woman's a complete whack job."

4

Standing at the front counter, watching Drayton pull down a tin of Empire Keemun tea, Theodosia said, "Do you know Cecily Conrad?"

Drayton pried off the lid and looked pensive for a moment as the heady scent perfumed the air around them. "Yes. If I remember correctly, Cecily moved here a year or so ago and got caught up with the Opera Society, even though she's a bit of a wild child. Her father is Colonel Josiah Conrad from down Savannah way." He measured out two heaping scoops of tea into a blue-and-white teapot. "You know, Cecily was at the museum opening last night."

"She was?" This was news to Theodosia. "Did you notice if she was, um, interacting in any way with Edgar Webster?"

Drayton looked at her sharply. "Why are you asking? For some reason, it feels like you have some sort of hidden agenda."

"Not so hidden at all," said Theodosia. "I just found out

from Delaine that Edgar Webster had been cheating on Charlotte and that Cecily was the so-called other woman. And to top things off with a nice, fat maraschino cherry, Webster apparently had a recent and highly volatile falling out with Cecily."

Drayton stared at her. "This is conjecture, right?"

"I know it sounds like an episode of *The Good Wife*, but I swear it's the honest truth."

"Hmm." Drayton seemed to mull everything over for a moment. "You're sure about this affair?"

"Pretty sure."

"Then your information, even though it's dreadful and gossipy, might possibly . . . um . . . impact the police investigation?"

"Is that a question?" said Theodosia.

"Mmn. No, I guess not."

"So you're saying that Tidwell and company might not look at suspects who are fairly close to home?" said Theodosia. "That the investigation could go off in a another direction? Maybe questioning past and current business associates, or something like that?"

"That could be the case," said Drayton, looking a little worried.

Theodosia drummed her fingers against the counter and fidgeted with a Royal Vale cup and saucer decorated with a sprightly yellow daffodil. "So both Charlotte and Cecily should probably be regarded as prime suspects," she said slowly.

"Your newly procured information," said Drayton, "even though it came from an unreliable source like Delaine, could definitely point to motive."

"Because Charlotte might have been jealous and Cecily might have been angry," said Theodosia. She tilted her head to one side. "So what do you think? Should I call Detective

Tidwell and drop a few heavy-handed hints about Webster's extracurricular activities? Sort of clue him in?"

Drayton stared back at her, his gray eyes practically boring into her, his brow furrowed. "Knowing what you do now, I think you have to share this information with him."

Theodosia set the cup and saucer down on the counter. "That's what I was afraid of."

They got busy then, brewing tea, ferrying plates of scones and pots of tea to all their customers. And because it was Friday, with its usual onslaught of weekend tourists as well as regulars, morning teatime at the Indigo Tea Shop stayed rush hour busy as they eased their way through the morning. And then, suddenly, it was time for Theodosia to duck into the kitchen and consult with Haley about lunch.

"The tea shop is jammed," Theodosia told her. "And in about two minutes we're going to have a few of our guests inquiring about lunch offerings."

Haley spun around like a ballerina, dipped a ladle into a pot of steaming sausage and gnocchi soup, tasted it, and said, "So you'd like to know what's on the menu?"

Theodosia smiled. "That would be the general idea, yes."

"Okay." Haley dug into the pocket of her apron and pulled out a three-by-five-inch index card. She glanced at it for all of one second, and then handed it over to Theodosia. "Here you go, boss."

"Thank you," said Theodosia. "And please don't call me boss."

Haley cocked her head. "Why not?"

"Because we're all in this together."

"You think?"

Theodosia chuckled. "I've always looked at it that way. Besides, I don't want to be that one lonely soldier who's always walking point." She scanned the card quickly. "Haley, this is just super." In her cramped, left-canted printing, Haley had listed sausage and gnocchi soup, chicken and wild rice salad, prosciutto and fig tea sandwiches, apple and Cheddar cheese scones, and chocolate cupcakes.

"I just hope our customers like everything," said Haley.

"Are you kidding? They'll love it."

And love it they did. Theodosia served bowls of soup until the pot was empty. Then she tried to steer customers to the salads. When those started to dwindle, she had Haley whip up extra prosciutto and fig sandwiches.

"Another success," said Drayton. He was lounging against the counter, his eyes focused on the busy café even as he sipped a cup of Darjeeling.

"Don't get too relaxed," Theodosia told him. "This is going to be a long slog of a weekend. Remember, we're going to be open on Sunday, too."

"How could I forget?" said Drayton, smiling. "Our *Titanic* Tea."

"A night to remember," said Haley as she dashed out to deliver a plate of fresh apple and Cheddar scones. "Just like the title of that old black-and-white *Titanic* disaster movie."

"And to think the *Titanic* Tea was all Drayton's grand idea," said Theodosia. "We could have gotten off easy by hanging up ghost and goblin decorations, but no, he wanted to go all out." Halloween would be arriving in a few days' time, and this Sunday's *Titanic* Tea was Drayton's clever *homage* to that quasi-holiday. No witches, ghosts, or goblins for him, just the grand, haunting memory of the *Titanic* tragedy.

"I think our guests will enjoy a Halloween tea without benefit of the same old ghoulies, don't you think?" said Drayton.

"I have to admit, I was nervous about the idea at first,"

said Theodosia. "But now that we're completely sold out, I take my hat off to you. It's a grand idea."

"Wait until you see the décor I've got planned," said Drayton. "It's going to blow your socks off."

"I even did research on some of the menus that the White Star Lines featured," said Haley. "So we'll be serving some of those actual dishes."

"You two," said Theodosia, shaking her head. When Drayton and Haley sunk their teeth into a new themed tea, it was like dealing with a couple of rabid jackals.

"But we're gonna decorate with a few ghoulies later on," said Haley. "After all, it is Halloween." She gave a little shiver. "One of my very favorite holidays."

"Why is that?" said Drayton. "Why do women go into an absolute swoon over Halloween?"

"I think it's because we get to wear a costume," said Theodosia. "For one crazy night, we can let ourselves be anybody or anything we want."

"Absolutely," said Haley. "Wicked witch costumes, fairy princesses, crazy ladies with ripped bodices . . ."

"So I suppose you two plan to be appropriately attired for our Tower of London Tea, as well?" said Drayton. This particular tea had been Theodosia's idea. A semi-spooky, British-themed tea to be held at lunch on Halloween day.

"Are you kidding?" said Haley. "I've got my Anne Boleyn costume ready and rarin' to go." She grinned at Drayton. "Who are you going to be?" she asked. "King Henry VIII?"

"Good heavens, no," said Drayton.

"Then who?" said Theodosia.

One of Drayton's brows lifted into an arch. "You'll just have to wait and see."

Just as Theodosia was serving plates of cupcakes and making a final round with a teapot filled with Keemun, Max came sauntering in. He stood by the front door, waiting patiently until she noticed him.

"Hey," she said, swinging by him. "Are you here for a late lunch?"

"I am if you've got any food left."

"I think we could scrape something up." Theodosia pointed to a small table wedged next to a highboy stacked with colorful tea tins. "You're lucky we even have one table left," she told him somewhat breathlessly. She was juggling desserts, trying to deliver checks to the guests who were finished, and still hadn't had a chance to run back to her office and call Tidwell. "I hope you don't mind perching at that smaller table?"

"Not a problem." Max gave her a sly wink. "Makes it easier to keep an eye on you."

She led him to the table, hastily laid out silverware, and poured him a glass of ice water. "So how are things at the museum today?"

"They're in turmoil, just as you might expect. Elliot Kern, our director, is pretty much yanking his hair out. What's left of it anyway."

"Have you heard anything specific? I mean . . . the police . . . Tidwell . . . have they been nosing around?"

"I was stuck in my office all morning, taking calls and fending off our local press, so I really couldn't say."

"Take a wild guess."

"Well, there was constant chatter and lots of urgent footsteps shuffling up and down the hallway. So, yes, the investigators were there all right. Probably wearing their little Sherlock Holmes caps while they tried to sniff out clues."

"I picked up a couple of interesting bits of information this morning," said Theodosia.

Max raised his eyebrows. "Concerning . . . ?"

Theodosia waved a hand. "They're just rumors really."

"Tell me anyway."

Theodosia quickly filled him in on the Charlotte-Edgar-Cecily love triangle.

Max tapped a finger against his water glass. "That's fairly weird. So what are you really saying?"

"Just that, I don't know . . ." She was a little nervous about sharing the gossip now. "That it was a strange situation, with no love lost between any of them?"

Max's eyes went suddenly huge. "Oh, jeez, Theo. But I do get your inference. You're saying that either of those two women could be a prime suspect in Webster's murder!"

"Well, that would be the general idea, yes."

"Holy crap," said Max. "Now there's a can of worms." He paused, studying Theodosia carefully as if she were a science project. "So . . . do you think you're going to kick that can wide open?"

"I'm planning to call Detective Tidwell, yes."

Max gazed at her. "To spill the beans about Charlotte and Cecily. Huh. You're really getting involved in this, aren't you?"

Theodosia lifted a shoulder. "I picked up some critical information that the police should probably know about."

Max made a sound that was somewhere between a sigh of resignation and a protest. "Okay, I'm sure you're going to relay all of this information to Tidwell. But that doesn't mean there's going to be any quid pro quo involved. I seriously doubt that he's going to open up to you about what *he's* already discovered."

"Probably not," said Theodosia. "But with this kind of information, I can at least prime the pump."

Theodosia took advantage of a lull in business a few minutes later. She whipped into her office, plunked herself down behind her desk, and dialed Tidwell's number. She didn't have the good detective on speed dial, but wondered if maybe she should.

It took a few minutes for Theodosia to bluff her way through Tidwell's gatekeepers, but finally she had him on the phone. Then she spent a fast three minutes bringing him up to speed on what she knew about Edgar and Charlotte Webster and Cecily Conrad. She laid her information out as smoothly as she could, hoping that this new information—well, some of it was hearsay—would spur him into action.

But when she was finished, there was dead silence.

"Detective Tidwell?" she said. "Have you heard any of this before?"

There were a few more moments of silence, then he said, "Miss Browning, this is all hearsay and conjecture on your part, correct?"

"It's information," said Theodosia. "A few basic facts that I think you should be aware of."

Tidwell sighed. "Please tell me you're not calling to horn in on my investigation."

"Of course I'm not." She grimaced. She kind of was. "I'm really just being a concerned citizen, trying to share some pertinent information."

"I see," said Tidwell.

"So did you know?" asked Theodosia. "About the . . . affair?"

"Yes, I did."

That brought her down a peg or two. "Oh."

"You sound disappointed."

"Not really. Oh, but I did want to ask you a question."

"Just one question?"

"Um . . . that's right."

"Then fire away with your single question, dear lady, so I can get back to work tout de suite."

"Did you have your technical forensic people tear that photo booth apart?"

"Yes."

"Yes what?"

"Yes, they ripped into it like a hungry dog gnawing a lamb shank."

Theodosia sighed. Dealing with Tidwell could be such a slog.

"You're rolling your eyes," said Tidwell. "I can hear them clicking inside your sweet little head."

"Look," said Theodosia, starting to get a little steamed. "I'm just wondering if the techs who examined that photo booth found anything pertinent?"

"Such as?"

"I don't know. Digital photos, images on the hard drive, old-fashioned negatives, *anything.* Basically anything that might be incriminating. Something that would point to the killer."

"I understand where you're going with this, Miss Browning. And it would be marvelous to push a button and have a photographic image of the killer pop out at us. Unfortunately, our clever killer chose to stab poor Mr. Webster rather than take time for a photo op."

"You're saying he's clever? Or she?"

"This one is, yes," said Tidwell. "Because an up-close, personal attack at a crowded party is always somewhat daring. But in the end, he or she will ultimately be apprehended."

"You're sure about that?" Theodosia looked up just as Max walked into her office. His cell phone was clenched in one hand, and his usually animated face wore a hard, unblinking stare.

"I'm as certain that we'll catch him as the sun rises each morning," Tidwell said into Theodosia's ear. There was a faint wheeze and then a loud *clunk.* He'd hung up.

"What's wrong?" Theodosia asked. Max looked like he'd just bitten into a sour pickle. Except they weren't serving sour pickles for lunch.

"You're not going to believe this," said Max. His jaw

seemed to be frozen as he moved woodenly toward her, almost gasping for air.

"What?" She leaned forward. "Max, what's wrong?"

Max lurched toward the plush chair that sat across from Theodosia's desk and eased himself down into it.

"I've just been fired."

5

Theodosia was dumbfounded. "What?" she yelped. Then she caught herself before she hit the red lever and her temper shot all the way up to DEFCON 4. She must not have heard Max correctly. Surely he hadn't just uttered the word *fired?* No, he couldn't have. That would never happen.

"What?" Theodosia said again, straining to hear what surely must be the correct words.

"I've been fired," Max repeated. He sat staring at her, his lips slightly parted, his brows pinched together. He looked disbelieving and totally in shock. "They told me not to come back to work today."

"Who told you that?" With a thud in her heart, Theodosia knew Max was absolutely serious. And that someone—his boss?—had just made a very grave mistake.

"Elliot Kern, the director. I just spoke to him. Or rather, he just called me on my cell phone."

"Wha . . . ?" Now Theodosia was the one who was in

shock. "Wait a minute." She held up a hand. "What exactly did Kern say to you?"

"He said I was on a permanent leave of absence until the Edgar Webster murder had been resolved."

"That was his explanation? That's ridiculous. There must be something else going on. There has to be an actual *reason*." She was starting to get really angry. "There has to be just cause!"

"Kern said that the board of directors had an emergency meeting this morning and decided to suspend me."

"They were meeting while you were hard at work?"

"Apparently."

"But why suspend *you?*" Theodosia knew she was sputtering but couldn't help herself. "Do you think it was because of the photo booth? Because it was your idea? Surely they can't hold that against you? It was just a stupid prop— a goofball amusement for wealthy donors. You didn't know someone was going to get *murdered* inside of it!"

Max was still dumbfounded. "Kern mentioned something about publicity, too. Or maybe it was press releases. I know that's what Webster was all fired up about last night."

"Over press releases?"

Max shook his head. "I don't know. I'm having a lot of trouble processing this whole thing."

"So am I," said Theodosia. None of this made a lick of sense to her. She knew, with all her heart, that Max would never willfully do anything to harm the reputation of the museum. And, as far as job performance went, he was an absolute whiz at publicity. He'd planted articles in *Charleston Weekly* and *Art Now*. Why, a couple of his press releases—ones about the contemporary southern art show and the Picasso ceramics show—had even been picked up by the Art & Design section of the *New York Times*!

"Even though Kern told me not to come back," said

Max, "I'm going to go back there anyway. See if I can sit down with him. Try to get some more . . . information."

"Good for you," said Theodosia. She stood up from her desk so fast, her chair almost flipped over backward. "You run over there and try to straighten out this whole ridiculous thing. Really, this firing can't even be legal." She came around her desk, put a hand on Max's shoulder, and rubbed it gently. "Nothing makes sense here. Maybe . . . it's some kind of Halloween prank?"

"Well, if it is," said Max, "it's not very funny."

"Oh my," said Drayton. "I don't mean to pry, Theo, but you look like you just received a nasty piece of news." He was setting out two dozen tiny blue-green ceramic Chinese cups without handles for a tea tasting that a table of customers had requested.

"I . . . we . . . did just get some terrible news," said Theodosia. And then, because there was no easy way to say it, she just blurted out, "Max was fired."

"No!" Drayton reared back. "I can't imagine that's true."

She swallowed hard. "Well, it is. It just happened. Like, five minutes ago."

Drayton peered over his half-glasses, looking concerned and slightly owlish. "Do you want me to make a phone call?" Besides being a permanent fixture on the board of directors at the Heritage Society, Drayton *knew* people. People in high places.

"I don't know. Max is on his way back to the museum right now to try to straighten things out with the director."

"So we should wait and see how this plays out?" said Drayton.

"I think so. For now anyway."

Drayton reached up and grabbed a tin of Fujian white tea.

"I think my ladies are going to enjoy this. Picked by hand for only a few choice days each spring from young, tender leaves. Sweet with a slight apricot fragrance . . ." He offered a reassuring smile. "Please don't worry, Theo. I'm sure this will all get straightened out. I'm sure there's a reasonable explanation."

But Theodosia was clearly flustered throughout the rest of their luncheon service. She delivered a pot of jasmine tea to Mrs. Biatek's table when she'd actually ordered rose tea. And a pot of East Frisian blend was misdirected to another table that had really wanted a Russian country blend.

"This isn't like me," Theodosia fretted to Drayton once she'd scurried back to the counter.

"Not to worry. This is all easily remedied with fresh pots of tea," he soothed.

"Still, to make such silly mistakes." She glanced down and saw that her hands were shaking. She clenched them hard to try to calm herself.

"You're way too hard on yourself," said Drayton.

"No," she said. "The board was way too hard on Max."

At midafternoon, down on her hands and knees, replenishing her shelves with DuBose Bees Honey and scone mixes, Theodosia looked up to find Bill Glass hovering over her.

"What are you doing here?" she asked him. Bill Glass was the smarmy, nosy publisher of *Shooting Star*, Charleston's very own gossip rag. Glass had founded it right after the tech boom and, like a really hideous reality show, it hadn't gone away. In fact, it had grown more and more popular every year until it had become a kitschy little weekly filled with glossy photos and bits of snide gossip that appealed to the nouveau riche.

"The-o-do-sia," said Glass, giving her one of his trademark toothy great white shark grins. "I heard you were swanning around last night at that very fancy but oh-so-disastrous museum party." The cameras strung around his neck clanked and clicked as if to punctuate his words.

Theodosia stumbled to her feet. "Where did you hear that?" She hated Glass for having such a tight little network of informers.

Glass held up a hand and made a fluttering motion. "A little bird told me. A little bird that siiiings." With his slicked-back hair and shiny suit, he reminded Theodosia of a sleazy used-car salesman. Or maybe somebody who sold advertising.

"Let me guess," said Theodosia. "You're here looking for inside information."

Bill Glass shot an index finger at her. "Right-o, sweetheart."

"I really don't know anything."

"Perfect. Pour me a cup of tea and tell me all about what you don't know," he said in a conspiratorial tone.

Theodosia considered him for a moment. Maybe Glass had picked up something that she could use. That's if she could muster the stamina to wheedle it out of him.

"Okay," said Theodosia. "Grab a seat at that table over there. But please, please don't disturb anyone."

"Gotcha."

Theodosia hurriedly poured a cup of Darjeeling for Glass. After a moment of deliberation, she also placed a scone and a dab of Devonshire cream on a plate. Carrying everything back to his table, she set the tea and scone down, and then slid into the chair across from him. She'd made up her mind that she would steer the conversation.

"What do you know about Charlotte Webster?" Theodosia asked Glass.

He had his teacup halfway to his mouth, but paused. "Big money," he said, then managed a noisy slurp. "Boatloads of money."

"That's what I've heard, too," said Theodosia.

Bill Glass broke off a piece of scone and popped it in his mouth. "You see, that's what I like about you." He tapped the side of his head. "You're smart. You're cognizant of the world around you."

"Thank you," said Theodosia. "I think."

"About last night?" said Glass. "If Vegas was making odds, I'd put my money squarely on good old Charlotte."

"You mean . . . ?"

"For the murder," Glass said hurriedly. "Here, let me lay it out for you."

"Please do."

"Charlotte's got money, status, and chutzpah, okay? But you know what's been dragging her down? That lying, cheating skunk of a husband. So . . ." Glass picked up a butter knife, twiddled it between his fingertips, then made a sharp, jabbing motion. "If there's no more good-time Edgar around, the problem is neatly solved."

"So you think Charlotte killed her own husband?" Somehow the murder didn't feel quite that cut-and-dried. There had to be more to it than an angry, vengeful wife, didn't there?

Glass shrugged. "She could have done it. Cops don't know for sure yet." He peered at her. "I was hoping you could help me fill in a few blanks."

"On what?"

"Sweet cakes, you were there last night. You bum around with all those swells. Your cuddle-bunny boyfriend works at the museum."

Not anymore, Theodosia thought to herself.

"Exactly what kind of information are you looking for?" she asked.

"Anything and everything," said Glass. "What society lady was cozying up with which gent? What businessman was trying to pick his buddy's pocket? What are the latest society rumbles and rumors?" He took a slurp of tea. "And I want to know if Cecily Conrad was there."

"What do you know about Cecily?" Theodosia asked.

Glass wrinkled his nose. "Ah . . . I hear she's a blue blood wannabe. A cute little piece of fluff who thinks she's God's gift to man and is trying her darnedest to claw her way into Charleston society."

"I have it from a reliable source that Cecily was there last night," said Theodosia.

"Aha. I thought as much."

Theodosia decided they'd come this far, why not keep going? In for a penny, in for a pound. "And you know that Cecily had been carrying on with Edgar Webster?"

Glass nodded. "Yup, heard that a while ago." He looked at Theodosia over his teacup. "Your mentioning Cecily like that . . . are you a little suspicious of her, too?"

"Not really." *At least not until I get some evidence on her.*

"But when you think about it," said Glass, "she does stack up as a pretty solid suspect."

"Maybe."

"So it's only logical to dig a little deeper," said Glass. "Since Cecily had been canoodling with Webster and then talked him into bankrolling her so-called design and furniture shop."

"Does everyone know about that?" said Theodosia.

Glass looked smug. "Cecily's a little girl with a great big mouth. She bragged about her big score all over town. You ask me, I think she even thought she might be the next Mrs. Edgar Webster."

"Not anymore she won't."

"Still," said Glass, getting more and more worked up, "you gotta admit there's a tasty catfight in the making. The widow pointing her finger at the girlfriend, the girlfriend dishing dirt on the widow."

Theodosia wondered if that might really happen. Then again, with a dead body in the morgue and big money on the line, anything could happen.

"I guess I'm gonna have to nose around some more," said Glass. "I hear Cecily's got some big shindig going on at her new shop. Maybe I'll get in touch with her and tease her with the possibility of a feature article."

Theodosia thought about the puddle of dark red blood that had oozed its way out from the photo booth last night. "Maybe you shouldn't do that," she told Glass.

"Aw"—he waved a hand—"don't worry about me. I can take care of myself."

Theodosia popped into the kitchen just as Haley pulled a pan of lemon scones from the oven. Besides the lemon scones, the intoxicating aromas of cinnamon, chocolate, and almonds also hung in the air.

"Do we have any scones left?" Theodosia asked.

Haley tilted her tray toward Theodosia. "These. Why?"

"I'm going to run over to Charlotte Webster's house. I'd like to take her some scones and a couple tins of tea."

"A care package."

"Something like that." Theodosia didn't want to admit to Haley, or even to herself, that she wanted to scope out the situation with Charlotte.

"Well, I can put something together easily enough," said Haley. "Can we spare one of those sweetgrass baskets from your office?"

"Sure. But you know what? I'll put the basket together. I've got time."

"Suit yourself," said Haley.

Theodosia swept into her office, grabbed one of the handle-style sweetgrass baskets that their friend Miss Josette had crafted by hand, and then ran out to study her shelves. She decided on tins of dragonwell and rosehips tea. Then, just because she knew Charlotte might perceive her as being a little bit nosy, tossed in jars of lemon curd, strawberry jam, and honey for good measure.

When she carried everything over to the counter, Drayton peered at her, and said, "That looks delightful. Who's it for?"

"I'm going to tie a ribbon on this and run it over to Charlotte Webster."

"A condolence gift of sorts?"

"I guess."

Drayton's furry brows arched. "And it wouldn't hurt to check out the situation over there, would it? To see if Charlotte really is the grieving widow."

"The thought had occurred to me."

"Good," said Drayton, "because it was top of mind with me, too."

Back in her office, Theodosia added Haley's cellophane-wrapped scones, and then tied a yellow ribbon around the handle of the basket.

Wait, was that too festive? Should she use a black ribbon? No, that seemed too funereal. She would stick with the yellow.

Then, just as Theodosia was about to duck out the back door, she called Max.

His cell phone rang six, seven, eight times, but Max wasn't answering.

Theodosia wasn't sure if this was good news or bad news. Or was no news good news? Whatever. When the beep for his voice mail sounded, she said, "I'm just wondering what's going on, sweetie, since I haven't heard from you. Call me when you get a chance. Oh, and come over to my house tonight. Okay, bye."

She hung up feeling oddly disquieted.

6

Charlotte Webster lived in a palatial home a few blocks over, on Meeting Street. Georgian in style, the home featured an enormous hipped roof, red box chimneys at either end, a belt of elaborately carved molding between the second floor and the third-floor ballroom, and a row of six pillars fronting the covered veranda, or what folks in Charleston usually called a piazza. The gardens that surrounded it were magnificent, though it was so late in the season that only a few hardy flowers bobbed their shaggy heads.

Jingling with nerves, hoping she wasn't butting in *too* much, Theodosia stood at the front double door and grabbed a brass knocker molded in the shape of a boar's head.

Bang, bang, bang.

Theodosia heard muffled metallic sounds ring out on the other side of the door. Her fingers had barely released the knocker when the front door popped open.

"Yes?" A middle-aged woman peeped through the four-inch crack of the opened door. In her black dress and tidy white apron, she was obviously the housekeeper or maid. But with her papery voice and gray hair unflinchingly scraped back from her forehead, she looked more like a character out of an old black-and-white movie from the forties.

"I just wanted to drop this off for Charlotte," said Theodosia, holding out her basket of goodies.

Expressionless, the maid opened the door so Theodosia could step inside. The door swung closed behind her.

"This way, miss," the maid said as she spun quickly.

"So I can . . . well, okay, then," said Theodosia. She followed the maid in her squeaky crepe-soled shoes as she led Theodosia across a green-tiled portico. They passed a wood-paneled library on the left and a staid-looking parlor on the right, and then headed down a long, dark hallway. On the walls, oil paintings depicting three generations of disapproving Websters glared down at them.

As they rounded a corner, Theodosia heard the murmur of low voices. Was Charlotte curled up in front of the TV, sniffling into a box of Kleenex tissues? Consoling herself with a box of chocolates and an episode of *Dr. Phil*? But no, it didn't sound like the good doctor's friendly Texas twang. Obviously, Charlotte was entertaining a visitor.

As Theodosia entered the room, Charlotte recognized her, jumped to her feet, and let loose a high-pitched squeal. "Theodosia! Bless your sweet little heart. I'm tickled to see you!" She did a quick hop across a room that was glassed in on three sides and filled with a heroic jumble of orchids, roses, palmetto trees, and other leafy green plants. Theodosia decided that solariums, if that's what people still called this type of room, always felt more like claustrophobic human terrariums.

Theodosia thrust her gift basket out in front of her. "I

just wanted to drop off some fresh-baked scones and a few tins of tea for you." She gazed at a thin, silver-haired man who occupied a nearby chair. "But apologies. I see you have company and certainly don't mean to interrupt."

"You're not interrupting at all," Charlotte beamed. She was barefoot and dressed in a canary yellow silk top and flowing slacks. Very Acapulco-ish. Her blond hair was swirled atop her head like a show pony. "Roger and I were just having drinks." The name Roger tripped off her tongue in a very familiar way.

Theodosia gazed at Roger, who'd barely stirred from his tufted leather chair. "Hello," she said, and gave a friendly wave.

"Oh," said Charlotte. "You two don't know each other?" She giggled coquettishly, and Theodosia decided Charlotte had already enjoyed a drink. Or two or three.

"We've not had the pleasure," said Theodosia. Since Charlotte held a half-full drink in her hand and had made no move to accept the basket, Theodosia placed it on a nearby wicker table.

"This dear fellow is Roger Greaves," said Charlotte. "Edgar's business partner at Datrex Technology."

Greaves hefted himself out of his chair and languidly crossed the floor so he could shake Theodosia's hand. "Nice to meet you," he said. He was dressed in khaki slacks, a pale peach golf shirt, and Tod's loafers. Casual but expensive.

"Nice to meet you, too," said Theodosia. "Considering the circumstances."

"Yes," said Greaves, struggling to look a little more somber. "Of course."

But Charlotte would have no part of it. "We were just having mint juleps, Theodosia. May I fix one for you?"

"No thanks," said Theodosia. "I can really only stay a couple of minutes."

Charlotte eyed Greaves. "I know I don't have to ask you twice."

He shrugged and went back to his chair.

"Come on over here," Charlotte waved. "Sit with me at the bar while I mix Roger another drink."

Theodosia perched on a high stool while Charlotte busied herself behind the bar.

"It's so sweet of you to drop by," said Charlotte. She reached for two cut-glass tumblers and set them on the counter in front of her.

"I wanted to extend my condolences," said Theodosia.

Charlotte gave a noncommittal nod. "Kind of you."

"And Drayton sends his sympathies as well."

"Dear Drayton," Charlotte murmured. "Always so proper." She dug into the freezer compartment of a small built-in refrigerator and pulled out a good-sized chunk of ice. "Such a traditional southern gentleman." She grabbed an ice pick and stabbed at the ice while it spun wildly on the counter. "Too bad there aren't more like him."

Theodosia watched Charlotte's strong, practiced hands as the gleaming metal tip flashed back and forth, hacking at the ice. She broke off one hunk and tossed it into a tumbler, where it clinked and spun around. She thrust the ice pick back into the block of ice and sheared off another shard. That went into the second tumbler.

Watching her was almost hypnotic. And the notion couldn't help but swirl inside Theodosia's head—was it possible that this woman had stabbed her own husband to death? Could she have done it with the same cool detachment that she was exhibiting right this very moment? Theodosia shook her head to rid herself of such an awful thought. But like a bad dream that lingers on into morning, it circled back and wouldn't go away.

"Theodosia?" said Charlotte. She was smiling, her eyes

shining bright like polished pennies, holding up a mint julep. Garnished with a sprig of fresh mint, no less.

"Excuse me . . . yes?" said Theodosia. While she'd been lost in her reverie, Charlotte had managed to whip together two fresh drinks.

"I know you said you didn't want a cocktail, but what's the harm, right? TGIF?"

"Right," said Theodosia, accepting the drink. The mingled scent of hothouse orchids and strong bourbon, plus Charlotte's constant prattle, made her feel slightly woozy. She put a hand on the counter to steady herself.

"Come over here and sit with us," said Charlotte, crossing the room and motioning to Theodosia. Charlotte handed a drink to Greaves, then plunked herself down on an overstuffed floral love seat and patted the space next to her.

Theodosia obliged.

Charlotte smiled at Theodosia, and said, "Thank you for the scones and tea, my dear. But . . . it feels like you might have come here for something else. Would I be correct in assuming that?"

Taken aback, Theodosia said, "Not really, I . . ."

Chuckling now, Charlotte held up a hand. "It's not a problem, Theo. I'm well aware of your . . . what shall we call them? Prodigious talents?"

"What on earth are you muttering about?" Greaves asked.

"Our dear Theodosia here," said Charlotte, "is a bit of an amateur investigator."

"Oh, not really," said Theodosia. She felt like shrinking into the furniture.

"Is that so?" said Greaves. He hunched forward, looking a little more interested now.

"Drayton Conneley speaks about you in glowing terms," Charlotte said to Theodosia. "He can positively enthrall with tales of your derring-do."

Thanks a lot, Drayton, Theodosia thought.

"How interesting," said Greaves. "Why don't we see if Theodosia has any insights into poor Edgar's untimely death? After all, she was a guest at the party last night."

"She was the one who found him," said Charlotte. "So I'd love to hear what she has to say." This time her gaze wasn't quite so friendly.

"The thing is," said Greaves, resting his drink on his knee, "something had been seriously bothering Edgar for the past couple of weeks."

"Do you have any idea what that might have been?" Theodosia asked.

Greaves shook his head. "None whatsoever."

"Oh, come on, now," said Charlotte. "Don't you think some of his distress had to do with your pushing him to take the company public?"

Greaves sighed. "Well . . . yes. You're probably right. Edgar was certainly upset over that." He gazed at Theodosia. "We were working to put together an IPO," he explained, "to finally take Datrex public."

"Except Edgar was extremely reluctant," said Charlotte. "He was dragging his feet."

"Why do you suppose that was?" said Theodosia.

"Fear of change?" said Greaves. "Fear of success? Edgar and I had been partners for eight and a half years, and in all that time, he generally preferred the status quo. He was never comfortable making major changes."

"He was an *engineer*," said Charlotte, as if that explained everything.

"But Datrex had clearly hit its stride," Greaves continued. "We were growing by leaps and bounds. Why, we even inked an agreement with the DOD a few weeks ago."

"The DOD?" said Theodosia.

"Department of Defense," said Greaves.

"For data mining," Charlotte said brightly.

"So there was a security clearance involved," said Theodosia.

"Yes, of course," said Greaves. "But aside from all that, this was an opportune time to make our grand move. An IPO would give Datrex a major infusion of cash and propel us to the next level."

"I take it your privately held shares would skyrocket in value?" said Theodosia. She wasn't immune to the intrigue of high finance and the stock market. She watched *Squawk Box* every morning.

"Oh, absolutely," said Charlotte. She put her lips together and pulled them downward into an unhappy face. "But Edgar was always too worked up to give the IPO serious consideration. To sign off on it."

"What do you think he was worried about?" said Theodosia. *Breaking up with Cecily? Or something else?*

"Oh," said Charlotte, "Edgar fretted about anything and everything. That's how he operated. There were always huge business concerns nagging at him, of course, but he also worried about getting the best seats at the orchestra. Or whether aphids were lunching on his precious cymbidium orchids."

"We always suspected Edgar was afflicted with OCD," said Greaves. "We tried to convince him there were good medications that might help—but to no avail."

"Because Edgar sat on the board at the museum," Charlotte continued, "he'd even worked himself up over that silly Chinese tea house. I know he called some art dealer over there just to check up on things."

"The man was conscientious," said Greaves. "You have to give him that."

"I think they'd even talked yesterday morning," Charlotte babbled. "Of course it would be a day later in China."

"Today?" said Greaves, looking puzzled.

"Well, now it's tomorrow," said Charlotte.

"Edgar was probably reassuring the Shanghai people

that the tea shop had arrived in fine condition," said Greaves, shaking his head. "And that it had been properly assembled in time for the reception."

Charlotte nodded sagely. "Oh, yes. That's typical Edgar. Very meticulous. Very thoughtful." Her voice hardened. "On *some* things, anyway."

"What's going to happen with Datrex's IPO now?" Theodosia asked, eager to get back to that particular subject. If she had been Edgar Webster, that's the item of business that would have kept *her* awake at night.

"Oh, we'll proceed with it," said Greaves. "No question."

"Nothing to hold it back now," chirped Charlotte.

She means no one *to hold it back*, thought Theodosia. Since the problem—the main sticking point—was now dead and buried. Well, not quite buried. Probably still lying on an autopsy table.

As if reading her mind, Charlotte said, "Theodosia, Roger and I paid a visit to Surley and Squire Funeral Home this morning. We're planning to hold Mr. Webster's funeral this coming Monday at nine AM." She referred to her husband as Mr. Webster, in the manner of the old South.

"I see," said Theodosia. She hoped the autopsy would be complete by then. She hoped there might be some definitive answers.

"Anyway," continued Charlotte, "the reason I tell you this is because we're holding the services at St. Philip's Church, which is just a half block down from the Indigo Tea Shop. Since the funeral is by invitation only, I was hoping we could have all our attendees drop by your place for a post-funeral luncheon. Do you think you could arrange that?"

"Yes, of course," said Theodosia. "I'd be happy to." She hesitated. "Well, not exactly happy, but I'd . . ."

Charlotte touched her arm. "Don't worry, dear, I know what you mean. And I'm sorry to give you such late notice."

"That's not a problem," said Theodosia. The tea shop was open tomorrow, Saturday, and would be open again on Sunday for the *Titanic* Tea, so it would be easy to pull Charlotte's luncheon together. Just one more event to rotate in.

"Probably just serve tea and tea sandwiches," said Charlotte, absently fingering a large coral ring.

"Along with scones and perhaps a small salad or fruit plate?" said Theodosia.

"Mmn, that does sound lovely," said Charlotte. "Yes, that would be perfect."

"Is there any particular tea you'd like to serve?"

Charlotte looked suddenly pained. "Perhaps you and Drayton could figure that out. You're the experts, after all."

"Of course."

A few minutes later, claiming the onset of a sudden headache, Charlotte shooed Theodosia and Greaves out the door.

"I'm sorry but I just can't . . ." said Charlotte. "I must . . ."

"We understand," said Theodosia. She figured the shock of her husband's death was finally catching up to Charlotte.

Standing on the front walk in fading October sunlight, with long shadows beginning to creep across the lawn, Theodosia and Greaves faced each other.

"May I speak to you frankly?" Theodosia asked.

Greaves gave an imperceptible nod.

"Charlotte never mentioned Cecily Conrad."

Greaves looked thoughtful. "No, she didn't. I think because her pride was . . . is . . . so deeply wounded."

Theodosia thought it was an interesting choice of words.

"Have there been any accusations from Charlotte that Cecily might have been the killer?"

Greaves stuck both hands in his pants pockets and jingled his change. Finally, he said, "Yes. In fact, it was the first thing she said to the detectives last night."

"Just to be clear," said Theodosia, "Charlotte made a direct accusation against Cecily?"

"She pretty much *hurled* an accusation," said Greaves. "Shrieked her head off to that rather large, stolid fellow. The one who heads the Robbery and Homicide Division."

"Detective Tidwell."

"Yes, that's the one. Tidwell."

"Do you think he took her seriously?"

"Hard to say," said Greaves. "He seemed to. Then again, Charlotte was beyond hysterical after the police hauled her husband's body away."

Theodosia hesitated. "What do *you* think, Mr. Greaves? Edgar Webster was your business partner for many years, you worked together closely, so you must have known something about Cecily." She'd tried to word her question carefully so as not to put Greaves on the defensive.

"Cecily was angry," said Greaves. "There's no doubt about that. Edgar cut off the relationship and asked her to pay back the money he'd loaned her. And Cecily pretty much spat in his face."

"Was he angry and demanding or . . . ?" What she really wanted to know was if he had provoked Cecily.

"No, no, Edgar was quite calm about the whole thing. He wanted to give her a reasonable amount of time and all that."

"Really?" said Theodosia. Then she added, "Do you think Cecily would have paid him back? I mean if she proved successful?"

Greaves shook his head. "Doubtful. I mean, Edgar was a pretty trusting sort of fellow. If you ask me, he pretty much just *gave* Cecily Conrad several hundred thousand dollars."

"I heard a half million."

"Maybe."

"And he didn't get anything in writing?" Theodosia asked. "Get her to sign some sort of note or contract?"

"Not that I know of," said Greaves.

"Which means, now that Webster is dead, Cecily really isn't obligated to pay the money back."

"That's right," said Greaves. "She's free and clear."

Maybe not that free and clear after all, Theodosia thought as she walked to her car.

7

Theodosia was lost in thought as she wove her way through the picturesque streets of the Historic District. She realized that, in just fifteen minutes' time, she'd stumbled upon quite a few relevant facts. She'd discovered that Charlotte Webster was not just crazy, as Delaine had warned, but that she was awfully cozy with Roger Greaves. Roger Greaves, on the other hand, with his cool, casual indifference, could be a raging sociopath who'd murdered his own partner in order to wrest control of the business and speed ahead with his IPO.

The third thing she knew for sure was that Max had been unjustly fired, no matter what crappy, rotten reason the museum board had drummed up.

And, yes, Theodosia had made up her mind that it was her mission in life to unravel this whole ridiculous mess. A man had been murdered in cold blood, Max desperately needed her help, and justice had to be served.

So where to start?

For one thing, Theodosia hoped that Max had gotten the voice mail she'd left him earlier and was waiting for her at home. Then they could sit down together, sort through the sordid details, and maybe figure a few things out. Or at least figure out where to start.

Hanging a right on Meeting Street, Theodosia bumped along toward her cottage, barely registering the fact that golden leaves were spinning down in miniature, swirling tornadoes. Charleston's hot, steamy summer was finally behind them, and the cooler, more temperate days of autumn were here.

She passed the historic Gunther-Melrose Home, a fine old Italianate mansion with rounded arches, balustrades, and a loggia. Unfortunately, its new owners, with their recently installed outdoor lighting, had managed to give it the garish appearance of a supper club. On the next block, the Granville Mansion stood hunkered in gloom. It was far more tastefully done, but was still waiting for a buyer after Dougan Granville, Delaine's fiancé and the home's owner, had been murdered last June. It had been priced high at almost four million dollars, so no takers thus far.

Then her headlights swept across the front of her own small cottage, and Theodosia's heart swelled with pride. Because she truly adored this cute little Queen Anne–style cottage that she had scrimped and saved for—her own little place, with the endearing name of Hazelhurst. How many plates of scones had she sold to make the down payment? How many pots of tea had she ferried to customers? It didn't matter; the Indigo Tea Shop was a labor of love, the home was in her name, and that was all that mattered.

Pulling to the curb, Theodosia gazed lovingly at the exterior. Her quirky little home fairly oozed street appeal, thanks to its slightly asymmetrical design and rough cedar tiles that replicated a thatched roof. The exterior walls were brick and stucco, and there was an arched door, wooden cross gables, and the blip of a two-story turret. To complete the look, lush curls of ivy meandered up the sides of her house.

Theodosia had barely gone three steps up the cobblestone walk when the front door flew open, and there stood Max with Earl Grey at his side. Earl Grey had been a terrified, half-starved puppy when she'd found him huddled in the rain in the alley behind the Indigo Tea Shop. Now he was a magnificent animal with his dappled coat (she thought of him as a Dalbrador), expressive eyes, and fine, aristocratic muzzle.

Bending forward, she clapped her hands together, and called, "Hey, pup!"

That was all Earl Grey needed. He dive-bombed toward her, almost knocking her off her feet as he buried his head in hands that moved gently and lovingly over him, patting ears, muzzle, and neck.

"Nice to see you, too," Theodosia told him.

"Rrwwr," said Earl Grey.

"I am home kind of late," said Theodosia. "Sorry about that." She looked up. "But I see Max dropped by. Were you two enjoying some playtime?"

"We went for a run together," said Max. "Down to the harbor."

"Great," said Theodosia. She threw Max a questioning look. "Well?" She hadn't heard from him all day and was dying to know what happened.

"I've definitely been fired," said Max. "There's not much else to say."

"Au contraire," said Theodosia, "there's a lot more to say." She dusted her hands together. "Why don't we go inside and you can tell me what's going on."

Max sat in a wooden Shaker-style rocking chair while Theodosia kicked off her shoes and curled up on her chintz-covered sofa. Earl Grey lay on the Aubusson carpet, equidistant between the two of them and looking a little nervous, as if he might be called upon to referee.

"So tell me," said Theodosia.

Max lifted one hand. "It's pretty much over. I'm not *technically* fired yet; I guess HR has to draw up some legal documents. But I've been put on unpaid leave."

"And why is that exactly? What reason did they give? Don't tell me this is because of the photo booth?" Theodosia had given some thought to the reason behind Max's firing and decided the photo booth couldn't be the *real* reason. It was far too petty. It had to be a smokescreen for something else.

Max shook his head. "Not the photo booth. That's really just an unfortunate add-on. Turns out the board was upset about an argument I had with Edgar Webster."

"You argued with him?" This was news to her. "When?"

"Couple days ago."

"Over what?"

"Oh, it was stupid, really," said Max. "Almost inconsequential."

"Obviously not."

"Our disagreement concerned publicity for the opening of the tea house."

Theodosia waggled her fingers. "Okay. Tell me more. Give me all the dirty details."

"I decided our private-donor party really didn't warrant any publicity," said Max. "I figured it was smarter to conserve our resources and garner as much press as possible for the public opening instead."

"Sounds right to me."

Max rocked forward in his chair and gazed at Theodosia earnestly. "It is right. I mean, think about it: Invitations had gone out and donors and Gold Circle patrons had already RSVP'd to the opening-night party. In my book, there's nothing worse than generating publicity for an event that the general public isn't invited to attend. Isn't *allowed* to attend. It's elitist and rude and defeats the purpose of presenting ourselves as a public institution."

"Absolutely," said Theodosia. Before opening the Indigo Tea Shop, she'd spent several years as a marketing executive. She understood the business of PR and media relations. "But you're telling me that Edgar Webster didn't agree with you."

"That's right. He had his heart set on a feature story in the *Post and Courier*. Apparently, he was fairly well connected with the arts editor, Phil Sirochi, and had it all ironed out."

"He wanted to toot his own horn," said Theodosia. "And that of the donors who paid to import the tea house."

"I'm fairly sure that was the gist of it," said Max. "But the story would have come off as a self-serving article about a bunch of rich guys."

"So you put the kibosh on it."

"Yes, I did," said Max. "I made a call to Sirochi, explained the situation, and that was the end of it. The other thing is, all publicity, all marketing efforts, are supposed to be run through me. We can't have everyone at the museum scurrying around like chickens with their heads cut off, writing their own press releases and sucking up to the media."

"That's right," said Theodosia. "The media is supposed to suck up to you, to the PR guy."

That brought a faint smile to Max's face. "Something like that, yes."

Theodosia gazed about her living room with its beamed ceiling, chintz and damask furniture, antique highboy, and elegant oil paintings, and said, "So that's why Webster was chewing you out last night? Because you pulled the plug on his publicity?"

"Yeah . . . and I have to admit I pretty much shrugged

him off. Nicely, of course. But now . . . now our confrontation has taken on new meaning and been blown completely out of proportion."

"And the board of directors really did vote to oust you?"

"Probably because they're running scared. They're worried about possible lawsuits from Charlotte Webster as well as from Edgar Webster's company. Or they're afraid of bad publicity, as well as backlash from board members, patrons, and donors—you name it."

"Cowards," said Theodosia.

"Looking for a fall guy," said Max. "Hey, for all I know one of the board members or Gold Circle patrons who was there last night could have stabbed Webster. I don't attend their board meetings and affinity groups, so I don't know what goes on. But I'm sure there's a fair amount of political maneuvering and backstabbing."

"Or ear stabbing," said Theodosia.

"Well, yes," said Max. "Unfortunately."

Theodosia thought about the situation. Pretty much every board of directors that she'd served on, with the exception of Big Paw Service Dogs, had been rife with infighting. It was the nature of the beast.

"So that's it," said Max. "In a nutshell."

"I have some news for you," said Theodosia. She quickly filled him in on her visit with Charlotte Webster and Roger Greaves, and what she perceived as a seemingly cozy and questionable relationship.

Max listened carefully.

"Oh, and there's something else," said Theodosia. "Webster was opposed to Greaves taking Datrex public with an IPO. But now, with Webster dead, there's nothing to stand in the way."

"Wow," said Max, when she'd finally finished. "All this information leaves me a little breathless."

"I haven't even gotten to Cecily Conrad," said Theodosia.

"The woman you mentioned this morning," said Max. "The one who was having the torrid affair with Webster."

"We've got to throw that little temptress into the mix as a possible suspect, too."

"So now we have three suspects. Each with a possible motive."

"A lot to think about," said Theodosia.

"How much do you know about Cecily Conrad?" asked Max.

"Not that much. Just that she's the proud owner of Pine Nut Décor and Custom Furniture."

"Okay."

"And, of course, Edgar Webster gave Cecily the money to open her store. I'd guess we're talking six months' rent, as well as money for interior renovation and decorating, fixtures, a complete inventory, custom woodworking shop . . . well, you name it. And the crazy thing is, I found out there was never any agreement in writing."

Max was listening carefully. "So now that Webster is dead, Cecily doesn't have to pay the money back."

Theodosia aimed an index finger at him. "Bingo."

"Theo," said Max, "you're getting that funny look in your eyes. You're leaning toward Cecily, aren't you? You think Cecily Conrad murdered Edgar Webster."

"Thinking is a long way from knowing."

"And you got most of this information from Delaine?"

"And I picked up a smattering from Roger Greaves," said Theodosia. "Who also had a serious motive to get rid of Webster."

"It seems like Delaine has the 411 on everybody."

"Telegraph, telephone, tell Delaine. Although, she's probably got her own podcast by now. And has raked in even more information since we talked this morning."

"You think it's worth calling her again? See if she's picked up anything new?"

"I suppose I could give her a ring."

"I'd appreciate it," said Max. "Especially since my neck is on the line here."

Theodosia pulled her cell phone from her bag and hastily punched in Delaine's number.

"Hello?" came a squawky, tremulous voice. Theodosia figured it had to be Aunt Astra.

"Is Delaine there?"

"Who wants to know?" Harsher now. Definitely Aunt Astra.

"It's her friend Theodosia."

"Hold."

When Delaine came on the line, Theodosia said, "Is Aunt Acid always that testy?"

"I warned you. Battery acid runs in that woman's veins."

"In that case, I hope you *can* pawn her off on one of your other relatives."

"I'm working on it, Theo, believe me. And while I have you on the phone, I want to remind you about the Hunt and Gather Market this Tuesday."

"The what?"

"Hunt and Gather Market," said Delaine. "Theo, don't tell me you forgot!"

"I . . ."

"You *guaranteed* me that the Indigo Tea Shop would have a table. In fact, I reserved one for you. I'm the chairwoman, don't you remember?"

"I guess it kind of slipped my mind."

Delaine released an unhappy-sounding sigh. "I thought that's why you might be calling."

"I was actually wondering if you'd picked up any more dirt . . . uh, information . . . on Cecily Conrad."

"Inquiring minds want to know, hmm?" said Delaine. "Well, it's funny you should ask, since I'm just off to her open house."

For the second time that day, Theodosia wasn't sure she'd heard Delaine correctly. "What did you just say?"

"Am I not making myself understood? I said I'm going to Cecily's open house at Pine Nut." Now Delaine lowered her voice. "And I'm dragging Aunt Acid along in hopes that I can dump the old bat on someone else."

"Wait a minute, back up," said Theodosia. "Cecily is actually having her open house the evening after her ex-boyfriend was murdered?"

Delaine made a *tsk-tsk* sound in the back of her throat. "Cecily didn't *plan* it that way, for goodness' sake. This open house has been on the schedule for a couple of weeks. Cecily wanted to wedge it in between the Lamplighter Tour and the opening of opera season."

"And you're really going?"

"Of course I'm going," said Delaine. "Good heavens, Theo, you don't expect me to stay home on a perfectly good Friday night, do you? There'll be interesting people there. Probably interesting men." She paused. "Come along if you want."

Theodosia thought for a moment. "You think that would be okay?"

"It's an *open house*, Theo. Not crashing a state dinner at the White House."

When Theodosia hung up the phone, she turned to Max, and said, "Guess where we're going tonight?"

"Ah . . . out to dinner?"

"That's right. We're going over to Drayton's for tuna and Tater Tot casserole."

"*That* doesn't sound like something Drayton would whip up."

"Then how about we attend the open house at Pine Nut?"

"Oh gosh," Max said, looking flustered. "That's Cecily's shop?" Then, "We're really going?"

"This is as good a time as any to sleuth around and try to pick up some more information on Webster's little tootsie."

"You just love rushing in where angels fear to tread, don't you?" said Max.

Theodosia gave him an easy smile. "But I never professed to be an angel. And we *are* doing this on your account." She held up a finger. "So give me a couple of minutes to change clothes, feed Earl Grey, and run a comb through my hair. Then we'll stop by your place so you can jump in the shower and get dressed."

"Okay," said Max. "But is it going to be fancy?"

"No," said Theodosia. "But it could be uncomfortable."

8

❧

Pine Nut was located on King Street, right in the heart of Charleston's upscale antique and art gallery district. Cecily's shop occupied the first floor of a redbrick building that was sandwiched between Dufrene's Antiques and the Sandager Gallery. The building, which looked old enough to be on the historic register, was dominated by tall windows accented with traditional white shutters. Palmetto trees, growing in large ceramic pots, flanked the front door, their tendrils waving in the cool evening breeze that swept in from the Cooper River.

"This must be the place," said Theodosia. She was wearing a crinkly black silk top with tapered black slacks. Max had changed into a camel sweater and gray slacks.

Rather than pull right up to the front door and leave her car with the hired valet, Theodosia had opted to park it further down the street. "The better to make a clean getaway," she'd joked to Max. Only she'd been half-serious.

"This isn't an open house, it's a mob scene," said Max.

They were standing on the sidewalk, gazing through the front windows. The words PINE NUT DÉCOR & CUSTOM FURNITURE had been lettered in gold Gothic script. Beneath it were the words CECILY CONRAD, PROPRIETOR. Along with the reproduction of a Louis XVI settee in the front window, nothing was understated.

"The fact that so many people turned out will make it easy for us to blend in," said Theodosia. She reached for Max's hand and squeezed it for good luck as they stepped across the threshold.

The shop was jammed wall-to-wall with furniture, lamps, mirrors, folding screens, and various pieces of upscale bric-a-brac. It was also packed tightly with crowds of decorators, designers, gallery owners, friends, and hangers-on who jostled each other like mad, trying to look glamorous while not spilling their drinks on the custom upholstered furniture.

Just to the left of the entrance was a bar where thirsty partygoers were packed in as tight as kippers. To their right, a slick-looking DJ with gelled hair and a black leather jacket worked his computer and mixing board setup. He twiddled a dial and "You're So Vain" by Marilyn Manson suddenly blasted through the shop. Behind him was a blinking red neon sign that said DJ MAD DOG.

"I'm pretty sure that's the same DJ we hired for the Matisse show," Max joked.

"Too bad you didn't hire him for last night's party," Theodosia shot back. "Instead of setting up that photo booth." When Max's lips pressed together, she said, "Dang, I didn't mean for that to come out so harshly. Sorry."

"It's okay," said Max. "I know what you mean. Heck, I feel the same way. I guess it was just my bad luck."

"No," said Theodosia. "It was Edgar Webster's bad luck."

Theodosia and Max pretty much abandoned all hope of getting a drink at the bar, but as they pressed their way toward the interior of shop, they encountered a cadre of white-coated waiters bearing silver trays heaped with appetizers.

"Thank goodness," said Max. "I haven't had a bite to eat since lunch."

"Me neither." Theodosia grabbed a cracker that was topped with a dab of pâte and accepted a paper napkin from a solicitous waiter.

"I wouldn't eat that if I were you," called out a brash, nasal voice.

Theodosia whirled around to find Bill Glass offering her a strangled grin. He was dressed in a ratty pinstriped suit that made him look like a mafioso or an actor from *Guys and Dolls.* A Nikon camera with a high-powered lens was slung around his neck.

Theodosia held up her cracker. "What's wrong with it?"

"That chicken pâte tastes like pet food," said Glass.

Theodosia popped the whole thing into her mouth and chewed. "Delicious," she proclaimed. But Glass was right. The chicken liver, or whatever mystery meat had been ground into submission, did taste like pet food.

"You obviously have a stronger constitution than I do," said Glass.

"All my tea drinking has build up certain immunities," said Theodosia, putting a topspin of bravado on her words. "Did you know that ginger tea is great for indigestion and that chamomile tea calms you down?"

"Very informative," said Glass. "And I hope you've got an emergency thermos of that ginger stuff tucked away somewhere."

"Afraid not," said Theodosia.

Glass aimed a perfunctory smile at Max. "Hey there," he said.

"Hello," said Max.

"I heard you got fired," said Glass.

"*Excuse* me," said Theodosia. She glared at Glass. "That's a rude way to start a conversation."

"Yeah," said Glass, "but it's relevant."

"You think?" Theodosia said coldly. What a pipsqueak Glass was!

Nonplussed, Glass hooked a thumb and jabbed it in Max's direction. "It's relevant because he didn't murder anyone."

"Of course, he didn't," said Theodosia.

"Of course, I didn't," said Max.

"But the swells at the museum aren't so sure about that," said Glass. "Deep inside their paranoid little minds, they think you might have done the deed." He made a slashing motion across his throat with his hand. "That's why you've been cast out."

"It sounds to me like you've done some more snooping around," said Theodosia. "Tell me, what exactly have you heard?"

"For one thing, your boyfriend here is probably going to be taken in for questioning," said Glass.

"I seriously doubt that," said Theodosia.

"I said *questioning*," said Glass. "Not *arrested*. There's a big difference."

"I already spoke to the police," said Max, "last night." He looked a little panicky.

"But that doesn't mean they got the answers they want," said Glass, "or picked your brain for possible leads."

"Do *you* have any leads?" Theodosia asked. Glass was a pain in the butt and an unmitigated snoop. But he was a *relentless* snoop. His blunt, somewhat unorthodox manner gave him an uncanny ability to draw answers out of people. He could interrogate people without them even realizing it.

"Leads?" said Glass. "Naw, I got nothin' concrete yet. But if we put our heads together, I bet we could come up with a few choice theories."

"You think we should work together?" said Max. "Are you serious?" He looked like he'd rather handle a rattlesnake.

"As serious as a tomb," said Glass.

"Not gonna happen," said Max.

"You might whistle a different tune when they haul you into that little room with the shiny bright lights and one-way mirror," said Glass. He grabbed another appetizer and popped it into his mouth.

"I thought you hated the pâte," said Theodosia.

Glass shrugged. "What can I say? It's hard to resist free food."

Theodosia propelled a nervous, jittery Max through the horde of people and headed for the relative calm and quiet at the back of the shop.

"The nerve of that guy," Max sputtered, "to imply that I'm a suspect." They stopped next to a pine highboy and gazed at each other.

"The thing is . . ." said Theodosia. She peeked at the price tag on the highboy. Twenty-six hundred dollars. Way overpriced for a not-so-great reproduction.

"What?" said Max.

"You *are* a suspect."

Max's shoulders sagged. "How did I go from being the unlucky PR guy to number one suspect in the course of twenty-four hours? I mean, what kind of loony tunes crap is that?"

"First off, you're not the number one suspect," said Theodosia, trying to calm him down. "You're one of dozens."

"Somehow it doesn't feel that way."

"Listen," said Theodosia, "you can't keep acting like a nervous cat, okay? You have to relax and project an air of cool and calm—and absolute self-assurance of your innocence."

Max swiped a hand across his cheek. "Okay." He didn't look convinced.

"Can you do that?" Theodosia pressed. "Because if you don't stay calm, the sharks will start to circle. They *will* smell blood."

"Jeez, Theo, you make it sound like I'm fighting for my life."

"No, Max, you're fighting for your job. You want it back, don't you?"

"Of course, I do. I love working at the museum. It means everything to me."

"Okay, then just stay frosty."

"And what are you going to do?" asked Max.

"Me?" Theodosia thought for a few seconds. "I'm going to do whatever it takes."

"Okay," said Max. "I'll play it your way. For now." He gazed earnestly at Theodosia. Then his eyes suddenly flicked past her. "There's Delaine over there. You think we should go talk to her?"

"I definitely think we should," said Theodosia. "It's one of the reasons we came here tonight."

Delaine had also spotted them and, like a heat-seeking missile, was scrambling in their direction.

"Goodness, what a ginormous crowd for such a pretentious little furniture store!" Delaine exclaimed. She looked extremely glam in a seafoam green beaded top, matching silk slacks, and silver Manolo Blahnik heels. Trailing in her wake, like a tiny remora fish, was Aunt Acid.

"It's nice to see you, too," said Theodosia. "We were wondering when you'd show up."

"Oh, I've been here for some time," said Delaine, "but I got stuck gabbing with that awful Monica Fontaine. She was bending my ear about Carol Bingham, who is *dying* to have her home on the Lamplighter Tour. Oh . . ." Delaine sniggered, "and did you see the hideous dress Cecily is wearing? It's the color of uncooked salmon. But that's neither here nor there. I'm thrilled to see the both of you, and I promise you my undivided attention. For now." She suddenly delivered air kisses to both Theodosia and Max, and then grudgingly introduced Aunt Acid to Max.

"Lovely to meet you," Max said to Aunt Acid.

"Whatever." Aunt Acid waved a hand, as if he were a buzzing mosquito sent to plague her.

"It's nice to see you again," Theodosia told Aunt Acid.

"What?" said Aunt Acid, cupping a hand behind her right ear.

"I said it's nice to see you again."

"Do I know you?" said Aunt Acid.

"You were just in my tea shop this morning," said Theodosia. She was smiling but found she was starting to clench her teeth. She could see Delaine's point. Dealing with Aunt Acid was a chore.

"You were the one who served those dry, crumbly scones?" said Aunt Acid.

Delaine rolled her eyes.

"I'm sorry you found them dry," said Theodosia.

"Whatever," said Aunt Acid. She waggled a glass that was half-filled with amber liquid.

Max, suddenly eager to make a getaway, said, "Can I fetch you ladies a drink? Or freshen one? The crowd around the bar seems to have thinned out some."

"A glass of champagne would be lovely," said Delaine.

"Ditto that," said Theodosia.

"Ma'am?" said Max, smiling at Aunt Acid.

"Thanks, sonny," said Aunt Acid. "Bourbon neat, skip the rocks."

"Gotcha," said Max as he scurried away.

"So," said Theodosia, once Max was out of earshot. "Have you heard anything new? About the . . . you know."

"Murrrrder," said Aunt Acid, obviously relishing the word.

"I talked to Brenda Gardner," said Delaine, "who heard it from one of the designers at Popple Hill that the police are going to be questioning Roger Greaves."

"I ran into him today," said Theodosia, "at Charlotte Webster's home."

Delaine's brows arched. "Did the two of them seem inordinately cozy?"

"Why do you ask?" said Theodosia. "Are there rumors going around about them?"

"Nothing all that specific," said Delaine. "But . . . you never know. That Charlotte's a sly one."

"Do you think Charlotte could have been having an affair with Greaves at the same time her husband was having an affair with Cecily?"

"Who's having an affair?" asked Aunt Acid.

"Nobody, dearie," said Delaine. But she tilted her head sideways and gave a little shrug that clearly said *maybe*.

"Wow," said Theodosia.

"It makes sense," said Delaine. "Charlotte and Greaves both have buckets of money, so at least it would be an equitable relationship."

"That would be a weird twist," said Theodosia.

"No kidding," said Delaine. "Of course, Greaves *is* married." She paused, glanced around, and said, "Where did Aunt Acid go?"

Theodosia blinked. "She was just here two seconds ago."

"She's such a little jitterbug," said Delaine, "always wandering off somewhere. I swear, we were down at the Battery the other day, and she climbed up on a cannon and practically took a nosedive into the water."

"I thought you were trying to dump her."

"I am, just not in the ocean."

A little stymied by Aunt Acid's hasty disappearance, Theodosia and Delaine checked the area around them.

There were lots of small women slugging liquor down their gullets, but no Aunt Acid.

"Oh, for crying out loud," said Delaine, lifting a hand to point, "there she is."

"Where?"

"On the other side of that window. She's wandered into the studio where they bang out the custom pieces."

Theodosia tilted her head, the better to see around a woman in a flamboyant black cape and red beret. "Oh, jeez, you're right. She's in the workroom."

"We have to grab her," said Delaine, "before she glues her feet to the floor or picks up a nail gun and . . ."

"Nails herself in the head," said Theodosia as they pushed their way through the crowd.

"Honestly, Auntie," Delaine said as they burst into the workroom, "I can't have you wandering off like this."

"We were worried about you," said Theodosia. The workroom was filled with all manner of finials, banisters, chair arms, and table legs. It carried the pleasant aroma of freshly planed wood, varnish, and lemon-scented polish.

"Hmmm?" Aunt Acid was balancing a tack hammer in her hand, looking like she wanted to smash something.

"Put that down," Delaine ordered.

"Don't yell at me, missy," said Aunt Acid. She stuck out her lower lip in an almost comical pout. "I got bored listening to you two jabber away mindlessly and was just looking around."

"Snooping," said Delaine.

Theodosia stepped in. "We just don't want you to get . . ." Her roving eyes suddenly fell upon a row of tools. ". . . hurt," she finished lamely.

"Now what's gotten into *you*?" Delaine asked, frowning at Theodosia.

"Look over there," said Theodosia. She pointed toward a

row of awls. Long, pointed instruments, all neatly arranged, smallest to largest, on a pegboard that hung on the wall. Awls that were used for carving, piercing, and punching holes.

"What are you . . . ?" Delaine began. Then her eyes took in the awls, and her brain flashed a quick connection. "Oh," she said. "Oh my. Those look so nasty and . . . sharp."

Theodosia stared at the woodworking tools, which bore a remarkable resemblance to ice picks. And, as her heart did a little *thump-bump* inside her chest, all she could think was: *Cecily?*

She wondered if Cecily Conrad could have jammed one of those nasty, pointy things into Edgar Webster's ear. And then, when the deed was done, when Webster's dying breath was nothing more than a sigh, had she carefully wiped the blood off an awl, one of *these* awls, and stashed it neatly inside her perky little Fendi bag?

And then what?

And then made her getaway, of course.

"I find these tools very disturbing," said Delaine, "in light of the, uh, murder."

"More like incriminating," said Theodosia. "I'd say any one of these awls could have made a perfect murder weapon." There, she'd said it. She'd spoken the words without having one shred of evidence. Except, of course, for Edgar Webster's poor dead body.

Delaine grimaced. "Do you think we should . . . ?"

"Tell someone?" said Theodosia. "Yes. I'll call Tidwell first thing tomorrow."

Delaine moved closer to her. "Why not call him right now?"

"Because I want to let this percolate," said Theodosia. "I want to . . ."

Her words were suddenly interrupted by a shrill aria of piercing screams and angry screeches.

"Now what's going on?" said Delaine, startled. "It sounds like a fight just broke out in the middle of the party." She put a hand to her chest and said, "Good glory, you can't even attend a fancy soiree anymore without somebody throwing down and starting a fight."

The awls suddenly forgotten, Theodosia, Delaine, and Aunt Acid rushed from the workshop into the main part of the store where all the action seemed to be taking place.

As if it were a good old-fashioned street fight, a tight circle of onlookers had gathered around two people who were apparently going at it tooth and nail. Theodosia could only hear raised voices, but from the tension in the room, it felt like they'd be throwing blows and ripping each other to shreds any minute now.

"What's going on?" Theodosia asked a tall man in a purple velvet jacket and matching paisley ascot. "What's it all about?"

"Our illustrious hostess is having a *Jerry Springer* moment," said the man, grinning.

"Who is?" said Delaine.

"Our hostess?" said Theodosia. Shocked now, she looked at Delaine, and said, "Cecily?"

"Cecily's in a fight?" said Delaine. "Whoa. This I gotta see. Maybe she'll even pitch a folding chair." Then, like a wide receiver running the ball in for a touchdown, Delaine sprinted into the crowd. She practically straight-armed a silver-haired lady, then dipped a shoulder and shoved a young woman in black leather out of the way. As Theodosia rode her coattails, Delaine zigged and zagged her way directly into the middle of the fray.

"Wait!" cried Theodosia. She was momentarily stalled behind a large man in a pink sweater.

"Hurry up," said Delaine. Her five-inch high heels didn't slow her down one iota. "We don't want to miss this."

Delaine popped out on one side of Marianne Petigru,

one of the decorators who owned Popple Hill Design Studio, while Theodosia ducked out on Marianne's other side.

Theodosia took one look and blinked in utter disbelief.

"Max!" she cried.

Her boyfriend was standing in the middle of the circle, while Cecily Conrad slapped at him and screamed like a crazed banshee.

"No!" Theodosia cried as she dove in to grab Max. "Stop it!"

Max continued to back away from an angry, red-faced Cecily Conrad. Her short, dark hair stuck up from her head as if she'd plunged her finger into a light socket. Her mouth was pulled into a tight, ugly grimace, and she looked as if clouds of steam were about to pour from her ears. About a hundred shocked but spellbound open house guests surrounded them. It looked, Theodosia thought, like a very classy rugby scrum.

"Get out of my shop!" Cecily screamed at Max.

Max held his hands high in a show of surrender. "I'm leaving, I'm leaving."

"You're a horrible, vicious excuse for a human," Cecily hurled at him.

Theodosia was suddenly at Max's side, latching onto his arm and pulling him away. "What happened?" she demanded. "Who started this?" The whole episode was embarrassing and humiliating for everyone.

"She did," someone said, pointing at Cecily.

Theodosia stared at Cecily, who was busy throwing the hissy fit of the century. And, at the exact moment Cecily screamed again, her mouth gaping so wide you could practically count her fillings, Bill Glass ducked in and took a picture.

"Get out of here!" Theodosia slapped at him.

Strobe lights flashed as Glass snapped another quick series of shots. *Pop, pop, pop.* He was Charleston's own unwelcome paparazzo.

"You're not helping," Theodosia hissed at Glass. She tried to wave him off at the same time she struggled to drag Max in the direction of the front door.

Cecily spun toward Theodosia like a rabid weasel and pointed a shaking finger. "Get him out of here!" she screamed.

"C'mon," said Theodosia. She'd sneaked an arm halfway around Max's waist and gave a series of urgent yanks. "Right *now*," she said, using her insistent "Don't you dare chew on that carpet, Earl Grey," tone of voice.

That seemed to get through to him.

"What?" Max said. He stared at her as if in a daze.

"Come with me," said Theodosia, "this instant." But this time she let a hint of gentleness seep into her voice.

"Yes, go!" Cecily shrilled. "You lying, freaking animal!"

Dodging and darting their way through the crowd, Theodosia and Max finally emerged onto the sidewalk. Cool air ruffled their hair, and darkness and quiet wrapped around them like a soft cloak.

"Okay," said Theodosia. She inhaled deeply. "That went well." She touched a hand to her hair and found that the heat, humidity, and the general aura of vitriol had caused it to expand. She smoothed it down, fearing she probably looked like a wild woman, too.

"Jeez," said Max. He touched a hand to his forehead and gave a mock wipe. "That woman's plum crazy."

"The thing I need to know," said Theodosia, "is what did you say to Cecily to make her flip out like that?"

"I was just minding my own business," said Max. "Standing at the bar and talking to that Bill Glass character."

"Oh, great."

"He was being snooty about the wine they were serving, making wisecracks about it coming in a box and all that. But then he apologized for the nasty shot he took at me earlier. I let him know it was cool, that I wasn't nursing any sort of grudge."

Theodosia made a rolling motion with her hand. "Yeah, yeah, and then what happened?"

"Then Glass mentioned Cecily, and I said something about her, and before you know it . . . she was right there in our faces, howling like a scalded cat."

Theodosia wrinkled her nose. "In what context did you mention her?"

Max just stared at her.

"As Edgar Webster's killer?"

"*Killer* is your word," said Max. "I only referred to her as a possible suspect."

"You did this right in the middle of her open house," said Theodosia, her tone getting a little rougher. "Where she or her friends could overhear you? Where she obviously *did* overhear you. Sheesh . . . no wonder the woman came unglued."

"I didn't *mean* for her to overhear me," Max muttered.

"You know what?" said Theodosia. "You think *I'm* the crazy one on this team?" She jabbed an index finger into the middle of his chest. "You're the one who's off his spindle."

"I'm sorry. I really am."

"Come on," said Theodosia. "Let get in the car. There's something important I have to tell you."

Max's face fell. "You're breaking up with me?"

"No," said Theodosia. "It's actually much worse."

When they were finally settled in Theodosia's Jeep with the engine running and the defroster pumping out a refreshing shot of cool air, she told him about the row of awls she'd seen in Pine Nut's workshop.

"Owls?" said Max. His brain was still a little discombobulated.

"No," Theodosia told him. "*Awls.*" She proceeded to give him a detailed description of her workshop discovery.

Max finally caught on. "Seriously?" His voice sounded strangled and his eyes went slightly crossed. "You're talking about those sharp, pointy things used in woodworking projects?"

"That's right. Kind of like ice picks, only probably made of stronger steel. Tempered steel."

"There you go!" said Max. "That could definitely point to Cecily being the killer."

"It could. Or it might just be a bizarre coincidence. I mean, who's crazy enough to stab somebody with an awl and then put it back in their own workshop for everyone to see? I mean, especially in the middle of a *party?*"

"Cecily's plan could be to hide the murder weapon in plain sight," said Max. "It's been done before."

"Sure, but mostly on reruns of *The Alfred Hitchcock Hour.*"

Max thought for a minute. "There's another possible explanation for her going all postal."

"Yeah?"

"What if Cecily did kill Webster, and the guilt is starting to eat away at her? That could explain why she went completely berserk."

Theodosia turned on the radio: WAAP, easy listening. Because, boy, did they ever need it. "It's a possibility."

"That's it? That's all you have to say? Theo, you just made a major discovery! One of those awls really could be the murder weapon."

"Calm down," said Theodosia. "Try to dial it back a little. I'm definitely going to run this awl thing past Tidwell."

"And tell him how whacked-out Cecily was?"

"Yes," said Theodosia. "If she really is guilty, she may be hitting her breaking point. Or, as you say, she's already lost it. And the awl thing . . . well, it's what you'd call an incriminating lead. Tidwell might even want to send in his crime-scene team."

"To test the awls for, like, blood?"

"Or tissue residue," said Theodosia. "But that's his call. The thing is, we've got other fish to fry."

"Now what are you talking about?"

"We have to think about getting your job back."

Max did a double take. "Kern was pretty adamant when I talked to him. He did everything but tell me to start punching up my résumé." He paused. "So I don't think getting my job back is even a possibility."

Theodosia gave him what she hoped was a reassuring smile. "Anything's possible. You just have to work it right and stay positive. Or at least *I* have to work it right."

"Wait a minute," said Max. "You're talking about getting my job back? When are you going to attempt this miracle?"

Theodosia reached across the console and squeezed his hand. "First thing tomorrow morning."

9

❧

Theodosia was as good as her word. Bright and early Saturday morning, she slipped into her midnight-blue Dior jacket, patted Earl Grey on his sweet little head, and hurried off to the Gibbes Museum.

She parked out front on Meeting Street, noting that two yellow school buses had just pulled up in front and disgorged at least three dozen museum-going youngsters.

This was good, she decided. The museum was back on track. Visitors, especially these kids, weren't going to be held hostage by what had taken place here Thursday night.

Of course, nothing was ever easy, and Mary Monica Diver, the director's longtime secretary and personal assistant, proved to be a formidable obstacle.

"He's extremely busy," Diver told her when Theodosia asked to see Elliot Kern.

"I imagine he is," said Theodosia. "The tragedy here . . . dealing with the aftermath . . . must be a trial for all of you." She was determined to keep the mood light and sweet. She'd dealt with Diver before and knew it would do no good to pressure her. Diver, who was pushing sixty, wore a beehive hairdo, brown pantsuit, and sensible shoes. She was as formidable and stolid as she looked, tenacious at running interference for her boss.

"I just need five minutes with him," Theodosia said.

Diver gave a passing glance at an appointment calendar and grimaced. "That's probably not going to happen."

"He's in a meeting?" said Theodosia. She leaned down and pulled a clear cellophane bag filled with toasted coconut scones from her tote bag. She'd stopped by the tea shop on her way over. Knowing Diver was a sugar freak of the first magnitude, she'd come armed for bear.

"Oh," said Diver when Theodosia plunked the scones down on her desk. Her squeaky little *oh* was the equivalent of the enemy blinking first.

"Because, if he's in a meeting, these scones might be a welcome addition," Theodosia said.

Diver stared at the scones as if she'd just discovered the treasure of the Sierra Madre.

"You know, I actually have an extra bag here," said Theodosia. She set the second bag on the counter. "Maybe *you'd* enjoy them."

Diver's brows knit together for a fraction of a second. "That's kind of you," she said slowly. "Generous, in fact." Her salivary glands seemed to be waging war with her no-nonsense attitude.

Theodosia gave an offhand wave. "Not a problem. Our scones are so popular, we pretty much bake them all day long. There's more where those came from."

Diver's hand snaked up to grab her bag.

"So . . . do you think Mr. Kern would have, like, two seconds to spare?" Theodosia asked.

Diver licked her lips. "He's awfully busy," she said, making a final pro forma protest, "but let me check." She stood up and smoothed the front of her jacket. "I'll just be a moment."

"Take your time," Theodosia said sweetly.

"I don't know how you weaseled your way in here," said Elliot Kern, "but I'm not about to discuss our employment policies with you." He was dressed casually in khaki slacks and a blue button-down oxford shirt and was bristling with outrage. His hawk nose seemed to vibrate and his lips were pulled tight. Theodosia thought that Kern still looked like one of the members of the Medici family. One of the bean-counter types.

Seated in a black leather club chair, Theodosia stared across an acre of mahogany library table that served as a desk in Kern's private office. If his words and attitude hadn't been so hostile, the meeting might have been downright cozy. Kern's floor-to-ceiling shelves held an array of art objects ranging from Greek vases to South Sea island masks to early American silver. Oil paintings and tapestries hung on the walls. His desk was peppered with tasty objects d'art such as brass candlesticks, geodes, and Chinese ink bottles. It was like taking a crash course in museology.

Theodosia placed the scones on his desk and offered a distracted smile. "I'm not here to discuss museum policy," she said. "I just want to get a few things straight."

Kern stared at her as if she were an unwelcome squatter. Which she pretty much was. "Such as?"

"You put Max on unpaid leave."

"Yes," said Kern. "I most certainly did."

"When do you expect him to return and be back on your payroll?"

Kern leaned forward. "Excuse me?"

"When will he be—"

Kern held up a hand. "No, I heard you just fine. I just can't believe you have the gall to ask that question."

"I don't mean to be galling," said Theodosia. *I just want a straight answer.*

"Look," said Kern, pressing his palms flat against his desk until his nail beds practically turned white. "I admire your loyalty. I even have a grudging respect for your chutzpah. But as far as Max's return to work . . ." He lifted both hands and his fingers flew apart, as if to indicate: Poof! There simply wasn't an answer to be found.

"Come on," said Theodosia. "You don't want to make Max the fall guy in Edgar Webster's death. In fact, you're completely off base if you do. Max is no killer and you know it. He's well liked in the community and has done an admirable job for the museum. When all the dust settles and the real killer is apprehended, you're going to look pretty darn silly."

"It's out of my hands," said Kern. "His dismissal wasn't an indictment; it was merely a recommendation that came straight from our board of directors."

Theodosia shoved the bag of scones toward Kern and smiled serenely. "I know quite a few of those board members," she told him. "Some are friends of mine, others are good friends of Drayton." Kern might regard Drayton as simply the local tea master and antiques buff, but Drayton was held in high esteem by many prominent families in the upper echelons of Charleston society. If Drayton gave Max his vote of confidence—and he certainly had—then that was serious currency. Something to be reckoned with.

"I don't care to be threatened, Miss Browning," said Kern.

Theodosia lifted her right eyebrow and let it quiver. "It's not a threat. I was merely stating a known fact."

"Then let me make myself perfectly clear," said a red-faced Kern, and this time all semblance of propriety seemed to have left him. "I heard all about that nasty squabble between Max and Cecily Conrad last night. Max caused quite a stir, so it's obvious to me that he's a hothead and a troublemaker. And, I can assure you, that is *not* the sort of person I want on staff at my museum!"

Theodosia didn't exactly storm out of Kern's office, but she exited in a distinct huff.

How dare *Kern slander Max like that,* she thought. Kern was a cowardly administrator who was hiding behind a bad decision that his board of directors had made. Or maybe it wasn't even the entire board. Maybe it had been just a few angry, paranoid old men. Either way, she was determined to turn the tide on this ridiculous ruling, no matter what it took. No matter how long it took.

Because the thing about Theodosia was . . . she was tenacious. Call it *wrong*; she'd prove it right. Tell her to back off; she'd dig in her heels. She was a woman who believed in equality and fairness. And no two-bit museum administrator was going to get the best of her!

Theodosia's heels sounded like castanets as she flew down the museum's central corridor, past Greek statues and elegant sixteenth century tapestries. In fact, her steps rang out so loudly, she barely heard the soft voice that called after her.

"Theodosia. Theodosia, hold up a moment."

She turned around with a flounce, her brows pinched together. "What?" she barked out.

Percy Capers, the curator of Asian art, hustled toward her. "I want to talk to you," he said. A stack of brochures fluttered in one hand—he must have been about to give a tour or lecture—and a look of concern lit his normally bland face. He was fairly young—not yet thirty—and wore round wire-rimmed glasses that gave him a friendly, studious look.

"What's up?" Theodosia asked.

Capers pulled up next to her and took in her expression. "Oh my, you don't look happy at all."

"I'm not," said Theodosia. "I just had an unsettling meeting with Elliot Kern."

Capers gave a knowing nod. "Fearless leader."

"Some leader," Theodosia snorted.

"I take it you were talking to him about Max's suspension?"

"Trying to," said Theodosia. She wondered how much Percy Capers knew about this.

Capers touched her arm gently. "If it's any consolation, please know that I'm on your side. And Max's side, too, of course. For Kern to have suspended him like that, with no evidence whatsoever, was unconscionable. That's not how we do things around here." He straightened the brochures that threatened to spill out of his hand. "We're gentlemen. And we conduct business as such."

"Thank you," said Theodosia. "It's nice to know we have a friend on the inside."

"Listen," Capers said hurriedly. "I *am* on the inside, and I promise I'll do everything in my power to help get Max reinstated. I believe in his innocence. Heck, I believe in *him*."

"You're very kind," said Theodosia.

"This is all a terrible misunderstanding," continued Capers. "Edgar Webster had enemies. That's who the police should be looking at. And I'm sure they are, but . . ."

Theodosia was slightly taken aback. "Wait a minute, what enemies are you referring to?"

"Certainly that crazy woman he was carousing with," said Capers. "I heard that she completely turned against him. As for his business partner . . . well, I'm not sure the two of them ever got along all that well."

"What about Charlotte, his wife?"

"That I couldn't say. Although . . ." Capers's eyes darted

from side to side and he glanced around, as if fearing he'd be overheard.

"What?" Theodosia pressed.

Capers dropped his voice to a minimal stage whisper. "I understand Charlotte is lobbying to take Edgar Webster's place on the board of directors."

"That's interesting," said Theodosia. She wondered if a woman would murder her husband just to improve her social standing. On the other hand, philandering husbands had been murdered for far less.

"I do find Charlotte's move a little strange," Capers admitted.

"Will you let me know if that happens? If Charlotte really does get invited onto the board?"

"Count on it," said Capers. He held up a finger. "And if there's anything else I can do . . ."

"You're an angel," said Theodosia.

Feeling somewhat mollified, Theodosia wandered into the museum's rotunda. Sunlight streamed down through the domed window overhead, dappling the marble floor and creating little prisms of warmth and cheerfulness.

And, almost on impulse, Theodosia found herself being drawn to the Chinese tea house. She threaded her way through groups of museumgoers until, finally, she was standing outside, once again marveling at the peaked roof and dark cypress walls.

When a group of three women exited the tea house, Theodosia seized the opportunity to duck inside. The interior was dark and peaceful, just as it had been two nights ago, the night of the opening reception. Candles flickered, tins of aromatic tea lined a single shelf, an antique tea chest rested near the small fireplace, where a cast-iron teapot hung. Lightly furnished with a teak tea table and four square Chinese benches, the tea house projected an aura of contemplation and peacefulness.

This transplanted bit of history was truly beautiful, Theodosia decided, from the ornately carved wooden screens right down to the antique scrolls hanging on the walls. It was everything you'd expect from a tea house where scholars and poets had once raised tea bowls filled with fine black tea and quoted the teachings and poetry of Lao Tse and Li Po.

Exhaling deeply, Theodosia settled onto one of the Chinese benches and pulled out her phone. It was time for ugly conversation number two. That is, it was time to call Detective Tidwell and clue him in about the woodworking awls.

Tidwell's gatekeepers were even gnarlier than Mary Monica Diver—they dug their heels in like a pack of unruly mules. But finally, after some serious wheedling, she got through.

"Speak," said Tidwell once he was finally on the line. He sounded gruff and harried.

"Do you have any news from the medical examiner regarding the murder weapon?" she asked.

"Why do you want to know?" said Tidwell. "Wait. Let me guess . . . You're planning to commit a copycat crime? You wish to add to my agitation."

"No, I was wondering if it really was an ice pick that penetrated Mr. Webber's frontal cortex."

"According to the ME's preliminary report," said Tidwell, "it was more likely his temporal lobe."

"In any case," said Theodosia, "I have some information that might interest you."

Her words were greeted by silence.

"Are you still there?" she asked.

"What is it you wish to tell me?" Teasing and taunting her, Tidwell was once again playing cat to her mouse.

"I happened to attend the open house last night at Cecily Conrad's new furniture shop."

"Ah, the rather aptly named Pine Nut."

"Where Max and Cecily got into a knock-down, drag-out screaming match. Or rather, Cecily did the screaming and I dragged Max out."

"Sounds like a lovely night on the town," said Tidwell. "Date night."

"There was also a workshop there," Theodosia continued. "One that was well stocked with woodworking tools."

"As one might expect," said Tidwell.

"Are you familiar with an awl? Or better yet, a row of awls of various lengths and sizes?"

Again there was a moment of silence. And then Tidwell said, "Are you telling me what I think you are?"

"What do you think I'm telling you?"

"That Cecily Conrad had ample access to what could possibly be a murder weapon?"

"My goodness, you're perceptive," said Theodosia. "It appears all that FBI field training paid off."

"No need to get snarky," said Tidwell, though he actually sounded excited. "It's quite unbecoming." Then he added, "This could yield a potential break."

"Yes. Cecily could be more than just a suspect. She could be the killer."

"But we must not leap to conclusions just yet," Tidwell cautioned.

"Really?" said Theodosia. "I've never seen you leap to anything at all."

"Dear girl," said Tidwell, sounding even more enthusiastic, "if this information pays off, I shall leap for joy."

Theodosia stashed her phone in her purse and stared at the scroll that hung on the wall opposite her. It was a lovely Chinese brushstroke painting of a swimming carp. With the fish's large eyes and scales and decorative ink swirls, the painting reminded her of a poem Drayton often quoted about heating water for tea.

Fish eyes going, carp eyes coming, soon will be the wind in the pines.

It referred, of course, to the small bubbles making way for larger, roiling bubbles, and the whistle of the teakettle.

"Excuse me," said a man's voice.

Startled, Theodosia practically jumped out of her chair. In fact, she half rose and spun around. It had been so quiet and restful in the tea house that she'd almost lost track of the fact that she was sitting in a public museum.

A man's face, large and ruddy, floated before her eyes.

"I didn't mean to startle you," said the man. He held his hand out in a gesture of greeting. "I just wanted to take a second look at this place."

Theodosia stared at him as she shook his hand. "I know you," she said. "Or at least you look familiar."

The man bobbed his head. "Yes, ma'am. I'm Harlan Duke." He reached into his jacket pocket, pulled out a crisp white business card, and handed it to her.

Theodosia scanned his card. "You're an art dealer." From the address on his card, it looked as though his shop was located maybe two blocks from Pine Nut.

Duke smiled happily as he sat down across from her. "I surely am." He extended a bulky fist and knocked it against one of the cypress posts of the tea house. "I'm also the man who located this baby in Shanghai, on one of the lanes behind Fuxing Road." He smiled. "And persuaded the owner to sell it."

"That couldn't have been easy."

"No, ma'am. Since this fine edifice had stood there since the middle eighteen hundreds, it took a fair amount of persuading."

"And a good deal of money, I would guess," said Theodosia.

Duke smiled. "I wasn't involved in that part. The financial negotiations were all handled by the folks here at the museum."

Theodosia studied Duke. With his string tie, brown

jacket embellished with swirls of fancy white topstitching, and Western boots, he presented quite a spectacle.

"You're not from around here, are you?" she said.

Duke gave a genial guffaw. "I'm from Texas. Dallas in particular. Newly transplanted."

"What brings you to Charleston?"

"Money," said Duke.

"Excuse me?" Theodosia had heard direct answers before, but this one took the cake.

Duke chuckled at her reaction. "You know who John Dillinger was?"

Theodosia gazed at him. "The gangster? Of course I do."

"When a famous newspaper reporter once asked Dillinger why he robbed banks, he replied, 'Because that's where the money is.'"

Theodosia tapped a finger against the table. "And you think this is where the money is?"

"Judging from what I've seen so far, I'd have to say yes. Why, Charleston's got all sorts of fine folks with great big houses, upscale taste, and a burning desire to spend some of that old family money to build up their art collections."

"So you're here to pick their pockets?" said Theodosia. But she said it with humor. She was warming up to this big Texan. He seemed straightforward and honest.

"In a way, yes," said Duke. "And it's been good so far. I'm in the process of selling a Tang horse to Percy Capers, the Asian curator here. And I've almost got Charlotte Webster talked into a pair of Ming tea bowls." He frowned slightly. "Of course, that poor lady's got more than tea bowls on her mind right now."

"I'm afraid she does," said Theodosia. "So . . . you attended the infamous soiree here two nights ago?"

"I sure did. And managed to catch the final act." Duke shook his head. "Never seen anything like it. Horrifying. I'd only met Edgar Webster a couple of times, but I liked him right off. He seemed like a real gentleman. And he was a real admirer of Chinese art. Actually *studied* it instead of just collecting it because it was the trendy, posh thing to do."

"So he was a true connoisseur. I hadn't realized that."

"Oh, yes," said Duke. "Mr. Webster not only knew his dynasties, he had a fairly keen eye." He stopped, adjusted his string tie, and said, "So I understand you're the proprietor of a tea shop?"

Theodosia glanced around. "Yes, but my tea shop isn't quite as historic or breathtaking as this one. It's the Indigo Tea Shop, just a few blocks over on Church Street."

"Sure, I know exactly where you're located. Near that lovely old church that juts out into the street." A broad grin split Duke's weathered face. "You know, I just happen to have a Chien-lung teapot that might interest you."

"You're taking a guess at my taste?"

"I consider myself a pretty good judge of people. And I pride myself on being able to match them up with lovely objects that they often can't resist." He gave a wink. "And this particular teapot that I have in mind has your name written all over it. What do you say, should I bring it by your tea shop so you can have a look?"

"Tell you what," said Theodosia. "You bring your teapot, and I'll at least fill it with tea."

Duke grinned. "You've got yourself a deal."

10

❧

By the time Theodosia got to the Indigo Tea Shop, it was almost eleven o'clock and the joint was jumping. Every table was occupied, and Haley was ferrying out plates of scones and green-tea donuts as well as small cut-glass bowls filled with Devonshire cream and lemon curd.

"There you are," said Drayton. "I was wondering if you'd ever get here. I thought we might have to send out a search party." He snapped the lid off a tin of Nilgiri tea. "We've been buzzing with customers all morning."

"Apologies," said Theodosia as she slipped a black Parisian waiter's apron over her head and tied it in back. "I got hung up at the museum."

Drayton measured out two heaping scoops and added his proverbial pinch. "Were you trying to get Max reinstated?"

"Something like that."

He glanced up. "Have any luck?"

"Not really."

"I'm surprised," said Drayton, as he carefully poured hot water into the teapot. "You're usually fairly keen at working your magic."

"It appears I'm all tapped out when it comes to spells and charms."

"Oh, I doubt that," Drayton chuckled. He set the teapot on a silver tray and added a small dish of lemon slices. "Can you run this over to table seven?"

"Of course," said Theodosia, all business now.

Theodosia delivered the tea, stopped to chat with a table of ladies who'd driven over from Goose Creek for the day, took a couple of orders, and then made the rounds pouring refills.

When Theodosia finally had a free moment, she said to Drayton, "Did you hear about the screaming match last night?"

Drayton offered a faint smile. "Delaine was in earlier and regaled us with all the sordid details. So, to answer your question, yes."

"Did she make it clear that it was Cecily Conrad who was doing all the screaming?"

"Oh, you know Delaine. She ratcheted up the drama to make it sound as if a pack of wolves were fighting over snippets of raw meat. But Haley and I pretty much picked up on the true gist of things, that Cecily overheard Max talking about suspects and sort of snapped."

"Did Delaine mention the carpentry awls?"

Drayton gave a disparaging look. "I'm afraid she took great pleasure in describing them. And insinuating that any one of them could have made a dandy murder weapon." Drayton fingered his bow tie nervously. "Have you informed Tidwell about this new development?"

"I called him half an hour ago, so he's on it."

"Good," said Drayton. He looked up. "What else have you got going on?"

"I ran into Percy Capers at the museum," said Theodosia. "The Asian art curator. Seems like a nice enough fellow."

"Capers mentioned to me that Charlotte is lobbying to get on the museum's board of directors."

"I find Charlotte's interest in the museum a little odd," said Drayton, "but I still don't see her stabbing her own husband. I mean, would she do it just to get a seat on the museum's board of directors? I think not."

"Remember, he'd been cheating on her, too," said Theodosia. "With Cecily." She picked up a tin of orchid plum tea, flipped the lid, and inhaled the sweet fragrance.

Drayton looked worried. "This all seems like a gigantic web of lies and deceit."

Theodosia snapped the lid back on the tin. "Don't forget murder."

Haley had designed the perfect autumn luncheon menu. Squash bisque topped with roasted pumpkin seeds, curried chicken salad tea sandwiches, cream cheese–and-strawberry tea sandwiches, and Cheddar and mushroom quiche.

As was expected, their customers dug into their lunches with relish. Which also meant that à la carte tea sandwiches were ordered, and as Haley's date-and-walnut tea bread and ginger scones emerged from the oven, they were voraciously snapped up, too.

"We're having one of our busiest Saturdays ever," Drayton proclaimed. "The food is selling like hotcakes, and people have been shopping our little gift area." He glanced over. "In fact, there's a woman fingering one of your home-made wreaths right now."

"Then I'd better go over and help her," said Theodosia.

"Did you make this?" the woman asked. She was holding a grapevine wreath woven with blue and gold silk ribbons and hung with miniature teacups and saucers.

"Guilty as charged," said Theodosia.

"You made the actual wreath, too?"

"It's just local grapevine that I pulled down out of trees." Theodosia had gone out to Cane Ridge Plantation, where her aunt Libby lived, and ripped the grapevine out of the trees it had been trying to choke the life out of. From there it had been a simple matter of wrapping her vines around a few old barrels and letting them dry for a couple of months. Then she wired the wreaths for stability and added the ribbons and teacups.

"Do you have any more of these wreaths?" asked the woman.

"How many would you like?" Theodosia smiled to herself. She had ten more wreaths stacked in her back office.

"This one and maybe two more," said the woman.

"I'll be back in a second."

Theodosia grabbed two wreaths from the tangle that sat in the corner of her office and carried them out to the front counter. Drayton helped her wrap each wreath in tissue paper and secure them in large plastic bags.

"Maybe you should have made more," said Drayton, once the wreaths had been rung up and the customer had departed.

"I did. There are another dozen barrels covered with grapevines out at Aunt Libby's. Stuck behind the old pump house."

"You're always thinking, aren't you?"

"Not really," said Theodosia. "That plantation is just terribly overgrown."

By two o'clock, most of their customers had cleared out and Theodosia was sitting in her office sipping a cup of Japanese green tea and nibbling a sandwich. She had gone to the museum's website, sought out their list of directors, and printed out that list.

Now she was muddling it over.

"Can I freshen that tea?" asked Drayton. He was standing

in the doorway holding a pink-and-green Famille rose teapot. With his ramrod posture and aristocratic bearing, he looked like an aging but fit ballet impresario.

"Thank you," said Theodosia, pushing her teacup across the desk.

As Drayton carefully filled her cup, he gazed at the list she'd been studying.

"The museum's illustrious board of directors," he said. "All ten of them in attendance at the reception Thursday night."

"And then there were nine," said Theodosia.

"I hope you don't think someone is trying to kill them off one at a time like some kind of bizarre Agatha Christie tale."

"Nothing quite that sinister," said Theodosia. "But someone certainly wanted to get rid of Edgar Webster."

"You think it was one of his fellow board members?"

"I suppose it's possible."

"Tricky," said Drayton. "Since all are well-heeled and quite powerful."

Theodosia picked up a pen and twiddled it. "Any one of them could probably buy and sell this tea shop without batting an eye. So I have to be careful who I mess with."

"Then don't mess with any of them," Drayton cautioned. "Stand back and let Tidwell do the heavy lifting."

Theodosia bit her lower lip.

"I take it you were thinking about making an appeal to one or several of these board members," said Drayton, "to try and get Max reinstated?"

"The thought had occurred to me. But I'm not sure I have an argument that's persuasive enough to change any-one's mind."

"You don't. That's why they're basically deferring to Elliot Kern."

"Then what's the answer?"

"I think," said Drayton, "that you should continue doing what you do best."

"Worry and bite my nails?"

The corners of Drayton's mouth twitched upward. "No, I mean investigate. But on the side. You know, run a kind of parallel investigation to the one Tidwell is doing."

"I think they call that a shadow investigation."

"That all sounds very drama filled, like the NSA. But I don't believe that national security is at stake."

"Just Max's job security," said Theodosia. "Which is hanging by a very tenuous thread. So thanks for your vote of confidence, Drayton, but I really am stumped. I'm not sure where to look next. Or who to look at." She thought for a few moments. "I suppose if I focused on figuring out some sort of motive . . ."

Drayton flashed her a look of encouragement. "When you find the motive . . ."

"It can lead to the killer," Theodosia said slowly.

"Then I'd say you have to cast a fairly wide net," said Drayton. "Take a look at all the guests who were at the event Thursday night. See how many you can connect directly to Webster."

"There could be quite a few."

"Or there might only be a handful," said Drayton.

"You make a good point," said Theodosia, "even though you are an optimist. So . . . I suppose I need to get my hands on a guest list."

"Which Max probably has at his office." Drayton cocked an eye at her. "If he can get to it."

Theodosia took a quick sip of tea. "So one more thing to worry about."

While Drayton and Haley finished putting the tea shop to rights, Theodosia took some time to handle a few items of business. There were bills to pay, orders that had to be e-mailed to vendors, and marketing decisions to be made.

And since she and Earl Grey were planning to run in the Halloween 5K race Tuesday night, there was the simple matter of figuring out a costume for him. Not an easy thing to do when he had to look cute and still be able to move.

Adding to that to-do list, the phone on her desk started to ring.

Theodosia snatched it up. "Yes?"

"What's going on?" asked Max.

"Oh. Hi. Well, just business as usual I guess." *Or is it business as unusual?*

"How was your meeting?" Max asked. "Did you talk to Kern?"

"I did, but he's still undecided as to when you can return." *Boy, is he ever.*

"It was sweet of you to plead my case," said Max. "But I didn't figure he'd welcome you with open arms."

Haley suddenly loomed in the doorway of Theodosia's office.

Theodosia dropped the phone away from her mouth, and said, "What?"

"Tidwell," Haley mouthed. "He's here. He wants to talk to you, like, now."

"Well, send him in."

"Something going on?" said Max.

"Sorry, but I have to hang up," said Theodosia.

"Customers?"

"Trouble."

Detective Burt Tidwell barely fit in Theodosia's office, even though the overstuffed chair across from her desk, the one she'd dubbed the tuffet, offered ample seating.

"Are you comfortable?" she asked him once he'd sat down.

"Fine," said Tidwell. Clearly he was not fine. He threw withering glances at the various stacks of baskets, red hats, and wreaths that clogged the office. It was all a little too girly for his cop sensibilities.

"May I offer you a cup of tea?" Theodosia asked.

Tidwell's lips pursed. "Do you still serve that lovely Japanese green tea with bits of cherry?"

"Of course," said Theodosia. She lifted the phone, buzzed Drayton on the intercom, and relayed the request.

"Should I bring in a couple of scones, too?" asked Drayton.

"What do you think?" said Theodosia. She hung up and smiled brightly at Tidwell. "What can I do for you?" She figured he was going to tell her about his investigation into the awls. Instead, he blindsided her.

"I need you to tell me about last night," said Tidwell. "The—how shall I phrase this?—the rather heated argument between Max and Cecily."

"Didn't I already mention that?" she said.

"Yes, but now I need to hear the full story. I just returned from Pine Nut, where Cecily Conrad, who feels much maligned, wasted a good deal of my time caterwauling in my ear."

"Let me guess," said Theodosia. "You asked her about the awls and she proclaimed complete and total innocence."

"That's a fair assessment," said Tidwell.

"But Cecily *could* have murdered Webster," said Theodosia. "She was angry at him, and she did have access to those wicked-looking weapons."

"My people are looking into it. Examining the awls carefully."

"Microscopically, I hope," said Theodosia.

"I have your tea," said Drayton, suddenly interrupting. He bustled into Theodosia's office with a large silver tray and placed it on her desk. He indicated the teapot. "Shall I pour?"

"Thank you, Drayton," said Theodosia. "I can manage."

Drayton spoke to Theodosia as he looked pointedly at

Tidwell. "Let me know if you need anything else. Tea, Devonshire cream, moral support."

"Thanks, Drayton, I will," said Theodosia. She poured a cup of tea for Tidwell and handed it to him. "And there are scones here, too. Please help yourself."

"Thank you," said Tidwell. He took a sip of tea and his eyes half closed. "Excellent. Such a lovely vegetal flavor contrasted with the sweetness of the cherry."

"You've become quite a tea connoisseur."

"And you're very clever at turning the conversation."

"I am?" said Theodosia.

"Last night," Tidwell reminded her.

"What was it you wanted to know?"

"The argument."

"I wasn't present when the fireworks started," said Theodosia. "I was in the workroom making what might be considered an important discovery."

Tidwell sipped his tea. "Nicely done. Still, you witnessed a good portion of the argument. Tell me, what exactly set Cecily off?"

Theodosia helped herself to a pumpkin scone. "Oh, Max apparently made some offhand comment to Bill Glass that Cecily overheard."

"About her being a suspect?"

"That was the general idea, yes."

"He didn't accuse Cecily of murder and then attack her?"

Theodosia broke off a piece of scone. "No, that's not Max's style."

"Still, she took umbrage at his remark," said Tidwell.

"No," said Theodosia. "Cecily completely flipped out. Big difference. Ask anyone who was there."

"I already have," said Tidwell.

Theodosia eyed him carefully. "Excuse me, why exactly are you doing this little tap dance? Are you trying to tell me that Max is a suspect?"

Tidwell shrugged.

"You are so barking up the wrong tree!" Theodosia cried. "You know who you should really be looking at?" Now she was practically shouting.

"Enlighten me," said Tidwell.

Theodosia held up a hand so she could tick off the suspects.

"Charlotte Webster. Edgar was cheating on her and making her look like a fool. Plus, Charlotte's no slouch with an ice pick. Just go check out her bar."

"I'll do that," said Tidwell.

"Two," said Theodosia. "Cecily. No more Edgar, no more repayment of the enormous debt that she incurred."

"Point taken."

"And three," said Theodosia. "Roger Greaves. He wanted to take Datrex public, and Edgar Webster was violently opposed to the idea. No more Edgar, no more barrier to an IPO." She sat back in her chair and said, "Get it?"

"I most certainly do," said Tidwell. The entire time she'd been ranting away he'd been nibbling his scone. Now he looked around. "Is there any more of that lovely almond-flavored Devonshire cream?" he asked.

"No," said Theodosia. She crossed her arms and stared at him. "We're all out."

"Are you finished with your rant?" said Tidwell.

"Yes," said Theodosia. "And you're finished, too. I'm afraid you'll have to leave now. I have a lot of work to catch up on."

Tidwell made no motion to leave. "It's funny you should mention the blocked IPO. Another person brought that up to me as well."

"Who was it? Cecily?"

"No, it was some transplanted art dealer that I inter-viewed yesterday."

"Harlan Duke?"

"Yes, that's the fellow. He worked closely with Webster on the importation of that tea house." He paused. "I take it you know him?"

"I met him this morning at the museum," said Theodosia. "He seemed very nice."

"Mmn," said Tidwell. He stood up and brushed at his tweed jacket, causing a miniature waterfall of crumbs to tumble down his lapels.

"Don't tell me poor Mr. Duke is on your suspect list, too," said Theodosia. She stood up to indicate the meeting really was over.

Tidwell just smiled at her. "I'm keeping all my options open."

"Good for you," said Theodosia. "Oh, and Drayton will give you a takeout box if you'd like. On your way out."

11

❧

"*He really sees* me as a suspect?" said Max. He was sitting across the dinner table from Theodosia in her small, elegant dining room. Candles flickered and paintings gleamed on the walls. Overhead, a small crystal chandelier cast a flattering pink glow. But Max was stewing as he fumbled his fork, and it clattered to the table.

"Tidwell was just trying to provoke me," said Theodosia. "He's playing his cards close to the vest, and I think his nose is a little out of joint because I stumbled upon those awls."

"But that's a *good* thing, a really tangible clue. So why is he still on my case?"

"You don't know Tidwell," said Theodosia. "Until a murder is solved, he's on everyone's case."

"Maybe so, but it's very unsettling."

"I know it is. And I wish I could have done more to dissuade him."

"He's a formidable presence," said Max.

"Which is why we want him squarely in our corner. We don't want to tick him off."

"I didn't think that I did," said Max. He looked at Theodosia expectantly. "Theo?"

She sighed. "I might have been a little forceful with him this afternoon."

"What did you do? Did you kick Tidwell out of your office?"

"Not exactly." *Gulp.* She knew she'd pretty much given him the bum's rush.

"Doggone," said Max. "Here you poached this wonderful salmon and made my favorite broccoli slaw, and now I've completely lost my appetite."

"I'm sorry to hear that," said Theodosia.

Earl Grey stood up suddenly. He'd been lazing under the table and enjoying a little doggy snooze. But now he gazed at them with an appraising eye. If there was spare food to be had, actual people food, he was more than willing to partake of his fair share.

"Rrrrr," he said.

"Yes, we know you're there," said Theodosia. She cut a bite of salmon and held it out to him.

Earl Grey's pink tongue shot out and, voilà: the salmon disappeared as if by magic. Now he was gazing at her again with sad, pleading eyes.

"Yes, I know," said Theodosia. "If I give you one more bite, you'll never, ever ask me for anything again, right?"

"Rrrrr."

"The killer," Max said slowly.

Theodosia glanced at him. "Mmn?"

"He had to have been in attendance Thursday night. *Had* to have been. This wasn't some random maniac who just wandered in from the street. Or who infiltrated the party at the last minute."

"Well . . . yes. I think that's pretty much a given."

"What we need to do," said Max, "is go over the guest list with a fine-tooth comb."

"Okay." Theodosia slipped another shred of salmon to Earl Grey. She'd been thinking about the guest list, too. In fact, she'd been thinking about it all day long.

"Will you help me do that?"

"You know I will," said Theodosia. "But we need to get our hands on that list. You have one, right?"

Max's face fell. "Sure, but it's locked away in my office."

"We can't just go get it?"

"I'm not sure I can waltz in and grab it, if that's what you mean. It would look . . . suspicious."

"How about if I waltzed in?"

"That's not such a great idea, either," said Max. He picked up his wineglass and took a sip.

"Then what do you say we sneak in and get it?" said Theodosia.

Max almost choked on his wine. "You mean now? Tonight?"

"No, next Tuesday," said Theodosia. "Yes, I mean now. Like, put your glass down and get your jacket on right this minute."

"But what if something's going on? Like a private event or a donor party?"

"Then we'll deal with it," said Theodosia. She flashed him a slightly crooked grin. "Max, what is it you don't understand about the words *sneak in*?"

They turned on Meeting Street, cruised past the museum, and then turned down a narrow alley. The night was full-on dark, and the tunnel of trees overhead seemed to make their mission feel slightly more ominous.

"Turn your lights off," said Max.

Theodosia flipped off her Jeep lights.

"What about the dome light?" said Max. "Won't it come on when I open the door?"

Theodosia hit a button. "Not anymore."

They sat there, the engine purring softly, both of them feeling a sense of nervous anticipation.

"Well?" said Theodosia. "It's now or never."

Max bent over and kissed her lightly on the lips. "Now," he said, then slipped quietly out the passenger door. He cut directly in front of her, and then crossed the back patio where, in warmer weather, outdoor receptions were often held.

Theodosia watched him carefully. Max wove his way through the statue garden, past a small fountain, and was closing in fast on the museum's back door. So far so good.

She saw him reach the door and stand there for a moment, as if assessing the situation. Then his hand reached out and punched his code into the keypad.

Good. He'll be inside in about two seconds flat.

But two seconds passed and Max was still fussing with the keypad.

What?

Ten seconds passed. Then twenty. She watched him, frustration building as Max continued to punch in numbers. Finally, in a gesture of exasperation, he threw his hands in the air and headed back toward her.

"What?" Theodosia said once Max had climbed back inside her Jeep.

"Crap!" said Max. He was practically shaking with anger.

"What?"

"They changed the code on the keypad."

"All because of you?"

"That snake Kern probably did it," said Max. "There's no way I'm going to get inside now."

Theodosia mulled this over. "How many numbers is the code usually?"

"Four."

"How hard can that be?" said Theodosia. "To come up with the correct sequence, I mean. Wait a minute." She made a few quick calculations and frowned. "Hmm, could there really be nine thousand nine hundred and ninety-nine possible combinations? Could that even be right?"

"I'm no math genius, but I'll bet it's something like that," said Max. "And if we enter too many false tries, it could trip a warning."

"Plan B then," said Theodosia.

"What exactly is plan B?"

Theodosia gripped the steering wheel. "I'm thinking."

"Jeez, Theo," said Max. "I thought you had this all figured out. You're always so good at this sleuthing thing."

"Chill. Please."

They sat there for a couple more minutes.

"Okay, I've got another idea," said Theodosia.

Max still looked defeated. "What now?"

"I ran into Percy Capers this morning, and he was kind enough to offer his help. He basically said he was in your corner one hundred percent."

"He really said that?" Max blinked rapidly and his voice suddenly sounded hoarse. "That's really something. I guess he is one of the good guys."

"I think we should call him," said Theodosia.

"I'd feel funny doing that," said Max.

"I wouldn't," said Theodosia.

The phone call took less than sixty seconds, and Percy Capers was there in under five minutes.

He came rolling down the dark alley and pulled up behind them, the engine of his bottle-green Jaguar XJ thrumming quietly.

"He's here," Theodosia whispered.

"What a guy," said Max. He sounded surprised. "Especially since he could be putting his job in jeopardy."

"I think I've got this worked out," said Theodosia. "Give me your office key."

"What?"

"If you go pussyfooting around inside the museum and get caught, it'll be your head on a platter. But if I go, no problem." She pushed an errant fluff of hair away from her darting eyes. "You don't think they changed the lock on your office, do you?"

"Probably not," said Max.

"Then give me your key."

"No way are you going in there," said Max.

"Sure I am. Where's your guest list stashed?"

"Top drawer on the left. But what if you get caught?"

"I told you, if I get caught, it's no big deal."

"Sure it is," said Max. "If they catch you, you'll be charged with breaking and entering."

"Not really," said Theodosia. "Because I won't be breaking anything."

Reluctantly, Max handed over his office key. "Only the law."

"Thank you for coming," Theodosia whispered to Capers. They were crouched between the two vehicles, whispering. It was so dark in the alley, she could barely see him.

"I never could stand a damsel in distress," Capers said. Then, "You want me to come with you? I assume you're making a foray into Max's office."

"I'm trying to retrieve the guest list."

"Ah."

"I really just need the code for the keypad," said Theodosia.

"The director changed it yesterday afternoon," said Capers. He reached into his jacket pocket, pulled out a slip of paper, and handed it to her. "Here. Good luck." A smile flickered across his face. "If you get caught, chew it up and swallow it or something. Anyway, don't get caught."

"I don't plan to," said Theodosia.

The code was one nine zero three. Theodosia was pretty sure it was the year the museum had been founded. Some code. If a thief really wanted to get inside and load up a pillow-case full of priceless artifacts, wouldn't he run through all the logical four-digit numbers that related to the museum? Sure, he would. In fact, that's what she would have done if she'd had more time.

As it was, the scenario was a simple *open sesame* all the way. Theodosia eased her way through the back door, tip-toed down a dimly lit hallway, then hooked a right down another hallway that led to the wing that housed the offices for the curators, administration, and support staff.

Max's office was the third door on the left.

She slipped the key into the lock, heard a click, and then turned it slowly. The heavy wooden door swung open and, just like that—bim, bam, boom—she was inside his office.

Theodosia closed the door and stood with her back pressed up against the cool wood. She waited a couple of minutes for her eyes to adjust to the darkness, and then headed straight for Max's desk. He told her he'd stuck the guest list in the top left drawer, so that's where she looked first.

Sliding the drawer open slowly, so there were no telltale creaks or squeaks, Theodosia peered in. And saw a jumble of papers. Hmm, Max wasn't as neat as she thought he was. She pulled out a handful of loose paper and piled it on top of his desk. Then—slowly, carefully—she turned on the small desk lamp.

The flash of light jolted her at first. It felt so bright, like a signal flare that would betray her presence at any moment. But when Theodosia didn't hear the clatter of footsteps running toward her, and when no armed guards appeared to haul her off to jail, she inched up her nerve and began to pour through the unruly nest of papers. There were press releases, expense reports, office memos, and dozens of other papers. She *really* hadn't realized that Max was such a pack rat. Not only that, he seemed to like to print out pages from his computer, whereas she was content to let her e-mails and memos reside on her computer in digital form for all eternity.

Still, she kept sorting and searching until, finally, there at the bottom of the pile was the guest list.

Eureka.

Theodosia folded up the single page and jammed it into her jacket pocket. Then she snapped off the lamp.

Retracing her steps, she put a hand on the doorknob, drew a hesitant breath, and turned it. When she was standing back outside in the hallway, she inserted the key and locked the door.

There. Done and done. Now to get out of here.

She glanced down the long, dark corridor and noticed a faint spill of light.

Unless . . .

Someone besides her was in the museum. Sitting in their office, late at night, all by themselves.

And they were doing . . . what?

Curiosity burned brightly within her. She knew she probably shouldn't risk it. On the other hand, she wondered if there might be some information to be gained.

Putting one hand against the wall to steady herself, Theodosia reached down and slipped off her loafers. Clutching them, she tiptoed soundlessly down the corridor in her stocking feet.

The light was on in Elliot Kern's office. For some reason, this didn't surprise her. Her meeting with him today had set off some low-level warning vibe, some sixth sense, as if the man knew more than he was letting on.

On the other hand, the culprit tonight could be his secretary, Mary Monica. Snarfing up the last bit of scone? Tidying up?

No, it wasn't Mary Monica, because as Theodosia crept down the hallway, one shoulder gently brushing the wall, she could hear a low voice, a masculine growl.

She reached the outer office and peered in. The room was dark and shadowy, Mary Monica's desk looming like a barrier in front of the door that led to Kern's office. The office that glowed with faint light. Where a voice could definitely be heard.

Up until just that second, Theodosia had been fairly certain that she wanted to satisfy her curiosity. Now she wasn't so sure. Sneaking into Max's office had been dangerous enough, but this might be pushing the envelope.

Still, she wondered what Kern was doing here all by his lonesome and so late at night. Reviewing the budget? Doubtful. Planning next year's exhibitions? Maybe. Trying to cover something up? Possibly.

Barely breathing, walking on tiptoe now, Theodosia moved closer to the door of Kern's office. It was half open, a V of yellow light spilling out into the dark outer office. And he was still talking on the phone, mumbling to someone.

What is he saying?

Throwing caution to the wind, Theodosia moved closer and put a hand up to cup her ear, just like she'd seen robbers and jewel thieves do in movies. She was vaguely aware that, should she get caught, she would probably be prosecuted in much the same manner as a jewel thief, her only consolation being that Burt Tidwell headed the Robbery and Homicide Division and might show her a sliver of mercy. Maybe.

Barely breathing and practically undulating toward the doorway, Theodosia crept forward. She'd determined that Kern was alone and talking on the phone, since the faint grunts and words she'd been hearing definitely sounded like a one-sided conversation.

She was closer now and could hear Kern's words a little more clearly. He was saying something about "a great deal of money." Then there was a pause, and he mumbled something that sounded like "probably in the clear."

A great deal of money for what? she wondered. And who was probably in the clear? Kern? Webster's killer?

The words struck Theodosia as being so ominous that suddenly all she wanted to do was get out of there. Holding her breath, she backed out of the office. When she hit the dark hallway, she spun around and ran soundlessly, as fast as her legs could carry her.

And when she burst through the back door and felt the cool night air brush across her face, all she could think was *Thank heavens!*

12

Back home at her cottage, Theodosia finally worked up the courage to tell Max about her very strange detour.

"Excuse me—you snuck down to Kern's office?" Max was flabbergasted. His face turned red, his voice grew strident, and his eyes fairly popped. "And he was actually *there*?"

Theodosia nodded. "All I did was tiptoe down the hallway and eavesdrop on his conversation. I didn't do anything else. I didn't want to risk it."

"Risk it? What you did was bad enough. Jeez, I wondered what took you so long. I was almost frantic, thinking the worst."

"Listen . . . Max." She clutched his arm. "What if Kern had something to do with Edgar Webster's death?"

Max looked stunned for a second time. "Why would you even say that? Yes, he's been harsh with me, but . . . Wait a minute, what exactly did you overhear tonight?"

"I heard Kern talking on the phone, mumbling something

about money," said Theodosia. "I think his exact words were 'a great deal of money.' And then he said something about being 'probably in the clear.'"

"But what does that mean?" said Max. "Taken out of context, it just sounds like a bunch of gibberish. It could be anything."

But Theodosia's eyes glowed hot with excitement. "Bear with me for a minute, because I have a theory. What if . . . what if this has something to do with Webster's company? With Datrex?"

"What are you talking about?"

"I think I told you—Webster's partner, Roger Greaves, was chomping at the bit to take the company public. That would have brought in a huge infusion of cash."

Max gazed at her. "Okay." He lifted a hand and waggled his fingers, making a "gimme more" gesture.

"But Webster was in a huge flap over the IPO," Theodosia continued. "He didn't want it to go through. But now that Webster's dead, that IPO will undoubtedly happen."

Max still wasn't following her completely. "Okay."

"So maybe there's some kind of slick deal going on. Maybe Kern is buying shares that will skyrocket once the IPO is announced."

"Isn't that what they call insider trading?" said Max.

"That's exactly right," said Theodosia.

"That would mean that Kern and Greaves are buddies."

"We don't know that they are," said Theodosia. "And they wouldn't have to be friendly buddies, but they could be in collusion."

"Okay," said Max, "and I am following your line of thought, albeit tenuously. What I think you're saying is that Kern could have . . . um . . . helped *facilitate* this deal by murdering Webster?"

"See?" said Theodosia. "You're becoming just as suspicious as I am."

"Maybe," said Max. "But if your theory is correct, that would be the craziest thing I've heard yet."

"But think about it," said Theodosia. "It tracks. You have to admit that it tracks."

"Somewhat."

"And Elliot Kern was in the perfect position to set you up. To frame you."

"Do you think Kern really believes *I'll* go down for the murder?" said Max.

"Maybe not. Probably not. But in the meantime, he's blown up a huge smokescreen around it. He's shunted the investigation away from him and put it squarely onto your shoulders."

"So Kern *is* a possible suspect," said Max. He said it slowly, almost as if he could taste the words forming in his mouth.

"In a kind of far-fetched way, I'd have to say yes," said Theodosia. "Yes, he is."

Max backed up against one of the dining room chairs and sat down heavily. "Cripes." Shoulders slumped, he gazed at her. "So what do we do now?"

Theodosia slid into the chair across from him and pulled the guest list from her pocket. "For one thing, we stick to our immediate plan. We keep an eye on Kern as a possible suspect, and we take a good, hard look at this guest list."

"The guest list," said Max, finally glancing at it. "With everything you've been laying on me, I almost forgot it was our original objective."

Theodosia smoothed out the wrinkled sheet of paper. "There must be fifty names here." She turned the list around and slid it across the table to Max.

"Sixty-two to be exact," said Max. "Not counting museum staff members who were also present."

"That's way too many people for us to investigate. What we need to do is eliminate as many names as possible. The ones who *feel* illogical anyway. You know, like interns, wives of board members, people who probably wouldn't have had anything to do with Webster."

"Okay," said Max. "Let's get out a red pen and try to do that."

Fifteen minutes later, they'd pared the list down to a more manageable twenty names. They crossed out names of people who were deemed far too mild-mannered to even consider committing murder, a few older ladies, several museum interns, and some people who just didn't seem logical or didn't fit the profile of a potential killer.

"Better," said Max.

"Now we're getting somewhere," said Theodosia. She ran her index finger down the list and hesitated when she came to Cecily's name. "Cecily Conrad," she said. "She's still one of our main suspects. And we know she had motive."

"Sure, but could she kill?" asked Max.

"You saw her the other night, when she turned her wrath on you. What do you think?"

"I feel like if she'd had a gun, she might have pulled the trigger."

"Well, there you go," said Theodosia. "So, from the looks of things, we have four main suspects—Cecily, Charlotte Webster, Roger Greaves, and now Elliot Kern. That's our A-list."

"And our B-list?"

"The other sixteen or so people."

"Whew," said Max. "A lot to think about." He ran the back of his hand across his mouth. "Makes me feel kind of shaky."

"Do you want something to eat?" said Theodosia. "Are you having a protein drop? You never really finished your dinner."

"I think maybe I've done enough eating, theorizing, and breaking and entering for the evening. Maybe I should just take off. Do something to calm my nerves."

Theodosia walked him to the entryway and watched him shrug into his suede jacket.

"Where are you off to?" She put her arms around him and gave him a squeeze. She hated the idea of Max just wandering around, fretting about his lost job and all the unfair accusations that went along with it.

"I don't know. Maybe I'll go home and change and then go for a late run. Blow out the carbon. Or maybe I'll head over to that cigar bar on Wentworth Street and hang out for a while."

Theodosia frowned. She didn't really like the sound of that. But if Max needed to walk and think or smoke and think, that certainly was his prerogative. "Whatever you do, be careful, okay?"

"Always," said Max. But to Theodosia's ears, his words sounded a little hollow.

Theodosia puttered around her house. She cleaned up in the kitchen, washed her wineglasses by hand, and let Earl Grey out into the backyard. When she was finished with her chores, she slipped outside to join him.

Earl Grey was snuffling about in the azalea bushes, hoping to rout out a ground squirrel or two. When that didn't work out, he trotted over to check the small fishpond. Marauding raccoons had dipped their paws in there on occasion, and he was determined it wouldn't happen again. Not on his watch anyway.

Theodosia reclined in a woven twig chair that sat at the edge of her free-form flagstone patio. The night air felt silky and smooth as it rustled the ivy on the back fence and swept her hair away from her face. Overhead, a handful of stars twinkled dully, looking like rough-cut diamonds that had been tossed carelessly into the blue-black sky.

She was letting her mind free-associate, thinking about Webster's murder and all the various connections, Max, and her crazy foray into the museum tonight. Other subjects floated into and out of her thoughts, too. Their *Titanic* Tea tomorrow, the Halloween week, all the little nits and nats of everyday business that needed to be taken care of.

As Earl Grey turned his attention to a clump of columbine that was making a heroic last stand, Theodosia was thinking about how she might stop at City Market first thing tomorrow and pick up a bushel basket of colorful gourds. With Halloween only four days away, plus the need for some general autumnal decorating in the tea shop, the gourds would be perfect. If all else failed, Haley could do something creative with them. Make them into soup? Or bread? Or cookies?

Theodosia smiled as she shook her head. No, gourd cookies didn't sound at all appetizing. They certainly wouldn't be in the same league with Haley's peanut butter cookies or her lemon marmalade cookies.

Suddenly feeling the stresses of the day weighing heavy upon her, Theodosia decided it was time to turn in. She whistled for Earl Grey, and together they padded inside, checked and locked all the doors, and retreated to their upstairs lair. Theodosia had basically turned her entire second floor into a bedroom, walk-in closet, and retreat room. And then there was her cozy turret room, where she enjoyed snuggling up in an easy chair with a good book.

Kicking off her shoes, she remembered how she'd carried them, just an hour or so ago, during her whacked-out ramble through the museum. Interestingly, the recollection brought a faint smile to her face. Perhaps she was getting good at this business of surreptitious activity? Or at least getting used to it?

She doubted Detective Tidwell would agree.

Yawning, she snapped on her small TV. Maybe she could catch the late headlines, see what else was going on in the world today. Surely, there had to be some good news somewhere. A rescued puppy? Returning soldiers enjoying a heartwarming reunion?

Just as she tossed a red-and-blue chintz throw pillow onto a matching chair, a familiar face suddenly loomed large on her TV screen.

What?

The image looked surprisingly like Detective Tidwell!

Wait a minute, that is *Detective Tidwell. The question is: What's he doing on TV?*

Well, for one thing, she could see that he was looking seriously annoyed while trying to escape the clutches of a television news reporter. The pretty blond lady from Channel Eight. Stephanie something.

Theodosia grabbed her remote control and beefed up the sound.

Stephanie Hayward, the reporter, faced the camera directly, and said, "For those of you just tuning in, a brutal assault took place just moments ago near the Lady Goodwood Inn."

A brutal assault? Moments ago? Theodosia wondered exactly what had brought Detective Tidwell out on a Saturday night. Hopefully, *assault* wasn't code for another murder.

"As chance would have it," Stephanie continued, "our WCTV van was cruising just blocks from where this attack took place. Which put us squarely on the scene to bring you this exclusive."

"An attack?" Theodosia said as Tidwell continued to look uncomfortable. "An attack on who?"

Stephanie smiled her dazzling smile and stuck her microphone back in Tidwell's face. "What can you tell us about the victim?" she asked.

"Nothing," Tidwell muttered. "Since this incident is currently under investigation, I'm unable to release any details."

Tidwell's words did little to deter the intrepid Stephanie. She adjusted her expression until she looked almost fearful, then continued. "But my sources are telling me that a woman by the name of Cecily Conrad was attacked after attending an event at the Lady Goodwood Inn."

"Cecily Conrad was attacked?" Theodosia cried out. Feeling like one of those rabid sports fans who screamed at the TV, she moved closer so she could get the full story.

On-screen, Tidwell looked supremely unhappy. "That is all we know so far."

"And Miss Conrad was attacked while walking to her car?"

"I do wish you'd stop using the word *attacked*," Tidwell said peevishly.

Startled by this bizarre turn of events, Theodosia hastily dialed Max's number. She wanted to bring him up to speed on what was going on. Could this assault—or whatever it was—on Cecily be intricately related to Webster's murder? Or was it just a strange coincidence?

Theodosia waited impatiently as she listened to the ringing of his cell phone.

Pick up, Max. Come on, pick up.

But there was no answer. She hung up and dialed his home phone. Did that three more times. Finally, just as she was kicked over to voice mail, Theodosia hung up. He wasn't there. He wasn't going to be there.

She turned and looked out her upstairs window. Saw only her reflection looking back at her. Saw worry in her face.

There's no way Max could be part of this, is there?

No, she told herself. No way. Max hadn't been that rattled by Cecily the other night. Had he? He wouldn't threaten her or . . .

Theodosia wandered over to her closet.

No, he wouldn't. Of course, he wouldn't.

She decided to lay out her clothes for tomorrow in an effort to calm her nerves. Unfortunately, it had the opposite effect.

Cecily attacked? Why? And by whom?

Against her better judgment, Theodosia decided she needed to find out a little more about this.

Okay, all cards on the table, I want to know a lot more.

Which meant that, five minutes later, Theodosia was in her Jeep, bumping down Tradd Street. When she got closer to the Lady Goodwood Inn, she could see flashing red and blue lights from three police cruisers and an ambulance. Plus it looked as if there were uniformed officers in orange vests blocking the street in an effort to keep gawkers away from the scene.

Theodosia circled around a block, then flipped a left on East Bay. She drove another half block or so, spotted a parking space, and pulled to the curb. From her nighttime jogs with Earl Grey, she knew this neighborhood like the back of her hand. She had complete familiarity with all the narrow alleys and lanes where palmetto fronds whispered in the night and where the right shortcut could sneak you in close, right to the scene of the crime.

Theodosia ducked down a small stone walkway that was tucked between two enormous Victorian homes. Brushing past a stand of dogwood, she dodged around a gently pattering three-tiered fountain and found herself on Longitude Lane. This was basically a grassy and broken rock path, an unimproved seventeenth-century country lane that passed behind several large and elegant homes. With its brick walls and overhanging shrubbery, Longitude Lane was practically hidden from view. Visitors rarely stumbled upon it unless they'd signed up for one of the special "hidden Charleston" walking tours.

Quietly, carefully, Theodosia emerged from the alley

and into a circle of lights and frenetic activity. Acting as if she belonged there—or better yet, lived there—she passed groups of neighbors who buzzed with excitement as they spoke to uniformed police officers. They were giving accounts of their stories—what they'd seen or heard.

Glancing around, trying to scope out the scene, Theodosia was startled when she spotted Cecily sitting in the back of an ambulance, being attended to by a youthful-looking African American woman. In her blue jumpsuit with red-and-white patches on her shoulders, the woman was clearly an EMT.

Theodosia walked slowly up to the ambulance. "Cecily," she said in what she hoped was a friendly, calming tone. "It's Theodosia. Remember me?"

Cecily lifted her head and stared at Theodosia. Her hair was disheveled, and her white blouse was ripped underneath one arm. There was a bruise on the right side of her face that would surely be the color of an eggplant by morning, and her knees were badly scuffed.

"I heard what happened," said Theodosia. She offered a sympathetic smile. "Are you okay?"

Cecily stared back for a few moments, then a hint of recognition flickered in her eyes. "Theodosia? The lady from the tea shop?"

"Yes, that's me," said Theodosia, moving a few steps closer. "Cecily, I just heard about your, um, attack, on TV." She glanced around. "We all did."

"Somebody leapt out at me in the dark!" Cecily howled. "It's a good thing I screamed and fought him off." She hiccupped loudly. "And that some nearby people helped scare him off."

Theodosia touched a hand to the shoulder of the lady EMT. Her nametag read CAROLINE BOWIE. "Miss Bowie," said Theodosia, "how is Cecily doing? What are the extent of her injuries?"

"He grabbed me and threw me to the sidewalk," Cecily whimpered. "Smacked me in the face!"

Caroline Bowie's almond-shaped eyes took in Theodosia. "Are you a friend?"

"Yes, I am. Please, does she need to be hospitalized?"

Caroline's Bowie's brown eyes crinkled warmly. "Call me Caroline. And there probably won't be any trip to the hospital tonight for Cecily. I'd say she's going to be just fine. She's sustained a few cuts and scrapes, and naturally she's a little shaken up."

"I'm a *lot* shaken up," Cecily sputtered. She was wearing an oxygen mask and kept trying to remove it so she could keep up her running commentary on how awful she felt. "I'm so angry, I'm about ready to jump out of my skin!"

"We can give you some meds for that," said Caroline.

"I'd rather have a drink," Cecily snapped.

"How did this happen?" Theodosia asked. She was a little surprised that Cecily was even talking to her. After all, they barely knew each other. Maybe Cecily was badly shaken up and her brain wasn't pumping out synaptic connections in the proper way. Maybe she'd forgotten that Theodosia was linked romantically with Max.

"I was . . . I was . . ." Cecily blubbered.

"Take your time," said Theodosia.

"I was coming from the Lady Goodwood Inn," said Cecily. Now tears coursed down her cheeks. "I had dinner and a . . . few drinks." She fanned her arms expressively. "On the way to my car . . ."

"Keep that oxygen on," Caroline advised.

"And somebody jumped you?" Theodosia prompted.

"A maniac!" said Cecily. "It was horrible. He came leaping out of the bushes and I . . . I had to fight for my life."

Theodosia patted Cecily's shoulder. "You poor thing."

"How could this happen?" Cecily screeched. "This is

genteel Charleston. People call it the Holy City because of all the churches!"

"I'm guessing your attacker doesn't regularly attend church," said Theodosia. She glanced sideways and saw Detective Tidwell issuing orders to two uniformed officers. Then, without looking over toward the ambulance, he cocked a thumb in its direction. She decided that if he was about to interview Cecily, this was probably her cue to get out of there.

"Take care, Cecily," said Theodosia. She gave a little wave. "Feel better."

"I . . . I just wanna . . ." said Cecily. Then she dissolved into loud, choking sobs.

Theodosia slipped back through the darkness of Longitude Lane. In all the time she'd jogged through this neighborhood, or walked home from parties, she'd never felt unsafe. She wondered if this assault on Cecily might change things for her.

But as she climbed into her Jeep and started the engine, other thoughts began to lodge in her head. Thoughts about Max. About his angry standoff with Cecily. Thoughts that could easily be construed as . . . doubts.

But as she drove down the street, she told herself, *No way. No, he couldn't have.*

13

❧

"*Where were you* last night?" Theodosia asked. It was barely seven AM and still dark. She'd just woken up, and the first thing she'd done was grab the phone and dial Max's number.

"Um . . . what?" Max said, sounding sleepy.

"Do you know what happened last night?"

"Uh . . . no. Why?" There was a soft rustling on his end of the line, as if he were struggling with the bed covers, trying to throw them off and sit upright. Then he said in a grumpy voice, "Jeez, Theo, do you know what the heck *time* it is?"

"Do you know what *happened* last night?"

"Didn't I just answer your question? No, I have no idea what happened."

Theodosia swallowed hard. Max sounded so . . . angry.

"I . . ." Max cleared his throat. "I'm sorry, I didn't mean to come across quite so obnoxious. What exactly happened that you're so upset about?"

"I'm not upset, I'm concerned."

"About . . . ?"

"Cecily Conrad was attacked last night."

"What!"

"I said Cecily . . ."

"I got that, I got that," said Max. "But what . . . ? Where . . . ? Maybe you better tell me what happened."

"I don't have all the details," said Theodosia. "But apparently she was attacked as she was leaving the Lady Goodwood Inn. I guess she'd met up with some friends there for dinner and drinks. Anyway, someone just . . . jumped out at her."

"Is she hurt badly?"

"She was bruised and extremely shaken up. The police called for an ambulance, but she wasn't seriously injured enough to warrant a trip to the hospital."

"Wait a minute," said Max. "It sounds as if you were there."

"I heard about it on the late news," said Theodosia. "So, yes, I went over there."

"And you talked to her?"

"Yup."

"She mention anything about our dustup on Saturday night?"

"Nope."

Max was quiet for a few seconds, and then he said, "It sounds as if someone was stalking her. Who would do something like that?"

"Um . . . maybe the same person who stabbed Edgar Webster?"

"Do you really think so?"

"I think it's certainly possible," said Theodosia.

"But why? Why go after Cecily?"

"Gee, I don't know," said Theodosia. She was suddenly annoyed that Max didn't seem to be taking this very seriously. "Maybe because Charlotte hates her. Maybe because

Cecily's privy to some sort of secret. Maybe because Cecily killed Edgar Webster and somebody was trying to get back at her. There are more than a few permutations that could explain this."

Max yawned loudly. "Or maybe it was completely random."

"Somehow," said Theodosia, "it doesn't feel that way to me."

Theodosia forgot all about stopping at City Market. Instead, she was anxious to get to the Indigo Tea Shop and talk to Drayton and Haley about this new twist of events. If Max didn't have any ideas—or didn't *want* to have any ideas— maybe they did.

But when she arrived, shortly before noon, Drayton and Haley had already heard the news about Cecily and were chattering about it, exchanging theories about the attack. And when Theodosia told them that she'd actually *gone* to the scene of the crime, that revelation ignited a whole new round of talk.

"I think last night's attack means that Cecily isn't the killer," said Drayton. "That she's definitely not the one who took an ice pick to Edgar Webster's ear."

"So she's free and clear?" said Haley. She brushed her stick-straight hair back from her face and stared confrontationally at Drayton.

"Not necessarily clear," said Drayton.

"So you're saying the killer is now targeting Cecily?" said Haley.

"If it was the killer," said Theodosia, jumping in, "then he almost got her. It's a good thing Cecily has a strong pair of lungs. She screamed for help, and people came running right away."

"Let me get this straight," said Haley. She was always a

stickler for nailing down details. "Have you guys crossed Cecily off your list as the possible killer?"

"Yes," said Drayton.

"No," said Theodosia.

"Ooh," said Haley, peering at Theodosia. "Aren't you the suspicious one?"

"The thing is," said Theodosia. "Cecily wasn't hurt all that badly. She could have . . . I don't know . . . staged the whole thing?" The idea had been percolating in her brain, but this was the first time she'd actually let herself vocalize it.

"You mean she *faked* being attacked?" said Haley. "To kick the investigation in a different direction? To have the police searching for some random guy? Hmm . . . that would mean she's a very clever girl."

"Not so clever at all," said Drayton. "Because if the police are the least bit suspicious about Cecily's cry-wolf scheme, they're going to be watching her even more carefully."

"Not just watching, but investigating," said Theodosia.

"Keeping an eye on her every move," said Haley.

"If you ask me," said Drayton, "I think Cecily *knows* something. That's why someone tried to kill her."

"What do you think she knows?" said Haley.

Drayton fingered his bright pink bow tie. "It's still unclear."

"Maybe it has something to do with Edgar Webster?" said Theodosia. "Or his company?" Theodosia knew there was the IPO to consider. She was sure that, at the start of business tomorrow, the IPO would be rammed through. Could Cecily somehow have a role in that? Well . . . maybe.

"Yes," said Drayton. "Cecily might possibly know something about Webster's company, some proprietary business secret. What's the company name . . . Datrex? That would be my guess, too."

They batted around theories for a few more minutes, then Haley retreated to her kitchen and Theodosia and Drayton got to work on the tea shop. Even though the *Titanic* Tea didn't kick off until five o'clock, they wanted to get things rolling. They started by draping starched white linen tablecloths across all the tables, and then put out the good crystal along with a set of antique Gorham sterling silver flatware in the Baronial Old pattern.

Haley had found photos depicting the *Titanic* leaving the dock at Southampton, as well as photos of some of the first-class passengers, and those had been blown up into posters and were now hung on the walls. And Drayton had brought in his personal collection of Royal Crown Derby English bone china, so that had to be unpacked and laid out carefully.

"It's looking good," said Theodosia as she placed bouquets of white lilies in the center of all the tables.

"Wait until you see what else I cooked up," said Drayton.

"Show me." Theodosia wasn't gung ho on surprises. Or waiting. She was an immediate-gratification type of gal.

Drayton ducked behind the counter and pulled out a large white box.

"What little trick do you have up your sleeve?" Now her curiosity had really been tweaked.

He popped the lid and tilted it toward Theodosia so she could take a peek.

"Oh my."

"I took the liberty," said Drayton, looking a little smug. He set the box down on the counter and pulled out a stack of white paper napkins emblazoned with the ubiquitous White Star Line logo. "First of all, monogrammed napkins from our friendly stationery store down the street."

"That monogram certainly lends a touch of authenticity," said Theodosia. "Our guests will be looking around for the lifeboats."

Drayton held up a finger. "Ah, but there's more." He dug into his box again and pulled out a small white ship, about ten inches long, with the White Star logo on its bow. "Actually, there are ten more ship models, to serve as proper décor for our tables."

"They're perfect. Well, maybe a little eerie, too."

"And I know you're not a fan of paper placemats," said Drayton. "But you might change your mind when you see these." He handed her a stack of placemats that were basically reproductions of the front page of the *London Herald*. The headline screamed "RMS *Titanic* Sinks" and depicted an antique etching of the ship.

Theodosia fingered them. "These are fantastic. You are so clever."

"And one last thing," said Drayton. He pulled out a small black tea tin. "Our friends at Harney and Sons created this lovely Titanic Tea. I wish I could say they made it just for us, but they've been offering it for quite some time."

Theodosia grinned as she studied the elegant black tea tin that featured the doomed *Titanic* ship surrounded by a gold porthole motif. "This is just fantastic." She balanced the tea tin in her hand. "Favors for our guests?"

Drayton nodded. "Everything but the icebergs."

"You really did it. You came up with a unique themed tea that actually works for Halloween. It's not spooky, but it certainly is haunting."

Drayton beamed. "And isn't that the whole idea?"

When Theodosia stepped into the kitchen to check on Haley, she was bombarded by a medley of enticing aromas coming from the stove, as well as English tea bread and éclairs baking in the oven.

"It smells like a genuine restaurant in here," Theodosia smiled.

Haley looked up from her stovetop. "Even though we're only working out of a postage stamp-size kitchen?"

"You're the one who said she doesn't ever want to move to a larger space."

"No, and neither does Drayton. We love it right here. Besides, I like walking to work." Haley now lived upstairs, in the apartment above the tea shop, where Theodosia had once lived. It was convenient, to say the least.

"I want to thank you for working today," said Theodosia. "I know you usually like to spend Sundays with your friends."

"Or reading in bed," said Haley. She grinned impishly, and added, "With my friends."

"Too much information," boomed Drayton. He was standing in the doorway, trying to muster a haughty demeanor. "Or, as your generation likes to say, Haley, TMI."

"Drayton's gettin' down," laughed Haley. "Pretty soon he's gonna turn hipster on us. He'll start dressing all in black and wear narrow ties. Maybe even affect a pork pie hat à la Justin Timberlake."

"Never," said Drayton.

"Do you even know who I'm talking about?" asked Haley.

"No," said Drayton. "And I don't care to know."

"Come on," Theodosia teased, getting into the act. "You can't tell me you don't sneak a peak at MTV once in a while. I happen to know you subscribe to cable TV."

"I capitulated only because I enjoy history and nature programs," said Drayton. And with that, he turned and disappeared.

"We tease him too much," said Theodosia.

"I don't think we tease him enough," replied Haley. She grabbed a large stainless steel bowl filled with sliced cucumbers.

"We kind of need to talk about the funeral luncheon tomorrow," said Theodosia.

"What are your thoughts on that?" asked Haley as she added a handful of fresh herbs.

"I suggested to Charlotte that we keep the menu fairly simple. Perhaps a salad or fruit plate, scones, and an assortment of tea sandwiches."

"Easy peasy. I could do a citrus salad, honey scones, and maybe three different tea sandwiches. Like . . . chicken and green goddess, cream cheese with crushed walnuts, and roast beef with thinly sliced Cheddar cheese. And maybe a dessert. What do you think?"

"It all sounds perfectly lovely. Can you get everything you need first thing tomorrow?"

"I'll make out my list this afternoon and e-mail it in. That way I can do morning tea and still get an early morning grocery delivery. Oh, what time do you think the luncheon guests will start arriving?"

"The funeral's set for ten," said Theodosia. "So I'm guessing everyone will start staggering in around eleven fifteen."

"Hmm, maybe we should just put a sign on the door that says CLOSED FOR PRIVATE PARTY?"

"You mean not be open for morning tea?" said Theodosia.

"Otherwise things could get a little sticky."

"You make a good point," said Theodosia. She thought for a few moments. "Okay, let's do that. We'll be closed for our private party until one o'clock. Then we'll open for afternoon tea."

"Works for me," said Haley.

Theodosia pursed her lips. "Now let's just hope it works for Drayton."

But Drayton was fine with the arrangement.

"A smart idea," he said. "That way we won't have two different groups to contend with."

"And we can attend the funeral," said Theodosia.

"*You* can attend the funeral," said Drayton. "I'll remain here to make sure everything is prepped and readied."

"And beat off any morning customers."

"Well . . . maybe we could accommodate our regulars with a scone and a cuppa to go?"

"I figured that's what you'd do," said Theodosia.

"What kind of tea does Charlotte want served to her guests tomorrow?"

"She said she'd leave the choice up to you."

"A wise decision." Drayton gazed at his floor-to-ceiling wall of tea tins and squinted. "I'm almost thinking the Sewpur Estate Assam. And perhaps an English breakfast tea. Both are a trifle bracing, which might be just the thing for a post-funeral luncheon. But I do want to noodle my choices around."

Bang, bang, bang.

Theodosia and Drayton turned toward the front door.

"Door," said Drayton.

"I hope it isn't an early guest," said Theodosia. She crossed the tearoom and peered through a sliver of wavering glass. It was Bill Glass.

"Glass," she said.

"Don't let him in," said Drayton. "Just ignore him."

But Theodosia was already unlatching the door. "The thing is, he might know something."

"What's up?" she asked, as Glass came crashing into the tea room. With his bulky photojournalist vest and cameras strung around his neck, he really was the proverbial bull in a china shop.

"Can you believe this latest turn of events?" asked Glass. He was practically chortling with excitement. "First Webster is killed, then his ex-girlfriend is attacked! This is shaking out to be a very crazy scenario."

"I don't think it's crazy at all," said Theodosia. "In fact, the scary thing is, it sounds like there's a master plan."

"Sure, but who's the mastermind?"

Theodosia shrugged. "There's the clincher. That's what we're all trying to figure out."

"So you guys haven't heard anything new?" asked Glass.

Drayton leaned forward, an inquisitive look on his face. "No. Have you?"

"Ah . . . I've been trying to pry some details out of a few cops I know," said Glass. "But they've been fairly close-mouthed about this whole thing." He peered at Theodosia. "You haven't spoken to Cecily, have you?"

"Not today, no," said Theodosia. She didn't feel like telling Glass that she'd talked to Cecily just after the attack, that she'd actually *rushed* to the scene of the crime.

"What I'm gonna do," said Glass, "is maybe snoop around the museum some more."

"You know Max is on leave," said Theodosia.

"Yeah," said Glass, "because he's a suspect."

"But he's innocent," Theodosia said hastily, her voice carrying a little bit of a tone.

"Of course he is," Drayton echoed.

Glass gazed at them mildly, as if he didn't want to interrupt his thought process. "And then I'm gonna circle back here and get a few snaps of your big shindig tonight."

"You want to photograph our *Titanic* Tea?" said Drayton. He sounded almost horrified.

"Yeah, sure," said Glass "Why not? You guys got something against a little free publicity?"

"I suppose not," said Theodosia. She hadn't figured on Glass trying to interject himself into the event. On the other hand, his presence, if she could keep a tight rein on him, might lend some excitement and media buzz, which was never a bad thing. "Okay, but don't show up until at least five thirty, okay? Let us at least get our guests settled."

Glass grinned and made a cheesy thumbs-up gesture. "Five thirty. You got it."

When they'd finally closed the door on him and turned the latch firmly, Drayton said, "Do you think you can control him?"

"I don't know," said Theodosia. "I wonder where I could buy a cattle prod."

"Very funny, but I still don't see why you're letting him attend our event."

"Because, like us, Glass has been nosing around about Webster's death. And he might just stumble onto something." She cocked an index finger at Drayton. "Hey, pal, you're the one who wanted a shadow investigation."

"Yes," said Drayton, "but I didn't think the shadow would be *Glass*."

"Well, he's what we've got. What we're stuck with for now."

"Just so long as Glass doesn't gum up the works," said Drayton. He glanced at his perpetually slow-running watch, and said, "I'd say we're just about set to go. With more than a little time to spare."

"Good," said Theodosia, "because your nemesis, Glass, just gave me an idea."

"Dare I ask?"

"I'm going to call Cecily and see if I can drop by her place."

"That's fairly gutsy."

"Maybe so, but is it smart?"

"I don't know," said Drayton. "Since she may or may not be a killer, the question is really up in the air."

"Cecily," Theodosia burbled into the phone, "I just wanted to call and wish you well. See how you're feeling."

"How do you *think* I'm feeling?" Cecily shot back. "I'm terrible. I'm battered and bruised and . . ."

"You know, I'd love to stop by for a quick visit," Theodosia said, cutting her off mid-rant. "Drop off a small care package for you."

"I'm not really in the mood for company. I prefer to be left alone."

"I can understand that," Theodosia said in her gentlest voice. "But I promise I won't take hardly any time at all."

"Seriously, Theodosia? Do you have any idea how absolutely *traumatized* I am?"

"I'll see you in ten minutes," said Theodosia, unwilling to take no for an answer.

14

❧

For the third time in three days, Haley's scones paved the way for Theodosia's investigation (some might call it meddling).

"I can't believe you came by anyway," Cecily said rather ungraciously as she opened the door to let Theodosia in. She lived in a small garden apartment that was part of a larger mansion on Legare Street. Her address was definitely upscale, but her entrance was down a crumbling brick path on the side of the home.

Theodosia handed her a small wicker basket. "Cranberry scones and English breakfast tea, guaranteed to brighten your day and help take your mind off last night."

Cecily let loose a snort. "That's fairly doubtful." But she led Theodosia down a narrow hallway and into a small room that was pleasantly furnished with two floral love seats and a few potted palms. French doors led out to a small garden, and with the late October sun lasering down full force, all the foliage looked golden and sun-kissed.

"How are you feeling?" Theodosia asked. She settled on

one of the love seats while Cecily eased herself down on the one across from her.

"I feel like I got hit by a two-ton truck, that's how I feel. I keep gobbling aspirin and pain meds, and nothing seems to help."

"I'm sure a lot of your trauma is psychological, too," said Theodosia.

"No kidding, Sherlock. Have *you* ever been attacked by a maniac? Been run roughshod over and then hurled to the ground?" Cecily's brows knit together as her voice erupted in anger. "No, I just bet you haven't."

As a matter of fact, Theodosia *had* been attacked. She'd even been shot at. But this wasn't the time or place to dredge that up. Instead she said, "And you're sure it was a man who came after you?"

"Absolutely," said Cecily. "He was a big, strong brute who tackled me like he was some kind of football player—I'm lucky I didn't break a few bones." She massaged her shoulder gingerly. "My collarbone or even my ribs."

"Were you able to give a decent description to the police?"

Cecily shrugged. "It was pitch-dark so I couldn't see much of anything. I especially didn't see his face."

So no description. Theodosia leaned forward. "What was your general impression of him?"

"What do you mean?"

"Was he angry and out of control, or was he cool and calculating? Was he trying to really hurt you, or do you think he was just trying to scare you?"

Cecily's upper teeth worried her lower lip. "He was big and strong, that's for sure. And you're right, he did seem a little . . . I know this is going to sound strange . . . detached. Oh, and his breath smelled bad, like he'd been eating onions or garlic."

"Did you share this with the police?"

"The police," Cecily spat out. "They were perfectly horrible!

They didn't care about me in the least. What's that stupid phrase? It's like déjà vu all over again."

"You're referring to their handling of the stabbing at the museum?"

"Yes," said Cecily. "I thought the police were bumbling incompetents then. Now they're just . . . Well, it's like they don't give a crap what happened to me!"

"I'm sure that's not the case at all," Theodosia said mildly. "I'm sure law enforcement is working hard to apprehend Edgar Webster's killer and find whoever attacked you."

Theodosia was secretly pleased that Cecily had brought up Webster's murder. It opened the door for a few more questions.

"Do you think your attack is somehow related to Webster's murder?" Theodosia asked.

Cecily dropped her head in her hands, and said, "I don't know. I really couldn't say."

"Considering the two of you were, um, close, your encounter last night doesn't exactly strike me as a coincidence."

"You know what?" said Cecily, giving her a baleful look. "I wish I'd never met Edgar Webster. Let alone gotten involved with him."

"Except you *were* involved with him."

"Biggest mistake of my life."

"But the man bankrolled your shop. You must feel some sense of gratitude."

"You don't know the Websters very well, do you? It wasn't like there was any long-term commitment. And you know what?" Cecily snapped her fingers. "About two minutes after we broke up, Edgar was demanding his money back. Said he needed it to help finance that stupid tea house at the museum. And now that he's gone, his witchy *wife* is coming after me. She wants all the money repaid and has threatened to sic her mad-dog attorneys on me if I don't cough it up!"

"I can't imagine Charlotte's topmost concern right now

is money," said Theodosia. "After all, she's got her husband's funeral to deal with tomorrow. That's going to be fairly traumatic."

"Oh yeah? That's what you think. Would you care to hear the voice mail Charlotte left me this morning?"

Theodosia hesitated. "Yes, I would."

Is there really a voice mail?

Cecily dug frantically in her Prada handbag. A wallet and keys were dumped out. A pack of tissues and a bottle of bloodred nail polish went flying by. Finally, she retrieved her cell phone. "Listen to this. Just *listen* to this." She manipulated a button.

Charlotte Webster's voice suddenly burst from the phone's speaker in a crackly, tinny tirade. "Cecily!" she shrieked. "I'm dead serious about getting that loan paid back! You'd better start making arrangements immediately or there's going to be hell to pay!"

"You see," said Cecily, "the woman's like a crazed rott-weiler. Somebody should throw her a chew bone."

"She did sound rather . . . emotional," said Theodosia.

Cecily stared at Theodosia, mouth open, eyes wide, looking slightly deranged. "It's like Edgar is coming at me from the grave. Only now it's his crone of a wife!"

On her way back to the tea shop, a million questions buzzed inside Theodosia's head. Could it have been Charlotte Web-ster who'd attacked Cecily last night? With her mind clouded by shock and fear, could Cecily have been mistaken about the size of her attacker? After all, the angry voice mail Charlotte had left positively dripped with malicious intent. Which indicated that Charlotte could have easily had a moment—or moments—of madness.

Or had Charlotte persuaded Roger Greaves to throw a scare into Cecily. And if so, why?

Or could Greaves have acted purely on his own? Trying to clean up some unfinished business?

On the other hand, the attacker could have been someone else entirely. The question was—who?

Was Elliot Kern, the museum director, involved?

Theodosia shook her head to try to dispel her imaginary swarm of angry hornets. There were so many questions, a roster of serious suspects, but not a whole lot of answers. The whole situation left her feeling queasy and nervous.

Still, she wasn't about to give up the hunt.

Leave it to Drayton to come up with the perfect costumes for the *Titanic* Tea.

"Come look at Drayton," Haley called as Theodosia slipped in the back door. "He's all decked out for our tea."

"He's what?" Theodosia dumped her bag on her desk, tossed her leather jacket on a chair, and headed into the tea room, where she skidded to a sudden stop. "Oh my."

"What do you think?" said Drayton. He extended his arms outward and did a half pivot so Theodosia could enjoy the full effect of his costume.

"Aren't you a vision in white," said Theodosia. Drayton wore a white jacket that had been duded up with a couple of shoulder epaulets, some gold braid, an eagle insignia, and a scattering of gold stars. He also wore matching white slacks and a jaunty-looking captain's hat.

"He's the epitome of the doomed captain on the *Titanic*," said Haley. "Don't you think?"

Theodosia couldn't help but chuckle, because Drayton really did look like he'd just stepped out of a wheelhouse. "I think he looks like he's about to meet up with Doc and Gopher on the Lido deck."

Haley doubled over with laughter. "*The Love Boat!* Ha, good one."

"Go ahead and laugh if you want," said Drayton, "but I did take it upon myself to procure costumes for everyone."

Haley stopped laughing immediately. "Wait." Now she looked wary. "By *everyone*, do you mean me, too?"

"Both of us?" said Theodosia. She hadn't counted on wearing a *costume.*

"That's right." Drayton held up two white frilly lace aprons and matching lace headpieces. "What do you think?"

Haley gaped at the costumes. "Are you sure these aren't naughty French maid costumes?" she asked suspiciously.

Drayton pursed his lips. "Please. I would *never.*"

Theodosia couldn't help but giggle. If they weren't going to wear those aprons over black slacks and white blouses, the costumes might have indeed exuded a certain Victoria's Secret vibe.

Haley gingerly accepted her apron and held it up in front of her. "And you're *sure* this is what the first-class waitresses wore?"

"No, Haley," said Drayton. "It's what the waitresses in steerage wore. *Of course*, I'm sure. I promise you these costumes are one hundred percent accurate." The corners of his mouth twitched. "Do you not trust that my research was exemplary?"

"What kind of research?" said Haley.

"We appreciate you going all out like this," said Theodosia, suppressing a smile. "And I'm sure our guests will, too."

"Historical accuracy is always important," said Drayton. He clapped his hands together. "Okay then, it's full speed ahead into that iceberg."

"Huh," said Haley. "More like iceberg lettuce."

Ten minutes later, with everyone looking like they'd just been beamed in from the year 1912, Max showed up.

"Hi," he said, glancing around the tea shop almost

furtively. "Oh, great costumes." He stopped in his tracks. "Is it okay to come in? Am I welcome here?"

"Of course, you are," Theodosia assured him. "But you realize we're completely sold out. Have been for a week. We don't have a single extra seat available."

"Oh no," said Max. "I didn't mean I was expecting dinner. I thought maybe I could help out in the kitchen or something."

Theodosia thought for a moment. "Maybe . . ."

"Get back here!" Haley screeched. "If you know how to zest a lemon, I'll put you to work as my sous chef."

"There you go," said Theodosia. "You are now gainfully employed in the kitchen."

Haley did put Max to work. He peeled and sliced asparagus, zested lemons, laid out plates for the appetizers, and generally did all of Haley's bidding. And when the customers began to show up just before five, the Indigo Tea Shop, if you closed your eyes in the flickering candlelight and drew upon your imagination, looked just like the first-class dining room on A deck of the RMS *Titanic*.

It took Theodosia and Drayton a good thirty minutes to greet all of their guests, lead them to their proper tables (as you would on any fine ocean liner), and then quickly serve steaming cups of Taiwanese Jing Shuan oolong tea and glasses of dry sherry.

At five fifteen, Drayton rang a brass bell that he'd borrowed from a yachting shop down the street. Having gained everyone's attention, he pulled himself up to his full height, ready to begin his welcoming speech. Just as she'd been cued, Theodosia dimmed the lights so the twinkling candles in glass hurricane lamps would enhance the mood.

"Welcome," Drayton intoned, "to our first annual *Titanic* Tea at the Indigo Tea Shop."

There was a smattering of enthusiastic applause.

Drayton continued. "On the evening of April fifteenth, in the year 1912, the first-class passengers of RMS *Titanic*, of the now-infamous and sadly defunct White Star Line, feasted on a sumptuous ten-course dinner. Only a few hours later, their ship struck an iceberg and, within the span of three hours, sank to the bottom of the Atlantic. Though tragically gone, the two thousand two hundred twenty-four passengers and crew are certainly not forgotten. They have been memorialized in movies, literature, and various documentaries." He paused. "And tonight we are going to partake of some of the very same gastronomic delights that the first-class passengers enjoyed at their historic and doomed 'last supper.'"

Theodosia stepped in now. "For your appetizer, we shall be serving chilled asparagus vinaigrette. Your second course will consist of sautéed chicken lyonnaise. Your rather lovely entrée will be poached salmon with cucumbers on a bed of rice. And, once dinner is concluded, gentlemen will *not* be required to retreat to the smoking lounge. Instead, you are invited to remain seated and enjoyed a rather ravishing desert of Waldorf pudding and chocolate éclairs." She paused dramatically. "And I can assure you all that, this evening, we are in no danger of sinking!"

Theodosia and Drayton got busy then. They each carried out large silver trays and placed plates of asparagus vinaigrette in front of each guest. That was followed by a slice of Haley's English tea bread placed on bread plates. As their guests chattered and openly admired the table décor, Theodosia circled back to the front counter.

"How do you think it's going?" she asked Drayton.

"Swimmingly," he said.

Theodosia lifted an eyebrow. "Really, Drayton?"

"No pun intended, I assure you," said Drayton, scuttling away.

As Theodosia circled one of the large tables with a teapot, an arm reached out to grab her.

"Hey there," said Harlan Duke. "We meet again."

"You," said Theodosia, smiling. "Fancy seeing you here."

"I heard about this *Titanic* Tea and got intrigued," said Duke. He pronounced it "Ti-*tan*-ic," with his Texas twang. "And then a couple of friends had an extra ticket, so they invited me to come along."

"I'm delighted you could make it," said Theodosia. She was pleased this Texas transplant was fitting in so well with her native Charlestonians.

"I've still got that teapot at my shop," said Duke. "The Chien-lung."

"You didn't bring it along?"

"Ah," said Duke, "I think you've got enough going on tonight."

"Okay, now you've definitely got me intrigued."

"Wonderful," said Duke. "I take that as a good sign."

While Theodosia was serving the second course, the chicken lyonnaise, she stopped to chat with Roger Greaves and his wife.

"Theodosia," said Greaves, "this is my wife, Dolores."

"Dolly, call me Dolly," said the woman. She had dancing blue eyes and a swirl of puffy hair that seemed to alternate in color between champagne blond and apricot. With a pair of red half-glasses perched on the tip of her nose, she looked like a slightly ditzy librarian. "And I'm thrilled to meet you." She gave a little shiver. "And to *be* here," she added. "This is so much fun."

"We're delighted you could make it," said Theodosia. "Do you have everything you need? Can I bring you anything else?"

"We're just great," said Greaves as he tucked into his chicken.

Seated at the table in the corner next to the stone fireplace,

Percy Capers was there with two other curators from the museum.

"We came to show the flag," Capers told Theodosia, "for Max." He looked around. "Is he here tonight?"

"Max is back in the kitchen with Haley," said Theodosia, "playing sous chef."

"Well, everything has been just wonderful so far," said one of the men with Capers. "I really didn't know what to expect, this being a tea shop and all. But your food is really delicious."

"Then we'll expect you back," Theodosia told him. She slid between the tables, checking to make sure everyone was happily feasting away. Then she spun around the corner and popped into the kitchen.

It was pure chaos. The stove was littered with steaming pots and pans, plates were laid out everywhere, and the temperature felt like it was ninety degrees. Haley had a red bandana tied around her head; Max had a blue one.

"Uh-oh," said Theodosia.

15

❧

Haley glanced up from a tray of salmon. "What?"

"Trouble?" said Theodosia. It looked to her like dinner might have gone off the rails.

Haley looked puzzled. "Why . . . no. Are *you* having problems?"

"It's just that . . ." Theodosia gestured with her hands. "Everything looks so . . ."

"Chaotic?" said Haley. "Yeah, well, this is my version of *controlled* chaos. Believe me, I'm on top of it."

"We're both on it," said Max. He was arranging pieces of kale on each plate along with a grilled tomato and a bed of rice. Obviously, the poached salmon would be placed atop the rice.

"Yeah, he's been a big help," said Haley. "Who'd ever guess that a PR dweeb could find his way around a kitchen. He even knows the difference between a potato peeler and a corn zipper."

"Okay then," said Theodosia, just as Drayton stuck his head in behind hers.

"We're ready for the next course," said Drayton. "Are you almost ready with the salmon entrées?"

"I was born ready," said Haley.

"Riiiiight," said Drayton as he quickly retreated.

"How long, really?" Theodosia asked.

Haley held up two fingers. "Two minutes. I guarantee your entrées will be plated and ready to serve in two minutes."

The poached salmon was pure perfection. How did they know? Because their guests exclaimed and raved over it again and again.

"Lovely," said Roger Greaves. "Just delicious."

"I'm going to get down on my hands and knees and *beg* for this recipe," said Dolly Greaves.

"This salmon's the best I've ever eaten," Percy Capers told Theodosia as she poured him a glass of chardonnay.

"Success," breathed Drayton, as he bumped into Theodosia rounding one of the tables.

"What is this delicious cream sauce with the salmon?" wondered Harlan Duke.

"That's a combination of béchamel and velouté," Theodosia told him. "One of our chef's own creations."

"Amazing," said Duke. He was practically scraping his plate with his fork.

Ten minutes later, with several bottles of chardonnay and white Côtes du Rhône having been consumed and the entrees almost finished, people began to get up and move around. They table-hopped, shook hands, and exchanged air kisses. Charleston was a social town, and these people were social animals, so pretty much every dinner party or charity event evolved into a friendly, chatty love fest.

Of course, they'd be seated again once the desserts were brought out.

Theodosia was standing behind the counter fixing a pot of gunpowder green tea when Percy Capers came up to greet her.

"A lovely evening," Capers told her. "Just perfect."

"Thank you." She measured four scoops of tea leaves into a Blue Willow teapot.

Capers dropped his voice so he wouldn't be overheard. "I trust you found everything you needed last night? You know, the guest list and whatever else you were hunting for."

"I did. And thank you so much for being such a knight in shining armor. Showing up like you did and giving us the new code. I know you took a risk."

"I was mostly worried about you," said Capers, "sneaking into the museum, especially in light of the stabbing at the big premiere party last Thursday. And then that attack last night."

"You're talking about Cecily Conrad?"

Capers nodded. "I read all about it in this morning's newspaper. She was the woman who Edgar Webster had been seeing, right?"

"Yes, but she seems to be relatively unhurt. In fact, I paid her a visit earlier today."

"You think it's a strange coincidence or . . . ?" His voice trailed off.

"No," said Theodosia. "Probably not a coincidence at all."

"Really? Whoa. That's not good. That means something fishy is going on."

"You know what else might not have been a coincidence?" said Theodosia. "Elliot Kern was in his office last night."

Capers looked suddenly concerned. "He was there when you went in? Oh boy, that could have made for a dangerous situation."

"After I found what I wanted in Max's office, I saw a spill

of light down the hallway. So I kind of tiptoed down there and listened outside Kern's office.

Capers gazed at her. "You like to live dangerously, don't you?" He dropped his voice to a whisper. "Okay, now you have to tell me. What did you see? Or hear?"

"Just Kern mumbling something about 'a great deal of money' and then something that sounded like 'probably in the clear.'"

"A great deal of money for what?" said Capers.

Theodosia shrugged. "No idea."

"Something to do with the museum?"

"I just don't know."

Capers's eyes narrowed. "And Kern actually said something about being in the clear? Do you think he meant someone was in the clear for . . . ah . . ." He looked pained. "For Webster's murder?"

"He . . . he could have meant that, I suppose."

"You must use extreme caution, then," warned Capers.

"So should you. After all, you have to work with the man."

"And promise me you'll relate your story to one of the investigating officers," Capers cautioned. "One of the detectives."

"I suppose I should," said Theodosia. "Though it's still only hearsay."

A brilliant flash startled them and left them dazed and seeing spots.

"I'll talk to you later," said Capers.

"Did you miss me?" said Bill Glass. He dumped a heavy canvas bag filled with camera gear onto the counter. "Sorry I'm late. Got held up." He pointed his camera into the crowd and clicked off a half dozen shots. "But I'm here now." He leaned forward and stared into his viewfinder. "Oh, here's a good one," he muttered. "That's not bad, either." He glanced up at Theodosia and gave a perfunctory grin. "How ya doin', sweetheart?"

"I'm not your sweetheart," said Theodosia.

"But you could be," said Glass.

"And please don't disturb my guests. You can circulate on the periphery of the room, but don't go blundering up to any of the tables. And please *ask* before you take any close-up shots. Okay?"

"You really like to lay down the law, don't you, lady?"

"Really," said Theodosia, "it's just a matter of simple etiquette."

Theodosia circled the tables, pouring tea, chatting with guests, watching them tuck into the chocolate éclairs and Waldorf pudding that Drayton and Haley had just delivered.

"Would you like a cup of gunpowder green tea?" she asked Roger Greaves. Dolly Greaves had jumped up earlier and was exploring the tea shop, looking at all the gift items.

"Please," he said, sliding his cup toward her. "These éclairs are delicious, by the way."

"Then you must be a chocolate lover," said Theodosia.

"I think it's all the theobromine," said Greaves. "The chemical that hits the feel-good receptor in your brain. Now Dolly . . . Dolly's not much for chocolate." He glanced over. "Shopping's her thing. She's gaga for shopping."

Theodosia followed his gaze. Dolly Greaves had grabbed one of their sweetgrass baskets and was filling it with jars of DuBose Bees Honey and some of Theodosia's own T-Bath products.

When Dolly saw the two of them looking at her, she grinned and gestured for Theodosia to come over and join her.

"You husband tells me you like to shop," said Theodosia.

"I do when the products are this intriguing," said Dolly. "Really, is this your proprietary bath oil?"

"It sure is. In fact, it's part of my T-Bath line, bath and skin-care products that are infused with various blends of tea. For example, there's Chamomile Calming Lotion, Lemon Verbena Hand Lotion, my new Hibiscus and Honey Butter, and a dozen or so more."

"I'm going to take one of each," said Dolly.

"Okay." *Wow. This is going to ring up as quite a hefty sale.*

As Dolly piled more products into her basket, she turned suddenly serious. "My husband tells me you're a bit of an amateur investigator."

"Oh, not really. I'm more of a crime-show fan. You know, *CSI* or *Criminal Minds.*"

"He told me that Charlotte Webster pretty much asked for your help."

"I think she really wanted moral support."

"Charlotte's a fairly smart lady," said Dolly. "She wouldn't have voted against the IPO for Datrex like her husband did."

"You think not?" said Theodosia. This conversation was suddenly veering into strange territory.

"An IPO can often raise millions of dollars and send the company's valuation into the billions," said Dolly. "Why, just look at all those West Coast tech companies with their mega-rich shareholders! I mean . . . Paul Allen and his yacht with a helicopter and a submarine? Just incredible. And to think that Edgar Webster didn't want any part of that." She sniffed. "He just wanted to wobble along like they always had. Ridiculous!"

"But things are about to change, aren't they," said Theodosia. It was a statement, not a question.

"Oh," said Dolly with a touch of smugness, "I'm fairly sure the IPO will move ahead now." The tip of her tongue flicked out and licked her lips, not unlike the tongues of the cotton-mouths that moved silently but deadly outside the perimeter of Theodosia's aunt Libby's plantation out on Rutledge Road.

Theodosia gazed at Dolly Greaves with her two-tone hair and her self-satisfied look. And suddenly, Roger's ditzy wife didn't seem quite so ditzy after all. "It sounds like you're privy to quite a few details."

Dolly nodded. "With seventy-five thousand shares of common stock at an initial public offering of twelve and a quarter . . . why, that's a hair over nine million dollars right there."

"And that would just be for openers," said Theodosia.

"Right," said Dolly with a vigorous bob of her head. She suddenly looked like she should be wearing a green eye-shade and peering at a computer spreadsheet. "I expect there'd be a nice, tasty run-up on the stock price, too."

"So who knows how high those shares could go?" said Theodosia.

"The sky's the limit," said Dolly.

"Interesting," Theodosia said in what she hoped was a neutral tone, though her heart was beating a little faster. After all, murdering Edgar Webster would definitely have been a strategy to move the IPO forward. And Dolly, charming little Dolly who just *loved* to shop, had been present the night Webster was killed.

Theodosia tried to put Dolly's talk of IPOs and yachts with helicopters out of her head for the time being. Tried to forget that Dolly seemed to have her finger on the pulse of Datrex's financial dealings. Instead, after shunting Glass out the front door, Theodosia stood there with Drayton, shaking hands and bidding farewells and saying multiple thank-you's to the guests who were slowly beginning to depart.

It was a long good-bye, replete with hugs and air kisses. But finally, everyone had gone.

"That's it," said Drayton. "Lock the door, pull up the drawbridge, and release the killer crocodiles."

Haley emerged from the kitchen, wiping her hands on her apron. She looked at Drayton, whose hat was canted at an odd angle, and grinned. "I feel like we should be playing the closing theme song from *The Love Boat.*"

"You think Drayton would get it?" Theodosia chuckled. "Do you think he's ever *heard* it?"

"Who cares?" said Haley. "It would be hysterical." She started to warble the song in a high-pitched voice: *"Love, exciting and new. Come aboard, we're expecting you."*

Drayton gazed at her. "Excuse me?" He was not amused.

Haley broke off her singing and turned away, pulling Theodosia along with her. "Come on back to the kitchen, we saved some food for you guys. You must be starving to death."

The kitchen didn't look half as bad as it had before. Dirty dishes had been stacked neatly in the commercial dishwasher, the stove wasn't steaming like Mount Vesuvius anymore, and Max was perched on a stool at the counter calmly eating a piece of salmon.

"How'd it go?" Max asked.

"Good. Actually, great," said Theodosia. "Percy Capers and a couple of the other curators were here. Said they came to show the flag. Solidarity and all that."

"I saw them," said Max. "I peeked around the corner right after you served the main course. Everybody seemed to be chowing down with great gusto."

"Absolutely they were," said Theodosia.

"Though *chowing down* is a rather inelegant way to phrase it," said Drayton as he suddenly appeared in the doorway.

"You want some poached salmon?" Haley asked him. "We have a few servings left. And sauce, too."

"I'd love some," said Drayton. "But what I need first is a bracing cup of tea."

"We should be able to manage that," said Theodosia. "In fact, why don't we brew a pot of that Castleton Estate that you like so much? Haven't we been saving it for a special occasion? A special triumph?"

"Let's do it," said Drayton.

"Go ahead," said Haley. "I'll fix a couple plates for you guys."

They walked out into the tea room.

"You okay?" Theodosia asked.

"Just a little tired," said Drayton.

"It's been a long day."

"Tell me about it," said Drayton as he reached up and grabbed a tin of tea.

"Is that the . . . ?" began Theodosia.

Her words were interrupted by a soft knock at the door.

"Now what?" said Drayton. "Oh dear, I suppose one of our guests left something behind."

Theodosia tiptoed to the door and peered out. "It's not a guest. It's Tidwell."

"Drat," said Drayton.

Theodosia pulled the door open a crack. "You're too late," she told him. "Dinner's over and done. Everyone's gone home."

"Ha," said Tidwell. He pushed the door open with a chubby paw. "I didn't come for dinner. I want to ask your friend a couple of questions."

Drayton took a step back. "What? You mean me?"

"Hardly," said Tidwell. "No, I meant Miss Browning's gentleman friend. Max Scofield."

"How did you know he was here?" said Theodosia.

Tidwell's mouth twitched. "Please."

When Max came out from the kitchen, he didn't look happy. "What now?" he asked.

"May we sit down?" asked Tidwell.

"I suppose," said Theodosia. She was curious as to what this was all about.

Tidwell wasted no time. "You know that Miss Cecily Conrad was attacked last night?"

Max's nod was imperceptible.

"What does that have to do with Max?" Theodosia asked.

Tidwell held up a hand. "Please." His large head swiveled toward Max. "I take it you have an alibi?"

"I was with Theodosia, and then I stopped at a cigar bar," said Max.

"Which one?" said Tidwell.

"DG Stogies. Over on Wentworth."

"And you were there from when to when?"

Max half closed his eyes, thinking. "Probably from about ten thirty to midnight."

"And you were not alone?"

"There were maybe a half dozen guys there. There was a rebroadcast of the Carolina Panthers game. We were watching it."

"And all of your football cronies would vouch for you?"

"Sure," said Max. "Why wouldn't they?"

"That's all I need to know," said Tidwell.

"That's it?" said Theodosia. She felt like they'd gotten off easy.

"That's it," said Tidwell. He gave a small smile. "Pro forma."

"Well, then . . . would you like a bite of poached salmon?" Theodosia asked him.

Tidwell looked suddenly delighted. His nose twitched, his eyes lit up, and he said, "Really?"

"I'll get an order," said Max. "Now that I know I'm not going to be burned at the stake." He jumped up and disappeared into the kitchen.

Theodosia looked over at Drayton, who was suddenly busy fixing his pot of tea.

"I met someone very interesting tonight," said Theodosia, leading Tidwell to a table that had been cleared.

"Pray tell," said Tidwell as they both sat down.

"Dolly Greaves, the wife of Roger Greaves."

"He of the murdered partner."

"Yes," said Theodosia. "Dolly is . . . well, she seems to be following the financial dealings of her husband's company rather closely."

"Meaning?"

"Dolly has a charming, jovial way about her," said Theodosia. "But she's extremely sharp, in a business sense."

"Most women are," said Tidwell.

"Still, Dolly seemed to take real pleasure in the fact that the Datrex IPO, the one Edgar Webster managed to postpone, is probably going to be happening now."

Tidwell held up a chubby hand. "Stop. What you're really saying is that Mrs. Greaves is a suspect. In your book, anyway."

"Yes," said Theodosia. "I guess I am. It's possible that Dolly could have been the one who killed Webster. After all, she knew him fairly well and she was at the event Thursday night."

"Interesting," said Tidwell, though the way he said it indicated he wasn't the least bit interested.

"Anyway," said Theodosia, "I'm just saying." She rose and grabbed a napkin, knife, fork, and spoon off the counter for Tidwell and arranged it in front of him.

Not thirty seconds later, Max set a dish of poached salmon in front of Tidwell. The dish was accompanied by Haley's cream sauce and a side of leftover asparagus vinaigrette.

Tidwell tucked his napkin into his shirt collar and dug in with relish.

"Mmn," he said at the first bite. "Good."

"I think the salmon turned out of be everyone's favorite," said Theodosia.

Tidwell took a second bite. "Really good. In fact, I am fairly trembling with pleasure."

"I'm not sure I've ever encountered *that* kind of reaction before," said Theodosia.

Tidwell glanced around as he continued eating. "What type of event took place here?" he asked.

"Our *Titanic* Tea," said Theodosia.

"*Titanic*? As in the ship? Really?" said Tidwell, never missing a beat.

"Think of it as a classy Halloween event," put in Drayton.

Tidwell inclined his head toward Theodosia. "And did you hire an orchestra to play 'Nearer, My God, to Thee?'"

"No," said Theodosia. "I'm afraid that would have been a little over the top."

"I'd have thought it highly appropriate," said Tidwell. "Considering that the one thing on your mind is murder."

16

❧

Church Street would never have been called Church Street if it weren't for St. Philip's Episcopal Church. Founded in 1681, constructed in 1836, the elegant-looking church with the circular front proudly extended out into the middle of Church Street for all to see.

Surrounded on three sides by centuries-old graveyards, St. Philip's seemed uniquely appropriate for Edgar Webster's funeral Monday morning. The choir sang a somber version of "How Great Thou Art" as the mourners quietly filed in. Theodosia, sitting in one of the back pews, recognized Roger Greaves and his wife, Dolly, and what was probably a contingent of Datrex employees crowded around them. There was also a bunch of Webster relatives.

Theodosia also noted that Elliot Kern was present and accounted for, as well as a number of curators and board members from the museum.

Stands to reason, she thought, since poor Webster had met his maker there. Too bad it hadn't happened in a picturesque garden or gallery. She couldn't imagine what it must have been like for Edgar to have gasped out his dying breath in a chrome yellow photo booth. The kind people rented for fairs or sweet sixteen parties. The kind Max had unfortunately rented. And it was too bad that Webster hadn't had the presence of mind to push the button and take a photo. Then his death—and his killer's identity—would have been recorded for posterity.

Squirming around in her seat, Theodosia noted that Tidwell was hunched in the very last pew. He seemed intent on ignoring everyone around him, though he was probably observing them like a hawk. And there was Bill Glass, skulking in with a load of cameras strung around his neck. He was here to capture the moment, she thought. But not for posterity. Any images he captured today would exist only for a day or two in his rag of a tabloid, then get tossed out with the next day's garbage.

As the choir finished their dirge and the organ music slowly died in the still air, there was a disturbance at the back of the church. The sound of doors opening, loud whispers, a hum of activity, and the *click-clack* of rolling metal wheels.

Theodosia swiveled around and saw that Edgar Webster's casket had been loaded onto a casket roller. Covered with the official state flag of South Carolina—bright blue with a white palmetto and crescent—that draped the casket and was topped with an enormous spray of white lilies.

Interesting, she thought. They were the same type of flowers used at the *Titanic* Tea last night. Only these lilies were larger and the presentation far more grand.

A hush came over the congregation, and the organ started up again as Charlotte Webster, hanging on the arm of Harlan Duke, came walking down the aisle. Charlotte wore a black jacket with a perky, stand-up collar, a ruffled skirt, and a black hat that was somewhere between a stovepipe and *The Cat in the Hat.* They were followed closely by Edgar Webster's casket. Flanked by six grim-faced pallbearers and an honor guard of four more men in black suits, it creaked noisily down the aisle.

In their dark suits, the men looked like a chorus of crows, Theodosia thought to herself. Although that might not have been the correct term for it. Maybe crows were a muster? Or a murder? She'd have to look that up.

But right now, she continued to watch Charlotte sniffle and shuffle her way to the front of the church.

When had Charlotte gotten so friendly with Harlan Duke, Theodosia wondered? And then she remembered that Duke had been the one who'd located the Chinese tea house in Shanghai, the tea house Edgar Webster had financed so heavily.

Once the casket had been rolled to the front and see-sawed into place, once the mourners had all taken their seats, the service began in earnest.

It was quite lovely, as funeral services go. Prayers, songs, moments of contemplation, and fine testimonials. Roger Greaves stood at the front of the church, gripping the podium as he delivered a rousing speech about Webster's amazing contributions at Datrex. Then another man— Theodosia thought it was their CEO—gave a shorter speech that was also filled with platitudes.

The Lord's Prayer ensued, and then everyone was asked to stand for a final blessing and what was to be the concluding hymn.

With the choir's last sad notes still hanging in the air, Theodosia slipped out the door and hurried down Church Street to the Indigo Tea Shop. She knew she had about five or ten minutes before they'd be besieged by mourners— after that much solemnity, she figured everyone would be hungry for lunch. And she wanted to make sure everything was set up and the tea shop was looking sharp.

But when Theodosia came crashing through the front door, she was greeted not by a frantic Drayton, but by a placid-looking Drayton.

"Hello," said Drayton. "How was the funeral?" He lounged casually behind the counter, sipping a cup of tea. In his brown tweed jacket and yellow bow tie, he looked like a gentleman of leisure, except for the half dozen tea tins that lined the counter. It would appear he was still mulling over his final choices.

"It was good," Theodosia responded. "Well, not *good* good. Really kind of sad." She blinked. "Is everything ready to go for the funeral luncheon?"

"See for yourself."

Theodosia glanced around. Tea lights flickered in small glass holders, the tables were set with their Royal Albert Old Country Roses china, and the floral bouquets from last night had been repurposed into smaller, more sedate arrangements set in simple milk glass vases.

"It looks lovely," said Theodosia.

Drayton smiled. "Thank you. Well, you can thank Haley, too. She did a lot of fine-tuning."

"I take it you didn't run into too much trouble with people showing up this morning to find us closed?"

"It was nothing we couldn't deal with," said Drayton.

"Well . . . okay. Then I guess we really are ready." Theodosia grabbed a long black apron off a peg, pointed to an easel that hadn't been there before, and said, "What's that?"

"One of the Datrex minions dropped it off right before the funeral," said Drayton.

"Okay," said Theodosia. She draped the apron around her neck and peered at the poster on the easel, which had obviously been created to memorialize Edgar Webster's life. There were photos of Webster playing golf with his buddies at Coosaw Creek, photos of Webster posing in a sunny garden with a smiling Charlotte, and photos of Webster looking large and in charge behind an enormous desk, a photo she assumed had been taken in his executive office at Datrex.

But no photos of Webster with Cecily. No, there wouldn't be, would there?

Of course not, since Charlotte had probably micromanaged this entire tribute and selected only the most flattering and appropriate shots.

Dozens of cards and condolence notes had been tacked beneath the photos. All seemed to profess extreme sympathy and grief for Webster's passing. Many of the notes were from Datrex employees, one was from the museum's board of directors, and one note was even from a Shanghai art dealer. Probably, Theodosia decided, it was the overseas dealer who'd helped arrange the purchase and shipment of the tea house.

"Hey," said Haley as she slipped out through the celadon green curtains, "how'd it go?"

"Okay," said Theodosia. "How are you managing with the tea sandwiches? I really appreciate your doing a big event right on the heels of last night."

"No problem," said Haley. "Today's luncheon isn't that much different from any other Monday morning."

"Except we might be a little more busy," said Drayton.

Haley walked to one of the front windows and pulled a chintz curtain aside. "Yeah, and I'm starting to see people heading this way. Probably coming from the funeral."

Drayton glanced at Theodosia. "Do you know, is this luncheon by invitation only? Do I have to collect cards or something?"

Theodosia thought for a moment. "I don't think the guests will be carrying formal invitations. I think there was just a kind of blanket announcement at the end of the ceremony."

"Ceremony?" said Haley.

"Um . . . funeral service," said Theodosia.

"So I should just let everyone in?" said Drayton.

"Until every seat is filled, I suppose," said Theodosia.

"And give preferential seating to all the people dressed in black?" said Drayton.

"They're all dressed in black," said Haley.

It was pretty much the same rogue's gallery that Theodosia had seen at the funeral service twenty minutes ago: Charlotte and a handful of Webster relatives. Roger and Dolly Greaves, accompanied by several Datrex employees. Elliot Kern with Harlan Duke and a couple of museum board members. And a bunch of people from the Historic District who Theodosia knew or vaguely knew.

Drayton gave Charlotte and her party preferential seating at the large round table, then seated the rest of the mourners as best he could. When there were maybe only three or four seats left, Delaine and Aunt Acid came straggling through the door.

"Were you at the funeral?" Theodosia asked Delaine. "Because I didn't see you there." She didn't think they were crashing. Then again . . .

"Yes, I was there," said Delaine, frowning. "You must have come in late. Were you late?"

"Not particularly." Theodosia regarded Aunt Acid. "Nice to see you again."

"Hello," said Aunt Acid, throwing her a slightly sour look.

"I see you still have your guest," said Theodosia, though she really wanted to say, *I see you're still stuck with the old bat.*

"Don't I know it," said Delaine.

"I can seat the two of you by the window if you'd like," said Theodosia.

"Thank you," said Delaine. She walked a few steps,

pointed to a captain's chair, and said, "Sit," to Aunt Acid. The old lady plopped down.

"How are things at Cotton Duck?" Theodosia asked. "Now that the weather's cooled down some, are you selling tons of fall and winter merchandise?"

"It's been crazy good," said Delaine as she spread a napkin in her lap. "Any shipment of cotton sweaters comes in, they just completely blow out the door. Same with slacks." She made a *ka-pow* sound. "We can't keep those in stock, either."

"A good problem to have," said Theodosia.

"Mmn. Theo, speaking of sales and merchandise, I hope you haven't forgotten about your participation in the Hunt and Gather Market."

"No, of course I haven't. When is that again?"

"Tuesday."

"*This* Tuesday?" said Theodosia. "You mean tomorrow?"

Delaine shook her head. "I knew it. You did forget."

"I didn't really forget. It just slipped my . . ."

"I have an eight-foot table *reserved* for you," said Delaine. "So you *have to* show up. Fifty percent of the sales go to charity, you know. To three different, very worthwhile animal organizations!"

"I'll be there," said Theodosia. "You can count on me." But what she was really thinking was, *Holy crap, how am I going to pull a rabbit out of a hat?*

"Theodosia?" Drayton was standing directly behind her.

Theodosia turned. She knew she'd kind of checked out for a few moments.

"Time to serve our fruit salads."

"I'm on it," said Theodosia.

She tucked the Hunt and Gather Market issue into the back of her brain for the time being and focused on getting the food out to their guests. Haley had prepared gorgeous little salads—field greens with slices of mandarin oranges, apples, and pears—for the first course. To accompany the salads, Haley's fresh-baked honey scones were stacked on plates, one plate for each table, and passed around to be enjoyed with Devonshire cream.

Drayton had finally settled on Nilgiri and Moroccan mint tea, so Theodosia made the rounds, a teapot in each hand. She filled teacups, refilled teacups, and accepted compliments on the salad and scones.

"I can't believe how well this is going," Theodosia said to Drayton when she circled back for refills on her tea. "And I was kind of jittery about pulling it off."

"Piece of cake," said Drayton. "And the tea sandwiches will be just as easy. Haley is going to arrange them on tiered tea trays, so our guests can just help themselves."

"I think I'll go check on the sandwiches," said Theodosia. "So . . . maybe you could handle the refills?"

"Consider it done," said Drayton.

Haley had everything under control in the kitchen as well.

"Just place the large trays on the larger tables and the smaller trays on the smaller tables," Haley instructed. "That way everybody can help themselves. And, if we need more, I made up a few dozen extra sandwiches just in case."

Haley's tea-sandwich repertoire consisted of chicken salad on whole wheat bread, cream cheese and crushed walnuts on pumpkin swirl bread, and roast beef and Cheddar cheese on dark bread. She'd made her sandwiches assembly-line style, then sliced off all the crusts and cut the sandwiches into triangles. Now, arranged on the tiered tea trays with a few bright red strawberries and some edible flowers sprinkled in, they looked elegant and appealing. Perfect enough to be photographed for a magazine spread.

Charlotte caught Theodosia by the arm just as she placed the last tea tray on one of the tables.

"This is just wonderful," Charlotte burbled. "I knew I could count on you."

Theodosia studied Charlotte's froufrou black skirt and high-necked black jacket. She didn't look exactly funereal, more like an expensively dressed vampire.

Interestingly, Harlan Duke had seated himself right next to her and was carefully ministering to her every need.

Theodosia touched Charlotte on the shoulder. "My condolences again. Helping with your luncheon was the least we could do."

"You are such a dear," said Charlotte. She turned and smiled at Duke. "Isn't Theodosia a dear?"

Duke beamed a solicitous smile. "She certainly is."

Theodosia had just grabbed a pitcher of ice water when she noticed the front door opening a crack.

Oh dear, I hope it's not folks looking for afternoon tea. Not this early.

No such luck. Because the woman who slipped soundlessly into the shop and looked around tentatively was none other than Cecily Conrad!

17

❦

Theodosia's heart lurched inside her chest.

Oh no. This has major disaster written all over it.

She scrambled toward Cecily like she was a sprinter heading for the finish line. Water splashed, chairs were bumped, a few people turned to stare.

"What are you *doing* here?" Theodosia hissed at Cecily. She wanted to head her off, turn her around, and get her out before something dire happened.

"I wanted to . . ." Cecily's voice sounded raw and dry.

"What do you want?" Theodosia was still hoping to stave off disaster. If she could just shepherd Cecily back out the door, tactfully oust the woman before too many people noticed . . .

But Cecily's feet seemed welded to the floor. And Theodosia tugging on her arm didn't seem to budge her, either.

"I wanted to be part of it," Cecily coughed out. "After all, I was . . ."

"You! What are *you* doing here?" a shrill voice rang out. It belonged unmistakably to Charlotte.

Theodosia's shoulders slumped. *Oh, great. Now Charlotte's going to get into the act. Here comes a full-blown three-ring circus.*

"How dare you show your face here!" Charlotte screamed. She scrambled to her feet, red-faced and indignant, and pointed a finger directly at Cecily. Now that she'd alerted all of Western civilization, every eye in the room turned toward Cecily.

"She was just leaving," said Theodosia. She was aware of indignant murmurs and the sound of chairs being slid back from tables. Were people getting ready for a knock-down, drag-out fight? She hoped not.

"You have to leave," Theodosia told Cecily. "This instant!"

But Cecily was staring at the easel that stood in the entryway. "Did *she* do that?" she demanded. "Because she never cared about him before."

Now Theodosia heard the *clack, clack, clack* of high-heeled pumps heading toward them. Which, to her, was the sound of impending doom. Then Charlotte's face bobbed like an angry pink balloon alongside Cecily's face.

"Get out, you little hussy!" Charlotte screeched. "Get out of here before we throw you out!"

"Please," said Theodosia, plucking at Cecily's sleeve. "It's time to leave."

"I'll leave with my dignity!" Cecily rasped at Charlotte.

Taken aback, Charlotte blinked as if she'd been slapped in the face. Then, eyes bulging, mouth pulled into an ugly pucker, she hauled her right arm back, swung it around in an arc, and punched Cecily right in the face!

It wasn't exactly a championship knockout; the blow glanced off at the last moment. But Cecily, caught completely unaware, staggered backward. She made an indelicate noise that sounded like *ptew* or *phu*, wobbled for a millisecond, and then collapsed to the floor like a cheap card table.

"Do something," Delaine screamed. "Somebody do something!"

Stunned beyond belief at the mayhem that was unfolding around them, Theodosia and Drayton both sprang into action. Drayton encircled his arms around Charlotte's waist and pulled her away from the scrum. Theodosia knelt down, wrestled an arm around a shocked and tearful Cecily, and basically hauled her up onto her feet.

"Get her out of here," Charlotte seethed. She sounded dangerous, like a hissing cobra.

"Consider her gone," said Theodosia. She pushed and prodded a shaken-up Cecily back through the curtain, past the kitchen, where Haley gazed in amazement, and into her office.

"What was *that* all about?" Theodosia asked Cecily. She was fuming, just this side of exploding.

But Cecily was wiping at her bloody nose, smearing the blood horribly, and trying to brush away a constant stream of tears at the same time. Then she gingerly pressed her hand against the side of her red, puffed-up face. "She hit me," she sobbed. "Did you see that? She *hit* me."

"Sit down," said Theodosia, grabbing Cecily by the shoulders and pushing her down onto the tuffet chair. She flew into the kitchen, grabbed a towel and some ice, and was back. "Put this on your face. It'll help knock down the swelling."

Cecily accepted the towel and touched it to her face. "Hurts," she murmured.

"I'm sure it does," said Theodosia. She felt sorry for Cecily. But, at the same time, knew that Cecily had gone out of her way to provoke Charlotte. She gazed at Cecily. "This was all so unnecessary, don't you agree?"

"I didn't mean to cause trouble," Cecily grumped. She wiped at her face again, smearing more blood.

"Sure, you did," said Theodosia. "Why else would you

have come here? Come on, dab that towel under your nose," she instructed, then sighed heavily. "You're a problem child, you know that?"

Cecily hiccupped loudly. "That's what my daddy always said, too."

"Well, guess what?" said Theodosia. "It's time to grow up. Time to act like an adult."

Cecily peered at her. "Huh?"

"Listen to me, Cecily. You've been smacked to the ground twice in three days. Does that tell you anything?"

"What do you mean?"

"Maybe you should start keeping a slightly lower profile," said Theodosia. "Stay out of the way for a while."

"I just . . . I just . . ."

"You just what?"

Cecily sucked in air and hiccupped again. "I went to Edgar's funeral, thinking it was out of a sense of duty. Then I got there and the songs and the eulogies sort of . . . Well, all the old memories came flooding back. And I guess I had kind of a meltdown."

"You both reacted badly," said Theodosia. "You and Charlotte."

Cecily looked up at her with a sidelong glance. "Do you think she killed him?"

"Do I think . . . ?" Theodosia suddenly snapped her mouth shut. Because one part of her still thought that Charlotte *might* have had a hand in her husband's death. And another part of her wasn't letting Cecily off the hook, either.

"I know the police have been talking to her," said Cecily.

"And I know the police have been talking to you," said Theodosia.

The girl's mouth fell open in shock. "You can't think that I . . . ?" Then her chin quivered and the waterworks started up again.

Theodosia handed Cecily a couple of tissues and waited patiently while she cried for a couple of minutes. Finally the girl sniffled, wiped at her tears, and said, "My eye and nose hurt like crazy."

"I'm sure it does."

She wiggled the bottom half of her face back and forth. "Do you think we should call the police?"

"You know what?" Theodosia gestured at the towel and the ice. "You can take that with you. And I think it'd be a smart idea if you left via the back door. Okay? Okay."

When Theodosia ducked back into the tea room, order seemed to have been restored. Tea was being sipped, the decibel level had returned to normal, and the funeral guests were munching their brownie bites and lemon bars. Even Charlotte looked relatively calm.

Drayton saw Theodosia and raised his eyebrows. "Is she gone?"

"Hopefully never to darken our doorway again," said Theodosia.

"That was something you don't see everyday."

"Except on WWE *SmackDown*."

The bell above the front door *da-dinged*.

"Now what?" said Drayton.

It was Bill Glass. He stepped inside and glanced around, a slightly suspicious look on his face.

"Did I just miss something?" Glass asked.

"Hmm?" said Drayton.

"Not really," said Theodosia.

"Because I would've sworn I saw Cecily Conrad dragging herself down Church Street," said Glass, "looking like she'd just been in the biggest cat fight of her life."

"Gee," said Theodosia. "I wouldn't know."

Glass edged closer to her. "Seeing Cecily looking so

bedraggled . . . something feels a little fishy. If I had to venture a guess, I'd say something went down in here."

Yeah, Theodosia thought. *Cecily went down. On her keister.*

Instead, she said, "Cecily dropped in but left immediately."

"I'm afraid she wasn't really welcome," said Drayton.

"That's it?" said Glass.

"That's it for now," said Theodosia.

Glass eyed them both suspiciously, then his head swiveled toward the café, and he said, "You guys got any of those dinky little sandwiches left?"

Relieved that Bill Glass seemed ready to drop the subject, Theodosia said, "Sure. In fact, there's a place open at Delaine's table." She led Glass over there and said, "Have a seat."

"What?" said Delaine, suddenly looking horrified. "He's going to sit *here?*"

"Is there a problem?" said Theodosia.

Delaine saw the set of Theodosia's jaw, and said, "Why, no. Actually, we were just leaving." She got up, slapped her hat on her head, and said, "Come along, Auntie."

"Have a nice day, ladies," said Glass, giving a mock salute.

"Hmph," said Aunt Acid.

As Roger Greaves and his employees started making motions to leave, Theodosia hurried over to them.

"This isn't the time or the place," Theodosia said to Greaves, "but I desperately need to talk to you."

Greaves stared at her. "About?"

"I just have a few questions."

"And why would *you* be asking me questions?"

"Because I promised to help Charlotte any way I could,"

said Theodosia. She knew it was a little white lie, but she wanted to get Greaves alone and on the hot seat. "You remember, when I brought the basket over to Charlotte? You were there, you heard her ask me."

He softened. "When you put it that way . . . I suppose."

"Thank you," said Theodosia, touching his arm gently. She knew men liked it when a woman touched their arms. It implied that you were addled and slightly helpless in their presence, and completely obscured the fact that you were manipulating the crap out of them.

"You can drop by my office later today. You know where we're located?"

"Um . . ."

"We're Digital Corridor members, so we've recently relocated over in the University District."

"Great," said Theodosia. "Many thanks. I look forward to meeting with you."

"Mmn," said Greaves.

As the luncheon dwindled to a close, a few of the guests wandered over to the highboys in the corner, where Theodosia had arranged a fresh stash of tea, honey, T-Bath products, antique teacups, and decorated sugar cubes.

"They're charmed by your shop," Drayton told Theodosia as they observed the luncheon guests mingling and looking about.

"You think?"

"Oh, absolutely. You've created everyone's ideal of what a tea shop should look like. The Indigo Tea Shop is small, cozy, and exudes that chintz-and-china aura . . . It's perfection."

"But they really come for our tea," said Theodosia. "As well as our sweets and savories."

"And for you," Drayton smiled.

"Excuse me?" said a male voice.

Theodosia turned to find Harlan Duke gazing at her intently. "Yes?" she said.

"Charlotte was wondering if she could have a word with you," said Duke.

Theodosia wondered who'd died and made him messenger, and then she remembered—Charlotte's husband had died. So she probably shouldn't be quite so snarky, as Duke seemed to be playing the nice guy and running interference.

"Of course," Theodosia said.

"It's a private matter," said Duke.

"Okay." Now her curiosity was piqued. She pointed over her shoulder. "In my office, then?"

"Perfect," said Duke. "I'll send her in."

Charlotte was fidgeting nervously as she walked into Theodosia's office.

"Won't you have a seat?" Theodosia said. She indicated the chair that Cecily had vacated some twenty minutes ago. The irony was not lost on Theodosia.

Charlotte plunked herself down and carefully arranged her black skirt. Then she looked up with a smile on her face. "Theodosia, dear, I want to ask you something."

"Yes?" Theodosia said. Warning bells started to clang in her head. Every time someone addressed her as "Theodosia, dear," they were generally trying to wangle something for nothing. Or trying to pull the wool over her eyes. But she wanted to give Charlotte the benefit of the doubt. After all, it had been a hard day for her. A hard couple of days.

"I'm chairperson of the Historic District's big Halloween event this year," said Charlotte. "But after everything that's happened . . ." She glanced around, exuding an air of helplessness.

"Yes?" Theodosia said again.

"Well, you've heard of the Bloody Mary Crawl and the Haunted Hayride?"

"Sure," said Theodosia. "It's the spooky walk and hayride that take place Halloween night." She was getting a good sense of what might be coming.

"Only it's so much more than just that," Charlotte enthused. "Historic homes will be all decorated and open to the public, and volunteers will be serving Bloody Marys, cider, and donuts. Then there are guided trips through the cemetery, and of course, a hayride with real live horses."

"I've never taken part in any of those events," said Theodosia. "But they sound like fun." She was still waiting for the other shoe to drop.

"Only now," said Charlotte, "my participation feels . . . well, rather unseemly. I mean, coming on the heels of poor Edgar's death"—she gave a dry cough that sounded a little phony—"and his subsequent burial."

That would be the usual order of things, Theodosia thought.

"Anyway," Charlotte continued, "long story short, I was wondering if *you* would agree to take over my duties as chairperson."

"What exactly would I have to do?" Theodosia felt sorry for Charlotte; she really did. A dead husband and Halloween didn't exactly go well together. At the same time, she was nervous about taking on an additional project. And a fairly big one at that.

"That's the beauty of it," said Charlotte. "You don't have to do much of anything. I mean . . . everything's been planned out, down to the last detail. Oh, sure, you'd have to be at the rallying point when the Bloody Mary Crawl kicks off and kind of ride herd on the volunteers. Then you'd have to make sure the open houses go off without a hitch, and that guides take visitors along Gateway Walk and through the cemeteries."

"How many volunteers do you have?"

Charlotte closed her eyes, thinking. Then they popped open. "We've signed up at least thirty."

"Oh, so a lot of volunteers."

"And the horses and hay wagons are all donated," said Charlotte. "From Equinox Equestrian Center."

"I don't have to worry about the horses, too?" said Theodosia.

"Not really. The hay wagon drivers will take care of trailering them in . . . and the hayride routes are all predetermined." Charlotte bobbed her head eagerly. "So you'll step in and do it?"

"Yes, I will," said Theodosia. "But I'd still need to get together with you and go over all the various aspects. Would that be possible?"

"Absolutely, it would. Maybe you could drop by my house tonight around seven. I could go over my notes with you—everything's organized in a binder. You should be able to pick up on the high points in about two seconds."

"Okay, I'll see you then," said Theodosia.

Charlotte reached out and grasped Theodosia's hand. "Thank you so much." She stood up, and said, "Oh, and some good news, too. I've been elected a board member at the museum." On this note she fairly beamed.

"You're taking your husband's place," Theodosia said slowly. "That's really quite . . . interesting."

"Interesting, yes," said Charlotte. "In fact, we have our very first meeting tomorrow night."

Ten minutes later, it was all over. The guests had departed, Theodosia had cleared away the debris, and Drayton had set up the tables for afternoon tea. Only Bill Glass lingered at his table, wolfing down a scone and slurping his third cup of tea.

"Are you just about done there?" Theodosia asked him. She worried that he might become a permanent fixture.

But Glass wasn't really listening. He was tuned in to his own wavelength.

"I am seriously suspicious of Harlan Duke," said Glass. "Did you see how he was making moves on Charlotte Webster?"

"Sitting next to her, being kind and comforting her. That's making moves?"

"If you could have seen them right after the funeral. He was escorting her out of the church, and she was positively leaning into him."

"Maybe because she was upset?"

"Or maybe because he was coming on to her."

"I don't know," said Theodosia. Although she was curious about their developing relationship herself.

"What if Harlan Duke killed Webster?" Glass blurted out.

"What?"

"I think you heard me just fine," said Glass.

Theodosia put a hand on her hip and regarded him. "Okay, smart guy, I'll bite: Why on earth would Duke kill Edgar Webster? What possible motive could he have had?"

Glass gave a nasty grin. "Duh . . . to get to the grieving widow? To get in line so he can be her next husband and heir to the throne?"

"The throne?"

"Well, all that money she's got squirreled away."

"That's an awful lot of speculation," said Theodosia. "But, okay, just for the sake of argument, let's just say Duke *did* kill Edgar Webster. Then does it follow that he also attacked Cecily Conrad?"

"He could have."

"But why? For what possible reason?"

Glass had an answer for this, too. "Maybe because Charlotte asked him to?"

"Then you're saying they're in collusion," said Theodosia.

"That's a possibility."

"And I think maybe you're completely off base." *Was he really?*

"Let's just say I haven't *rounded* the bases yet," said Glass. "But I think I might have hit a decent line drive."

"You're crazy, you know that?" said Theodosia.

"Admit it," said Glass. "There's something going on."

"Something, yes. We just don't know what."

Glass held up a finger. "But we will. I know we'll figure it out."

18

"*They left their* easel behind," said Theodosia. She glanced around as if she expected it to toddle off by itself. "Drayton?"

Drayton looked up from where he was fixing a pot of Earl Grey. Afternoon tea was in full swing and almost half the tables were occupied. Haley had baked a batch of orange scones, and those were being enjoyed along with cups of chocolate hazelnut and ginger peach tea.

"The easel," said Drayton. "Yes, I guess it is still here. I suppose Charlotte was supposed to take it. Or the Datrex people."

Theodosia grabbed the tag board with the photos and notes stuck to it and propped it behind the counter. Then she gathered up the wooden easel and carried it into her office. "We don't need people tripping over this," she muttered.

She shoved the easel up against a wall, struck her toe on the corner of a cardboard box filled with straw hats, and clambered over to her desk. Yes, her office was messy. She was the first one to admit it. But only because it was jam-packed with boxes of tea, honey, Tea Shirts, and her trademark indigo-blue shopping bags. To say nothing of the stacks of sweetgrass baskets, wreaths, and red hats.

Sitting at her desk now, she leaned back, and thought, *Why did I come in here again?* She let her mind wander for a few moments. *Oh, yes. I need to focus on Delaine's Hunt and Gather Market.*

She really had forgotten all about it. Forgotten that she'd promised Delaine months ago that she'd take part. That, along with forty or so other merchants who Delaine had coerced, she'd sell some of her tea or T-Bath products at the one-day street market.

Delaine was certainly flamboyant and a little maddening, but she was a whirling dervish when it came to fundraising. The Heritage Society, the Charleston Opera, and especially animal-welfare organizations benefitted from her fiendish ways. When it came to opening doors, prying open checkbooks, and garnering substantial pledges, nobody could hold a candle to Delaine.

Theodosia picked up a tea catalog, flipped through a few pages, and then, feeling restless, tossed it aside. She still had to figure something out for the Hunt and Gather Market. She supposed she could sell some of their proprietary blended tea. They still had beaucoup bags of their Housewarming Blend, a Chinese black tea blended with a hint of citrus and ginger. And there was a good stock of Honey Hibiscus tea, too, a mild black tea blended with hibiscus blossoms, rosehips, and a touch of honey.

Sure, that should work.

"You look puzzled," said Drayton. "Are you deep in thought?" He was standing in the doorway, smiling.

"I have to come up with something to sell at tomorrow's Hunt and Gather Market," said Theodosia.

"Yes, I heard Delaine banging away about that."

"It slipped my mind."

"You've had a lot going on." Drayton took a step forward. "You know, I've just worked up a new tea blend."

"Another one?" Drayton came up with the most wonderful proprietary blends. And they were all good sellers, too.

"If Haley and I put in an extra half hour or so this afternoon, we could probably package up a few bags for you."

"To sell at Delaine's market?" said Theodosia. "That would be super. And thanks for the rescue, I owe you one."

"Don't you even want to taste the tea?" asked Drayton.

"Well . . . sure."

He held up a finger. "I shall return."

Theodosia was halfway through the afternoon mail—mostly junk—when Drayton came back with a small pot of tea. "It's ready," he told her. "Perfectly steeped." He poured out a cup and handed it to her.

"What is it?" she asked.

"Better you should try it first."

So Theodosia did.

"This is delicious," she said. "It tastes like . . ." She smiled. "The outdoors." Taking another sip, she let the warm liquid roll across her tongue. "What do you call this?"

"This is my English Hedgerow tea," said Drayton. "A rich black tea with chamomile, lemongrass, cornflower, and rose petals. It's basically a floral and grassy blend that I find reminiscent of the English countryside and its hedgerows."

"This is magnificent," said Theodosia. "No wonder you're the tea blender and I'm the tea taster."

"We'll package up . . . what? Maybe four dozen bags for you?"

"That should do it." Theodosia stood up and came around her desk, feeling like a weight had been lifted from her shoulders. She nodded toward the tea room. "Do you need me out there?"

"Couldn't hurt," said Drayton.

Together they strolled out into the tea room, Theodosia

still enjoying her cup of tea. "You know I'm going to pay a visit to Datrex later on today."

"For what reason?"

"I still get a weird feeling about Roger Greaves," said Theodosia. "I thought if I saw the company, talked to him a little more, that something might pop."

"This whole thing is a skull cracker, isn't it?" said Drayton.

"Yes, and there's something I need to ask you," said Theodosia. "You know about the Bloody Mary Crawl and Haunted Hayride?"

"The events taking place on All Hallows Eve," said Drayton.

"Well, Charlotte asked me to take over her role as chairperson."

"That sounds like an awfully big job. Isn't her request coming a trifle late?"

"It is, but I still told her yes anyway. The thing is, I'm going to drop by her house tonight and go over the final plans." Theodosia hesitated. "I was wondering if you'd come along with me."

Drayton looked pained. "You're not going to ask me to dress up as a ghoul or a ghost are you?"

"No, no, you'd be coming along strictly as moral support. And because you're smart and because I'm still a tiny bit suspicious of Charlotte." *Especially after Bill Glass got done spinning all his wild theories.*

"I see," said Drayton.

"So. Will you? Come along, I mean?"

"You know I will."

"Thank you," said Theodosia.

Drayton cocked his head to one side and peered around Theodosia. "Exactly what are you doing, Haley?"

"Oh," said Haley. She was struggling with an enormous

cardboard box. "I dug out our Halloween decorations. I thought I'd put them up."

"Now?" said Theodosia.

"We couldn't do it any earlier," said Haley, sounding a little defensive. "I mean, how would it have looked? The tea room festooned with ghosts and skeletons while a funeral luncheon was taking place? That would have been way too macabre. But now . . ."

"I suppose it's okay," said Drayton, looking pained. "At least our lovely tea room will only resemble Dante's *Inferno* for three days." He turned to pluck a tea tin from one of the shelves. "Though it will *feel* like an eternity," he muttered.

"I heard that," said Haley.

Theodosia was just about to leave when Detective Tidwell came striding in. He was accompanied by another detective in a worn-looking brown leather jacket, a man he introduced as Detective Tuck Samuels. She recognized Samuels as one of the men who'd been at the scene of Cecily's attack on Saturday night.

"Miss Browning," said Tidwell. A grin stretched across his wide face. "It looks as if we almost missed you. Are you dashing off somewhere?"

"Just running errands," said Theodosia. No way was she going to tell him that she was headed for a meeting with Roger Greaves.

"I have a few questions," said Tidwell. He glanced at Samuels. "Actually, *we* have a few questions. Could you spare a moment of your time?"

"A moment," said Theodosia. She turned to Drayton. "Drayton, could you . . . ?"

"My pleasure," said Drayton.

Theodosia led the men to a table, and said, "Won't you

sit down? Drayton is going to bring you some tea and scones. Unfortunately, I can't join you. My schedule . . ."

"Wonderful," said Samuels. He'd been sniffing the air like an overeager bird dog, obviously entranced by the aroma of tea and muffins and scones.

"Detective Samuels means it's wonderful that you're offering us some refreshments," said Tidwell. "Don't you, Detective?"

Samuels nodded. "That's right."

"And I believe you had some questions for Miss Browning?" said Tidwell.

"I thought *you* had the questions," Theodosia said to Tidwell. What was this, anyway? A rehashed version of good cop, bad cop?

"Kindly bear with us," said Tidwell as Samuels dug a spiral notebook and pen from his jacket pocket.

Samuels cleared his throat. "How long have you known Max Scofield?" he asked.

"Why are you asking?" said Theodosia.

"We're trying to clear him," Samuels said matter-of-factly.

Theodosia focused a level gaze at Tidwell. "I thought Max was already cleared."

"The board of directors at the museum has asked us to take a more careful look at everyone involved," said Tidwell.

"Everyone?" said Theodosia. "Does that mean everyone who was at the grand opening party for the Chinese tea house?"

"Almost everyone," said Samuels.

"You care to tell me who else you're talking to?" said Theodosia.

"No," said Tidwell.

"That's not how it's done," said Samuels just as Drayton showed up with a pot of tea and a plate of scones.

"Now, we also have some blueberry muffins if you'd prefer," said Drayton.

"No," said Theodosia. "This is just fine. This is all these gentlemen have time for." When she saw disappointment register on Tidwell's face, she added, "They're extremely busy. They have a lot more people to question."

Theodosia was still miffed as she drove down Calhoun Street heading for Datrex.

The nerve of Tidwell. Didn't he know her better than that? Did he really think she'd have anything to do with Max if she'd caught even a *whiff* that he'd been involved in Webster's murder?

As if to reinforce her indignation, Theodosia pulled out her cell phone and called Max. He answered right away.

"Hello?"

"Hi," she said. "Me. What are you doing?"

"Working on my résumé," said Max.

"Seriously?"

"Yes. It feels like I'm going to be persona non grata around here for quite some time."

"So you're really going to look at other jobs?" She felt unsettled by the news. "Um . . . where?"

"Well," said Max. "I did have that offer from Savannah a couple of months ago. At the College of Art and Design."

Theodosia's heart caught in her throat. "So what does that mean?" she asked. What she really meant was, *What does that mean for us? Living almost one hundred miles apart?*

"It means I'm actively looking," said Max. He fell silent for a few moments, and then said, "How did your luncheon go?"

"It was fine." It really hadn't been fine at all, but she didn't feel like rehashing the Cecily-Charlotte grudge match with him. "Okay, I just wanted to check in and say hi."

"You still want to go for that jog? Get one last good workout in before you run the five-K tomorrow night?"

"Sure, but it's going to have to be later tonight. Maybe nine-ish?"

"I'll see you then."

The corporate headquarters for Datrex looked like it had been conceived by an architecture student who was torn between the Bauhaus and Buck Rogers. A three-story trapezoid of shimmering blue glass, Theodosia thought the building stuck out like a sore thumb in a neighborhood that offered Ivy League–style buildings as well as cute little Charleston single houses. But there was guest parking, a friendly receptionist, and a respectable-looking Aubusson carpet on the floor of the lobby.

Theodosia had barely cracked the pages of the new *Fortune* magazine when she was greeted and led to Roger Greaves's rather comfortable office.

"We meet again," said Greaves. He came around the side of his large desk to shake hands with her.

"Thanks for taking time out of your busy day," she told him. "Although, with the funeral this morning, I doubt you got much work done today."

Greaves indicated a leather chair embellished with old-fashioned hobnails, and she sat down in it. Greaves settled in behind his desk. While the Datrex headquarters may have looked ultramodern, Greaves' office was furnished fairly traditionally. Touches of wood, some large green plants, and a few paintings and what appeared to be several shadow boxes hung on the walls.

"You seemed so anxious to talk to me before," said Greaves. He offered a pleasant smile. "What's so important that it warrants a special visit?"

"As I mentioned before," said Theodosia, "Charlotte asked me to look into things."

"Isn't that what the police are doing?"

"Absolutely," said Theodosia. "Which is why I'm doing it from a civilian's point of view."

"Interesting," said Greaves. "But I don't see what you can learn from me. I mean, Charlotte and I have spoken fairly regularly since her husband's murder. I've done my best to keep her in the loop."

"And she's still okay about the IPO going through?"

"We talked about it at lunch. It's practically a done deal."

Theodosia glanced at a photo that sat on Greaves's desk. It showed a number of executives standing in a semicircle. Edgar Webster was in the middle.

She indicated the photo. "I take it Edgar Webster was the senior partner?"

"Yes, but only because he provided most of the initial financing," said Greaves. "But you have to understand, Edgar wasn't exactly a tech guy per se. That was my baili-wick. I worked in Silicon Valley during the nineties and kind of cut my teeth on databases and data mining."

"That's how the DOD contract came about?"

Greaves nodded. "They purchased our Versus product. We have a full suite of products, but that one's become our bread and butter. Our real claim to fame."

"And this Versus," said Theodosia. "This is the one that will drive your IPO? Will make investors excited about you?"

"Hopefully," he said. He balled a fist and rapped it softly against his desk. "Knock on wood. It's what we should have done two years ago."

"Will the IPO make you all rich?" said Theodosia.

"Comfortable anyway." Greaves pressed his hands against his desk and pushed himself up. "Which means I should get to work." He forced a hearty smile. "It's nice we had this time to chat."

Short as it was, Theodosia thought. She stood as well and glanced about his office. He was giving her the bum's rush and she knew it. Resented it.

"You have some lovely artwork here," she said. She edged her way toward an oil painting of Charleston Harbor. It was sketchy and spattery, not her taste at all. "This one's gorgeous, just look at all those colors."

"It's an original by Easley Harper. You know his work?"

"Some," said Theodosia, though she'd never heard of him before. She shifted her gaze to the shadow box that hung next to it. It had a dozen small nooks and crannies of various sizes, kind of like an old-fashioned type box, and was about two inches deep with a glass cover. Each cubbyhole held a small medal or patch.

"This is interesting," she said. "Are you a collector of military memorabilia?" She knew that Charleston was filled with memorabilia collectors, most of them Civil War buffs. But she didn't recognize these patches, and they didn't look particularly old.

"Oh, those," said Greaves, looking a little sheepish. "They're personal. From a long time ago."

"Yes?" Theodosia gave him the kind of bright, anticipatory smile that begs for more information.

"I earned them."

"You were in the military," said Theodosia. Now they were getting somewhere.

"Yes."

Her smiled widened. "Which branch?"

"Special Forces."

"How very interesting," said Theodosia. "And I imagine challenging, too." She turned to face Greaves. Now that she looked at him, really studied him, she saw that, beneath that conservative three-piece suit, he was trim and fairly well muscled. Still in very good shape.

"In which parts of the world did you serve?" Her smile beamed even brighter, but her words were clipped and to the point.

"All over, really," said Greaves. "Angola, Mogadishu . . ."

His voice faded out, as if he'd rather not rekindle old memories. Or not reveal those rougher, more lawless parts of the world where his missions had taken him.

"In other words," said Theodosia, "you know how to kill a person with your bare hands."

Greaves offered her a thin smile. "Not exactly."

But from the way he said it, Theodosia knew that he could probably snap someone's neck like a matchstick. Or, without even breaking a sweat, whip an ice pick into someone's ear.

19

❧

Drayton lived just a few blocks from Theodosia in the heart of Charleston's Historic District. His quaint, 160-year-old home was a single-story cottage with a gabled roof and a narrow brick front set with elegant dark blue shutters. Now on the historic register, it had once been owned by a prominent Civil War doctor.

With the last vestiges of light fading, Theodosia hurried along the bumpy cobblestone walk toward the screened side piazza. She stepped inside and knocked on the kitchen door.

"Entre!" Drayton called out, and Theodosia went in.

She was immediately enveloped in not just a steamy warmth, but also a mixture of tantalizing aromas. Her nose picked up bay leaves, coriander, and . . . *Good heavens, is that curry?*

"What are you cooking?" Theodosia asked. "Indian food?"

Drayton shrugged into a brown tweed jacket and slid

his wallet into his inside pocket. "I'm making a huge pot of country captain."

"Oh, of course." Country captain was a low-country tradition. Basically a chicken curry stew with lots of freshly ground and roasted spices.

"I hope the aroma isn't too overwhelming."

"It's very nice," said Theodosia. "Particularly this time of year, when you start craving heartier dishes and stews." She glanced around Drayton's kitchen. It was a neat and tidy bachelor's kitchen with fine Carolina pine cupboards that he'd accented with dozens of tasty little eye catchers. A sterling silver cream and sugar set sat on the counter, several teapots from his extensive collection peered down from the shelves, and a small box of gleaming cutlery rested on a small kitchen table, which looked spindly and tippy but was really genuine Hepplewhite. She pointed at the cutlery, and said, "Are those new?" Then, "What are they exactly? Forks?"

Drayton grinned. "I finally lucked out and located that set of kipper forks I wanted."

"Kipper forks," she said. Trust Drayton to ferret out something as strange and obscure as kipper forks.

"You see"—he picked up one of the forks and made a jabbing motion—"you simply ease these two long prongs under the back of your kipper's head once it's fully roasted."

Theodosia wrinkled her nose. "No, that's what you do when *your* kipper is fully roasted," she said. She wasn't a big fish eater and wasn't thrilled with the idea of being served fish with the head still on. She didn't like food that looked back at her.

"Then you pop the spine up," Drayton continued, "and zip it all the way out, working from head to tail."

Drayton was still rhapsodizing about his kipper forks when they climbed into Theodosia's Jeep. She started the engine and pulled away from the curb.

"Are you sure you want me to come along?" Drayton asked suddenly.

"It's a little late to be worrying about that now. But, yes, I absolutely do."

"Tell me why again."

"For moral support, of course."

"And because you think Charlotte might be dangerous?"

Theodosia gripped the steering wheel harder. "There's that. And something else I need to talk to you about."

"What?"

"When I visited Roger Greaves this afternoon . . ."

"At his office, yes," said Drayton.

"Turns out he had a nice little display of patches and emblems from his days spent with Special Forces."

"Are those the soldiers that . . . ?"

"Yes," said Theodosia, as they shot through an intersection. "They most certainly do."

"Which means he could have easily . . ."

"Yes," Theodosia said again. "He certainly could have."

Charlotte welcomed them into her home like she hadn't seen them in two years.

"Theodosia," Charlotte cooed. "And Drayton. Come right in and make yourselves at home." Wearing a fluttering pink-and-purple caftan, she led them down her hallway, past her gallery of paintings, and into her jumble of a solarium. With it full-on dark now, the glass-walled room didn't have quite the presence or punch it had with bright sunlight streaming through.

"Sit down, sit down," said Charlotte. "Can I get you anything? A refreshing beverage perhaps?" She looked hopeful. "Glass of wine? Something stronger?"

"Nothing," said Theodosia.

"No, thank you," said Drayton.

"I suppose you just want to get to it, then," said Charlotte.

"You said you'd put together a notebook?" said Theodosia. She didn't meant to be brusque, but this wasn't exactly a social call. Besides, she had a date to go running later tonight.

"Yes, of course," said Charlotte. She toddled over to a table, grabbed a white plastic binder, and carried it back to Theodosia. "It's all in here. The various events and plans."

Theodosia thumbed through the binder. Much to Charlotte's credit, the Bloody Mary Crawl and Haunted Hayride did seem to be fairly well-thought-out. Either Charlotte wasn't as frenetic as she appeared to be, or there were some fairly savvy volunteers with good organizational skills. Theodosia suspected the latter.

"As you can see," said Charlotte, "there are three aspects to the event. The open houses . . ."

"How many homes will be open for visitors to tour?" Theodosia asked.

"Four lovely homes," said Charlotte. "Three of them located right along Meeting Street, one just around the corner. You see, there are even photos of the homes." She tapped a finger against a plasticized page.

"Very impressive," said Drayton. Two of them were private homes that were opening their doors to the public, and two of them were bed-and-breakfasts.

"And they're all going to be decorated for Halloween?" said Theodosia. "And serving Bloody Marys?"

"Yes," said Charlotte. "The décor is completely up to the home owner, of course. It can be as elaborate as they choose. But the really great thing is that all of the homes have good-size backyards and patios, so tables and chairs can be easily accommodated." She smiled. "As well as the Bloody Mary bars."

"Will nonalcoholic drinks be available, too?" Theodosia asked. She assumed this was something children might enjoy, too. After all, it was Halloween. What kid didn't love Halloween?

Charlotte nodded. "We'll provide hot cocoa and cider."

"And will appetizers be served?" asked Drayton.

"Yes, it's all being catered by Vicks and Von Catering," said Charlotte. "This may be a Halloween event, but it's an *upscale* event. I mean, tickets weren't cheap. Forty dollars each."

"And they've all been sold?" said Drayton.

"Sold out as of yesterday," said Charlotte. The phone rang suddenly, and she jumped up to answer it. "Excuse me," and then: "Hello?"

Theodosia and Drayton could hear a loud voice booming through the phone, though they couldn't make out the exact words.

But Charlotte certainly could. "No," she told her caller, "you're not interrupting me at all." She turned and winked at Theodosia and Drayton. "Oh, you did?" Now she turned her back to them, hunched her shoulders, and lowered her voice. "Yes, that sounds lovely. I think I'd like that very much."

"Get a load of her," Drayton whispered to Theodosia. "She sounds like she's flirting. Hmm . . . the grieving widow."

They waited patiently while Charlotte talked for another three or four minutes. Finally she hung up.

"Apologies," said Charlotte. She sat down across from them. "That was Harlan Duke. He is such a *dear* man. He's been an absolute rock for me these past few days."

"I'm sure he has," said Theodosia, suddenly recalling Bill Glass's crack about Duke being next in line.

Drayton, meanwhile, had been speed-reading Charlotte's binder. "So let me get this straight," he said. "There are the home tours, the Bloody Mary Crawl, and then there's the Haunted Hayride."

"And a few walking tours down Gateway Walk," said Charlotte. Gateway Walk was the three-block walking path that meandered from Archdale Street, crossed King Street, wound past the Charleston Library Society and the Gibbes Museum of Art, and ended up in the ancient grave-yards behind St. Philip's Church.

"That's right," said Charlotte. "As you can see, the entire area will be a kind of Halloween epicenter."

"And there are guides lined up for the Gateway Walk tours?" said Theodosia.

"Yes. In fact, there's a complete list of names in the binder. Volunteers for all the venues."

Drayton let loose a little snort. "Gateway Walk. Always purported to be haunted."

"But it is!" Charlotte cried. "People have seen all sorts of strange things there at night. Ghosts and spooky vapors and glowing orbs, and . . ."

CRASH!

Out of nowhere, a flaming bottle suddenly slammed through one of the floor-to-ceiling windows that overlooked the back garden. Glass shards exploded everywhere, creating a dangerous hailstorm of sparks and needlelike splin-ters. Then the flaming bottle hit the tile floor with a loud *thwack*, whirled wildly like some unholy game of spin the bottle, and exploded. Flaming bits of Molotov cocktail blew out everywhere into the room!

"Holy croakers!" Charlotte screamed. She jumped up from her seat and went bug-eyed as sparks burned instant holes in draperies, scatter rugs, and a slipcovered chair. Within an instant, orange and yellow flames flickered brightly and began licking their way up the side of a linen cloth that hung down from a small table.

"Whoa!" said Theodosia. She grabbed her handbag and pulled out her phone. Hurriedly poked out 911 with trem-bling fingers.

While Theodosia was jabbering into the phone to the dispatcher, Charlotte's single contribution to the growing conflagration was to jump up and down, wave her arms wildly, and continue to shriek at the top of her lungs.

"You hear that?" Theodosia said into her phone. *"That's* why we need the fire department!"

Much to Drayton's credit, he leapt toward the bar area, pawed around under the sink, and came up with a small fire extinguisher. He fiddled with it for a few moments, then pointed the nozzle at the worst of the flames, and pushed a red tab. A shot of white foam spewed out.

"Watch the curtains!" Charlotte screamed. "That fabric is Brunschwig and Fils. Ninety dollars a yard!"

Drayton ignored Charlotte's warning and doused the curtains where tiny burn holes smoldered.

Once Theodosia had been assured that the fire department was on its way, she rushed to the back door, flung it open, and dashed out into the backyard.

Because maybe, just maybe, she could catch the jerk who was responsible for this firebombing. Or see him running down the alley. Or leaping into his car.

Or maybe not.

The backyard was quiet and dark. Palm fronds rustled in the night wind, a tiny fountain pattered away in the corner of the patio. No sign of the jackhole who'd pitched the flaming bottle through the window.

And why a flaming bottle? Theodosia wondered. Had it been directed at Charlotte? Because . . . Well, she didn't know what the reason might be.

Maybe to scare her? Or to warn her? Or was this just unrelated mischief?

Now Theodosia could hear the distinct shrill of sirens as they headed their way. She walked back into the house, feeling unsettled.

Mischief? No, she didn't think so. Somehow this was all connected. She just couldn't figure out how.

The firefighters were wonderful. They charged in like knights on white horses, calmed everyone down, and put out the last of the firestorm. Then they checked everywhere for any sign of burning embers.

"An improvised incendiary weapon," said the company officer, a man with a handlebar mustache, kind brown eyes, and a nametag that read CAPT. WILL SCHAFER. "You don't see that too often. You think it was neighborhood kids?"

"No," said Theodosia. "I think it was someone intent on scaring the homeowner to death."

"Well, they certainly managed to do exactly that," Charlotte cried. She put a hanky to her face and collapsed limply into a chair, coughing out sobs.

One of the other firefighters had opened a black case and was gathering up little burned and charred bits, samples for analysis. "Probably gasoline or turpentine," he said. "We'll know for sure in a couple of days."

Somewhere along the line, Drayton had sustained a small burn on his right hand, so one of the firefighters hauled out a first-aid kit and smeared cortisone cream on the burn area. Then he covered it with a soft bandage.

Captain Schafer tried to question Charlotte, but she was no help at all. She vacillated between tears, gasps, and stiff warnings to the firefighters about damaging any of her precious Limoges figurines.

Theodosia pulled Schafer aside, and said, "This particular home owner has been embroiled in a bit of controversy lately. Her husband was murdered at the museum last Thursday night . . ."

His brows knit together. "Okay. Interesting."

"Do you know Detective Burt Tidwell?"

"I do."

"I think he should be informed about this."

Schafer nodded at her. "We're the AHJ here—authority having jurisdiction—but I'll make sure Tidwell's in the loop. File my incident report and fire it off to him right away."

"Thank you."

It was all over except for a few more tears. The firefighters left, Charlotte wept as she fixed herself a bourbon and water, and Theodosia tucked the white notebook under her arm.

"What a terrible night," moaned Charlotte. She took a sip of her drink, grimaced, and then took a longer sip.

Theodosia had a feeling Charlotte's night wasn't going to get much better. And if she continued drinking, her morning would be even worse.

"Take care," said Drayton as they headed for the door. He never looked back; he couldn't get out of there fast enough.

Charlotte offered an apathetic wave. "I think I'm just going to remain sequestered for a while," she called after them.

"That's probably a good idea," said Theodosia.

She and Drayton walked down the sidewalk. The air felt clean and fresh, with a nip of salt blowing in from the Atlantic. Dry leaves scuttled about in the street. Streetlamps glowed orange in the darkness.

"Whew," said Drayton as they climbed into the Jeep. "What a night."

"How's your poor hand?" Theodosia asked. "Are you feeling okay, or should we stop at one of those doc-in-the-box places and get it looked at?" She pulled her seatbelt across, ready to hustle Drayton off to the nearest burn ward.

"I'm fine. It's nothing," said Drayton. He seemed to have shaken off the incident, though he was cradling his injured hand. He turned to gaze at Theodosia. "You don't believe that Molotov cocktail was any kind of accident, do you? That it was random kids or neighborhood crazies?"

"I do not."

"Then what?"

Theodosia shrugged. "Not sure. Maybe someone feels strongly about not wanting Charlotte on the board of directors at the museum?"

"Call me dubious," said Drayton, "but I have a hard time envisioning sixty- or seventy-year-old men running down a back alley carrying flaming bottles aloft." Clearly, he wasn't buying it.

"Maybe her husband's killer came back to try to finish her off?"

"That's a fairly grisly notion."

"Or maybe the killer was just trying to throw her off the scent," said Theodosia.

"I'd say it's more likely he was trying to throw *you* off the scent," said Drayton.

Theodosia's heart did an impromptu flip-flop. "Uh . . . what did you say?"

"Think about it," Drayton continued. "You're the one who's been doing a fair amount of poking around. Maybe that flaming bottle was meant to scare you."

Theodosia cranked the key hard in the ignition and her Jeep roared to life.

"You're going to have to be a lot more careful," said Drayton.

"If the killer *was* after me," Theodosia snarled, "this isn't going to be the end of it. I'll track him down like a rented mule!"

Theodosia dropped off Drayton and drove back to her house. Max was waiting for her, standing in the front yard, doing leg swings and walking lunges, stretching his muscles in anticipation of their run.

He broke into a smile when he saw her. "Hey." Then he saw the look of deep consternation on her face. "Hoo boy, what's wrong now?"

Theodosia told him about the flaming bottle crashing through Charlotte's window, the shards flying everywhere, and Drayton getting a nasty burn.

"You're the one who risks getting burned," said Max, "hanging around with crazy old Charlotte."

"I think you might be right."

"Which means you've got to seriously bug out of this thing," said Max. "Let the police handle it."

"They're already all over it. And they're not doing a very good job."

"You don't know that. They might have somebody in custody right now."

"Doubtful," said Theodosia. She didn't think the police were any closer to solving Webster's murder, apprehending Cecily's attacker, or figuring out Charlotte's firebombing than she was. In fact, they were probably treating them as three separate incidents. Whereas she was linking them . . .

"Jeez, Theo." Max broke into her thoughts. "You can't solve *every* crime that comes along."

"I don't try to, I really don't," she said. "But the things that have happened lately are starting to feel . . . very personal."

Max stared at her. "Wait a minute. Are you saying . . . Do you think the killer might have his eye trained on *you?*"

"That's what Drayton thinks."

"Drayton's a smart guy," said Max. "In fact, he's downright brilliant. So if he thinks you're in danger, then you've got to step away from this immediately."

"Maybe so," said Theodosia. But deep in her heart she was thinking, *Never. Now I'm never going to let this go.*

20

The Harlan Duke Gallery was located on King Street, right in the very heart of Charleston's antique district. It was housed in a ubiquitous redbrick building, narrow but three stories tall, with slender, arched windows framed by elegant white shutters.

It was bright and early Tuesday morning, and Theodosia peered in the front window, trying to gauge exactly what kind of merchandise Duke's gallery carried. She saw a Japanese tea set, an antique Japanese sword, a bronze Chinese vessel, a set of antique calligraphy brushes, and an array of carved Chinese jade statues. They all looked like exquisite pieces.

Pushing open the front door, Theodosia figured she was probably the first customer of the day.

An older woman, her silver-gray hair the precise color of her silk blouse, smiled from behind a mahogany counter that had probably been around since the eighteen hundreds.

"Good morning," said the clerk. "How may I help you?"

"I'm looking for Harlan Duke," said Theodosia. "Is he here?"

"I'm sorry, he's not," said the woman. "Did you have an appointment? Please don't tell me he forgot." A sly smile crept across her face. "I've only worked for Mr. Duke for a few weeks, but in that time I've discovered that he's much more of a big-picture person. Buying, selling, wheeling, dealing.

"But"—she gave a little shrug—"details do seem to elude him."

"Actually," said Theodosia, "I don't have an appointment. I was just in the neighborhood and thought I'd drop by." She hesitated. "Mr. Duke had mentioned something to me about an antique Chinese teapot?"

"Oh, yes," said the woman, quickly threading her way past an altar table that held a pair of blue-and-white vases, and around a coromandel screen. "We have several, but I think the one you're referring to is right over here. An absolute beauty."

The Chinese teapot had been accorded its own black lacquered stand. And it was a beauty. Plump and rounded—a real teapot's teapot—it was done in oxblood enamel with gold edging around the lid and bottom rim. In the center of the teapot's body was a white seal that held a scramble of calligraphy. It was, quite simply, a gorgeous piece.

Sensing Theodosia's interest, the clerk carried the teapot to the counter and gingerly set it down on a square of black velvet fabric. "Are you a collector of teapots?"

"I have my fair share," said Theodosia. Actually, she was edging toward owning almost fifty different teapots. Nowhere near Drayton's collection, but getting there.

"This one's got some age on it," said the woman.

"It's lovely," said Theodosia. "Chien-lung?"

"Ah." The clerk smiled. "I see you know your Chinese antiques."

"I know a *little* bit about ceramics. Obviously there's a lot to learn."

"Tell me about it," said the woman. "I'm always discovering some new little nugget of information."

Theodosia moved her hands toward the teapot. "May I?"

"Please," said the woman as Theodosia picked it up and turned it over.

When Theodosia saw the faint maker's mark on the bottom, she said, "It's from one of the imperial kilns?"

"Why, yes."

"And what is the price?"

The woman fingered a small white tag. "We have it marked at twenty-two hundred, but I know Mr. Duke's prices are always negotiable."

"Mmn."

"You know," the clerk said, in a conspiratorial tone, "I'm not allowed to negotiate prices. But if you want to speak with Mr. Duke, I happen to know he had an errand at a friend's house, and then he was going to be at the Equinox Equestrian Center. Just over in Mount Pleasant. I'm sure he's there now and that he'd be pleased if you dropped by."

Theodosia wondered if the friend Duke had gone to see was Charlotte Webster.

"I take it Mr. Duke is a horse lover, too?"

"Brought his two thoroughbreds all the way up from Texas. Drove the truck himself."

"There's dedication for you," said Theodosia.

Back out in her car, Theodosia called the Indigo Tea Shop. Drayton picked up on the first ring.

"Indigo Tea Shop," he said in finely modulated tones.

"Drayton, it's me. How's your hand feeling today?"

"Fine. No problem," Drayton responded. "I've been burned worse fixing tea. Scalding water and all that."

"Still," said Theodosia. "I feel bad. I feel like your getting burned last night was my fault. If I hadn't pressured you to come along . . ."

"If you want to feel guilty," said Drayton, "then be my guest. But there's really no need." He paused. "Are you on your way in?"

"That's why I called. I just stopped in at Harlan Duke's gallery, but he wasn't there. His assistant tells me he's out at the Equinox Equestrian Center."

"So I'm guessing that's where you're off to?"

"That's right."

"Haley's been bugging me about our Tower of London Tea. Trying to finalize tomorrow's menu and all."

"I'm sure she has," said Theodosia.

"Oh, and I have all your English Hedgerow tea packaged up for Delaine's Hunt and Gather Market."

"How can I ever thank you?" said Theodosia. "You're a lifesaver."

"I'll tell you how you can thank me," said Drayton. "You can be careful."

"You mean . . . ?"

"Please," said Drayton. "Exercise some caution. There have been too many strange goings-on lately. Which means I'm in a constant state of worry."

"You know I'll be careful," said Theodosia.

Drayton sighed. "Actually, I don't know that at all."

Theodosia didn't have any particular reason to talk to Harlan Duke, other than that she was still curious about him. Bill Glass might have been right—Duke had insinuated himself into Charlotte's life awfully fast. Then again, if the woman's husband had been having a torrid affair, maybe she simply needed a shoulder to cry on.

Maybe.

Theodosia couldn't help but smile as she drove onto the grounds of the Equinox Equestrian Center. Horses peeked over white fences from where they grazed in a dozen different paddocks. Yearlings played in a pasture. Over in a riding ring, a jumping lesson was taking place. Riders in velvet caps—elegant hardhats, really—their arms outstretched, reins draped loosely around their horses' necks, were sailing blithely over a one-foot-high jump. Learning the basics.

A rider all her life, Theodosia loved the sounds and smells that surrounded horses. She loved the rich, robust scent of saddle leather. The vegetal scent of fresh hay, almost like a cup of Japanese green tea. And she loved the musical jingle of bridles and the soft stomping and gentle nickering of the horses themselves.

Theodosia found Harlan Duke working away in a large, white, hip-roofed barn. He was standing in the aisle between two rows of box stalls, running a metal currycomb down the flanks of a large chestnut horse. Dressed in a plaid shirt, khaki slacks, and English riding boots, he had a brown leather apron tied around his waist, the kind a farrier might favor to protect his clothing and hold his tools.

"The lady at your gallery told me I'd find you here," said Theodosia.

Duke whirled around at the sound of her voice, and his face lit up with delight when he recognized her. "Hey, there. How are you doing? I hope you brought along a picnic lunch for us to enjoy." He chuckled heartily. "I guess you can tell I've been dreaming about your wonderful food. Particularly those honey scones."

Theodosia walked slowly toward Duke and his horse. "I'm afraid I arrived empty-handed," she said. "But you can drop by the tea shop any time you like." She ran a hand down the horse's fine nose, across its velvet muzzle, and under its stubbly chin. "This is a beautiful horse you have here."

"This is Lady Veronique Begonia. But I just call her Begonia."

"Nice to meet you, Begonia," said Theodosia.

"Do you ride?" Duke asked.

"I do."

"Jump?"

"I've been known to tackle my share of poles and gates," said Theodosia. "Though not all that well." She gave Begonia a final pat and focused all her attention on Duke. "I take it you heard about the firebombing at Charlotte's house last night?"

Duke turned suddenly serious. "Oh my, did I ever! Charlotte called me right after you left. Right after the firefighters left. She was in hysterics, poor woman. She seemed completely unhinged."

"It's good you were able to comfort her," said Theodosia, watching Duke closely.

"Yes, it's been a tough week for her." Duke shook his head. "Really miserable. Anyone with less strength would have completely fallen to pieces."

She did fall to pieces, Theodosia thought to herself. *Or was it a masterful bit of play acting? Is Charlotte a candidate for* Inside the Actors Studio?

"Charlotte tells me you're going to be stepping in for her as chairman of the Bloody Mary Crawl."

"And the Haunted Hayride. That's right."

"They're bringing in horses from right here, you know. Four nice Percherons from over in the next barn."

"Great," said Theodosia. Then she added, "Have you spoken to Charlotte today? Do you know if she's heard anything back from the fire department? Or from the police?"

"I dropped by for all of five minutes early this morning," said Duke. "She was subdued, as one might expect. She said she was still waiting for a call from that police detective. Tidlow."

"Tidwell."

"Ah yes, that's it."

"Good," said Theodosia. "I'm glad he's on it." She was watching Duke's hands. He'd just set down his brush and was digging in the pockets of his leather apron.

"I'm hoping," said Duke as a piece of metal flashed in his hand, "that Charlotte will feel well enough to attend her first museum board meeting."

Theodosia heard his words as if off in the distance. Because her eyes were fixed on the metal tool that Duke wielded in his hands. He switched it back and forth, from one hand to the other, then leaned forward and, with practiced efficiency, picked up Begonia's right front leg.

Theodosia watched, fascinated, as the sharp metal hoof pick dug into Begonia's hoofs. And she wondered—could a stainless steel hoof pick like that have killed Edgar Webster? Was that tool long enough, sharp enough, to slide into someone's ear and turn off his lights for good?

She took a step backward.

She was pretty sure it was.

Her smile merely pasted on her face now, Theodosia listened but didn't really hear Duke as he chattered away.

All she could think was, *Is Harlan Duke the killer?* And, if he had killed Webster, what had been his motive?

"I . . . I have to take off now," said Theodosia.

Duke looked up, surprised. "Okay, then. Nice to see you." He pointed the pick directly at her and smiled. "I'll probably be dropping by your tea shop real soon."

"Do that," said Theodosia, though the words tasted dry and dusty in her mouth.

Driving back toward the Indigo Tea Shop, the chill that Theodosia felt in her stomach had crawled all the way up to her heart.

Was it possible that Harlan Duke was the killer? He could be. And might he have also attacked Cecily? Possibly. But . . . what could have motivated him to do such terrible deeds?

Was Duke really and truly trying to worm himself into Charlotte's good graces? And eventually win her love as husband number two? Or at least be the one who catered to her incessant neediness?

Theodosia flew across the Cooper River Bridge. Normally, the dizzying height and awesome span of the cable bridge caught her attention and gave her a little thrill. Not today. Today she was too caught up in the Edgar Webster murder mystery and all the strange permutations that seemed to surround it.

As she spun down Bay Street, an idea tickled at Theodosia's brain. All the bizarre events that had taken place in the last few days had been set in motion since Edgar Webster's murder the night of the Chinese tea house gala.

So . . . did the tea house somehow figure into this? After all, Harlan Duke was the art dealer who'd located the tea house in Shanghai and arranged for it to be shipped to Charleston. And Edgar Webster had been its biggest booster.

Theodosia puzzled over this notion for a few minutes. Was it possible that the tea house was a fake? Had Edgar Webster, who knew a fair amount about Chinese antiques, suspected as much and then confronted Duke?

And then, had Harlan Duke, fearing that he'd be exposed as a fraud, boldly and cold-bloodedly murdered Webster?

The whole thing sounded awfully far-fetched. In fact, it was pure conjecture, like a made-for-TV movie. Still, the more Theodosia thought through her scenario, the more she felt a tingle of excitement building, a vibe that told her she could be onto something.

"I'm going to stop at the museum," she said out loud. "I want to take another look at that tea house."

She turned right on Broad, hooked a left on Meeting Street, and turned down the alley behind the museum. She pulled into one of the parking spaces that said RESERVED FOR MUSEUM PERSONNEL. She didn't care if she wasn't supposed to park there. Nobody was going to shoo her away or tow her car. She wouldn't be inside long enough.

This morning, the back door was unlocked. Theodosia pushed her way through, recalling her covert operation on Saturday night. Down the corridor she hurried, heading directly for Percy Capers's office. He was a friend and an Asian expert, so maybe he could render a learned opinion. Or maybe . . . maybe he harbored a few suspicions, too.

Theodosia knocked on a frosted glass door that had two names with titles stenciled on it in gold ink—PERCY CAPERS, ASIAN ART and SUMNER MOTTE, AMERICAN ART.

Without waiting for an answer, she twisted the knob and barged in.

A man looked up from a sheaf of papers and smiled at her. "Hello," he said, pleasantly. He had messy Albert Einstein hair and narrow, tortoiseshell glasses, and wore a black turtleneck. Theodosia thought he looked like a beatnik, or what a beatnik from central casting might look like. She also recognized him as one of the curators who'd accompanied Capers to the *Titanic* Tea.

"I was looking for Percy Capers," she said.

Sumner Motte touched the eraser end of a yellow pencil to the tip of his nose. "I'm afraid you just missed him. He drove over to Columbia this morning to meet with some people at their museum of art. We're thinking of doing a kind of South Carolina version of *Antiques Roadshow* and are putting our heads together to hammer out some of the details."

"That sounds like a lot of fun," said Theodosia. "I'm sorry I missed him."

"That sure was a lovely tea you put on Sunday night," said Motte. "We enjoyed it immensely." He twiddled his pencil.

"I'm glad you did," she said, backing out of his office. "And just FYI, we're having a Tower of London Tea tomorrow."

He smiled. "Sounds like it's been especially themed for Halloween."

"That's right."

"You've got a pretty clever gang over there."

Theodosia gave a quick wave. "Drop by anytime."

Because Theodosia's curiosity was still running at a fever pitch, she hurried down the corridor and popped out into the central rotunda.

Museums were traditionally closed to the public on Mondays, and this one was no exception. So she had the place pretty much to herself. Off to her right, a group of art students—probably from the museum's Fine Arts Program—were bent over large pads of paper. They clutched sticks of charcoal and were diligently sketching their version of a statue done by Charleston sculptor Willard Hirsch.

Theodosia turned left and headed for the museum's newest acquisition—the Chinese tea house.

Once again, the blue ceramic roof tiles; smooth, weathered wood; and the architecture in general looked and felt genuine to her. She stepped inside into the calm and quiet to take an even closer look.

She was struck again by the utter serenity of the place. Tea houses—tea pavilions—had been constructed in ancient China as simple, elegant retreats to foster the poetic feeling that was long associated with tea drinking. And most tea houses, like this one in particular, typified an ancient ideal of simplicity. Hence the rustic feel, unadorned walls, and natural colors of rice paper and bamboo. Nothing was supposed to intrude or jar the tea drinker's sensibilities. She'd even heard that a tune played on a lute in a tea house should be no louder than the hum of a bumblebee.

Theodosia reached out and touched the interior wall. The wood felt ancient and soft, as if it had been rubbed smooth by a thousand loving hands.

She smiled softly. This tea house was the genuine article, all right. It was everything else surrounding it that felt false and brittle.

21

❧

"*Hey, you're finally* here," said Haley. She poked her head out of the kitchen as Theodosia rushed by. "It's important that we talk."

"About the menu for the Tower of London Tea," said Theodosia. "I know. Drayton mentioned it to me."

"When's good?" called Haley.

"Not this minute," Theodosia sang over her shoulder as she continued on toward the tea shop. It was late morning, and customers would be arriving for lunch, if some hadn't shown up already. Job one was to assist Drayton and make sure all the tables were polished and pretty and ready to go.

Turns out they'd already been set up. In a Halloweenish sort of way. Their standard white tapers had been swapped out for orange candles, filmy ghosts floated from the rafters, and plastic skeletons clicked and clacked in the breeze. Seemingly overnight, her chintz-and-china tea shop had gone over to the dark side with broomsticks and bones.

"You've been busy," said Theodosia, slightly taken aback

by the tea room's changed appearance. "And I see everything's already set up for lunch."

"It's set up," said Drayton, "just not to my particular
taste. As you can see, Haley's been indulging herself in a
Halloween fantasy."

Haley sauntered toward them carrying a fat orange
pumpkin that she'd carved. "Theo, you had a couple of
phone calls."

"Who needs me now?" Theodosia asked. She reached
out and rapped the top of the grinning pumpkin with her
knuckles. "Knock, knock. Nobody home?"

"Hah," said Haley, pleased. "Detective Tidwell called.
He wants you to call him back ASAP."

"Okay," said Theodosia. "And who else?"

Haley snickered. "Delaine. She says you're late."

"I'm what?" That stopped Theodosia dead in her tracks.
"Wait a minute, what time is the Hunt and Gather Market
supposed to start?"

"I believe it kicks off at one o'clock," said Drayton.

Theodosia checked her watch. "It's just eleven." She
decided Delaine was certifiably Type-A crazy.

"There you go," said Drayton. "You have plenty of time
to help with lunch, go set up your table, and prove Delaine
wrong." He let loose a dignified snort. "As if *that's* ever
going to happen."

"Right," echoed Haley.

While Drayton and Haley argued about where to display
the pumpkin, Theodosia went back to her office and called
Tidwell. She was put on hold for what seemed like an inter-
minable amount of time before he finally came on the line.

"What?" Tidwell barked.

"Hey, you called me," said Theodosia.

"Oh, yes. So I did."

Theodosia heard papers rustling, as if he were combing
distractedly through a stack of scribbled notes.

"Probably concerning the firebombing at Charlotte Webster's last night?" she prompted.

"Why were you there?" Tidwell asked brusquely.

"Not that it's any of your business," said Theodosia, "but Charlotte asked me to step in and take over her Bloody Mary Crawl."

"So you are honchoing yet another event." For some reason he sounded put out.

"My world and welcome to it. So . . . what part of the walk is bugging you the most? Me, Bloody Marys, or the ghosts?"

He ignored her question. "I'm reading the report filed by the engine company captain," said Tidwell. "An incendiary device was actually *hurled* through Mrs. Webster's back window?"

"If that's what it says, then that's what happened."

"Do you know any reason why a person might throw something like that?"

"As you keep reminding me," said Theodosia, "*you're* the detective, not me."

"But if you could venture a guess?"

"You want me to speculate? Detective Tidwell, you're always cautioning me never to speculate." Theodosia was enjoying herself. This little joust with Tidwell was invigorating. Just what she needed to lighten her mood.

"I'm glad you find our conversation so amusing," said Tidwell. "But, need I remind you, there is a murderer on the loose."

"And a stalker and now an arsonist," said Theodosia. "Which means you have a lot on your plate." She hesitated, wanting to go on, but deciding not to. "But, I promise you, I will think about your question and get back to you."

"Sooner rather than later," said Tidwell. There was a distinct click. He'd hung up.

Theodosia had wanted to tell Tidwell about Harlan

Duke and the dangerous-looking hoof pick. She really had. And she'd wanted to share her concerns about the Chinese tea house—how something seemed not quite right to her about it. That the tea house felt like it could be some weird nexus for all the events that had taken place. But she'd consciously held back her information.

Why? Fear of ridicule? No, not at all. Tidwell had never actually pooh-poohed any of her theories.

No, Theodosia decided she wanted to keep these little tidbits of information tucked away for herself. It would give her a chance to noodle things around and see if her hunches led anywhere else.

With her phone still in her hand, Theodosia dialed Max's number. He answered right away.

"Hey, how's it going?" asked Max.

"Busy," said Theodosia. "Par for the course. How are things with you?"

"Making calls," said Max. "Just putting the word out."

Doggone, she thought. "I was wondering if you're still planning to run with us tonight in the five-K?"

"Of course, I am. We can't let Earl Grey down, after all. Hey, how's his costume coming?"

Theodosia looked over at a puddle of brown fur that sat on one of her office shelves. "It's coming."

"Okay," said Max. "See you tonight?"

"See you," said Theodosia. She leaned sideways and grabbed the hunk of brown fur that was supposed to be Earl Grey's costume.

She'd gone to the fabric store last week with an idea in mind of creating a Chia Pet costume. If she could just find some shaggy green fabric, then maybe she could fashion it into a kind of wrap for Earl Grey. But then she'd seen a hunk of golden-brown fake fur. And it seemed to cry out *lion's mane*. So it seemed easier, in the long run, to just fashion a collar for Earl Grey that would resemble a lion's mane.

She was already going as a witch, so why couldn't they be *The Lion, the Witch and the Wardrobe?*

Theodosia pulled the needle out from where she'd stuck it earlier, when she'd been in the middle of whipstitching the last seam. Just a few more stitches and . . .

"Now can we go over that menu for our Tower of London Tea?" asked Haley. She was standing in the doorway, fanning an index card that was clutched in her hand. Her tall, white chef's hat was canted jauntily to one side as if she'd been caught in a strong wind and spun about.

"Sure," said Theodosia. "But I thought you had everything pretty much set to your liking."

"But is it to *your* liking?" said Haley. "You know I prefer to run everything by you."

Theodosia smiled as she leaned back in her chair. She and Drayton knew who the real boss was—it was the diminutive Haley who ruled the kitchen with an iron potholder. "Okay, then. What's on your menu?"

"We kick off with crown jewel scones," said Haley. "Which are really cream scones chockablock with candied fruit. Those are followed by Anne Boleyn chocolate-dipped strawberries."

Theodosia grinned. "You had me at crown jewel scones."

Haley held up a finger. "But there's more. Tea sandwiches of honey-roasted ham and English mustard on caraway seed bread. And English smoked salmon with cream cheese on brown bread."

"Wonderful."

"And for dessert," said Haley, "I was thinking about chutney crescents and Victoria sponge cake."

"It all sounds great, but what about the teas? Has Drayton worked out his tea offerings yet?"

Haley nodded. "He's got something called Lady Jane Grey, which is a variation on Earl Grey. And then a War of the Roses tea, which is basically his own blend of a Ceylon black tea infused with rose petals."

"Perfect," said Theodosia. "And tickets are all sold out?"

"Oh yeah. Have been for a couple of days. We're gonna have another full house tomorrow."

"I think we've discovered the magic key," Theodosia mused. "Maybe we should just switch to having themed teas."

Haley looked shocked. "You mean every day, all the time?"

"Well . . . maybe two or three a week?"

Haley shook her head so vigorously, her curtain of long blond hair swished about her shoulders. "No way. Then people would start taking our themed teas for granted. No, we need to keep them in reserve for special occasions only."

Theodosia had to smile at Haley's intensity. "I see your point. Okay, we'll do it your way."

"Whew." Haley touched a hand to her chest. "I don't like to rock the boat, but . . ."

"You prefer to stick to a routine. Same as Drayton does."

Haley nodded sagely. "Routines are good. It's what keeps us all sane."

"I could use a little more sanity in my life," said Theodosia. "Especially after the past couple days."

"You've been running yourself ragged all over the place. And now you're off to that Hunt and Gather thing?"

"Afraid so."

"Does it feel like you're chasing your tail?"

"Truer words were never spoken, Haley. Because the crazy thing is, Earl Grey and I are supposed to run in tonight's Halloween five-K."

"Oh, Earl Grey's a marathoner now?"

"I guess so, since we're entered in Big Paw's Run and Romp Division." Big Paw was a local service-dog organization that both Theodosia and Earl Grey volunteered with.

"You guys are regular little Energizer Bunnies, aren't you? Me, I'm just gonna stay home tonight and loaf on the sofa, watch a chick flick, and down a bag of Chips Ahoy!"

Theodosia tipped her head. "Haley. Really?"

"You think my own scones or muffins would be better?"

"Infinitely."

Lunch was busy, which kept Theodosia and Drayton hopping from table to table. They served croque monsieur sandwiches, citrus salads, and egg white omelets accompanied by spiced plum and Ceylon black teas. At twelve forty-five, Theodosia glanced at her watch and said, "Uh-oh."

"What?" said Drayton.

"I've got, like, fifteen minutes to get to Delaine's market and set up my table."

"I already loaded the tea into the back of your Jeep if that's any consolation."

"Thank you." Theodosia glanced at her watch again.

"Now you've got fourteen minutes," said Drayton. "Perhaps you'd best get moving."

"I . . . I need to tell you something."

"What's that?" He picked up a Meissen teapot decorated with a swirl of pink peonies.

"When I drove out to the equestrian center this morning to talk to Harlan Duke . . ."

"I hadn't realized he had horses," said Drayton.

"He has horses and a very sharp hoof pick," said Theodosia.

That got Drayton's immediate attention.

So Theodosia told him about the shiny metal hoof pick and how she wondered if something like that could have served as a murder weapon to kill Edgar Webster.

"I suppose it could have," said Drayton. "Did you tell Tidwell about this?"

"No."

"Keeping a lot from him, aren't you? Do you think that's wise?"

"I don't know. Maybe not. Probably not."

"Well, think about telling him, okay?"

"I'll think about it." Theodosia glanced at her watch again. "Are you going to be okay here without me? You and Haley are literally a skeleton crew."

Drayton gave her a deadpan look. "Please."

Theodosia ran into her office, snatched up her jacket and bag without missing a beat, and was out the back door. Then it was a matter of a five-minute drive down to Queen Street, where Delaine's market was setting up.

Luckily, Theodosia found a parking spot just a block away. A woman in a white Escalade was just pulling out, and Theodosia was able to nose into the vacated spot.

Thank you, parking space fairy godmother.

And, once she'd grabbed her cardboard boxes filled with tea and sprinted the block to her table, she arrived with about one minute to spare.

Good thing Delaine was nowhere in sight. She would have had a major conniption.

Theodosia whipped an indigo blue cloth onto her table, and then quickly arranged her packages of English Hedgerow tea in neat little rows. She'd printed out a sign that said INDIGO TEA SHOP, ENGLISH HEDGEROW TEA, $6.99 A BAG, so that went into a plastic table topper for all to see.

Theodosia took a deep breath and looked around. Tables stretched to either side of her as far as she could see. They held dried flower arrangements, jams and jellies, pottery, jewelry, fluttering scarves, and even used books.

There were food stands, too. In fact, Theodosia could smell the mingled aromas of fried shrimp, fresh-baked muffins, and fresh-roasted coffee.

And just as Theodosia was wondering if any shoppers would show up, if maybe the whole thing would turn out to be a bust, the proverbial floodgates opened and crowds descended upon them.

Theodosia sold tea like it was going out of style. Forty-five minutes into the event, she'd sold out more than half her merchandise. *Now what?* Well, she could call Drayton and ask him to grab some bags of tea and tea accoutrements off the shelf and pack them up.

She did exactly that. And, some twenty minutes later, Haley showed up, red-faced and lugging an enormous card-board box.

"The cavalry to the rescue," announced Haley. She thumped her box down on Theodosia's table and scrambled to help unpack.

"I'm sorry you had to drop everything and rush this over," said Theodosia. She was delighted to see that Drayton had packed thirty more bags of tea, as well as teacups and saucers, jars of honey, and a few T-Bath products.

"Don't be," said Haley. "It's no trouble. We weren't all that busy." She looked around. "I guess everybody's over here."

"So you can hang around for a while?"

"Well . . . maybe I ought to get back. I hate for Drayton to be the lone wolf."

"Thank you, Haley," said Theodosia, "for bringing this over. And thank Dayton for packing all this up at the last minute."

Theodosia got busy again, arranging her merchandise, selling tea, and chatting with the women who had tables on either side of her. Finally, she caught a glimpse of Delaine.

"Theodosia!" said Delaine as she careened toward her. She held a clipboard in her hand and had two harried-looking interns following her like a pair of ducklings. "How's it going?"

"Very well," said Theodosia. "I already had to restock."

"We've had a fantastic turnout," said Delaine. She looked about distractedly. "I can't quite believe it. The animal groups are going to be so thrilled." And with that she dashed off.

Theodosia wrapped a teacup and saucer in tissue paper for one buyer and explained to another how to heat water just so for brewing the perfect cup of tea. When she finally dared to draw a relaxing breath and look around, she saw Elliot Kern standing at her table. He had picked up a bag of tea and was studying the label.

"Can I help you?" said Theodosia. She was a little surprised that he'd even stopped at her table. Her meeting with him had reeked of hostility.

Kern looked up when he heard Theodosia's voice. Suddenly recognizing her, he looked so startled one would have thought he'd just been doused in hot oil.

"Oh . . . h-hello," Kern stuttered. Then he looked down at the packages of tea again and glanced back at Theodosia, reluctantly making the connection. "I should have guessed you'd be the one selling tea," he said in a flat tone of voice.

"Yes, well, I'm sure there are other sellers here if you'd prefer," Theodosia replied.

"No, no," said Kern, backpedaling slightly and trying to cover his unease. "This looks like lovely tea. It's your special blend, I take it?"

Theodosia gave a tight nod. "It's one of our proprietary blends, yes."

Kern stared at her, a look that was both imperious and challenging. "You really don't like me, do you?"

The first thought that popped into Theodosia's head was, *No, I really don't.* Instead, she bit her tongue and reminded herself of the old adage about catching more flies with honey. And maybe more information, too.

"I really don't know you," said Theodosia.

"But you're still upset about Max being put on leave."

"Max is upset about Max being put on leave."

"I understand he's already been approached by another museum," said Kern.

Theodosia ignored his somewhat probing remark. Instead she said, "When do you intend to invite him back?"

"That's hard to say," said Kern.

"I can't imagine it's that difficult. You're the museum's director, after all. It's your job to weigh the various options and make tough decisions." Her smile was a half snarl. "It's why they pay you the big bucks."

Kern cleared his throat, clearly uneasy.

"By the way," Theodosia continued, "I hope you're excited to have Charlotte Webster on your board of directors. Especially in light of the firebombing at her home last night. You did hear about that, didn't you?"

Kern gave a sober nod. "I did. It sounded awful."

"If you ask me," said Theodosia, "someone doesn't want Charlotte around. Kind of like someone didn't want her husband around." She realized that her resolve to catch more flies with honey had been kicked to the curb. But she was angry and rolling now.

Kern's brows pinched together and he scowled. "If you're implying that I had something to do with either of those things . . ."

"I don't know," said Theodosia. "Did you? Someone clearly didn't want Edgar Webster poking his nose into museum business. And now someone might feel the same way about Charlotte." She glared daggers at him.

"I don't need to take this," Kern snarled. He tossed the bag of tea down on the table and spun away from her. He disappeared into the crowd.

Theodosia watched him go and wondered. Was Elliot Kern the man who'd been orchestrating all this mayhem? Was he a killer and a madman? Or was someone else to blame? Someone she hadn't yet tumbled to. Someone *nobody* had tumbled to?

22

❧

Feeling tired and a little worn out, Theodosia arrived back at the Indigo Tea Shop just after five o'clock.

The place was closed, and the curtains were drawn. Drayton had long since gone home for the day, and she could hear the rafters creaking as Haley rattled around upstairs.

That was good, Theodosia decided. She thought she could use a little peace and quiet to help her get her head back together. Meeting with Harlan Duke this morning and realizing he was a potential suspect—and then running into Elliot Kern—had rattled her. She now understood that either of those men might have had an ax to grind against Edgar Webster. And that either of them could have harassed Charlotte last night. Duke, to send her running in his direction, and Kern, to frighten her away.

As Theodosia walked out into the tea room, the lingering aromas of gunpowder green and Indian spice teas made her decide to fix herself a cuppa. She was running a 5K in a matter of hours, and a convenient hit of caffeine would definitely help spike her energy level.

But as she pulled a tin of Assam down from the shelf, her eyes landed on the Edgar Webster tribute poster that she'd stuck behind the counter. And the note from the Shanghai art dealer that was still tacked to it.

Theodosia plucked the note from the poster and stared at it. And wondered—what time was it in Shanghai?

She knew that, because of the international date line, it was already tomorrow in China. That meant it would be first thing Wednesday morning in Shanghai, seeing as how that city was something like thirteen or fourteen hours ahead of Eastern Standard Time.

Should she call the art dealer, whose name was . . . ? Her eyes traveled to the bottom of the note.

MR. FANG LIU OF MANDARIN ART AND ANTIQUES.

Should she venture a few questions to Mr. Liu about the Chinese tea house? Theodosia put a hand up and massaged the back of her neck. And decided . . . yes. Yes, she would.

Sitting at her computer, feeling like she was about to sail into uncharted waters, she Googled Mandarin Art and Antiques. There it was, located on Moganshan Road in Shanghai, with a phone number listed and everything. She flipped through a phone directory and located the country code. From there it was a small matter of dialing the number.

After a few clicks and clacks, a crisp male voice answered on the other end.

"*Ni hao,*" said the voice.

"Hello?" said Theodosia. The connection sounded hollow, and there was a time delay of a couple seconds.

The man's voice changed to cultured English. "Good morning. How may I help you?"

"Hello," said Theodosia. "I'm trying to get hold of Mr. Liu."

"Speaking."

"Oh, Mr. Liu, this is Theodosia Browning calling from Charleston. In the United States?"

"Yes?" Now he sounded slightly wary.

"I just wanted to tell you how thrilled we all are with the Chinese tea house," Theodosia burbled. She was making things up as she went along. "It's absolutely gorgeous."

That warmed him up.

"I'm so very glad," said Mr. Liu.

"It's almost hard to believe that it's . . . authentic," said Theodosia.

Mr. Liu chuckled. "I can assure you that it's perfectly legitimate, right down to the floorboards."

"That's what Mr. Harlan Duke told us, too."

"Ah yes, Mr. Duke. He has a discerning eye for Chinese antiquities. It was a pleasure to work with him."

"I imagine a Chinese tea house is not that easy to come by anymore," said Theodosia. *Please, please, please, take the hint and follow my lead.*

"Luckily, the city of Shanghai is still blessed with a number of such structures," said Mr. Liu. "However, with the current building explosion that's going on here . . ." A note of regret crept into his voice. "Well, we are gratified to see these tea houses go to public institutions, where they will be honored and appreciated."

"Our museum in Charleston really *loves* it," Theodosia assured him. "It's very popular."

"Right now there is another museum that is also looking to secure one," said Mr. Liu.

Theodosia's ears perked up. "Oh really? Which museum is that?"

"The Crenshaw Museum," said Mr. Liu. "In Upstate New York. They are in the process of raising funds to complete their purchase."

"Well, thank you so much," said Theodosia. "It was very nice talking to you."

As she hung up the phone, Theodosia wondered if it was too late to call the Crenshaw Museum. Yes, she decided, it probably was. But first thing tomorrow, she would make that call. Because if Shanghai tea houses were somehow tied to these recent crimes, she was determined to get to the bottom of it.

"You look adorable, you know that?" Theodosia was back home in her kitchen, smiling at Earl Grey, trying to cajole him with the upbeat sound of her voice.

The dog wasn't buying it.

Standing there in his lion costume, Earl Grey was a very reluctant participant. His tail was down and his shoulders slumped. He looked . . . embarrassed.

"You know," said Theodosia, trying her best to pump up some enthusiasm, "I hand stitched that costume just for you. Went to the fabric store, found that nice shaggy orange fun fur, and created your cool lion's mane."

Earl Grey let loose a delicate sigh.

Theodosia decided to approach it from a different angle. "You only have to wear your costume for an hour or so. We're going to jog over to White Point Gardens, run in the Big Paw five-K, and then blow that pop stand."

This time Earl Grey rolled his eyes.

"And look," Theodosia continued, "I'm going to wear a costume, too." She put on her witch's hat. "See?" She gazed at him hopefully, and then said, "I still haven't convinced you, have I? You know what? I understand how you feel. I get that dogs hate Halloween because it's the worst holiday of the year. It's one long litany of ringing doorbells, kids in scary costumes, and chocolate that's bad for you. And I'm sorry about that, I truly am. But what we're doing tonight is going to benefit a lot of people and dogs."

He lifted his muzzle and gazed at her.

"That's right, it's a *good* thing. We're trying to raise money so we can train more service dogs."

Earl Grey took a step toward her and touched his nose to her hand. Gave her a nudge.

"Thank you," said Theodosia. "I see we're finally on the same wavelength. Okay, let me put on my cape and slip into my running shoes. Then we're outta here."

Strings of purple and orange lights glowed in the dark. An enormous circle of carved pumpkins with flickering candles gave the impression of a witches' convocation. And rumbling fog machines pumped out great gluts of ethereal white vapor, making White Point Gardens look very much like a haunted theme park.

Theodosia and Earl Grey picked their way through throngs of costumed people and dogs, heading for the registration table that was staffed by Big Paw volunteers.

"Hey there," Theodosia said to Helen, one of the volunteers and race organizers. "We're here to pick up our numbers."

Helen consulted her list and then shuffled through a dozen or so cardboard tags. "Let's see, Theodosia and Earl Grey. Here you go. You're team number forty-five."

Theodosia pinned her number to her sleeve and grinned. "Everything looks so nice and spooky tonight."

"Can you believe it?" said Helen. She was short and cute with curly dark hair, the owner of a wonderful white poodle named Shawn. "We didn't really need to rent a fog machine." She waved an arm. "The Atlantic Ocean seems to be providing us with a good supply of the real thing."

"It certainly adds to the moodiness," agreed Theodosia. "Oh, do you have Max's number, too? He'll be running with us."

"He's already picked it up," said Helen.

"Max is here?"

"Somewhere," said Helen as she went on to help the next runner, a man with an exuberant boxer in a red devil costume.

"Okay, thanks," said Theodosia.

She found Max snarfing down a funnel cake. "Aren't you afraid that glop of sugar and grease is going to slow you down?" she asked.

Max had just taken a huge bite of his funnel cake, so he had to chew and swallow hard before answering. "Uh-uh. The carbs are guaranteed to give me an extra shot of energy."

"In other words, you skipped dinner?"

"Afraid so."

"Me, too."

"We're both running on empty, then," said Max. He reached down and scratched Earl Grey behind the ears. "Hey there."

"At least it's a short race," said Theodosia. She took in his Lycra pants and nylon hoodie. "I see you didn't wear a costume."

"No time," said Max. He turned his attention back to Earl Grey. "But hey, buddy, *your* costume looks great."

"He hates it," said Theodosia.

"Nooo," said Max as he continued to rub Earl Grey's ears. "I bet you feel like a big, tough lion in that costume, don't you?"

Earl Grey stared at Max as if he'd just committed a major faux pas (or would that be faux paw?).

"I see the costume is kind of a sore point," said Max. "Like you already said, good thing it's a short race." He sidled closer to Theodosia. "You look cute tonight. Very witchy and mysterious."

"Max," said Theodosia, turning serious, "I have to tell you something."

He tilted his head toward her. "What?"

She pulled him away from the crowd and into a quiet area. "I stopped by Harlan Duke's antique shop this morning."

"Okay."

"He wasn't there, but I was able to catch up with him at the Equinox Equestrian Center."

"Is this your way of telling me you bought a horse? Or that you're going to run away and join the rodeo?"

"No, but . . ." Theodosia drew a deep breath, and then proceeded to tell Max about Duke, his horses, and his casual handling of the dangerous looking hoof pick.

As she talked, Max's expression changed from one of mild interest to one of great concern. "Whoa. Time out. Are you implying that Duke might have used a hoof pick to dispatch Edgar Webster?"

"The thought did cross my mind."

"The saga of Webster's murder just keeps getting stranger and stranger."

"Doesn't it?"

"Theo, did you tell Detective Tidwell about the hoof pick?"

"I was going to," said Theodosia. "Drayton said I should. But I haven't yet." When Max gave her a troubled look, she added, "Mostly because I was so darned busy today with lunch and then running off to the Hunt and Gather Market."

"I think you have to tell him."

They stood there as a pair of Jack Russell terriers romped by, barking and spinning happily.

"Here's the problem," said Theodosia. "Whenever I bring up a random suggestion or share a bit of information, Tidwell goes all law enforcement on me and accuses me of meddling."

"But a razor-sharp hoof pick isn't exactly random," said

Max. "Especially when it's connected to the art dealer who located the Chinese tea house and who's also connected to the murdered man who helped fund it."

"But it's still not direct evidence," said Theodosia. "It's circumstantial at best."

Max took her arm and slowly led her toward the starting line, where the runners—both humans and dogs—were beginning to line up. "I'd like to come to the Indigo Tea Shop tomorrow and help out if I could."

"Wait a minute. Why the sudden change of subject? You . . . you want to help with our Tower of London Tea?"

"Actually," said Max, "I want to be there so I can keep you safe and sound."

Theodosia adjusted Earl Grey's lion's mane. "I'm sure I'll be perfectly fine."

"That's probably what Edgar Webster thought, too," said Max. "As well as Cecily and Charlotte just before they were attacked."

"But I'll be surrounded by lots of people."

"Kind of like Edgar Webster was at the museum?" They stepped over a trio of dachshunds and a tangle of leashes.

"Tell you what," said Theodosia. "We've got Miss Dimple coming in to help serve tea. But what if you lent a hand tomorrow night at the Bloody Mary Crawl and Haunted Hayride?"

"I think that might be a smart idea," said Max. There was a long pause as he gave her a curious look.

"Now what?" said Theodosia.

"Nothing."

"Something." She knew him better than that. Something was brewing and it wasn't a pot of tea.

"I got a job offer today," said Max.

"Seriously?"

"No," said Max. "They're probably just yanking my chain."

"I'm sorry," said Theodosia. "It's just that . . . well, I'm a little bit shocked. But a genuine job offer . . . I suppose that really is good news."

"I thought so," said Max.

"Was your offer from the Savannah College of Art and Design?"

"That's right."

"Hmm. A long ways away."

"Just ninety miles, give or take," said Max. "Seems to me you never mind breezing down to Savannah when you need to pick up tea and supplies."

Theodosia thought for a minute. "So we'd do long distance?"

"I don't see why not."

"And there's no possible chance of your returning to your old job here?"

"Kern doesn't want me and I don't want him."

"What if Kern left the museum? What if he was fired or something?" Tucked in the back of Theodosia's mind was the notion that Kern was also a viable suspect. If it was proved that *he* was the one who'd murdered Edgar Webster, then everything could be set right again.

"Excuse me," said Max. "Do you know something I don't?"

Theodosia sighed. "No, probably not."

"Okay," said Max. As he did a couple of slow knee bends to warm up, his knee joints popped audibly. "Jeez, I hope we're not in the greyhound division."

When the race started—there was no starter's gun because it would have spooked the dogs—the entire group took off in a mad rush. Dogs barked, tails wagged, and collars jingled as they dashed across the park. The group thundered past a plaque commemorating the hanging of Stede Bonnet and his pirates, following a path that had been clearly marked by orange lanterns and glittering arrows. It took them around Oyster Point and past a group of cannons. Just as they ran past the bandstand, the course suddenly split into two separate race courses. One was the 5K, the other a much shorter course, designed especially for non-runners as well as smaller dogs.

Because Theodosia, Earl Grey, and Max were all seasoned runners, they headed down the 5K track and soon found themselves out front, pacing the pack. Now the marked course took them down South Battery, past dozens of enormous mansions. In daylight, these mansions, painted in the French palette of pink, eggshell, and pastel blue, were as delightful as a plate of macarons. Now, in the spirit of Halloween, many were decorated.

There were action-figure witches sitting on side piazzas and stirring cauldrons, ghosts hanging from finials and balustrades, and skeletons standing guard on both sides of driveways. One home even had a full-scale headless horseman on its front lawn.

"I had no idea these homes would be so lavishly decorated," said Max.

"Some of them must be taking part in the Bloody Mary Crawl tomorrow night," said Theodosia.

"And the Haunted Hayride," said Max. "Don't forget the hayride."

They huffed their way down King Street, then turned down Ladson.

"Looks like this route is taking us past the museum," said Max. He didn't sound particularly happy, but Earl Grey wagged his tail.

"Buck up, mister," said Theodosia. "You've got an ace in the hole now. You just scored a serious job offer." She wasn't crazy about Max moving to Savannah, but she knew his career and self-esteem were definitely at stake.

Rounding a corner, they chugged down Meeting, headed

toward the museum. As they approached, they saw that a small crowd had gathered outside. They clapped and cheered mightily when Theodosia, Earl Grey, and Max came into view and continued their raucous cheers as more runners came pounding down the street.

"See," said Theodosia once they'd breezed past. "That wasn't so bad. I think I even saw a couple of your friends out there waving to us." She was pretty sure she'd caught sight of Sumner Motte and his wild, flyaway hair, as well as Percy Capers. But there'd been no sign of Elliot Kern.

They blew down Atlantic Street, a few more runners closer on their heels now, and then followed the markers until they were sent down Church Street.

"We're running right past the Indigo Tea Shop," said Max.

"The home stretch," said Theodosia.

From there it was just a few more blocks until they hit White Point Gardens again. As they spun across the finish line, there were cheers, shouts, and barks from the waiting crowd. Then everyone who finished was awarded an orange ribbon, and all dogs were presented with bowls of water.

"Come and get your picture taken," urged Helen. She was waving at Theodosia and company as well as several other race finishers.

So Theodosia led her gang of three over to the bandstand, where cameras clicked and strobe lights flashed.

And, wouldn't you know it, Bill Glass was also there taking pictures.

"What are you doing here?" Theodosia asked him as he aimed his camera at an enormous harlequin Great Dane. "You're not the official race photographer, are you?" She didn't think Big Paw had hired him. At least, she hoped they hadn't, since he was such a squirrel to deal with.

"Oh, heck no," said Glass. "I'm just hanging around, taking a few snaps of these mutts and their people. Hoping to catch something interesting."

"And have you?"

"Not here." But Glass suddenly pursed his lips and looked smug.

"What?" said Theodosia.

He started to smile. "You never know. I might have stumbled onto a couple leads concerning the Webster murder."

"What are you talking about?" said Theodosia, as Earl Grey pulled Max over to a bunch of dogs and people.

Glass waggled a finger at her. "No, you don't, Nancy Drew. I'm not about to share any information with you. You'd try to scoop me."

"No, I wouldn't." *Yes, I would.* "C'mon, what are you talking about? Who are you looking at?"

"I've got my sources."

"You'd better be careful," said Theodosia. Max's warning was still echoing in her head. "Somebody fairly close to us wants to shut this investigation down completely."

"Yeah, yeah, don't go worrying about me," said Glass. "I'm one slippery guy. I can take care of myself." And, with that, he dashed off into a swirl of fog and purple lights.

23

"*Happy Halloween!*" *cried* Haley. Theodosia had just ducked in the back door this Wednesday morning as Haley popped out of her kitchen. She was suited up in a biker-chick costume, complete with studded black leather jacket, miniskirt, and boots.

"Haley," said Theodosia, a little taken aback. "You're wearing a costume. Wait a minute, weren't you going to wear an Anne Boleyn costume?"

Haley grinned. "She got kicked to the curb. This is way more cool."

Theodosia glanced toward the front of the tea shop, looking puzzled.

"I . . . wait a minute. Was I supposed to wear a costume, too? Did I not get the memo?"

"Naw, I'm all dressed up because I felt like it. I tried to talk Drayton into wearing his captain's outfit again, but he said once was enough. And he *hated* the idea of wearing a Beefeater costume. You know, in honor of our Tower of London Tea? I thought it'd be neat if he wore a costume like all the fancy pants guards at Buckingham Palace wear. But he said no way." She looked downright sad. "What a party pooper."

Theodosia chuckled as they walked out into the tea room together. "Face it, Haley, Drayton's not exactly a costume-wearing, popper-popping, streamer-tossing kind of guy."

Haley considered Theodosia's words for a moment. "I suppose you're right. That type of wild and crazy guy I can find in any . . ."

"Local gin joint," said Drayton. He stood behind the counter looking askance at both of them. "Is Haley still whining pitifully because I won't wear a costume?"

"Would you consider a simple werewolf mask?" asked Haley.

"No, thank you," said Drayton. "I'm grouchy enough as it is today." He reached up, grabbed a tin of tea, and a black plastic spider tumbled down onto the counter. "Haley!" he cried. But she'd already disappeared into her kitchen amid a riot of giggles.

Because it was Halloween, there seemed to be an extra dollop of excitement thrumming in the air. Customers rushed in and grabbed tables. Yellow-and-red horse-drawn jitneys pulled up outside and disgorged more customers. Local shopkeepers, many wearing costumes, ducked in for their morning takeaway of a cuppa and scones.

Haley's cherry banana bread and maple scones were a huge hit. Along with Drayton's choice of teas.

"I'm calling them my daily brews," Drayton told Theodosia. "In honor of Halloween."

"And what teas are you featuring this morning?"

Drayton held up a Chinese teapot with a sacred bird-and-butterfly motif. "A blend called Jasmine Mountain. Chinese black tea with a hint of jasmine blossoms and strawberries. And my own proprietary blend, Autumn Cornucopia."

"The one with black cherries and currants," said Theodosia. "I love that tea blend."

"Though I tend to be more of a purist," said Drayton, "I must say the aroma in our tea room today is extraordinary."

"Tea aromatherapy," Theodosia agreed. "Nothing better. And you're ready with your Lady Jane Grey tea and your War of the Roses tea?"

Drayton smiled. "All set to go."

"Helloooo! Toodles all!" a familiar voice sang out.

Theodosia couldn't help but chuckle. Miss Dimple, their friendly tea-drinking octogenarian bookkeeper, had just arrived in a flurry of silver hair, pink cheeks, and layers of ruffles.

"Miss Dimple," said Drayton. "Thank goodness. You're just the woman I was looking for."

Miss Dimple toddled over to the counter on short, plump legs. "What can I do for you, Drayton?" Though she was here to help serve tea, Miss Dimple always made it a point to be extra sweet to Drayton. In her mind, he was the one who really ran the tea shop. He was the major domo who could spout volumes of tea lore. And that was just fine with Theodosia. As long as all the work got done and their customers were happy, why worry about who was in charge?

"I want you to taste this tea," said Drayton. He poured a steaming serving of tea into a small handmade Japanese teacup. "I need you to render your expert opinion."

Miss Dimple chuckled. She loved nothing better than to render an opinion.

"Now I must warn you," said Drayton, "this tea is a Formosan Lung Ching green tea. It's quite different than your usual preference for Japanese Genmaicha."

Game for anything, Miss Dimple took a sip. She squeezed her eyes shut for a second, then opened them wide. "Lovely. This tea is bright but not too brisk."

"Very good," said Drayton. "You've become a real connoisseur."

"I have?" she said, pleased. "Really?"

"Our customers rely on you to help them select the best teas," said Theodosia, stepping in.

"I knew there was a reason I loved working here," said Miss Dimple. She spun around and finally noticed Haley's decorations. "Oh my. I see we've had a small infestation of witches and ghosts. Is that Haley's doing?"

"No, the decorations were Drayton's idea," said Theodosia, laughing as she said it.

"Oh, you two!" said Miss Dimple. She let loose another chuckle and then got serious. "Say, I was so sorry I wasn't able to help out with your *Titanic* Tea. But my cousins from Murrells Inlet were visiting."

"We would have loved to have you," said Theodosia. "But we made out just fine."

"Still, I would have given anything to see Drayton in his captain's uniform."

Drayton lifted an eyebrow. "Who told you about that?"

"Haley," said Miss Dimple. "Who else?"

"She would," said Drayton.

"I bet it was quite a sight," said Miss Dimple. "I mean, who doesn't love a man in uniform?"

With Miss Dimple serving morning tea, Theodosia took time out to put in a call to the Crenshaw Museum in New York. She was curious about them buying a Chinese tea house. And wondered if they were being guided by Harlan Duke, as well.

When she reached the museum, she was told she needed

to speak with a Mr. Allan Abrams. But when she was connected, she was bumped over to his voice mail. Theodosia waited for the beep, then said, "Please call me as soon as possible. I'd like to ask you a few questions about the Chinese tea house you're thinking of purchasing." She left her name and number. And, as an afterword, said, "Please call any time. It's really quite urgent."

Theodosia was still thinking about Chinese tea houses and Harlan Duke's connection, when her phone rang. She picked it up, figuring it was someone hoping to grab a late reservation for the Tower of London Tea.

It wasn't.

"Theodosia?" said a crackly voice. It was a voice she knew but for some reason couldn't quite place.

She clutched the phone tighter to her ear. "Who is this? Speak up, please."

"It's me, Glass."

"*Bill* Glass?" *What does he want?* "What do you want?" she said. "What's up?"

"I'll tell you what's up," Glass suddenly spat out. "I'm in the hospital!"

Was this a joke?

"What?" she said. "Are you trying to be funny? Because if you are, it's not work—"

"This is about as funny as a crutch, which I'm going to be needing for the next couple of days!"

"You're really in the hospital?" said Theodosia.

"Yes!"

"What happened?" *Oh my goodness*, she thought. Another attack, another injury, maybe another attempted murder? What was going on?

"Can you come over here?" Glass asked.

"What? You mean now?"

"Yes, now. I'm at Mercy Medical Center. I need to talk to you. There's something fishy going on."

"You think?" said Theodosia.

"I don't need sarcasm," said Glass. "I need sympathy."

"You know what?" said Theodosia. "You're probably going to have to settle for the sarcasm."

"But you'll still come?"

Theodosia sighed. "I'm on my way."

She flew out into the tea room, almost colliding with Miss Dimple.

"Oh dear," Miss Dimple exclaimed. "I almost poured my pot of English breakfast tea all over you. We wouldn't want that, would we?"

Drayton glanced up. "What's wrong?" he asked.

"I have to duck out for a short while."

"Now?" He frowned and consulted his watch. "You're aware our Tower of London Tea starts in less than two hours?"

"Bill Glass was attacked late night," said Theodosia. "He's in the hospital."

Drayton did a slow blink. "Dear lord."

"Bill Glass, that silly photographer?" said Miss Dimple.

"That's right," said Theodosia. "I want to run over and see him, but I'll be back in plenty of time for the luncheon, I promise."

Miss Dimple patted her on the shoulder. "Don't worry, dear. We'll take care of things."

But can I? Theodosia wondered.

The heels of Theodosia's Coach loafers drummed a staccato beat on the marble floor of the hospital lobby. She glanced around, saw two wheelchairs sitting empty, a cart full of flowers trundling by, and a receptionist sitting at the front desk.

Definitely need to start at the front desk, she told herself. She approached quickly and smiled at a stern-looking woman with curly red hair. She wore a badge that said LAILA, MMC VOLUNTEER.

"Excuse me," Theodosia said. "Can you tell me which room Bill Glass is in?"

The woman's eyes squeezed shut at the sound of Glass's name, and then she focused a cool, appraising look at Theodosia.

"Are you another one of Mr. Glass's *girl*friends?" the woman asked. Her tone was just short of unfriendly. "We've had a couple of ladies call for him already."

"What?" said Theodosia. She reared back, a little unsettled by the question. "No, I'm not a girlfriend. Certainly not. I'm just . . . look, could you please just give me his room number? I'm in kind of a hurry."

"Four six seven," said the woman. She seemed to take pleasure in carefully enunciating each and every syllable.

Theodosia hurried toward the elevators, wondering just how many girlfriends Bill Glass might have? And had they really been calling him? She'd never thought of the man as a devil-may-care bachelor. Now there appeared to be another side to Glass, a side she really didn't want to know too much about.

Stepping out of the elevator on the fourth floor, Theodosia was almost mowed down by a linen cart. She pressed her back against the wall, vowing not to be involved in a hit-and-run with a stack of starched hospital sheets. She glanced at the signage on the wall, decided she needed to hang a left, and struck off down the corridor.

She still had to dodge busy nurses, rattling carts, and a couple of concerned-looking visitors, but she managed to find Glass's room.

"Four six seven," Theodosia murmured to herself as she knocked on the door.

"Yeah?" Glass called out in a loud, caustic bray. "Door's open. Come on in."

Theodosia pushed her way into Bill Glass's room. He was sitting up in bed in a perfectly ordinary hospital room that had a sliver of a view of the Ashley River. There was a white bandage wrapped around his head that caused his dark hair to stick up wildly. His right eye was badly bruised and ringed in colors of purple and black. He looked as if someone had used him as a personal punching bag.

"Look at this dump of a room," Glass suddenly shouted, waving an arm at her in protest. "It's just short of a *charity* ward. The sheets are scratchy and the entire place reeks of disinfectant. There aren't any RNs to plump my pillows, not even a lousy candy striper!"

"It looks fine to me," Theodosia said. Because it really did look fine. Crisp and clean and antiseptic. Although he was right about the odor of disinfectant. That was downright nasty.

"You know what else?" said Glass. "I was lying in bed this morning, barely able to twitch a single sore and battered muscle, when some idiot barges into my room with a breakfast tray."

"Okay," said Theodosia. She took a few steps forward and eased herself down into a vinyl-covered chair. She decided to let him ramble, because it seemed like he needed to blow off steam.

"So, anyway," said Glass, "this idiot yells out, 'Dietary!' and then slams down my breakfast tray on the cupboard over there. You see?" He flailed an arm out. "My breakfast is *still* sitting over there, because I'm unable to *limp* over and get it," he sputtered. "Now I ask you, what good is breakfast if it's not *served* to you properly?"

Theodosia was suddenly having trouble keeping a straight face.

"How are you feeling?" Theodosia asked.

"Terrible," said Glass. "Never felt worse in my entire life."

"Would you like me to run down to the cafeteria and get you something to eat?" she offered. "Some toast and juice, perhaps?"

"No, no." Glass placed a hand on top of his sheet and patted his midsection gingerly. "The thing is, I have this extremely sensitive stomach. Powdered eggs, cold toast, that kind of crap will give me the urps all afternoon."

"I'm sorry to hear that." Theodosia also hadn't realized that Bill Glass was such a crybaby. He'd always come off like a cigar-chomping tough guy.

Glass fixed her with a slightly lopsided gaze. "How do I look?"

"Excuse me?"

"Is my face all banged up? Do you have a mirror or something so I can take a look?"

Theodosia dug into her handbag and pulled out a small compact. She flipped it open and handed it to Glass.

He gazed in the mirror and flinched. "Oh, howdy! I look like a bit player from *The Walking Dead*." He put a hand up, touched his forehead, and winced. "Feel like one, too. Except my entrails aren't hanging out all over the darn place."

"So there's a bright spot after all," said Theodosia.

"Oh, man." Glass was still groaning as he inspected himself in the mirror. "And I think my front tooth is chipped. Crap on a cracker. That's gonna cost a fortune to fix." His gaze shifted to Theodosia. "Do you hear a whistle when I talk? I thought I just heard a whistle, and I don't think it's from my nose. Oh, man, if it's my tooth . . ."

"Do you want to tell me what happened?" Theodosia interrupted. *After all, you wanted me to drop everything and race right over here.*

Glass snapped her compact closed and handed it back to her. "You know what's so strange? I really don't know *what* happened last night."

"You don't know what happened to you?"

Glass made a grimace. "I know some creep clobbered me on the head with a baseball bat or something."

"Were you robbed? Were any of your cameras stolen?"

"Nope. They were still strung around my neck when the ambulance showed up."

"Do you think your assault had something to do with the fact that you were investigating Edgar Webster's murder?"

"Well," Glass said slowly, "I think that might be it exactly."

"Did you get a look at your attacker?"

"Afraid not."

"Did you get any sort of general impression?"

"Only, you know, that the person who hit me had some heft to him."

"Heft," said Theodosia.

A cagey look spread across his face. "But you know what I did after they loaded me into the ambulance?"

"What?"

"I called Charlotte Webster's house," said Glass. "Just because . . . well, you know why."

"To see if she was home," said Theodosia.

Glass nodded. "But she was there."

Theodosia leaned forward in her chair. "Last night, you mentioned that you might have a lead on someone."

"That's not what I said."

"Some evidence, then," said Theodosia. "Which I have a feeling you might want to share with me now?"

"Aw," said Glass.

"Come on, what gives?"

Glass hunched his shoulders forward and glanced about his room as if somebody might be listening in.

"What's wrong?" said Theodosia.

"Somebody could overhear us."

"There's just us and that hemostat stand over there. And I don't think it's going to blab."

"The thing is," said Glass, "I talked to this guy at the museum . . ."

"What guy?"

"A guy who works there."

"A curator?"

"No, no, he's in building maintenance. You know, like a janitor."

"Okay." This was brutal, like pulling teeth.

"Anyway," said Glass, "my guy tells me there are all these late-night meetings and things going on."

"Staff or board members?"

"He wasn't completely clear on that."

"So what are these meetings supposedly about?" said Theodosia.

"He wasn't sure. But he said it was the first time anything like that ever happened there."

"And it's also the first time a murder ever occurred at the museum," said Theodosia. "So it's reasonable to expect a little extra activity. A little nocturnal action."

"And then I was nosing around and asking questions as well," said Glass, "of the staff and whoever else I could buttonhole."

"And you think what?" said Theodosia. "What's the bottom line here?"

Glass crooked a finger at his bandaged head. "I think somebody at the museum didn't want me hanging around asking all those questions."

"You think that's why you were attacked?"

Glass gnashed his teeth together. "I *know* that's why I was attacked."

24

Tea kettles chirped and teacups rattled softly as Miss Dimple scurried from counter to table.

"I'm back," said Theodosia, suddenly putting in an appearance at the front counter. "What did I miss?"

"Just good food and fun," said Miss Dimple. She shot a sly glance at Drayton. "And Drayton's amazing nonstop comments. It's like being part of a tea documentary."

"I prefer to think of it as encouragement," said Drayton.

It was eleven fifteen, and the Indigo Tea Shop was half-filled with customers. Miss Dimple had already reset the empty tables for the Tower of London Tea, which kicked off at noon, so there wasn't all that much to do, thank goodness.

"I see we're using the Coalport china," said Theodosia.

"What else?" said Drayton. In his mind it was a fait accompli.

"And the Edinburgh crystal?"

"Tell me what other maker crafts fine leaded glasses in that English thistle-cut pattern?"

"You must have quite a collection of china and glassware at home," Miss Dimple said to Drayton.

The corners of his mouth crooked upward. "You have no idea."

"And teapots," put in Theodosia. "Our Drayton's a bit of a hoarder. Only he's a very organized, OCD-type of hoarder."

"Everything in its place," said Drayton. "Carefully and neatly categorized and stored."

"And labeled," said Theodosia. "Drayton still uses one of those old-fashioned plastic labeling guns."

"The kind that makes letters and spits out little plastic tape?" said Miss Dimple. "Oh my, that's quite a relic."

"Not if it still does the job," Drayton replied.

Finally, when the last of their morning customers had departed, Theodosia flew around the tea shop, cleaning and resetting the rest of the tables, making last-minute preparations. As candles were lit and the polished crystal and silver caught the morning light, the shop sparkled like a miniature jewel box.

And Drayton was front and center with a few surprises.

First off, there were tiny bouquets of pink English roses that he'd ordered from Floradora. Those went on the tables in crystal vases, along with miniature Union Jack flags stuck in place card holders. And there were favors, too. Each guest would receive an individual packet of English shortbread along with a miniature jar of marmalade.

"It looks like merry old England in here," Miss Dimple marveled. "Like some charming little tea shop you'd visit in the Cotswolds."

Theodosia scrutinized the tables. "You don't think our

table décor is slightly at odds with the Halloween décor?" In what world, she wondered, did ghosts and witches rub their bony shoulders with sweet marmalade and tea roses?

"But it's a Tower of London Tea," Miss Dimple chortled. "In honor of Halloween. I think you folks struck just the perfect balance."

"If you say so," said Theodosia. She decided she'd just go along with the whole thing. Haley adored the theme, the tickets had all been sold, Miss Dimple was a perennial cheerleader, and Drayton . . . well, Drayton was still gloating over his tea choices.

At eleven forty-five a line began to form outside the Indigo Tea Shop. It continued to swell until, at precisely twelve o'clock, Drayton threw open the front door and welcomed their guests in his inimitable hale-hearty style. Dozens of folks poured in and began to mill about excitedly. They exclaimed over the Halloween décor, *ooh*ed and *ah*ed over the lovely tables, and then wandered happily about, searching for their place cards.

The few customers who showed up without reservations were regretfully turned away as even more guests rolled in.

"Theodosia!" cried Delaine. Looking like a contemporary witch in a slithery black shift, shiny black leather boots, and a floofy hat, she waved at Theodosia from across the tea room.

Theodosia noticed Delaine windmilling her arms and waved back. Then Theodosia hurried to join her, noting that Aunt Acid was still stuck to her like a tick on a hound dog.

"We're so glad you could make it," Theodosia said.

"So am I," said Delaine. "It was touch and go there for a minute. Whew." She made a big production out of exhaling loudly. "I've been crazy busy, dancing as fast as I can. Well . . . you saw me at the Hunt and Gather Market yesterday. Insane! But we did manage to raise a pile of money."

"That's wonderful," said Theodosia. "And as a special reward, I have a table for you and your aunt right over here." She took Delaine by the elbow and guided her to a table.

"Thank you," said Delaine. "Come along, Auntie." The two of them plopped down in their chairs. "Oh, I hear you got roped into honchoing the Bloody Mary Crawl and Haunted Hayride tonight."

"I'm afraid so," said Theodosia.

"Good old Charlotte twisted your arm?" Delaine said in a wry voice. Then she added, "The woman's completely nutters, you realize."

"Charlotte has a lot on her plate right now," said Theodosia. "I'm just trying to lend a hand." She glanced over at the front door and saw a familiar puff of multicolored hair. *Who is that again? Oh no, it's Dolly Greaves, Roger Greaves's wife.* "Excuse me."

But Dolly Greaves had seen Theodosia and was already making a beeline for her.

"We meet again!" Dolly squealed. She reached out and clamped her fingers down on Theodosia's shoulders, pulling her forward in a tight embrace.

"Welcome back to the tea shop," said Theodosia, trying to pull herself away.

"I have to tell you," said Dolly, looking back over her shoulder at the two other women who'd come in with her. "I had such a fabulous time Sunday night that I just couldn't stay away." She grinned at Theodosia. "So you see? I brought two of my BFFs along."

"We're thrilled to have you," said Theodosia, finally managing to escape Dolly's clawlike clutches. "You're right over . . . well, let's put you here at table five."

It was another five minutes before all the guests were seated, but Theodosia and Miss Dimple had already grabbed steaming pots of tea and were busily filling teacups.

Then, finally, as all the guests sipped, chatted with each other, and looked around expectantly, Drayton stepped to the front of the room.

"Welcome," he intoned in his best Heritage Society lecturer voice. "Welcome to our first ever Tower of London Tea."

There was a spatter of applause.

"The Tower of London has always enjoyed a dark and storied history," Drayton continued. "It has been the scene of beheadings and imprisonments, and many dour legends abound. But today, with this special themed tea, we plan to present our own lighthearted version of the Tower of London. Yes, tonight is Halloween, when mischief will abound. And some of you may even subscribe to the notion of orbs, haunts, and spirits that make up so many of our low-country legends." He gestured for Theodosia to join him.

Theodosia stepped in front of the group and smiled. "But today we shall eat and enjoy a civilized tea. In fact, we hope our sweets and savories will completely captivate you, and you'll never think of the Tower of London in the same way again."

With that, Haley and Miss Dimple each appeared with a towering four-tiered tray chock-full of food. Upon seeing this amazing presentation, the room erupted in applause. Then, as Haley and Miss Dimple carried their trays to the two round tables, Theodosia and Drayton ducked into the kitchen, grabbed two more trays, and began delivering food to the rest of the tables.

As the tiered trays were placed in the middle of each table, there were questions galore.

"What kind of scones are these?" Delaine demanded.

"On the top tier of our Tower of London you'll find our crown jewel scones," said Theodosia, "which are cream scones packed full of delicious candied fruit."

"And then what?" someone asked.

"On the next tier," said Theodosia, "you'll find Anne

Boleyn chocolate-dipped strawberries, in both milk and dark chocolate."

"And what is this delightful little tea sandwich?" Dolly Greaves asked. She was pointing and chattering away like a manic magpie.

"That particular tea sandwich is honey-roasted ham and English mustard on caraway seed bread," said Drayton. "And the other one is English smoked salmon with cream cheese and chives on brown bread."

"And once you nosh your way down to our dessert tier," said Theodosia, indicating the bottom tier of the tea tray, "you'll find chutney crescents and individual Victoria sponge cakes."

It was, as they say, your basic piece of cake. Besides enjoying the sweets and savories that were so elegantly presented, their guests were literally eating out of their hands. Nobody complained, everyone seemed deliriously happy, and cup after cup of tea was being sipped with great gusto.

"This was so much easier than I thought it would be," Theodosia whispered to Drayton.

He nodded. "We should make use of our tiered tea trays more often."

"It's the presentation that wows them," said Miss Dimple as she swung by the counter. "Customers see four layers of goodies interspersed with edible flowers, and they just melt. You see, everybody's still grinning like crazy."

"You're sure that's not gas?" Theodosia joked.

"Theo!" said Drayton, pretending to be horrified.

Miss Dimple just chuckled.

As Theodosia made a slow circle around the tea room refilling tea cups, Maggie Twining reached out to stop her. Maggie was a local real estate agent who'd sold Theodosia's cottage to her. She had a friendly, open face surrounded by a tumble of gray hair. Today she wore a nubby turquoise sweater with half-glasses on a chain to match.

"Theo," said Maggie, "this is a wonderful tea. Just amazing."

"Thank you," said Theodosia. "It was fun putting it together."

"And I so love your décor," said Maggie. She pointed to a diaphanous ghost that floated overhead and gave a slow wink. "Reminds me of all our local haunted mansions." Maggie specialized in homes "below Broad," meaning south of Broad Street, which was the expensive, upper-crust part of Charleston.

"I think you've probably sold a few haunted mansions in your career, haven't you?" Theodosia joked.

"I surely have. In fact, I just sold a grand old Italianate-style place over on Lenwood that's supposedly haunted by a Civil War soldier. The former owner swears he heard spurs and sabers clanking in the night."

"I believe it," Theodosia giggled.

"Speaking of Halloween," said Maggie, "I understand you've been strong-armed to chair that Bloody Mary Crawl tonight."

"And the Haunted Hayride," said Theodosia. "Lucky me."

"Still," said Maggie. "It sounds like a fun time."

Theodosia refilled her teacup. "Then I expect to see you there."

Maggie smiled back. "I just might take you up on that."

The bonhomie and good feelings lasted for another hour and a half, basically until Dolly Greaves was just about ready to leave. She was chatting with her friends and a few other departing guests when she spotted Theodosia. She frowned, held up an imperious finger, and then reached out to pull Theodosia aside.

"My husband mentioned that you stopped by his office the other day," Dolly said to Theodosia.

"That's right." Theodosia figured she pretty much had to play it straight. That way nothing could circle back to bite you.

"I didn't give your little visit much consideration," said Dolly, "until I happened to overhear someone at the next table today. They were talking about how you're quite the amateur investigator."

"Oh, not really," said Theodosia. Oops, something *had* just circled back to bite her.

"That's not what I heard," said Dolly. She flashed a lop-sided smile that was chilly at best. "Or overheard."

"Just whose conversation were you listening in on?"

Dolly snapped a hand at Delaine.

"Oh."

Dolly's tone grew insistent and her words terse. "So I have to ask myself—are you investigating the murder of Edgar Webster? And, if so, are you trying to pin it on my husband?" Her eyes narrowed to slits. "Which, of course, would be utterly despicable. I mean, my poor Roger is prostrate with grief!"

"You know what?" said Theodosia. "I was just asking a few questions for Charlotte's sake."

"That's *so* interesting," Dolly snapped. "Considering Charlotte Webster is one of the prime suspects." Her tongue darted out to lick her lips. "Don't you know that the wife is *always* a suspect when her husband is murdered? Especially when serious money is involved."

Theodosia was about to counter Dolly's words when Drayton suddenly cut in to their conversation.

"Thank you for coming," Drayton said to Dolly. "I hope you and your friends had a lovely time." He was smiling and flushed with excitement, bouncing on the balls of his feet.

"It was *most* enlightening," Dolly said in a snide tone. She'd gone from snappy to downright hostile.

"I'm sorry," said Drayton, taking a step back. "Did I just interrupt something?"

"I'm sure Theodosia will tell you all about it," said Dolly, practically spitting out her words. "Aren't you her little confidant? Or would that be Detective Tidwell?" Then, without waiting for any kind of response, Dolly Greaves flounced out of the tea shop.

"What was *that* all about?" asked Drayton, gazing after her. "Clearly, the woman's feathers have been ruffled."

"Dolly thinks that I think her husband might have killed Edgar Webster," said Theodosia.

Drayton's eyes slid toward her and he suppressed a small "told you so" smile. "Isn't that exactly what you think? I mean, isn't Roger Greaves a logical suspect?"

"I don't know," said Theodosia. "The problem is, there's a whole raft of logical suspects."

With Drayton and Miss Dimple cleaning away the detritus of the tea party, Theodosia was back in her office. She was bound and determined to get through to Allan Abrams at the Crenshaw Museum.

But when she placed another call, Mr. Abrams still wasn't answering his phone. So she left another voice message, this one just the teensiest bit more pleading for him to call.

With that unfinished business hanging over her head, Theodosia decided she still wasn't any closer to figuring out Webster's murder.

But something was bound to pop, she decided. She just didn't know what.

"Do you want me to wrap these two teapots in bubble wrap?" Theodosia asked. Drayton had brought along his basalt Capri teapot and majolica blueberry-pattern teapot to use today,

and now Theodosia wanted to make sure they were returned to him in pristine condition. In other words, unbroken.

"Please," said Drayton. He was standing behind the counter, tallying up the day's receipts. Theodosia and Miss Dimple were packing up all the teapots, dishes, and glassware that Drayton had loaned them. The tables were bare, the floor had been swept clean, and now there were just a few final chores left to do.

"Knock knock," called out a tentative female voice.

Everyone looked up from what they were doing to stare at the front door. It was crooked halfway open now, and Cecily Conrad was peering in at them.

Drayton pushed his tortoiseshell half-glasses up on his nose. "What on earth?" he said.

"Cecily," said Theodosia. "Can we help you?"

Cecily took a step into the tea room. "Can I come in? I mean, is it okay?"

Drayton glanced down at his receipts again, so it was left to Theodosia to say, "Yes, Cecily, come in. What can we do for you?"

Cecily looked nervous and a little fearful. "Can we talk?"

"You want to talk to me?" said Theodosia. She looked around, but Drayton and Miss Dimple were giving her no help at all. *Some allies they are.*

"It'll only take a minute," said Cecily.

"Sure," said Theodosia. "Okay. I guess we can . . ." She made a pointing gesture. "We can talk in my office."

Cecily bobbed her head and followed Theodosia without saying another word.

When they were both in her office, Theodosia closed the door and slid behind her desk.

"Are you feeling okay?" Theodosia asked. "You've got a bit of a shiner on your right eye."

"It's not too bad," said Cecily, once she'd settled across from Theodosia. "Charlotte didn't hit me that hard."

"What's up?" said Theodosia. She didn't have a lot of time to waste. The tea shop still needed to be put shipshape for tomorrow morning, then she had to run home and change, and then rush off to the Bloody Mary Crawl. And, oh, yes, the Haunted Hayride.

But Cecily was clearly in no hurry. She twirled a finger in her hair and cleared her throat.

"How can I help?" Theodosia said again, trying to convey a note of urgency.

"I appreciate that you were being helpful the other day," said Cecily, "when you dropped by with your tea basket."

"Uh-huh."

"And I didn't know until I talked to Detective Tidwell again this morning that you were so smart at investigating."

Theodosia smiled faintly. "What exactly did Tidwell say?"

"Just that you were clever and sometimes got involved where you probably shouldn't."

"That was kind of him," Theodosia said in a semi-sarcastic tone.

"No, I think he was trying to pay you a compliment," said Cecily. "Except that he . . . he's not very adept at that kind of thing."

Theodosia leaned back in her chair and steepled her fingers. "So I've noticed."

"The thing is," said Cecily, "when I heard Detective Tidwell sort of . . . well, *vouch* for you, I decided that maybe I should have you on my side."

"Cecily, is this leading somewhere? Do you have some information for me?" Theodosia paused. "Or do you need to get something off your conscience?"

"Not really," said Cecily. But the expression on her face belied her answer.

She does want to tell me something, but she's afraid.

"I think you do know something," said Theodosia. "I think you know more than you're letting on."

"No, I don't," said Cecily. She looked like she was ready to cry.

"You say you talked to Detective Tidwell . . ."

"Just this morning."

"And he questioned you some more regarding . . . the attack on you?"

"That and Edgar Webster's murder," Cecily grumped.

"Okay."

"But I told him I didn't *know* anything about that. That I'm going to try and forget I ever knew the man!"

"But you have a sort of suspicion."

Cecily shrugged.

"Cecily . . ."

"Okay!" Cecily blurted out. "I've had my suspicions all along, but now . . . now I'm too scared to say anything!"

"Surely you can tell the police."

Tears rolled down Cecily's face. "No, I can't. What if I'm wrong? Worse yet, what if I'm *right?* What if the killer comes after me? I mean, he already did once, I think. How do I protect myself?"

Theodosia stood up and came around her desk. She sat down next to Cecily on the wide, cushy chair. "Cecily, there's nothing you can't tell me."

"I can't. I'm too afraid."

Still Theodosia pushed her. "Cecily, you came here today for a reason. So why not share your suspicions—if that's what they are—and let me be the judge of what's going to get you in trouble or not?"

But Cecily just pursed her mouth tightly and shook her head from side to side, looking like a five-year-old who's not about to tattle.

25

"*I see Mother* Nature's fog machine is at work again," said Theodosia. She was standing on Meeting Street just outside the historic Heywood House. The place was a large Greek Revival home that, tonight, was lit up in spectacular fashion. Orange spotlights splashed up the sides of the home, causing it to glow like a jack-o'-lantern in the dark night. Some sort of green rotating projector cast ever-changing images against the front of the house, enticing streams of visitors through its front doors. And, with most of them clutching plastic cups, the Bloody Mary Crawl was clearly in full swing.

Two volunteers, Mary Grace and Katina, were standing with Theodosia on the sidewalk, taking in the spectacle. Meeting Street had been cordoned off for almost three blocks, so only foot traffic was allowed. Still the crowd continued to swell.

"I had no idea so many people would come out for this,"

Theodosia marveled. She clutched the binder Charlotte had given her as if it were a lifeline.

"Oh, yes," said Katina. She was cute and blond and dressed in a kind of red beetle costume. "And most of them are even wearing costumes."

Theodosia smiled. "I can see that."

"But we have a small problem," said Mary Grace. She was dark-haired and petite, the more serious-looking of the two volunteers. No costume for her.

"What's that?" said Theodosia. This was why she was here tonight, hopefully to solve problems.

"The hay wagons haven't arrived yet," said Mary Grace.

"That is a problem," said Katina. "The hayrides are one of our major draws. Particularly for families."

Theodosia flipped open the white binder and ran her finger down a contact sheet until she found the number for the Equinox Equestrian Center. "Let me make a call and see what the holdup is."

But just as she grabbed her phone, the *clip-clop* of hooves rang out sharply from down the block.

All three of them turned at once to watch as two enormous black horses steamed directly toward them, pulling an enormous hay wagon. The horses tossed their heads and jingled their harnesses as they pranced right down the middle of the street. Behind that first wagon, Theodosia could see another set of horses pulling a second wagon.

"Problem solved," said Theodosia. "They're here." If all problems were resolved this simply, it was going to be an easy, fun night.

"Those are awfully big boys," said Katina as the first horse-drawn wagon rumbled past.

"Percherons," said Theodosia. "Horses that were originally bred in France and used as war horses." She noted that the wooden wagons were stuffed with hay and looked like they could easily accommodate twenty-five or thirty people. That was good, because kids and their parents were already lining up.

The first wagon shuddered to a stop next to a large red barrel with a sign that said HAY RIDES LOAD HERE. Theodosia strolled down there to get a closer look at the monster-sized team.

"These are gorgeous horses," she said, looking up at the driver. Then she did a double take when she recognized just who was holding the reins. It was Harlan Duke!

"What are *you* doing here?" Theodosia asked. Duke was all gussied up in a western hat and long, white drover's coat.

Duke grinned down at her. "Bet you didn't expect to see me!"

"No, I didn't," said Theodosia. "But it's a nice surprise." At least she hoped it was.

"Carriage driving is one of my hobbies," said Duke. "So I thought I'd help out tonight. I heard that Charlotte roped you in, too."

"She sure did," said Theodosia. "You didn't drive those horses all the way in from the equestrian center, did you?"

"Naw, we trailered these big boys to the parking lot at the Coast Guard station and unloaded there. The wagons were hauled in by tractor."

"Neat."

"Well . . ." Duke glanced back and saw that he had a full passenger load already. He tipped his hat to her. "Got to get going."

"Good luck," she said. "Be safe."

Pleased that the hayrides were finally under way, Theodosia decided to do a quick inspection of the Heywood House. She strolled up the front walk, which was lined with silver and gold luminaries, and stepped inside.

It was absolutely amazing what the owners had done.

They'd turned the entire first floor of their home into a haunted wedding tableau. There was a ghost bride and her four bridesmaids getting gussied up in the front parlor. The hallway was draped in white gauze and fake cobwebs. In the library, on the other side of a white velvet rope, a ghost groom and his groomsmen preened in black and Day-Glo orange tuxedos. And in the large family room, folding chairs held a family of wedding ghosts—*er, guests*, Theodosia thought. She could just imagine them tapping their bony fingers, anxiously awaiting the ceremony.

Just wonderful, she thought. The home owners had really gone to a lot of effort. In fact, it looked as if they'd brought in a professional set decorator.

Outside, the expansive back patio was lit by hundreds of flickering candles. Flaming torches surrounded a long reflecting pool. Nearby, a Bloody Mary bar had been set up. Guests with the appropriate color wristbands were helping themselves to drinks and garnishing them with olives, shrimp kabobs, pickles, and lettuce stalks. Theodosia was happy to see that there was also plenty of apple cider and soft drinks available for the kids.

Thank goodness for all these hard-working volunteers, she thought. All these venues had been planned and plotted, and all she had to do was serve as the pro forma chairperson. Really, she thought, if Charlotte Webster had been only 2 percent involved in all of this, she still deserved a ton of credit.

As Theodosia was exiting the house, she ran smack dab into Max.

"There you are," said Max. "I've been looking all over for you." He smiled warmly. "But, hey, you didn't wear your costume. I thought for sure you'd wear that witchy thing."

"I thought I'd be better off in jeans and sneaks tonight," said Theodosia. "Makes it easier to move around. Sneak around."

Max spread his arms wide apart. "What can I do to help?"

Theodosia thought for a moment. "You know what? I haven't been over to Gateway Walk yet. Do you think you could take a stroll over there and see how the cemetery tours are going?"

"Of course."

"That would be great."

They walked down Meeting Street together, dodging people, bumping shoulders, ducking around lampposts strung with twinkle lights. The street was getting more and more crowded, and there was a crackle of excitement in the air. It felt like a thousand people had turned out this Halloween night. Maybe even some that weren't wearing wristbands? Probably, but Theodosia wasn't going to worry about it. As long as everyone enjoyed the open houses, hayrides, and cemetery ramble, she figured she was way ahead of the game.

As Theodosia turned into the Featherbed House, Max continued on to the cemetery. She smiled as she climbed the steps to the lovely large front porch. Her friend, Angie Congdon, was the proprietor of the Featherbed House, and Theodosia had always found it to be one of the cutest, quaintest B and Bs in the entire area.

Stepping across the threshold, Theodosia was struck by the pitch-perfect mix of elegance and hominess. Quilted patchwork geese, carved wooden geese, and plaster geese were everywhere. Needlepoint pillows with geese motifs were propped on overstuffed chintz sofas and matching chairs. The lobby didn't look spooky at all, but there was a life-sized witch with one boney hand pointing toward the outdoor patio. The sign hung around her neck read HAUNTED GARDEN.

That must be the place, Theodosia decided. She crossed the lobby and stepped outside. And practically laughed out loud.

It looked like an outdoor woodland café with the wicked witch from "Hansel and Gretel" as the hostess and proprietor. Trees were strung with orange, purple, and green lights, extra palm trees had been brought in to give the feeling of abundant flora and fauna, and papier-mâché gremlins and trolls peeped out from various groves of shrubbery.

And there, in the corner, sitting at a wrought-iron table, was Drayton. And, glory be, Charlotte Webster and Roger Greaves were also at his table!

Theodosia ducked under hanging branches and tiptoed around a large clump of palmettos.

"Hello there," she said, popping out at them fast.

"Aiiii!" cried Charlotte, giving a little scream. When she recognized Theodosia, she said, "You scared the living daylights out of me."

"Just trying to put you in the Halloween mood," said Theodosia.

Drayton stood up and pulled a chair out for her. "Sit down, sit down. How's it going out there?"

"I'd have to say everything's running smoothly," said Theodosia. She reached across the table and touched Charlotte's hand. "And it's all due to your good planning."

"Thank you," said Charlotte, beaming. "But I had a lot of help from some awfully good volunteers. Everybody really pitched in."

"From my perspective," said Theodosia, "it feels like a huge success."

Charlotte looked suddenly serious. "Thank you so much, Theodosia, for taking this off my hands. I really appreciate it."

"No problem," said Theodosia. Because there really hadn't been any problems.

Charlotte glanced sideways at Roger Greaves, then back at Theodosia. "I wanted to come out and thank you earlier," she said, "but I was nervous about coming on my own." She gave a little shiver. "There are so many people, so much going on, and . . . well, you know my circumstances." She fluttered a hand to her chest. "Anyway, I was lucky that Roger agreed to serve as escort." She smiled now. "I figured if I hung out back here, you'd turn up sooner or later."

"And here I am," said Theodosia. "I've been making the rounds . . ." She pushed back her chair and stood up. "And now I'd better continue doing so."

"Can't you stay for a drink?" said Charlotte. She looked pleadingly at Greaves. "Make her stay. Just one little drink?"

But Theodosia was insistent. "No, I've got four more venues to visit yet. If everything goes well, I'll try to swing back here a little later."

Drayton stood up, too. "I have to take off, as well." He nodded toward Charlotte and Greaves and wished them a pleasant evening. Then he turned to Theodosia, and said, "I'll stroll with you for a while."

Back out on Meeting Street, things were getting wild. There were throngs of people wearing masks and costumes, and kids running wild. Fog streamed in from the Atlantic, and the evening had turned considerably cooler and darker. A vampire swooped by in a velvet cape, five teenaged boys wearing green alien masks charged past en masse, and a Venetian lord scrambled onto a front porch.

"I should check things out at the Ames-Parker House," Theodosia told Drayton.

"Let's do that," said Drayton. "I haven't been there in ages, and I've always been enamored of that free-floating staircase in the entry hall."

When they went in, the staircase was still there, but it was decorated with bats and spiders.

"Dear me," said Drayton. "They've gone positively batty."

"Still," said Theodosia, "it's kind of cute."

"If you like that sort of thing."

They pushed their way through a library that had been decorated in a Sherlock Holmes theme, and headed out to the back patio. As they stood on the back stoop, Theodosia caught a glimpse of Elliot Kern, the museum director. He was sitting at a table with several other people, enjoying a drink.

Hmm. Maybe a quick visit is all that's needed here.

But just as they turned to go, they ran into Percy Capers.

"Hello, you two," said Capers, grinning at them. He was holding a Bloody Mary in a plastic cup and dressed in a black ninja costume.

"Fancy meeting you here," said Theodosia. She took a second look at his costume. "I hope you're going on to another party," she said in a good-natured tone.

"I am," said Capers. "One of the other curators, Donald Ross—I don't know if you know him—is having a party. But it doesn't start until much later."

"An adult party," said Drayton.

"That's right," said Capers. "No dunking for apples, no mob of trick-or-treaters." He held up his glass. "Just adult beverages and conversation."

"What's not to like?" said Theodosia. They walked back outside with Capers. As he wandered down the street, Delaine and Aunt Acid were just coming up the walk.

"Ha," said Drayton. "You two are the last people I ever expected to see at this mob scene."

"Mostly we're just going to drop by the Featherbed House," said Delaine. "I hear their Haunted Garden is really something."

"You'll enjoy it," Drayton promised.

"And then we're going to ride the hay wagon," said Aunt Acid.

Delaine wrinkled her nose. "Seriously, Auntie? Horses are awfully . . . How shall I put this? Aromatic?"

"Stinky?" said Aunt Acid, smirking.

"Well, yes," said Delaine.

"I still want to ride," said Aunt Acid.

Delaine shrugged at Theodosia. "What can I say? She wants to ride."

"Don't let the haunts get you," Drayton said to Aunt Acid with a twinkle in his eye.

"If they try," said Aunt Acid, "I'll give 'em a shot of my pepper spray!"

"Get a load of her," said Delaine. "She thinks she's my personal bodyguard."

"Good luck," said Theodosia. She gave a little wave as she and Drayton headed down the street in the direction of another house on her list. But they'd only gotten twenty feet or so when Max came running toward them. He was waving his arms, trying to get their attention.

"What's wrong?" Theodosia asked as he huffed up to meet her.

"Aw, they're completely swamped over at the cemetery," said Max. "One of the guides from the Heritage Society, the lady who was doing a lovely lesson on the history of the place, just went home sick."

Theodosia turned immediately to Drayton. "Drayton, can you do it? Can you lead the tour?"

"What?" His eyes widened and he touched a hand to his chest. "Me? You want *me* to lead a tour? What do I know about Gateway Walk and the program the guides are supposed to be presenting?"

"Are you serious?" said Theodosia. She practically laughed out loud. "Drayton, you know just about *everything* there is to know. I mean, you're on the board of the Heritage Society. You're probably one of the most knowledgeable people concerning legends and lore in this area."

"You think so?" said Drayton.

"I know so," said Theodosia. "So . . . will you do it?"

Drayton nodded. "For you, Theo, yes. I'll try to muddle through."

"Thank you," said Theodosia. "Max, will you take Drayton over to Gateway Walk and get him set up?"

"You got it," said Max.

As Theodosia watched the two of them disappear into a swirl of revelers, her cell phone began to hum. She dug for it in the bottom of her bag, fumbled it once, and then finally said, "Hello?" She hoped there wasn't another problem somewhere along the route.

"Ms. Browning?" said the voice on the other end of the line. "Theodosia Browning?"

"Yes, that's me." She didn't recognize the voice.

"This is Allan Abrams from the Crenshaw Museum. You wanted me to call you back?"

"Oh, yes, thank you!"

"I hope I didn't catch you at a bad time, but the voice mails you left were awfully insistent."

"I do appreciate the call back," said Theodosia.

"What was it you needed to know?" asked Abrams

"Just some basic information. I understand your museum is buying a Chinese tea house? From Mandarin Art and Antiques in Shanghai?"

"We're *trying* to buy it," said Abrams. "We're in the process now of rallying support from the arts community and staging a number of fund-raisers." He hesitated, sounding a little wistful. "Still, one-point-two million dollars is a lot of money."

"Excuse me?" said Theodosia.

Abrams repeated himself, speaking up louder. "I said one-point-two million dollars is a lot of money."

"Yes, it is," said Theodosia. Somewhere in the back of her mind, that figure sounded way low. Hadn't the Gibbes Museum paid considerably more for their tea house? She thought they had. "You know," she said, "we have a tea house here in Charleston."

"Yes," said Abrams. "I saw the photos on your museum's website. It's a gorgeous tea house. Almost identical, I'd say, to the one we're trying to buy."

"Almost identical," said Theodosia. Her mind was suddenly in a tumble. "Well, thank you," she told Abrams. "Thank you for calling back."

She punched the Off button on her phone and practically swayed as crowds streamed past her. Why was there such a discrepancy in price between the two tea houses? she wondered.

Why had the Charleston museum paid . . . what was the figure? She thought it was something like $2.3 million. But the Crenshaw Museum was only trying to raise $1.2 million for their tea house. That was a difference of $1.1 million.

Maybe the discrepancy didn't mean anything. Maybe the two tea houses were completely different. They could be. They could be as different as night and day.

Or maybe my recollection is wrong.

Theodosia suddenly wondered if Charlotte Webster was still sitting in the Haunted Garden over at the Featherbed House. She drew a breath and glanced around. Only one way to find out.

Theodosia tore down the street and into the Featherbed House. She glanced right and left inside the lobby, then bolted out the back door and into the garden.

Charlotte was still there all right, sitting on the back patio with Roger Greaves, drinking what was probably her second or third Bloody Mary. She looked like she wasn't feeling any pain.

Theodosia dashed over to her table.

"Charlotte!"

Charlotte looked up with a question on her face. "Theodosia?" Her bewilderment was soon replaced by worry. "Is something wrong? I mean, you look like you're positively frantic. Please tell me something hasn't turned disastrous."

"Sorry, I didn't mean to come careening up to you like that," said Theodosia. "But I have to ask you something. It's really important."

Charlotte leaned forward. "Something about tonight's event? I'd help if I could, but I'm just not—"

"No," said Theodosia, interrupting. "I need to ask you about the Chinese tea house that you and your husband helped finance."

At that, tears sprang to Charlotte's eyes. "The tea house," she said, almost blubbering. "It was the fulfillment of Edgar's dream. His legacy."

Theodosia tried to pull Charlotte back into the here and now. "Do you remember the price that the museum paid for it?"

Charlotte swallowed hard and did a sort of double take. "The price?"

"Yes. Do you remember the exact amount the museum paid for it?"

"Of course, I do," said Charlotte. "I have a very good head for numbers."

"And that number was?"

Charlotte didn't hesitate. "All in, the price was two-point-three million dollars."

"Quite a pretty penny," said Roger Greaves, finally interjecting himself into the conversation.

"Yes, it is," said Theodosia. She backed away from the table. "Thank you. Thank you very much."

"Theodosia?" Charlotte gazed at her sharply. "What's wrong? Why are you asking about the tea house? And why do you look as if you've just seen a ghost?"

Theodosia mustered a faint smile. "Because maybe I have." *A ghost of an idea, anyway.* "So I just need to . . . um . . . take care of a couple of things." She took off hurriedly, leaving a very puzzled Charlotte in her wake.

26

Back out on the street, standing in a puddle of yellow light cast by a flickering street lamp, Theodosia ran the numbers in her head again. Just to make sure.

Okay, the Gibbes Museum paid $1.1 million *more* than the Crenshaw Museum planned to pay for their Chinese tea house. That was an awfully big discrepancy. Too big to ignore. So . . . was it possible . . . could someone have lined their pockets with that $1.1 million? She clenched her fists tightly. They *must* have. That had to be the answer.

Theodosia spun quickly and practically swayed in her tracks from the effort. So who had absconded with all that money? And—here was the kicker—had the thief *murdered* Edgar Webster because he'd discovered the theft?

Oh, dear.

This was big. This was too big for Theodosia to deal with all by herself. She needed to bring in reinforcements. Not just Drayton, not just Max, but the big guns: Detective Tidwell and his crew of detectives and uniformed officers.

Walking slowly down the street, Theodosia knew what she had to do. She turned down an alley where she could have a little privacy. Cool wind rushed past her, dried leaves swirled, footsteps echoed behind her.

She whirled around, saw no one, and smiled faintly.

Nobody there. Just ghosts.

Theodosia pulled out her phone and made the call to Tidwell. There was no answer. All she could do was leave a message. Tidwell was probably sitting at home in an over-sized bathrobe, reading Plato or something incredibly academic. On the flip side, he might be watching trash TV.

Theodosia tried to keep her message as short and succinct as possible. She fought hard to modulate her voice, but she was aware that it was starting to rise—just like the panic that fluttered deep inside her chest.

What do I do now?

She dropped her phone inside her bag, hoping Tidwell would get her message and call back as soon as possible. Or rush over here as soon as possible.

In the meantime . . .

Maybe she could figure out exactly who had absconded with the money?

It didn't seem as if Charlotte or Roger Graves could have pocketed the difference, since they had no idea that the museum had grossly overpaid for the tea house. So that meant they were free and clear as suspects.

Okay, what about Cecily? She might not be the most forthright person in the world, but she couldn't have had anything to do with the actual transaction. She wasn't involved with the museum, so there was no way any money had passed through her hands. There was no way she could have skimmed such a large amount.

So who was Cecily so afraid of? Who did that leave as suspects?

Well, it left the two people who'd been most involved in

the importation and installation of the Chinese tea house, that's who: Harlan Duke and Elliot Kern.

Harlan Duke was occupied right now, driving the hay wagon, but Theodosia wondered if Elliot Kern was still over at the Ames-Parker House? And, if so, what would happen if she went over there and accused him outright?

He'd deny it, of course. But her threat of unmasking him might also set something in motion. He might flee, he might hire an attorney, he might go into total denial, or he might beg for mercy. Really, anything could happen.

So . . . was she willing to take that risk? Did she feel comfortable confronting Kern to see what his reaction might be?

Theodosia wasn't sure.

On the other hand, maybe she could drop a very broad hint and see if he flinched.

If he's even still there.

Theodosia turned and hurried back toward the Ames-Parker House, still unsure of how she was going to play it. *If* she was going to play it. Her nerves were completely jangled, and she constantly had the feeling that her footsteps were being dogged. But when she looked back, she could see . . . nothing.

Back at the mansion, Theodosia crept past the bat-infested staircase, past the Sherlock Holmes room. She exploded out onto the back patio and looked around, ready for a cataclysmic confrontation with Kern.

He wasn't there. The table where he'd been sitting was now occupied by a gaggle of women.

Feeling defeated, questioning her own reasoning now, Theodosia hauled herself back out to the street. Maybe Kern had gone to the Halloween party that Percy Capers had been headed to? She'd go after him if she could get the address. Try to pin his wily little ears back against his head. But she didn't have the address. Who would know? Max?

No, he'd been out of the museum loop for a few days, so that possibility was slim to none.

Disgruntled, Theodosia walked slowly down the street.

"Theodosia?"

She looked up. Maggie Twining, her Realtor friend, was smiling at her. But when Maggie saw the worried look on Theodosia's face, her smile slipped a few degrees.

"Theo, are you okay?" Maggie asked.

"I'm just . . . Oh, I'm fine," said Theodosia. "Just in a quandary over something."

"You look pretty upset. I could tell straight away." Maggie hesitated. "You're investigating something, aren't you?"

Theodosia's brows pinched together. "Why would you say that?"

Maggie fixed her with a kind smile. "Because that's what you do, hon. That's what you're good at. I mean . . . besides tea. Drayton mentioned it to me just the other day when I dropped in to grab some tea and scones. He's very proud of your sleuthing skills."

"Okay," said Theodosia. "I'll admit it. I am on the trail of something."

Maggie seemed pleased. "I'll just bet you're following up on the murder of Edgar Webster. That's all people have been talking about lately. That and the lovely tea house he helped bring to the museum."

Theodosia stared at her. "You're good."

"Did I guess right?"

Theodosia nodded.

Maggie put a hand on Theodosia's arm. "I hope your friend Max isn't involved."

Theodosia stiffened. "Why would you say that?"

"Oh, just because he handles PR at the museum," said Maggie. "I'd hate to see him pulled into any kind of witch hunt over there."

She doesn't know, thought Theodosia.

Theodosia desperately wanted to tell Maggie about Max being fired, but she didn't want to lay a total bummer on this lovely woman.

"You know," said Maggie. "I'm working with one of Max's colleagues right now."

"Oh, really?" Theodosia was only half listening. Her brain was still whirling like a cyclone, trying to figure out who might have benefitted financially from the tea house purchase. Could it have been the dealer in Shanghai?

"He's buying a gorgeous townhouse on St. Michaels Aly," Maggie continued. "Expensive, but positively steeped in history, with a walled courtyard garden to boot. Still, he's putting a half million down. I had no idea those museum positions paid so well."

Theo's ears suddenly perked up.

"Huh? Excuse me, *who's* buying it?"

"Percy Capers," said Maggie. "You know, the Asian curator?"

The light instantaneously snapped on for Theodosia. (There was, in fact, an audible *click* inside her head, as if she could physically feel the lightbulb being turned on.)

Taking a deep breath and a step backward, Theodosia stared off into the distance, thinking. Percy Capers. Yes, he was most certainly the *Asian* curator. If anybody could have masterminded a swindle, it could have been him.

Feeling as if Max had been partially vindicated, Theodosia cast her eyes around and was rocked to the core when she suddenly saw the dark eyes of Percy Capers staring directly at her. He was practically hidden, crouched way back in the shadows, where a narrow walled alley led to a private garden. But she could tell he was staring fixedly at her and Maggie, his eyes as flat as a reptile's, desperately trying to listen in on their conversation!

Theodosia tried to remain calm as Capers shifted slightly

and continued to study her. She didn't want to let on that she'd seen him.

Panic bubbled up inside her like hot lava, and there was a loud whooshing sound in her ears. *What to do? How to get help?* Most of all, she didn't want to trigger a bad situation that would put this crowd of parents and kids in any sort of danger!

Theodosia tried to pull it together. She squared her shoulders and set her jaw in a hard line. She hadn't intended to convey her fear to Capers, to give him what a Vegas card player might call a "tell." Unfortunately, she probably *had* telegraphed the anxiety and fright that was prickling her senses and flooding her brain.

Oh, yes, she had, because Percy Capers suddenly broke cover and took off running down the block at full speed.

That was all Theodosia needed. She shoved her binder into the hands of a surprised Maggie Twining and, without really thinking about it, dashed after him.

Capers spun down the sidewalk, dodging people, slamming into a couple of older women, then dashing up onto a lawn and vaulting a flowerbed. Then he was careening down the middle of the street, feet slapping hard against the pavement.

"Stop!" Theodosia cried as she ran after him. "Stop right there!"

Capers continued his flight with Theodosia running hard right behind him. Startled by this impromptu chase, the crowd seemed to magically part as Theodosia—legs pumping, hair flying—tried to chase him down.

They may have been roughly around the same age, but Theodosia figured she could take him. She was in far better shape, her muscles toned and tight from daily runs. Her lung capacity was the best it had ever been.

Legs flying, arms akimbo, Percy Capers dared to turn

his head and sneak a glance back at Theodosia. Fear registered on his face when he saw that she was gaining on him fast. He'd started out with a half-block lead, and now Theodosia was a hundred yards back, running flat out with a cold, determined look on her face. And a battle song in her heart that said, *I'm going to run you down, punk, and knock you flat to the ground.*

Percy Capers did what all cowards seemed to do. He panicked. His mouth gaped open, and his pinched face took on the appearance of a cornered rat. He spun wildly around one of the red barrels that marked the hay wagon–loading station, bumping people left and right. The wagon had just emptied out, and the driver was standing on the street, talking to a group of small kids. Without breaking stride, Capers shoved his way past the startled driver and sprang up onto the front wheel of the hay wagon. He landed on the flat wooden seat with a thud and snatched up the reins. Giving them a furious shake, he let loose a loud cry and took off!

Metal horseshoes grated against cobblestones as the two giant horses struggled to gain traction. Gentle in nature, not built for speed, they'd been pulling the wagon at a nice sedate pace all night, and this new driver had shocked their equine sensibilities to the max.

"Oh no, you don't!" Theodosia shouted after Capers as she raised a fist at him.

With barely a glance around, she leapt on board the second hay wagon. Floundering through a foot of loose hay, she scrambled madly toward the front seat and plopped down right next to Harlan Duke.

"Follow that wagon!" Theodosia screamed.

If it hadn't been so dangerous, it would have been the Keystone Cops meets the wild, wild West.

Capers's wagon roared down Meeting Street, shuddering

and rocking, scaring everyone silly and causing innocent bystanders to run for their lives.

"You've got to catch him!" Theodosia shouted to Duke. "Capers killed Edgar Webster!"

Duke's wagon was rolling fast and picking up speed. "You serious?" Duke shouted back to her.

Theodosia gritted her teeth and nodded. "I think he stole a big chunk of money and Webster found out."

Comprehension dawned on Duke's broad face. "He's the one who handled the final . . ." He ground his teeth together and leaned forward, urging his pair of Percherons on harder. "The final sale," he grunted out.

Theodosia grabbed his arm. "Be careful. We don't want to kill anyone!"

"Brace yourself," cried Duke as they spun around a corner.

Capers had turned his wagon onto South Battery, urging his horses to run full tilt. Not used to such a rough, unskilled driver at the reins, the nervous team plunged from left to right, changing lanes haphazardly. The hay wagon swung back and forth wildly, its wheels jouncing up over curbs and trampling flowerbeds. The wagon was swaying so violently that it slammed into a couple of parked cars.

"Ouch," said Theodosia. "I think he just creamed a Volvo."

"There goes a BMW," said Duke.

"Pull over!" Theodosia screamed at Capers. But he ignored her and just kept going on his wild, destructive ride.

"Where's he gonna run to?" wondered Duke.

"He's headed straight for White Point Gardens," said Theodosia. And, indeed, Capers drove his team right up over the sidewalk and into the park, clipping a magnolia tree and barely missing a row of Civil War–era cannons.

Clods of earth flew at Theodosia and Duke as both sets of horses dug their pounding hooves deep and hard into the turf.

"You're finished, Capers!" Theodosia shouted after him. "Give it up!"

As if in answer, Capers yanked his reins wildly, causing his team of horses to spin right, turning so sharply that his wagon almost tipped over.

"He's going back onto Murray Boulevard," Theodosia yelled.

"Giddyup!" cried a voice from behind her.

Theodosia spun around in surprise and saw Aunt Acid lying in the far back corner of the hay wagon. She was giggling like mad and hanging on for dear life.

"We've got a passenger," Theodosia told Duke.

But Duke's face was set in a grim line. "Tell her to hang on tight."

"You hear that?" Theodosia asked Aunt Acid. "You've got to hang on."

"Giddyup!" the old lady cried again.

"What's that up ahead?" asked Duke. They were running full tilt now and starting to close on Capers's wagon.

"Holy guacamole," said Theodosia. "It's the WCTV van. I think they're conducting some sort of interview."

The two wagons flew directly toward a shiny white TV van with a satellite dish on top, toward the bright glow of lights where Stephanie Hayward was conducting what was probably a slice-of-life Halloween interview. She was leaning down, talking to a group of costumed trick-or-treaters. Doing what the station would call a human-interest story.

Stephanie, her cameraman, and the kids saw the first wagon coming and jumped out of the way, just in the nick of time. Then Theodosia's wagon bore down upon them.

"Stephanie!" Theodosia yelled as they spun past. The cameraman, a seasoned correspondent who knew his trade, immediately swung his camera toward them and managed a fairly decent tracking shot as they raced by.

"Yeehaw," cried Duke. "Now we're on TV."

"Dear lord," Theodosia muttered as the hay wagons rocked and creaked and plunged through the dark night.

Of course Tidwell picked that exact moment to call her back!

Bracing herself, hanging on tight, Theodosia grabbed her phone, and said, "What took you so long?"

"It depends on what you want," Tidwell grumped.

"Backup!" Theodosia shouted. She was hanging on for dear life as the wagon careened onto Ashley Street.

"What are you talking about?" said Tidwell. Then, sounding suspicious, he barked, "Where are you?"

"If you turn on WCTV right now," Theodosia told him, "I think our hay-wagon chase is being broadcast live!"

"Hay wagons?" screeched Tidwell. "Live?"

"From the Haunted Hayride," cried Theodosia. "Just please hurry up and get over here with as many squad cars as you can spare. Try to set up some sort of barricade across Montagu. Or maybe Calhoun Street! I mean, you're going to have to stop a whole lot of horsepower!"

"Miss Browning!" came his shout, but she was already hanging up on him.

"Your man's turning again," shouted Duke.

"Dear lord," said Theodosia. Was Capers going to head back into the Historic District? What new havoc would this cause?

But just as Capers rounded a corner, his right front wagon wheel caught the corner of a wrought-iron fence. There was an agonizing screech of metal, a sudden shuddering of the entire wagon, and then the vehicle began to tip.

"Noooo!" Capers screamed.

His cry sent shivers down Theodosia's spine.

Duke pulled back on the reins to slow their wagon as they both watched in horror. Slowly, inexorably, Capers's runaway wagon tipped up onto two wheels. It seemed to teeter for a moment, as if undecided. Then a sudden jerk from his team of horses sounded its death knell. The wagon rolled over onto its side with a thunderous crash. Hay bales tumbled, wood shattered, and Percy Capers was pitched headlong onto the cobblestone street!

His wagon dragged and screeched for another twenty feet. Then the horses, who'd clearly had enough, came to a stop.

Theodosia jumped out while Duke stayed behind to secure his team. She ran to Capers, slewed to a stop, and gazed down at him.

Capers hadn't fared well. He'd fallen hard and landed badly on his side. And from the way he was crying and whimpering, he had probably broken a couple of bones.

Capers tried to roll over, then caught sight of Theodosia. "Help me," he cried in a dry, papery voice. "I'm hurt." His eyes traveled upward, finally meeting her stony gaze. "You've got to help me," he pleaded.

Theodosia knelt down next to him and thrust her cell phone in his face. "You help me, I'll help you," she said in a flat voice. "A little quid pro quo. I think that's reasonable, don't you?"

"What?" Capers gasped.

"Did you kill Edgar Webster?" she asked.

"Help me," said Capers. His voice was a wet sigh. "Call for an ambulance."

"I'm going to, I really am," said Theodosia. "But you have to give me something in return."

Capers gritted his teeth. "Okay, yes."

"Webster," she repeated.

"It was an accident, I swear."

"An ice pick in the ear was an accident?" Theodosia shook her head. "Now, about the money . . ."

"Please," groaned Capers. "I'm hurt bad."

Duke came over and stood next to Theodosia. "Jeez," he

said. "The guy's in kind of a bad way. We should get him to a hospital."

"Almost done here," said Theodosia. She leaned closer to Capers and practically whispered in his ear. "You were the intermediary, weren't you? You handled the purchase of the tea house?"

"Yessss." His voice was a low hiss.

"And you dipped your beak into a pile of money. To the tune of one-point-one million dollars, am I right?"

Capers writhed on the ground, practically gnashing his teeth. "All right, yes!"

"But Edgar Webster caught you with your hand in the cookie jar," said Theodosia.

"Jeez," said Duke. He hooked his thumbs in his belt. "He really stole the money?"

Theodosia gave a thin smile. "Webster caught you stealing the money, didn't he, Percy? And that's why you killed him."

Capers groaned.

"Was that a yes?" said Theodosia.

"Yes," said Capers.

"Good." Theodosia stood up and clicked off the recorder on her phone. Five seconds later it rang. It was Tidwell again, talking a mile a minute, rocketing questions at her.

Theodosia listened for a few moments, and then said, "It's over. Percy Capers's wagon overturned and he was pitched out into the street."

That put an end to Tidwell's rant. "Is he hurt?"

"I imagine he could use an ambulance," said Theodosia. "And an armed guard. The man's dangerous, after all. He killed Edgar Webster."

"Capers did?" Tidwell started squawking like an angry crow. "Capers *told* you that?"

Theodosia glanced around. Duke had gone back to tend to the horses. "Full confession," she said. "Caught on tape."

"What else?" said Tidwell. "What else is Capers saying?"

Capers twisted abruptly. Quick as a snapping turtle, one hand shot out and closed hard around Theodosia's ankle. With an iron grasp and a sharp yank, he wrenched her leg out from under her.

Theodosia crashed to the pavement with a bone-jarring thump.

"Gotcha!" Capers hissed malevolently. "Now give me that phone!"

That was when Aunt Acid stepped in, cool as you please, and hit him in the face with a shot of her pepper spray. "Take that!" she cried. "Don't you dare mess with my favorite tea lady!"

"Owwwww!" were Capers's final words.

27

The ambulance showed up some two minutes later. Tidwell rolled to the scene in his Crown Victoria five minutes after that. He stomped around, grumbling like an angry bear and looking generally unhappy.

But Tidwell was smart enough to listen patiently as Theodosia and Harlan Duke filled him in as best they could. Tidwell asked a few questions, then got Elliot Kern on the phone and related the complete Percy Capers story to the museum director. Elliot must have thanked Tidwell profusely or said something highly complimentary, because he suddenly became a little more human.

Theodosia, meanwhile, had called Max. "It's all over," she told him with a long sigh.

"Not quite," said Max. "Drayton's just finishing up with the last tour."

Theodosia had to chuckle. He didn't know. Of course, he didn't know. "I didn't mean the tour," said Theodosia. "I meant the whole murder-mystery thing."

"What!" Max screeched.

"Tell you what," said Theodosia. "I'll explain everything to you real soon. If you and Drayton walk over to Church Street, we'll swing by and pick you up."

"Pick us up?" said Max, sounding confused. "Pick us up in what?"

"In a hay wagon," said Theodosia.

Theodosia was as good as her word. Ten minutes later, she and Harlan Duke *clip-clop*ped down Church Street to where Max and Drayton were waiting for them. Somewhere along the line they'd picked up a frantic Delaine, who was now sitting in the back of the wagon, cradling her feisty little aunt.

"You expect me to ride in that?" said Drayton when he saw the wagon.

"Hop aboard," said Duke, "for the tea shop express."

Drayton clambered on board, looking a little nervous. "We're really going to the tea shop?"

"Tidwell's going to meet us there," said Theodosia.

"We're having tea?" asked Aunt Acid. "Oh, joy."

And they really did have tea. Drayton bustled about preparing pots of chamomile and black plum. Haley, in her apartment upstairs, heard the commotion and came shuffling down to help. She laid out cups, saucers, and plates, and then warmed up a batch of cherry scones.

By the time Detective Tidwell had arrived, the whole sorry story had been spilled, mopped up, and retold.

"I can't believe I'm in the clear," said Max.

"You were always in the clear," said Tidwell. He was seated at the head of the table in one of their ample captain's chairs. "Thanks to Miss Browning here."

"Did you get in touch with Charlotte?" Theodosia asked him.

Tidwell nodded. "Yes. And I managed to speak with Roger Greaves, too. Needless to say, he was very much relieved that his business partner's killer has finally been apprehended."

"We have to contact Cecily Conrad, too," said Theodosia. "I think she was fairly convinced it was someone from the museum who killed Webster and then came after her. She just wasn't sure who."

"Percy Capers," Drayton spat out. "He probably figured Cecily knew something. That's why he went after her."

"Probably," said Theodosia. "And Capers was trying to scare everybody else off, too. Tossing that flaming bottle through Charlotte's window, roughing up Bill Glass."

"Throw up a big smokescreen," said Max. "Go big or go home."

"Or go to jail," said Tidwell.

Theodosia passed a scone to Tidwell, and said, "When you question Capers, I hope you squeeze him like a Florida orange. In fact, when you question him, I wouldn't mind being there."

"Really, Miss Browning," said Tidwell. He was pretending to be perturbed but not doing a very good job of it. He beetled his brow and forced a stern look on his face. "Haven't you meddled enough? And then to engineer that wild hay-wagon chase through the Historic District? My goodness. What do you have to say for yourself?"

Theodosia lifted her teacup and smiled serenely. "Film at eleven?"

FAVORITE RECIPES FROM

The Indigo Tea Shop

Sausage and Gnocchi Soup

½ lb. sweet Italian sausage (ground, not links)
2 cups water
1 package vacuum-packed gnocchi (Bellino or Vigo)
2 cups beef broth
1 can (14 oz.) Italian-style stewed tomatoes (chopped, not
   drained)
½ cup Parmesan cheese (fresh grated)

COOK sausage in large saucepan until browned. Add
water, gnocchi, beef broth, and tomatoes. Bring to a boil,
then reduce heat and allow to simmer for 5 to 6 minutes,
or until gnocchi float to the top. Ladle soup into bowls and
top with grated Parmesan. Yields 4 servings.

Prosciutto and Fig Tea Sandwiches

6 slices white sandwich bread
Butter
Fig jam
Prosciutto, 6 thin slices
1 pear, peeled and sliced thin

SPREAD 3 slices of bread with butter and 3 slices with fig jam. Layer prosciutto and pear slices on the buttered bread, then top with the fig jam slices. Slice off crusts and cut into triangles. Yields 12 small sandwiches.

Green Tea Donuts

1¼ cup flour
¾ cup sugar
½ tsp. baking soda
½ tsp. salt
½ tsp. matcha green tea powder
⅔ cup oil
½ cup buttermilk
1 egg
½ tsp. white vinegar
½ tsp. vanilla extract

PREHEAT oven to 350 degrees. Combine flour, sugar, baking soda, salt, and green tea powder in a bowl. In another bowl, combine oil, buttermilk, egg, vinegar, and vanilla. Pour the wet ingredients into the dry ingredients and stir until just combined. Fill a greased donut pan about two-thirds full and bake for 12 to 14 minutes. Add your own frosting or glaze. Yields 12 donuts.

Cream Cheese and Strawberry Tea Sandwiches

1 loaf date nut bread
Cream cheese, softened
Strawberries, hulled and sliced

SLICE date nut bread and spread each piece with cream cheese. Arrange sliced strawberries on top and serve open-faced.

Church Street Peanut Butter Cookies

1 cup butter (2 sticks), softened
1 cup peanut butter
1 cup sugar
1 cup brown sugar, packed
2 eggs
2 cups flour
1 tsp. baking soda
½ tsp. vanilla extract

PREHEAT oven to 325 degrees. Combine butter, peanut butter, both sugars, and eggs. Mix in flour, baking soda, and vanilla. Drop by the teaspoonful onto a greased baking sheet, leaving at least 1 inch between cookies. Bake for 10 to 12 minutes, or until cookies are set. Yields 4 dozen cookies.

Blueberry Sour Cream Muffins

2 eggs
1 cup sugar
½ cup vegetable oil
½ tsp. vanilla extract
2 cups flour
½ tsp. salt
½ tsp. baking soda
1 cup sour cream
1 cup blueberries

PREHEAT oven to 400 degrees. In large bowl beat eggs, gradually adding sugar. Continue beating and pour in oil and vanilla. In a separate bowl, stir together flour, salt, and baking soda. Stir dry ingredients into egg mixture, gradually incorporating sour cream. Gently fold in blueberries. Scoop batter into a greased muffin tin. Bake for 20 minutes. Yields 12 muffins.

Chicken and Green Goddess Tea Sandwiches

6 slices whole wheat bread
Green goddess dressing
Chicken, cooked and sliced
Avocado, pealed and sliced thin
Salt and pepper

SPREAD each slice of bread with a thin layer of green goddess dressing. Arrange chicken slices on 3 pieces of bread. Top the chicken with avocado slices, then salt and pepper to taste. Top sandwiches with the remaining 3 slices of bread. Trim off crusts and cut into triangles. Yields 12 tea sandwiches.

Haley's Honey Scones

2 cups flour
1 Tbsp. baking powder
¼ tsp. salt
5 Tbsp. butter, cold and diced
¼ cup sour cream
4 Tbsp. honey
1 cup cream, plus 3 Tbsp.
Sugar

PREHEAT oven to 350 degrees. Mix together flour, baking powder, and salt. Cut butter into mixture until crumbly, then stir in sour cream. In a small bowl, mix together honey and 1 cup of cream. Add cream mixture to flour mixture, stirring until a soft dough forms. Place dough on a lightly floured work surface and roll out to about ¾ inch thickness. Using a circular cutter, cut out scones. Places scones on a baking sheet that has been lined with parchment paper. Use a pastry brush to coat the tops of scones with the extra 3 Tbsp. of cream. Sprinkle with sugar and bake for 15 to 18 minutes or until golden brown. Serve with Devonshire cream or whipped cream. Yields about 16 scones.

English Tea Bread

1½ cups dates, chopped and pitted
1½ cups sugar
1 tsp. salt
2 Tbsp. butter
1½ cups boiling water
1 egg, lightly beaten
2¾ cups flour
1 tsp. baking soda
1 tsp. cream of tartar
1½ tsp. vanilla extract
1 cup walnuts, chopped

PREHEAT oven to 350 degrees. Place dates, sugar, salt, and butter into a bowl. Pour in the boiling water and stir. Set aside to cool. Once cool, mix in the egg. Stir flour, baking soda, and cream of tartar in a large bowl. Add the date mixture to the flour mixture and stir to combine. Mix in the vanilla extract and walnuts. Pour batter into a greased 9" x 5" loaf pan. Bake for 1 hour and 15 minutes. Cool in pan before turning out onto a rack to cool completely. Slice and spread with cream cheese or wrap in foil and store in refrigerator.

Chutney Crescents

½ cup butter (1 stick)
1 small package cream cheese (3 oz.)
1 cup flour, sifted

½ cup chutney (prepared)
⅓ cup sugar
1 tsp. ground cinnamon

PREHEAT oven to 375 degrees. Cream butter and cream cheese together. Beat in flour until dough forms a smooth ball. Wrap in aluminum foil and chill overnight. Remove dough from refrigerator 30 minutes before using. Roll dough out to ⅛-inch thickness and cut with round 3-inch cookie cutter. Place a small spoonful of chutney in the center of each round. Fold over and gently press together. Bake on an ungreased baking sheet for about 15 minutes. When cooled, roll in mixture of sugar and ground cinnamon.

Cherry Banana Bread

1 cup sugar
½ cup butter (1 stick)
2 eggs
3 bananas, mashed
2 cups flour
1 tsp. baking powder
1 jar maraschino cherries (10 oz.), chopped with juice

PREHEAT oven to 350 degrees. Cream together sugar and butter. Beat in eggs and bananas. Blend in flour and baking powder. Stir in cherries and juice. Pour batter into 3 small, greased loaf pans and bake for about 45 minutes. Yields 3 small loaves.

TEA TIME TIPS FROM
Laura Childs

Sherlock Holmes Tea

Dim the lights, throw on a dark green tablecloth, and make your tea table look as British as possible. That means decorating with a stack of books, a magnifying glass, and brass candlesticks. Copy and enlarge pages from a Sherlock Holmes mystery to use as placemats and use plaid or herringbone napkins. If you can add a Sherlock Holmes hat, so much the better. You'll want to serve currant scones or oat cakes with lemon curd and jam, hearty roast beef and cheddar cheese sandwiches, and strong black tea. (Note: Mystery book clubs, this is for you!)

Russian Tea

Delicious Russian Caravan tea sets the theme here. This traditional blend is usually served with heartier savories, so consider blinis with cream cheese, dark bread with eggplant spread, potato dumplings, and beet borscht. For dessert, cakes and small pastries fill the bill. And don't forget the sugar, since Russian Caravan tea is often drunk with two or even three cubes.

Ming Tea (without the Murder!)

Make this an occasion to pull out all your chinoiserie—your blue and white dishes, Chinese figurines, and Chinese teapots. Decorate your tea table with paper fans or even a bonsai or *penjing*. Serve miniature egg rolls, a Chinese chicken salad, and steamed dumplings. And remember, Chinese black tea is always more authentic when served in small tea bowls.

Van Gogh Sunflower Tea

For this afternoon tea, your table should resemble a painterly still life. Think an enormous vase of sunflowers, yellow dishes and napkins, and a wooden bowl heaped with oranges. Van Gogh postcards are readily available in gift shops, so they make perfect invitations. There are also van Gogh tea towels and teapots to be had. Serve sunflower seed scones, cream cheese and roasted red peppers on brown bread, and ham and apple slices on French bread. Choose a light Formosan oolong for your tea, and pipe yellow frosting into sunflower designs on chocolate cookies.

Floral Tea

This tea table calls for a floral tablecloth, floral patterned dishes, and masses of flowers in vases. Start with a quiche accented with edible flowers, and move on to egg salad tea sandwiches on whole wheat bread as well as ricotta cheese mixed with bits of orange and spread on hearty white bread. Serve a delicate chamomile tea and don't forget sugar swizzle sticks or orange sticks covered with chocolate. If you can have your Floral Tea outdoors—in the garden or on the patio—so much the better.

French Tea

Elegance is the watchword here, so set your tea table with interesting textiles, fine china, and cut glass. Add candles and put on some soothing music. Cream scones are always a delicious starter. Your tea sandwiches might include crab salad on croissants, brie cheese and strawberry jam on baguettes, and cream cheese and sliced cucumbers on whole wheat bread. Serve a lovely Ceylon black tea, and don't forget the macarons or chocolate truffles for dessert.

TEA RESOURCES

TEA PUBLICATIONS

TeaTime—A luscious magazine profiling tea and tea lore. Filled with glossy photos and wonderful recipes. (teatimemagazine.com)

Southern Lady—From the publishers of *Tea Time*, a magazine with a focus on people and places in the South as well as wonderful teatime recipes. (southernladymagazine.com)

The Tea House Times—Go to theteahousetimes.com for subscription information and dozens of links to tea shops, purveyors of tea, gift shops, and tea events.

Victoria—A magazine including articles and pictorials on homes, home design, gardens, and tea. (victoriamag.com)

Tea in Texas—A magazine highlighting Texas tea rooms and tea events. (teaintexas.com)

Margaret Thornby's Tea & Tea Room Talk Magazine—A magazine covering tea news and tea shops in Britain. (teatalkmagazine .co.uk)

Fresh Cup Magazine—A magazine for tea and coffee professionals. (freshcup.com)

Tea & Coffee—A trade journal for the tea and coffee industry. (teaandcoffee.net)

Bruce Richardson—This author has written several definitive books on tea. (elmwoodinn.com/books)

Jane Pettigrew—This author has written thirteen books on various aspects of tea and its history and culture. (janepettigrew .com/books)

A Tea Reader—an anthology of tea stories and reflections by Katrina Avila Munichiello.

AMERICAN TEA PLANTATIONS

Charleston Tea Plantation—The oldest and largest tea plantation in the United States. Order their fine black tea or schedule a visit at bigelowtea.com.

Fairhope Tea Plantation—A tea plantation in Fairhope, Alabama.

FiLoLi Tea Farm—An up-and-coming Mississippi tea farm about ready to go into production. (filoliteafarm.com)

Sakuma Bros. Farm & Market—This tea garden just outside Burlington, Washington, has been growing white and green tea for more than a dozen years. (sakumamarket.com)

Big Island Tea—An organic artisan tea from Hawaii. (bigisland-tea.com)

Mauna Kea Tea—An organic green and oolong tea from Hawaii's Big Island. (maunakeatea.com)

Onomea Tea Company—A nine-acre tea estate near Hilo, Hawaii. (onomeatea.com)

Moonrise Tea Garden—Organic teas grown on Hawaii's Big Island and packed in rice-paper pouches. (moonrisetea.com)

TEA WEBSITES AND INTERESTING BLOGS

Teamap.com—A directory of hundreds of tea shops in the U.S. and Canada.

Greattearoomsofamerica.com—An excellent tea shop guide.

Afternoontea.co.uk—A guide to tea rooms in the U.K.

Cookingwithideas.typepad.com—Recipes and book reviews for the bibliochef.

Cuppatea4sheri.blogspot.com—Amazing recipes.

Seedrack.com—Order camellia sinensis seeds and grow your own tea!

Friendshiptea.net—Tea shop reviews, recipes, and more.

RTbookreviews.com—A wonderful romance and mystery book review site.

Adelightsomelife.com—Tea, gardening, and cottage crafts.

Theladiestea.com—A networking platform for women.

Jennybakes.com—Fabulous recipes from a real make-it-from-scratch baker.

Lattedavotion.wordpress.com—Coffee, tea, and book reviews.

Southernwritersmagazine.com—Inspiration, writing advice, and author interviews with Southern writers.

Allteapots.com—Teapots from around the world.

Thedailytea.com—Formerly *Tea Magazine*, this online publication is filled with tea news, recipes, inspiration, and tea travel.

Fireflyvodka.com—South Carolina purveyors of Sweet Tea vodka, Raspberry Tea vodka, Peach Tea vodka, and more. Just visiting this website is a trip in itself!

Teasquared.blogspot.com—A fun, well-written blog with musings about tea and tea shops.

Blog.bernideens.com—Tea, baking, decorations, and gardening.

Teapages.net—All things tea.

Possibili-teas.net—Tea consultants with a terrific monthly newsletter.

Relevanttealeaf.blogspot.com—All about tea.

Baking.about.com—Carroll Pellegrinelli writes a terrific baking blog, complete with recipes and photo instructions.

Stephcupoftea.blogspot.com—Blog on tea, food, and inspiration.

Teawithfriends.blogspot.com—Lovely blog on tea, friendship, and tea accoutrements.

Garden-of-books.com—Terrific book reviews by an entertainment journalist.

Teaescapade.wordpress.com—An enjoyable tea blog.

Bellaonline.com/site/tea—Features and forums on tea.

Lattesandlife.com—Witty musings on life.

Napkinfoldingguide.com—Photo illustrations of twenty-seven different (and sometimes elaborate) napkin folds.

Worldteaexpo.com—This premier business-to-business trade show features more than three hundred tea suppliers, vendors, and tea innovators.

Sweetgrassbaskets.net—One of several websites where you can buy sweetgrass baskets direct from the artists.

Goldendelighthoney.com—Carolina honey to sweeten your tea.

Fatcatscones.com—Frozen ready-to-bake scones.

Kingarthurflour.com—One of the best flours for baking. This is what many professional pastry chefs use.

Teagw.com—Visit this website and click on Products to find dreamy tea pillows filled with jasmine, rose, lavender, and green tea.

Californiateahouse.com—Order Machu's Blend, a special herbal tea for dogs that promotes healthy skin, lowers stress, and aids digestion.

Vintageteaworks.com—This company offers six unique wine-flavored tea blends that celebrate wine and respect the tea.

Downtonabbeycooks.com—A *Downton Abbey* blog with news and recipes. You can also order their book *Abbey Cooks.*

Auntannie.com—Crafting site that will teach you how to make your own petal envelopes, pillow boxes, gift bags, etc.

Bostonteaparty.com—Mark T. Wendell is the U.S. distributor for Davison Newman & Co Ltd of London, original suppliers of tea for the historic Boston Tea Parties of 1773–1774.

Victorianhousescones.com—Scone, biscuit, and cookie mixes for both retail and wholesale orders. Plus baking and scone-making tips.

Harney.com—Contact Harney & Sons to order their Titanic loose leaf blend tea or their RMS Titanic tea sachets.

PURVEYORS OF FINE TEA
Adagio.com
Harney.com
Stashtea.com
Republicoftea.com
Teazaanti.com
Bigelowtea.com
Celestialseasonings.com
Goldenmoontea.com
Uptontea.com

VISITING CHARLESTON
Charleston.com—Travel and hotel guide.

Charlestoncvb.com—The official Charleston convention and visitor bureau.

Charlestontour.wordpress.com—Private tours of homes and gardens, some including lunch or tea.

Charlestonplace.com—Charleston Place Hotel serves an excellent afternoon tea, Thursday through Saturday, 1:00 p.m. to 3:00 p.m.

Culinarytoursofcharleston.com—Sample specialties from Charleston's local eateries, markets, and bakeries.

Charlestonteaco.com—This small café on Ann Street sells loose leaf and iced teas, and serves breakfast and lunch. They have even blended a special medicinal migraine tea.

Poogansporch.com—This restored Victorian house serves traditional low-country cuisine. Be sure to ask about Poogan!

Preservationsociety.org—Hosts Charleston's annual Fall Candlelight Tour.

Palmettocarriage.com—Horse-drawn carriage rides.

Charlestonharbortours.com—Boat tours and harbor cruises.

Ghostwalk.net—Stroll into Charleston's haunted history. Ask them about the "original" Theodosia!

Charlestontours.net—Ghost tours plus tours of plantations and historic homes.

Follybeach.com—Official guide to Folly Beach activities, hotels, rentals, restaurants, and events.

TURN THE PAGE FOR A PREVIEW OF
LAURA CHILDS'S
NEXT SCRAPBOOKING MYSTERY . . .

Parchment and Old Lace

COMING OCTOBER 2015 IN HARDCOVER
FROM BERKLEY PRIME CRIME!

Commander's Palace wasn't just the most storied restaurant in New Orleans—for Carmela Bertrand it was pure magic.

Carmela knew this for a fact because she was sitting in their Garden Room at this very minute. And not only was she nibbling soft-shell crab and drinking an awesome Montrachet, but she was staring into the inquisitive blue eyes of her fella du jour, Detective Edgar Babcock.

Maybe it was the wine, no doubt crafted by Bacchus himself, that had cast such a luscious spell. Or maybe it was soft, warm light from the gilded candelabras, the old-world charm and formality of the place, or that crazy second course of oysters baked in absinthe and buttered crumbs. Whatever the reason, Carmela was definitely feeling it. Luxuriance, exhilaration, and romance. Sweet, bubbly romance.

"This is so lovely," Carmela said, trying to pitch her voice an octave lower so it was sexy and seductive, kind of like

Kathleen Turner in *Body Heat*. Or maybe Lauren Bacall in one of those old black-and-white movies from the forties.

"You're lovely," replied Babcock.

And Carmela really was. Her porcelain-blue eyes, fine features, and tawny-colored hair (this week's color, anyway) gave her an air of exuberance and creative curiosity. She was toned and fairly athletic from lots of dog walking, but still enjoyed a few sweet curves. And, yes, she could be a bit stubborn, but she was generally quick to administer a kind word followed by a hug.

Carmela took another sip of wine. "I have to say, this dinner has been pure perfection. If every restaurant reviewer in the universe hadn't already bequeathed four stars to this place, I would have sprinkled them on myself."

Babcock smiled and reached across the table to gently take her hand.

"Why are you talking that way?" he asked.

Carmela's eyes went slightly round. "What way?"

"Like you've got the beginnings of a head cold. Or are doing an imitation of a character from *The Simpsons*."

"Oh." Then, "I didn't mean to."

"You've just fallen completely under my spell, is that it?"

"Well . . . yeah," said Carmela, reverting to valley girl. Now she wasn't sure if he was flirting with her or putting her on.

Babcock gave a low chuckle. "You're such a little cutie, you know that? One of these days we're seriously going to have to . . ."

"Carmela!" A loud, impassioned shriek suddenly split the air.

Startled, Carmela and Babcock both whipped their heads sideways, only to find an exuberant-looking blond woman grinning at them, all teeth and gums and big southern hair.

"Uh . . . hi," said Carmela as she scrambled to dredge

her memory, to put a name to this face. "Isabelle?" She said it tentatively because she really wasn't sure that was the name of this young woman who'd just hit an ear-splitting high C as she stormed their table like a pirate commandeering one of the king's galleons.

Isabelle's smile got even wider and brighter, and she said, "You remembered."

"How could I forget?" Carmela said, when she really had forgotten. Well, almost.

"Has Ellie been keeping you in the loop about all my big wedding plans?" Isabelle asked. Ellie was Eldora Black, Isabelle's sister and the tarot card reader who worked at Juju Voodoo, the little shop across the courtyard from Carmela's French Quarter apartment. The voodoo shop, a kind of funky, fun tourist trap, was owned by Carmela's very best friend Ava Gruiex.

"Ellie *has* shared a few things with me," Carmela said, lying as gracefully as she could. She glanced over at Babcock. "With us." Now she gave Babcock an encouraging nod. "You remember Isabelle, don't you? She's one of the assistant district attorneys."

"We've met," Babcock said politely.

"Just two more weeks," Isabelle said. She held up two fingers and then fluttered her hand nervously as her engagement ring caught the light and glittered like a disco ball.

"That's some gorgeous ring," Carmela said.

Now Isabelle preened a bit. "Isn't it? Three carats, a VS2."

"Sweet," Babcock said, gamely trying to interject himself in a conversation that had suddenly turned girly.

Flustered by the attention, Isabelle took a step back from their table. "I hope you two are still planning to attend my wedding."

"Absolutely," Carmela said. She had an awful feeling that she hadn't actually mailed back her RSVP. She'd been busy and scattered lately, what with teaching a series of card making classes at her scrapbook shop, Memory Mine. Oh well, maybe she could short-circuit things and give her reply to Ellie. Yeah, that oughta work just fine.

Isabelle glanced across the room where two of her friends waved at her. One tall and blond, the other short and dark-haired. "Well, I'm afraid I have to hustle off. I've been tasting cakes with Naomi and Cynthia and a few other folks from the wedding party." She rolled her eyes. "And now I have a thousand other things to nail down."

"I'll bet you do," Carmela said. "Bye-bye," she gave a little wave as Isabelle scampered away. "Good luck." Then, when Isabelle and her friends were out of both sight and earshot, she leaned across the table and said, "Do you recall me inviting you to her wedding?"

Babcock shook his head. "Nope."

"Do you want to go? Do you want to be my plus one?"

Another head shake. "Nope."

"Come on," said Carmela. "Don't be an old poop. Weddings are exciting, romantic events filled with dancing, champagne, good food, and excellent cake." Carmela was particularly fond of cake, though champagne wasn't too far down on her list either.

"I'm pretty sure I have to work," Babcock said.

"You don't even know when her wedding is," Carmela said. "So how do you know if you'll be called upon to bust up an international smuggling ring of ladies' designer flip-flops or chase down some homicidal maniac?"

But Babcock didn't answer. He was suddenly frowning at the check that had been surreptitiously deposited at their table, running quick fractions in his head.

Hmm. He was good at dodging bullets, that's for sure, Carmela decided. Probably from all the practice he got as a police detective.

She narrowed her eyes and studied him carefully. He was quite a catch, this guy. Tall, lanky, ginger-colored hair, nice high cheekbones. A man who walked into a room and immediately projected a certain weighty presence. Plus he had a penchant for snazzy clothes. Really snazzy clothes, like Ralph Lauren Black Label and Moncler. Tonight he was wearing a Burberry Brit jacket that widened his shoulders and nipped his waist. Always a good thing.

Babcock glanced up and gave her a warm smile. "Ready to go?"

"Sure." Carmela returned his smile. "I could get used to this, you know." She meant the dinner, the togetherness, and then some. The *and then some* meaning the two of them would eventually head back to her place for a nice Sunday night canoodle.

"So could I," Babcock said. He held out a hand and helped her up from the chair. Then, he slid both arms around her, pulled her close, and gave her a quick kiss.

"Uh-oh," Carmela cautioned. "PDA."

Babcock arched back an inch. "What's PDA? Some kind of women's political group? A new design project?"

She brushed her lips across his cheek, feeling his warmth and energy. "You know, public display of affection."

"Oh, that." He chuckled and grabbed her hand. "Come on."

Outside the restaurant, the November evening had turned cool and breezy. Though it was full-on dark, the exterior of Commander's Palace twinkled with multiple strands of lights. Turrets, columns, gingerbread swirls, and balustrades were all shown off to their best advantage, gilded and glittering like a Mardi Gras float. Turquoise and white awnings flip-flapped in the wind while the restaurant's trademark neon sign hummed brightly.

The whole of the Garden District was spread out around them, stately and sublime, as if it were its own proud principality governed by some unseen archduke. Lush gardens and wrought-iron fences surrounded block after block of palatial Greek Revival homes, with a few Queen Annes and Victorians thrown in for good measure. And, if you strolled down First Street, you might even encounter a fanciful Gothic home, owned by a famous author of vampire books.

Carmela and Babcock walked down Coliseum Street, heading for Babcock's blue BMW, which was parked at the end of the block. Across the scuffed blacktop, where dry leaves scritched and scratched as they were hurried along by little puffs of wind, stood the infamous Lafayette Cemetery. Dark and ominous-looking, this was one of New Orleans's oldest and most infamous Cities of the Dead. Here, crumbling tombs, ancient crypts, and hulking mausoleums stood shoulder to somber shoulder, more than seven thousand residents interred in a one-block area, attracting and terrifying swarms of tourists as well as locals.

A chill gust of wind suddenly blasted them, and Carmela turned her face into Babcock's shoulder.

"I was thinking that we should—" she began.

An ungodly scream suddenly pierced what felt like a fragile night.

"Heeeeeelp!"

Carmela clutched Babcock's arm. "What was that?"

"Nooo!"

Another agonizing scream rolled out but was immediately cut off.

Babcock swiveled his head like a periscope. "Cemetery," he said sharply. He took off running, as if a starter's gun had sounded, leaving Carmela standing all by herself on the sidewalk. In the dark.

She weighed her options for all of one second. "Wait!" she cried. And took off after him.

But Babcock's longer legs had put him easily twenty strides ahead of her. And when he reached the cemetery's fence, he simply grabbed hold of the top tines, wedged a toe into a curlicue, and vaulted over it slick as you please.

"Where are you . . . ? Oh, jeez!" cried Carmela. She knew she couldn't climb over that foreboding-looking fence in her tight skirt, so she pounded down the block to the formal entrance at the corner, lost her balance and almost spun out, then ducked through the narrow entryway.

"Babcock," she called out. "Where are you?" She slid to a stop and listened intently. When she didn't hear anything, she called again, "What's going on?" Then, "Are you okay?"

"Over here." Babcock's faint shout drifted toward her.

Carmela glanced around, decided that his voice had to be coming from practically the epicenter of the cemetery, and then took off at a gallop. She dodged around a row of low, flat, humpy-looking tombs, then sped down a narrow gravel walkway between two mausoleums that were iced by a finger of moonlight. The night felt even darker in here, more dangerous. Fear trickled coldly down her spine, and the exertion of a full-out sprint made the blood pound in her ears.

Still she kept going, moving and darting ahead.

What could have happened? Carmela wondered. Had someone been attacked? That had to be it. None of New Orleans' cemeteries were particularly safe after dark, and visitors were constantly being cautioned to avoid them. Had Babcock been able to foil this robbery attempt or attack or whatever it had been? Had he given chase to the attacker?

Carmela spun around a stone angel whose upturned face had eroded away over the years from the constant onslaught of heat, wind, humidity, and hurricanes. She dashed past a row of oven tombs and stumbled as her toe caught on the corner of a marble tablet that the earth had heaved up.

Righting herself, she listened again but didn't hear anything. So she ran left in a sort of zigzag pattern, still trying to get a bead on where Babcock had called to her from.

Gray clouds boiled up, and the sliver of moon, which had served as a small guiding beacon, slipped behind them. Now Carmela was practically running blind, feeling her way along, touching and grasping cold stone. If only she could . . .

She ran her fingers along the edge of a marble tomb, cool and smooth as picked bones. She glanced up—hoping that a crescent of moon might put in an appearance again. But the night seemed to turn darker, holding a hint of even more danger.

Carmela scuffed along quietly. She figured she was fairly close to where Babcock might have called to her from. Now if she could only see . . .

A sound, soft and muffled, as if someone might be hunching themselves back into the shadows and hiding from her, caused Carmela to stop dead in her tracks. On high alert, hair on the back of her neck prickling like crazy, Carmela listened as though her life depended on it. And maybe it did.

What was it? What did I hear?

She flattened herself against the side of a large, hulking crypt and tried to modulate her breathing as best she could, tried to make every sense keenly alert to what was going on around her.

But, after a few moments, she heard—and felt—nothing.

Carmela slowly released a breath. She was spooked, yes, but she wasn't going to let her emotions run wild on her. She was going to keep bumbling along and find Babcock. After all, he was in here somewhere.

Carmela moved ahead two steps, then three, her right shoulder still brushing against the side of the crypt, using it as a sort of touch point. She was just about to cry out to

Babcock again, to try to get a fix on his position, when she heard a strange, low creaking sound and caught a flash of something.

The initial spark in Carmela's brain told her it was a shadow coming at her—a grid of light and dark projected by a far-off passing car. At the last moment, she realized it was a rusty iron gate. The heavy, flaking wrought-iron door of the crypt had been flung open on squeaking hinges and was creaking inexorably toward her.

Shocked, totally unprepared, Carmela had barely two seconds to get a hand up in front of her face, a pro forma protest at best, before the gate struck hard against her, pinning her tightly against the crypt's outside wall.

She let loose a startled yelp as her forehead went numb and bright stars danced and flashed before her eyes. She suddenly felt like a captured butterfly pinned inside a display case. Angry, stunned, and struggling to pull herself back to the here and now, she gripped the gate with her hands and managed to croak out, "Help!"

Then she heard footsteps lightly running away from her as she was finally able to shove the heavy door or metal gate or whatever it was away from her.

"Stop!" she cried out. Now her fear had been replaced with fury.

But whoever had smacked her with the gate was long gone.

Carmela gently touched a hand to her nose, mindful of sudden tears that clouded her eyes.

Broken?

She prodded carefully. No, she didn't think so. Just sore. But whoever had tried to waylay her had been fairly successful. They'd stopped her cold. And she knew she'd probably feel battered and bruised come tomorrow morning.

Deciding the smartest thing, the *safest* thing, to do right now was get herself out of the cemetery as fast as she could,

Carmela scuttled left, found a sort of pathway, and hurried along it. She was feeling angry and scared and hurt. If she could make it out to Babcock's car, she'd hopefully meet up with him there.

Boy, did she have a story to tell!

But as Carmela lurched along, her eyes scanning to either side of the path, she almost tripped again. She caught herself at the last moment, glanced forward, and let loose a startled cry.

What is that? What am I seeing now?

Someone had flung a coat across a gravestone?

Carmela blinked and struggled to focus. Wait a minute. Maybe that wasn't a coat?

Is that a person lying there? Oh dear lord!

Carmela moved forward as if in a trance. She was suddenly hyperaware of every crunch of gravel underfoot, every looming grave, every sigh and hiss of the wind.

Who is it? Is it the person we heard screaming?

Had to be.

As if compelled to bear witness, Carmela drew closer and closer to the grave where someone—she was pretty sure it was a woman—was sprawled in a totally unnatural pose, as if they'd been hurled there by some uncaring, unfeeling giant.

Carmela was five feet away when her brain blipped out a warning message: Be careful, be careful.

Babcock. Where was Babcock? Now she really had to find him.

She opened her mouth to yell out, but no sound emerged. Because, by this time, she was standing directly in front of the slumped body (slumped *dead* body?), experiencing not only shock, but paralyzing fear.

Get a grip, she told herself. *Try to breathe. Make a sound. Any sound.*

Carmela gritted her teeth and tried to rally her courage.

She wasn't sure if the woman was dead or very badly injured. But she knew she had to try to make a determination. Because if there was any chance she could help this poor soul . . .

Tentatively, Carmela reached out a hand. And just as the tips of her fingers were about to touch the woman . . .

"Carmela!" came a harsh voice. "No!"